NOW IT'S
INESCAPABLE

Bill Mccausland

authorHOUSE®

AuthorHouse™
1663 Liberty Drive
Bloomington, IN 47403
www.authorhouse.com
Phone: 1 (800) 839-8640

Published by AuthorHouse 02/23/2018

ISBN: 978-1-5462-3078-6 (sc)
ISBN: 978-1-5462-3077-9 (e)

Print information available on the last page.

CHAPTER ONE

Susan was screaming at me. She's probably a Valium addict—I know all the signs—who's an unhinged wreck today, since she ran out of her sedative-hypnotic drugs. And I recalled that she's off the deep end in other ways, regardless of the meds being interwoven into her mind. I moved the receiver away from my ear, since she screamed so loudly.

"You left me high and dry just like everybody else!"

"On the contrary," I shot back, checking my watch, already late for my next surgery, "I did more follow-up with you than any other patient that week." I was trying to remember her face. I could see her nose, the excellent job I did on it, then remembered our interview in my office before her surgery, the way she would deliberately lower her head and inspected me with her upturned and narrowed eyes. I should have known she was nutso. And talking to her had been like facing a menacing tight spot head-on. My neck felt stiff.

"You messed my nose up on purpose! I look ghastly!"

I was in a tailspin about how to manage her screaming rage because of what she was putting me through, but her lunatic, obsessed and wild take on the surgery was real to her. "Why would I want to make you look ghastly?" I began to worry she might be hinting at blackmail, suing me or reporting me to the Medical Board of California.

"I don't know! But I do! I can see it in the mirror!"

"It was a big change, I know. But now your nose is in proportion to the rest of your face. And that bump is all gone—your profile is straight as an arrow now. The bulbous shape on the tip of your nose is now perfectly formed. Your nostrils were the size of dimes before I reconstructed them. It was close to an ideal rhinoplasty."

"Yeah, and then I got an infection after the surgery and had to take those goddamn antibiotics you prescribed."

"We discussed you stopping smoking before the procedure because of the risk of infection and you said you'd stop, but didn't."

"Aaaahhhhhhgh!" she screamed again into the phone. I really had to get down to the operating room. I cut her off—

"Why don't you speak with my secretary and make an appointment so we can discuss this in person. I can show you the old pictures if you like—" I really need to leave. If my hands were to be steady in surgery I'd need some help before I enter the operating theather. I found my last bottle of oxycodone in the top desk drawer, and downed a couple.

I heard the line go dead. I head down the hallway and thoughts about Susan race through my mind. Troubling was she put a grip around my throat and I didn't have any sensation until I gagged. The assaults driven by Susan's jumbled brain—coded in disaster—frayed my edges. I was a tough guy Army doc when I did war trauma surgery, but I had no clue about the fragility she imposed on me until I felt it. Maybe I just need to get out of Susan's way, rather than being absorbed in her frontal attack.

I showed too much presumption when I first met Susan. She had pessimistic expectations about the procedure. And this was counterbalanced with the anticipation that she would finally look like a movie star. I make people look pretty damn good, but movie stardom is not in my bag of surgical tricks.

I knew she was unbalanced. This caused me to take a history. She said at times she's rash, having the impulse to break down and end it all. On a par with this was her history of making slashes on her arms. She showed me the scarring. The disfigurements were all perfectly perpendicular to the long axis of her arms. The scarier part was Susan said a lot of pressure would build up and making the gashes on her arms actually gave her relief.

Susan mentioned she felt empty and nothing fills her, but she thought the nose procedure would do the trick for her to finally feel complete. So, who's the dummy? I am. She was a god awful candidate for any type of plastic surgery. I stumbled with my harebrained judgment, thinking I could overcome these obstacles because she emotionally begged me to do the surgery. She hoped the rhinoplasty would for once put her in a stable relationship with someone if she finally looked beautiful and had a good picture of herself in her mind. She thought the procedure would miraculously say she's okay. I knew the surgery would make her look good, but it wouldn't solve what ricochets around in her unhinged mind.

I needed to wipe the sweat off the palm of my hand after hung up the receiver. And there were still creases of worry across my forehead. I had no trouble putting two and two together. I recognized what would come in the future: a lengthy process to clear myself if she sued me and made a report to the Medical Board. And then I get scared that some dreaded secrets about me might come out. Scared? No, bump that up to terrified.

Trying to backpedal, bad judgment mistake number two happens. I offer to reevaluate the outcome of her rhinoplasty procedure. That was really dumb to get her to calm down and get her off my back. For being so intelligence, I sure can make some stupid judgments sometimes. There's the pressure and trepidation of what she's going to pull next and it's a crap shoot about what I should expect. But I know it won't be good. I feel a kind of urgent rashness and I have to reel myself in, but I'm not doing a very good job of it.

I have to admit that I'm kind of a cowboy doctor who is good at hogtieing patients into going along with me. But after talking to Susan, I'm a wreck. She emotionally jerked me around so much that I'm distracted and have problems concentrating on surgery that's in front of me for today.

I walk into the space where we do procedures. The thirty-five thousand dollar operating table is in the center of my office-based windowless surgical suite. The pricy table rings bells in my head. What if Susan gets a judgment against me. And what if my covert charade that I keep out of view gets blown out of the water and exposed to the world. My insurance company is sure to drop me if they have to do a payout of Susan. I've seen the same carrier dismiss other doctors who were sued. Maybe I could manage being bareback and not have insurance. But if she reports me to the Medical Board and they suspend my license that thirty-five thousand dollar operating table isn't going to do zip for me. I'm feeling impetuous and imagining a big dose of despair is on the horizon before anything has happened. Susan had that affect on me.

I mull over what I have and struggle to gather myself up. The framework of the surgical suite is so professionally and impressively organized no one supposes my mind's perception occupies its own closed in universe. My mind lays bare a secret spectacle of stars and constellations, stirred by an imaginary vision. The suite is a container, yet the spell I'm under has the movement of a crescendo. Where it will lead I don't know and not being able to see what will happen in the future sets off alarms in my head that I'd do everything possible to squelch. An uneasiness and fright accumulates envisioning a devastating collapse that hasn't happened yet. I've lost the direction of my heart, or maybe I never really know its course. The clinic is my isolated and private domain, where a sense of freedom is a trick of the mind. The surgical suite is also my prison, since here all my well-guarded secrets envelop me.

I go to the reception area where the fax machine is located. I send off the order form to our medication distributor. My nurse anesthetist comes up behind me. She's thirtyish and svelte. She's a longhaired brunette with luminous expressive china blue eyes. Jackie's presence throws me out of balance. She's prepossessing and spicy lovely looks absorbs my mind, especially stirred by her trim and willowy hourglass figure. I want to be coolheaded around her to keep my composure. But I lapse back into thinking about when we were both hurting at the same time and how we soothed each other and whether it will ever happen again. We went too far, but maybe too far is where we needed to be to take the ache away. Jackie says, "Glen, I can order those medications for you. I'm clued into what the total needs of the office are…for the patients and etcetera." She has a pleasant, almost cutesy smile. The allure of her grin pulls me in.

I have my personal agenda. I make the drug supply dance and it's choreographed for my self-possessed concealed compulsion. "I don't mind steering the show when it comes to ordering the meds. I know you can do it, but I'd prefer keeping tabs on the medication flow myself." The one thing I make sure of is that the supply is not short-sheeted.

"I can make sure there's always an abundant supply for all the office needs." Now she's speaking in code because the receptionist is overhearing our conversation.

I add up the things that I need to be in control of, and this one heads the list. Some skepticism and suspecting something is motivating Jackie seeps in. "Is there some consideration that I don't know about?"

"No. I'm just trying to be the helpful me." Her smile drops a notch. "It was just an offer. You keep up the ordering if that is what you *need*… excuse me…*want* to do." She practically makes a movement like a curtsy and turns to walk out of the reception area.

Another reason for having a private surgical suite is to escape the scrutiny of operating at the hospital, where I would have to submit myself to other physicians or nurses breathing down my neck, inspecting my every move. So except for reconstructive surgery, I avoid the complicated cases that require more intensive layout of the hospital.

Maintaining an office practice means fewer bucks for Julie and me. Julie is business minded and she is concerned about the lost income, but not too much since we're not extravagant like some other docs and their wives or husbands. I don't have to be pestered by every goddamn pismire hymenopterous insect bopping around on the swarming anthill of life—all that boring medical system political bullshit.

I have a pain management subspecialty, with enormous drug ordering ability with the regulatory agencies, and my clinic has a pharmacy license in addition to my DEA license. The pharmacy board—backed up by the DEA—oversees the clinic, but they don't see all the covert shit that transpires. I have the system pretty well scoped out. I've been getting away with it for a long, long time, avoiding detection. Am I smart, or charmed at rolling the dice?

Jackie comes into my office to sort out the case for this morning. "Hey, Glen. There's a combination mastopexy and breast augmentation on the schedule for this morning." Her eyelashes flutter. Jackie is my linchpin member of the surgical team and she's key in making the cogs of the operation mesh exactly. She likes to take charge to make sure I don't mess up.

"Right-o." I look Jackie in the eye, followed with an easy nod and smile. "You've all the skids greased?"

"Sure." Jackie runs through the routine. She'll start with Versed, and when the patient is calm she'll add intravenous fentanyl to induce anesthesia and move to propofol for deep sedation. And then the standard antibiotics as one measure against postoperative infection. For the recovery Jackie will use bupivacaine for the long acting local anesthesia and give the patient Vicodin via IV. Jackie runs her hands through her hair, maybe to get my attention since I have glazed over listening to the conventional formula. I wake both of us up by playing with Jackie and caressing her cheek. She answers back with a glowing smile.

"Oh, stop teasing me." Jackie is flirty for half a second. "It's the routine drill." But she makes sure the routine works. "You ready to setup for the patient?" Jackie's voice has an absent sound, flat and salted down with no modulation. I go with the change of subject. It's a relief.

"Absolutely." I look down for half a second and then back at Jackie. "Is the medication safe open?"

It's open. And Jackie knows damn well it's unlocked. "Yeah, I already did the combinations."

The scrub nurse, Lana, and circulating nurse come into my office. While Ann is subordinately hushed, Lana says, "Okay Dr. Glen, we're set to go. Colette Hardel is ready in the operating suite. She's pretty antsy."

The antsy comment tips me and sets off a thrumming sensation, since the conversation with Susan flashes back in my mind. I change into scrubs and join the surgical team in the suite. The room doesn't have much of a smell, except for the residual faint odors of disinfectant and cleaning solution, since the cubic feet per minute (CFM) filter setting sweeps and sanitizes the air giving it a mostly neutral smell.

The surgical platform's positioning functions are run by a handheld control device. The operating table has the capacity to handle up to a seven hundred pound person. God save me if I ever have to operate on someone that heavy. The three pieces of wall art are dreamy mystical looking landscapes, setting the stage for the patient to drift off into the ether. Overhead are two large disc-shaped adjustable and movable operating lights.

Jackie actively checks the functions of the anesthesia machine and oversees the vital signs monitor, each situated above and to the left of where the patient's head will be. The scrub nurse places the surgical instruments and drapes on a narrow rolling table—and it's situated to be moved closer or out of the way depending on my surgical needs—to the left of the operating table. The stainless steel table holds other surgical supplies, such as Betadine microbicide surgical scrub to topically degerm the patient's skin before surgery.

Blue drapes cover the patient during surgery and generally expose only the operating surface. There is an endotracheal tube to maintain intubation to secure the airway of the patient, and if needed a stream of nitrous oxide. The suite has oxygen, and IV fluids to hydrate the patient. The circulating nurse keeps things clean and tidy. The four person team makes the day's work unwrinkled and sleekly done.

The tirade Susan put me through ruffles in my mind and I want to talk with the surgical staff about it because they are aware of how twisted this patient is, but I stop myself because Colette is in the room.

Colette is already dressed in a surgical gown. Her hair neatly enveloped in a clear head cover. I take her hand and gratuitously say, "Are you ready to become more beautiful?" I can't seem to get the hackneyed starch out of my voice, a duplicate retell with each patient. I despise myself for being so rote and lacking the authenticity to be more genuine.

"I've been up and down getting ready—anticipating this operation. My husband has big…expectations." She bites the corner of her lip. "He's looking forward to the new me." Colette is twisting her wedding band, then clutches the fabric of her gown. "He thinks I'll look like I've stepped out of a magazine."

"You must be a little apprehensive." My two comments so far sound like I've hit the replay button on a tape recorder. Jackie and Lana and Ann turn bland smiles.

"Tense? Yeah. On edge, yeah, but I still want it." Colette looks off for a moment, like she's in another universe. She stares back at me as if Colette desperately wants me to understand, to take good care of her. "It's like I fear waking up in the middle of the operation and I won't be able to talk. Or I won't be able to wake up at all."

"You know what that says?"

"What?"

"You're on target. Those are the usual apprehensions that most every patient has before the procedure."

"So, I'm normal?"

"Yes. We'd be concerned if you didn't have some uneasiness." I'm disconnected, faking good doctor bedside manner. Then I start to feel slightly more revved up about the procedure that increases compassion and rapport with the patient. I tell Colette we'll first administer a sedative which is short-acting and high potency. It's amnestic, meaning she won't remember much after taking it, and then when she's calm we'll start the anesthesia. I tell her each step and in my head I'm saying blah, blah, blah, as my lips mechanically make the right cooing sounds.

The nurses feign thoughtful expressions helping to hide how phony I sound "Jackie will send you home with instructions, so you don't need to remember what we just went over."

Colette shifts on the surgical table, looking like she can't get comfortable. "What else?"

I turn on some soft music—a Mozart violin piece, and then go to a cabinet and pull out a couple of magazines. "Let's look at some possibilities. The surgical lift will restore your breasts after the wear and tear of having two kids. But don't you want to make your breasts more of a work of beauty?" I thumb though a *Playboy* magazine to demonstrate some luscious examples of well-shaped breasts.

Colette lets out a little yelp. "I can't believe you're doing this." She fans herself. "But I have to admit those uptight medical before and after photos you also showed me at our initial consultation were boring. You know, the somber straight-faced women with the big boobs and with their backs up against what looked like a baby blue curtain."

Ann is hiding a mixed twinge of repugnance because of the magazine and the kick she gets out of it. Her cheeks and corners of her mouth pull up, cracking a smile.

Lana says, "He's not fooling around showing you the sexy chicks. Dr. Coyle will create a new you."

Ann blurts out, "Yeah, be ready for a hot rack!" We all look at her, and Ann rolls her eyes. Still, the quips ease Colette's pre-surgical anxiety.

She scrutinizes the magazine pictures and then her eyes widen. She points, "Just like that. I won't be able to get my husband off me. Now, that's what he would call walking right out of a magazine."

It's time to turn back on the serious-doctor act. "Colette, let's double check your medical status that we initially talked about."

We go over bits and pieces about her history and their possible effects on the procedure. The hum of the suction device and the anesthesia machine start up. The monitor displays the patient's vital signs. Lana stands by the surgical instruments, ready to assist me. Jackie begins the sedation, followed by the fentanyl for anesthesia. We insert the breathing tube for tracheal intubation, followed by the propofol for deep anesthesia, and a small dose of antibiotics for infection prophylaxis. Colette drifts to a faraway place.

I say, "Ann, enough of the spa experience. Turn off that goddamn Mozart and put on the Eric Clapton and crank up the volume. When we get to the serious part of the operation turn on Whitney Houston and toward the end let's hear Adele's *Rolling in the Deep*." I mark up Colette's chest where I'll make the incisions.

Jackie messes with me, "I get a kick out of that girly magazine routine you pull. They're shocked at first, and then they get the mental image of looking like a Bunny."

But Lana seems oblivious. She chortles, "No kidding. Plus when she goes home and looks in the mirror at her great breasts, and then looks at her face and says, 'Oh shit.'" She snorts. "Now we have a repeat customer."

And then Lana's torso vibrates when she cackles. "Here's your instrument, Dr. C."

Ann adjusts the sound on the music system. "So, Dr. Glen we've all taken some time off. When is your turn?"

I'm already getting hammered by Julie on the subject. Now the surgery staff is getting on my case. "Have you been conspiring with Julie?"

"What?"

"This morning Julie asked me the same thing."

Jackie says, "Well, it's been a while since you've taken time off."

"I've got this and that to consider before taking time away from the office." Straight-faced, I disguise my tension and agonize to refocus on the mastopexy, and then look to the side for a second, fumbling and dropping the scalpel. It dances off the hard linoleum floor and makes a clanging sound when the scalpel ricochets off the stainless steel leg of the instrument table.

Jackie and Lana and Ann say zip, leaving only a silence that's filled by the sounds of the suction and anesthesia machines. Lana stoically hands me another scalpel, while Ann picks up the blood-tinged stainless steel instrument from the floor. She wipes the ruby shaped and colored blood specks off the operating deck.

The machines drone in my ears. My distraction about being cut off from my drug supply overrides being embarrassed about dropping the scalpel. Jackie says, "Good thing the scalpel didn't spear you in the foot, Glen. It'd be a real scene seeing you hopping around the surgical suite on one foot." Jackie and Lana and Ann fudge imitation laughter. The scalpel distraction eases me off the hook.

"I want to tell the three of you something. Before the procedure today I got a call from a patient, Susan, who was yelling at me over the phone and she was being a lunatic. You remember the one, where I did the rhinoplasty, and despite my misgivings about the case, I went ahead and did it anyway.

The procedure came out perfectly, but she constantly looks in the mirror and screamed at me that I purposely botched it."

Jackie says, "Yeah, I know. She is one batty woman." She pauses for a second. "Hey, I have an idea. Give her a list of all the plastic surgeons in the county and tell her go have a second opinion about the results of the rhinoplasty. Let her make the choice about who to see, so she isn't suspicious that you put a bug in the doctor's ear."

"Clever idea. That's just what I'll do." I take in a breath to get rid of my nervousness. "I blew it by accepting her as a patient…a momentary lapse in judgment. Now I'm paying for it. The doc giving the second opinion will undoubtedly say the rhinoplasty turned out perfectly. I know the logic of what the doc says won't take hold for Susan. It's not about her nose. It's about all the bananas thoughts and emotions that shoot around in her mind. She thought the nose job would reposition her life. The only thing it shaped up was her nose and it wasn't a fix for everything else that crazes her mind. But the second opinion would support my defensive posture to shield me against litigation or a report to the Medical Board."

My cell phone rings. "Ann, will you get that."

She picks up the telephone and looks at the screen. "It's Julie." And pushes the speak button. "Hi Julie. Glen is in the middle of a procedure." She listens for a couple of seconds. "Glen, she is nailing down plans to go to Colorado and wants to know the dates you can go."

"Tell her I'll check." But really I want to put her off. Distressed, I feel the pressure I'm putting on the scalpel and ease up. I think about the harangue that Susan put me through and I don't want to mess up the operation on Colette.

"Did you hear that? No? Glen said he'd check." Ann takes note. "Okay, goodbye." She puts down the phone and turns to me. "Julie has been checking flights out of San Francisco and wants to hook up with her triathlon friend to work out with in Colorado and to see her parents." We haven't seen her parents for ages for good reason. Her mind must be numb if she is thinking of stepping into that horror show. She hates them more than I do. Still, who am I kidding? I know the obligatory visit to Colorado is inescapable.

I robotically work on the routine breast lift and augmentation procedures. The surgical team runs as a tight multi-operational unit despite all my preoccupations—amazing how well we get the job done given they have a maniac of a surgeon to work with. But they can't keep a bead on everything. What if I screw up and my whole surgical world swirls down the drain.

After I have finished up and the patient is wheeled away, I say, "Jackie, while you work with Colette in recovery, I'll take care of wasting the unspent drugs." My voice isn't overly dismissive, since she is supposed to watch me waste the drugs. She gets what I'm up to, though. I'll take the remaining drugs to my office, but I won't waste them. I'll deposit them in my cache to protect the supply. I touch Jackie's shoulder and ease my hand around her back to her other shoulder and pull her close. Her eyes coyly connect with mine. Jackie leaves to attend to Colette in the recovery room.

I glance up and look at and the receptionist who has materialized in front of my desk. "Tara Swan called…" Jackie reappears. The receptionist goes on, "…she has a postoperative infection."

"Call her back and tell her to have her primary care physician to take care of it."

"She already contacted her PCP. He told her to call you since you are the treating physician who is responsible for the surgery."

I'm preoccupied with the unused drugs from the procedure. "Okay." Her primary care physician is an uptight asshole. "We'll take care of it."

The receptionist leaves. Jackie is a nurse practitioner and licensed to recommend medications under a physician's supervision. She says, "Glen, do you want me to call Tara and check it out? Should be a quick fix to prescribe some meds—antibiotics."

"Sure. Thanks. You know the drill."

Jackie takes two steps and does an about face, stepping close to me. She wrings her hands. "I have to say something that can't wait."

The look on Jackie's face unnerves me. "So what's the urgency?" My loose hand turns into a tight fist.

"The practice has been dotted with more and more outcome problems lately. I mean the procedures are great, but the rate of infection is above the norm."

"You think there's erosion?" I feel the creases form in my forehead, thinking Jackie is going to turn on me and I'll get hammered by her.

"I think you'd better watch it."

"And if—"

"I don't think Lana or Ann is a whistleblower, but if more patient complaints get generated there could be a report to the Medical Board of California or an inquiry by the Physician Well Being Committee at the hospital." A sense of alarm is in Jackie's voice.

I jerk back. "Those goddamn women are not following the postoperative instructions."

"Look, I'm your friend."

I laugh. "I'd like to think it's a tad more than that."

"Come on Glen, not right now. No bullshit, you don't look right in morning until the mediation safe is opened up."

"I have a pulse on what is going on and I can handle it. It's not like I'm absorbed in some sort of dark vortex that's sucking me down to hell." I'm draw back. I must be making myself look small in Jackie's eyes.

"Glen, I love you, but I hate…"

My fists get tighter. I tense up, thinking she's going to throw me off a cliff. "Finish your sentence."

"There's a lot at stake. I don't know what's going to happen next. I mean goddamn it, Glen, you scare me. Stop it."

"Is that it?"

Jackie leaves. I know she's in a huff, but disguises it.

Jackie has just defied me to face up to what I keep in hiding. I always want the warm fuzzy stuff from her and now here I am being challenged to meet the most threatening pieces of my life. At least there's no contest about the clash of my duplicity between Jackie and Julie. My mind becomes pelted with anticipation, some unrecognizable slice that's yet to come.

It's going to be dicey pulling through a visit with Julie's parents since I haven't seen them since I got back from that god forsaken war-torn mess. The obligation to visit them is a liability. Julie must being screening out her daunting past. She doesn't get what this visit is going to add up to.

CHAPTER TWO

The overhead announcements say what flights are boarding and to report to the authorities any unattended luggage. Julie is wearing Lycra athletic pants, running shoes and a hooded navy blue sweatshirt that has the Boston Marathon lettered on it in white. Her hair is pulled back in a swishy ponytail. Julie and I go through security at the San Francisco airport to board our two and a half hour flight to Denver. I get jumpy when I put my carryon bag on the conveyer belt to be scanned. The X-ray machine spins around us while we hold our arms up as we individually go through the TSA inspection.

I don't pack the medication in case the twit airline loses our bags. Maybe it's dim-witted, but I take only the standard maximum daily dose of the opiate, Vicodin—eight tablets per day for seven days and an extra day in case there's some SNAFU flight delay. Sixty-four of the hydrocodone and acetaminophen tabs to get me through the week. It's my attempt at control. Is this dumb or smart or really stupid? Maybe no sweat—I think. I have the medication in a container with Julie's name on it and the prescription signature for dosage. Should security fuck with me I'll lean on her to cover me and say the drugs belong to her. I wrote the prescription for her. Julie knows about my little hiding game and she's acquiescent to make my covert cover-up possible. There's no way I'd write it for myself—a set up for justice to step in and bust me.

I'm frayed, anticipating the TSA security people are going to hassle me about the drugs I'm carrying. Feeling skinless, my hypervigilant gaze darts from place to place while going through security. I have strange sensations, being hyped on opiates, mixed with adrenaline. But the place is packed and we slide through.

The actual or imagined strain is off my back. "Those TSA people really get on my nerves. I'm so relieved they didn't harass us. Trying to slide through these functionaries is such an annoyance."

"Goddamn, Glen, don't be so pestered. I mean you're kind of doing a number on yourself."

• • •

Julie and I tap on the door. I see a simultaneously conflicting look of horror and hope on Julie's face, a crease across her forehead and uplifted cheeks from her smile. We walk in her childhood upscale but skimpily maintained home. The terrible two—Tess and Thad—hug and pull us into the house. I smell a gush of his alcoholic acetaldehyde breath left over from yesterday's drinking.

The expectancy of sweet honey turning to sticky glue is sickening. I want to defend Julie against what's coming next. Thad rubs his hands together. His eyes brighten, "I just made a pitcher of vodka martinis. Let me pour you a good one." Tess jerks her head up and down. Her bubbly grin puffs up her spider veined cheeks.

They always offer us drinks the split second after we walk through the door. And they're so pushy; it agitates the hell out of me. "We've been here thirty seconds and you want to get us juiced."

I love bright minded and beautiful Julie, and then there's having to buy into the gooey mess of having Thad and Tess for in-laws. They are about to shit on Julie and she's oblivious about all the crap that's about to get dumped on her, despite being through it a million times before. "Hey Glen, good to see yeah, son." Thad leans his head back and chortles while he puts his hands on top of his paunch. "Come on in."

I see the change on Julie's face. The picture frames must be flashing in Julie's mind, like she's swimming in the morass of her toxic childhood. "Hello, Dad." She pats him on his shoulder to get his attention.

Thad perks up to give her a bear hug. He looks as if he's about to crush her ribs. "Okay, darling." He pulls back. His beaming smile shows two rows of straight teeth. They must be veneers—too perfect and overly white, almost looking iridescent. "Let me get you a drink."

"No thanks. I'm in training for the Ironman in Hawaii this October. Liz and I are doing a hundred miler road bike training ride tomorrow." Julie wrinkles her nose. "Drinking is out and nutrition is in." Her words sound stiffened, on the inelastic hard side.

Tess furrows her brow. "When'd you get so pure on us?" I double check the veins on her spidery looking cheeks.

It's no news that Julie has always wanted her folks to say she's okay, and they're so preoccupied with themselves the two of them never say Julie is okay or anything about her accomplishments or that she's got something going for her. I get this every time we're around them—with her emotionally getting down on her knees and begging like she a five year old waif. "You've got a pretty hot daughter. Her prowess as a long distance runner is over the top. You see it, right?" And then I shrink inside myself, knowing I got sucked into a cesspool.

Tess shrugs it off. "Well honey, don't you think all that athleticism for someone your age is a waste of time. I mean to say, we put you through the wonderful education at Scripps College and the only good that came from it was meeting Glen."

I think about the amazing good fortune of going to Pomona to put me practically right next door to Julie and hooking up with her. But Tess's inaccurate analysis of Julie misses the mark. And how could a mother not know what a gifted daughter she has.

Julie puts both of her hands on the side of her head like she's covering her ears. She drops her arms. "It's what I want to do." I'm slightly relieved that Julie was able to counter with a little moxie to defy toxic waste that Thad and Tess dump on her.

Thad muscles in, "You really like all that running around, treading water and pushing pedals?" His voice booms. "An educated girl like you."

I always have to protect Julie from her parents. "Yeah, Thad, Julie loves it so goddamn much she can't get enough of it." I'm worked up, grind my teeth until they hurt. But Thad and Tess are so insensible, it's like I'm looking at two perfunctory blank faces. Why don't I shut up? Because I can't. "And Julie is so educated she's a whizz kid at cocktail party conversations."

Thad flips the conversation. He slaps me on the back. "Say son, I'm glad you're in one piece. Did you almost get your ass shot off over there in Iraq?"

I feel a burning anger toward Thad who never served in combat. And then I grasp some self-possession. I'd like to return the favor by slapping Thad so hard on his back that he'd fall face first onto the hardwood floor.

Julie's face is ashen. Tess's smiling self shows zero comprehension and the force of her oblivion. "Yeah, I almost got my ass shot off some of the time."

I flashback to how shots and IEDs resulted in wounds of the poor souls I was pasting back together in the OR. Whole faces were penetrated by debris from IEDs or part of their faces had been blown off. The slap on the back and my ass almost being shot off comment cheapens what happened in the war theater. The painstaking procedures turned devastating injuries and disfigurements to appearances of normalcy.

Tess looks at Thad. "Let's have that drink now."

I feel like projectile vomiting when I'm around Tess and Thad. And they waddle around with a martini glass in their hands. At least my sloshed father said I was a meaningless piece of shit to my face without being furtive or devious about it. I look at Julie. She's so turbulent, she must have turned numb. I think of Thad and Tess as being two turds floating in an alcoholic punch bowl. I say, "I need to use the bathroom."

Tess gulps down a third of her martini. "Use the bathroom in the master bedroom. The plunger in the guest bathroom is broken." They're so sidetracked with getting loaded that Thad and Tess can't be bothered with minor household repairs.

I walk out of the room. Julie is on my tail. When we get the bedroom she grabs me. I tightly hold her. She says, "Goddamn it. Every time I think it is going to be different with them and it's always the same." A pained and pale vacuousness occupies her face. The sensation of how Julie feels transmits she's downcast and dejected. It's all too familiar to me. With her folks the roots of her existence are intensely poisonous, but she gives my misdoings a break.

"Stop needing their approval, because…guess what?"

"I know, but I always get sucked back into it."

"Capricious dipsomanic assholes."

"Say what?"

"Unpredictable boozers."

"Let's go."

I'm going to have a look to see if they have anything stashed in the medicine cabinet. "Okay. I need to use the bathroom before we go."

Julie leaves the room. I close the door the bathroom. Shit, I've been here one day and already burned through twenty tabs of my stash. I poke around the medicine chest and drawers. Eureka. I feel high finding the stuff and even before taking this crap. OxyContin and Dilaudid and Xanax. I check the expiration dates. I'm good to go. There're about ten tabs in each container. A knee-jerk physical craving jacks up and I feel like gulping the meds. Ravenous gluttony is a virtue in my little self-indulgent notebook. One pill each isn't going to lift me half an inch off the ground. I've got forty-four tabs left in my stash, so I'll take half of asshole mom and pop's Rx while they can settle their nerves and enjoy pain control with their old buddy vodka. Fuck 'em. Especially after Thad's mindless back slapping number.

I do my duty, shake three times, and thoroughly wash up. All that hand washing is blazed in my brain from my undergraduate advanced classes in microbiology. Sometimes I have a hard time believing stuff like that sticks with me. I toss down two OxyContin and Dialaudid and those drugs perk me up where they would lay out ordinary people. I rejoin Tess and Thad who are halfway through another martini. Or did they slip another one or two in while I was in the head? Who cares, I'm not keeping track of them. And they don't keep track of what they do. Julie is sitting hunched over with her forehead resting on her palms, fingers splayed back on her scalp.

Julie elevates her head to glance at me. She's so downcast that her face looks like it has been run over, leaving a tread mark. Her eyes link up with mine, like it's a message that I'm her ticket out of here. "Glen, I told mom and dad we have to go."

"You told them why, right?"

"Yeah, I have a touch of—"

"A touch of consternation driven home by Julie being a wonderfully accomplished person defined by her magnanimous station and accomplishments in life…" I sound like an asshole, but I don't give a fuck. "…but lacking validation by the genetic protoplasm that coalesced to bring such a wonderful being to our universe."

Tess toasts me not knowing she spilt a fourth of her drink on the floor. Stupefied and not having a clue about what I just said. With an impassive intonation she says, "Glen, do you want a drink before you go?"

CHAPTER THREE

I leave the bed and breakfast place where we are staying, while Julie is with her triathlon girlfriend getting loads of miles in on their road bicycles. She no doubt assumes I'll run my own maneuvers while she's out with her training buddy. I'm out of my pharmaceuticals that keep the balance going and have twinges of withdrawal warning signs. I know what's on the horizon is going to hit me full force. I'm angst-ridden about what I'll try next, since it's new and not my style, being out of my element. I'll work a pharmacy to get what I need.

"Hi, could you help me out with something?" My smile is effusive, unrestrained. "And by the way, how are you today?" Underneath my grinning face is a tension I have to restrain or it will explode.

"Fine." The florescent lights glare on the pharmacy technician, making her face look pasty and her hair a strangely fixed blondish color. She's a slight woman with long hair pulled back in a ponytail.

"I am a physician from California and I'm in a bit of a prescription jam." I shift to seriousness, trying to stop my foot from bouncing to calm down my restless legs. My eyebrows pull together. "I should say, my wife has a problem. We flew here to Colorado and she packed her medication in her suitcase—something I've advised her not to do—and the airlines lost our luggage. We have contacted them several times and there's no sign of our baggage."

The tech's neck bends forward. She scratches her jaw. "Yes, sir."

I look at the nameplate pinned to her chest. "You see, Margaret, my wife has severe radiculopathy and the nerve compression in her spine is causing acute pain." I try to deepen my shallow breathing. What's rushing through my veins is a feeling of desperation and I have to make this scam work. "And unfortunately, she has a history of chronic fibromyalgia, which overlays the radiculopathy making for acute and unrelenting pain."

"That's a lot of explanation." She lifts one eyebrow. I see her suspiciousness. Margaret's disbelief unsettles me. "And what is it that you want?"

This woman isn't buying it. My stomach tightens. "I have a current DEA license, but I'm not licensed as a physician in Colorado." I work at having a relaxed appearance, but I'm speaking too rapidly. Damn it. I slow it down. "Please extend me the courtesy of writing her a prescription for pain medication so we can get her some relief."

The tech is openly staring at me. "And why isn't she with you, now?"

What runs through my mind is Julie is on a goddamn hundred-mile road bike ride with Liz and then she's going to swim two miles. "Her pain is quite intractable and she simply couldn't make the car ride to get here."

"Are you sure?"

My stomach constricts another notch. "Sure I'm sure."

"I assume you have a prescription pad and identification."

I overenthusiastically smile. "Of course. I never leave home without them." I pull back, realizing this was a lame thing to say.

"Dr...."

"Dr. Coyle. Dr. Glen Coyle."

"Dr. Coyle, would you please step over to the consultation line and I will have the pharmacist in charge speak with you."

I wait for five minutes. The PIC arrives at the consultation station. He moves his glasses down his nose and looks over the top of the rim. His face conveys dubious skepticism. "Hello, sir, the pharmacy tech told me your situation in detail." The PIC's name badge says Kyle Geiger with Pharmacist in Charge written in smaller letter below his name. Geiger is thick through the chest. He has a heavy jaw.

I start to blurt out the explanation again. "My wife—"

"I have the details already, no need to repeat them." Geiger rubs his eyebrow. "Since you are not licensed in Colorado, but have a DEA license I will need to call California to check on the regulatory requirements for prescription writing for controlled substances." He quickly blinks a couple of times. The tone of his voice tells me this is some kind of pro forma routine he's doing to get me out of his hair. "Do you want me to do that?"

"Sure. Yes, please."

"And what exactly are you wanting...in terms of pain medication?"

"We are going to be here for about two more weeks. One hundred and twenty Vicodin should get her through." I pleasantly smile, while my clinched jaw is grinding my back molars.

"Dr...."

"Coyle."

Geiger crosses his arms across his chest. "Dr. Coyle, we're not going to fill this prescription." The PIC has a neutral look on his face. "I suggest since your wife is in that much pain that you take her to an urgent care clinic to be evaluated by a physician and appropriately prescribed medication."

My eyes narrow. "I am a physician and know what my wife needs." This guy is shooing me out the door. I'm about to snap at this guy, but stop myself.

Geiger's hands drop to his sides. "We just can't fulfill your request. Please accept it."

"And why the hell not?" My cheeks get hot. They must be red.

"You're sure you want to know?"

I practically spit at Geiger. "Yes I do. An explanation would be—"

"How many people a day do you think we get in the pharmacy with a story like yours? You're a physician. But the way you are asking for what you want is...well, odd. Like others, you're very friendly. Explain the situation with elaborate and too much detail. Something happened to the medication and you have an unusual refill request. And it's not for antibiotics or medication that isn't subject to abuse. When people like you come in it's pain medication or benzodiazepines. And the amount—"

I'm burning up and my temples are moist. "Are you suggesting—"

"We have one to two people per day come into this pharmacy that approximately duplicate what you are saying. To us it's obvious. I am not judging you as a person, I am simply saying no to your request. Good afternoon." The PIC turns and walks away.

I spin around and make my way toward the door. I feel slighted being rejected by this attempt and moist creases form across my forehead. I grumble under my breath, "Fuck you, asshole." I sit in the rental car and grip the steering wheel, observing my knuckles turning white like my hands are disassociated from my body. I contemplate my next move. Geiger told me how they profile drug seeking behavior. I know this shit. I recapitulate what I just said—how it went. Too stupid. And then what jumps in my mind are the chronic pain patients, a lot of whom work me over for drug prescriptions and early refills and all the trauma drama telephone calls during the week and weekends with the flimflam excuses—this and that bullshit story—the scams to the max. But the empathic me gives in and prescribes their meds. Those sons of bitches better not be calling me Dr. Feel Good behind my back

And there's that competition body builder psycho woman whose moods are up and down like a yoyo because of steroid-induced labile swings. We augmented her flat chest with fist sized breasts and made her nipples look like erasers and made her little tummy flat as a board. And then she constantly bugs me to prescribe her steroids. I feel like some kind of heavy weight she's bench pressing.

Should I try another pharmacy? If I don't, I'll be in the pit of withdrawal symptoms. Here's the next plan. I'll go to a mom and pop operation rather than a big chain pharmacy where they have vodka and beer and pink toenail polish on sale. Change the story. Take the chance and write a prescription for myself. I look up Boulder pharmacies on my iPhone. Here we go. Dunwoody Pharmacy. That's a mom and pop shop.

Driving over to the next pharmacy my crafty self comes out full force—no being undone again. I fiddle with the stations on the radio. My hands on the steering wheel are like Vice Grips. I blast the car's horn at a jaywalker in front of me and yell, "Fuck you." I try to reel myself in and then say the hell with it. My skin was moist at Geiger's pharmacy and now I'm getting sweatier. I better not get jerked around at the next pharmacy. I park in front.

"Good afternoon." I have a cordial and not an overdone smile. "Here's a prescription I'd like filled." My stomach churns. But my expression remains neutral.

The pharmacy tech has bleached hair with black roots. She's dumpy, but looks pleasant. Her nameplate reads Karen. She reads the prescription and signature, and looks up. "This is for you and written by you?"

"That's correct. I have a chronic back condition."

"And you're from out of state?"

"Yes. But my DEA license is current and valid."

"The PIC will have to discuss this with you."

"And that is Mr. Dunwoody?"

"No, he retired and Peter Enright is the new owner. The name was retained because of the pharmacy's long history in the area." She glances down at the prescription again. And without looking at me she says, "Excuse me, I will get Mr. Enright. He will meet you at the consultation window."

Here we go again. I feel a bead of sweat at my temple. I need to relax my squint and loosen my steal trap jaw. Jesus.

A clean cut man in his mid-forties appears at the consultation window. He smiles and extends his hand to shake mine. "Dr. Coyle, I am Peter Enright the owner and PIC of the pharmacy." He clears his throat. "There are a couple of gaps here. Would you please fill me in on the details of you being from out of state and writing your own prescription, so we can best address your needs?" He respectfully smiles, but his grin looks suspiciously fake.

"Certainly. I have a chronic back condition from being in odd positions from performing surgery and then having to twist when I assist my staff in lifting the patient from the operating table to the gurney to be taken to the recovery room." I look away for a second to collect myself, wondering if this sounds too lame. I notice his eyes have a penetrating quality to them, despite the cordiality of his facial expression. "My medication for the trip was packed in a suitcase and the airlines lost our bags. And they don't seem to be able to recover their whereabouts. I always pack my medication in my carryon bag, but I'll be damned if I know what happened. The telephone rang while I was packing and I must have inadvertently been distracted and my preoccupation caused me to slip up and forget to pack my medication, or I must have put the medication in my luggage that went on the plane. I'm always on top of the physician-medication procedures, but even I can do some really dumb things sometimes."

I wish he'd get that shit eating grin off his face. "I have an idea. You packed your medications and did not carry them on your person. *O-o-kay.* Do you mind holding on for a second? I need to check something out."

"Sure, fine." Son-of-a-bitch, this isn't going to work either.

"I'll be right back." Enright does an about face.

Apprehension turns into a feeling of alarm. I can't pull the reins back to curb myself and have some restraint. A frenzied feeling affects the beginning stages of withdrawal that magnifies dysphoric physical sensations and whirl upset in my stomach and a jitteriness crawls across my skin.

He returns in five minutes. My face is pinched. I shift my weight from side to side. I say, "What do you have in mind?" I'm wringing my hands behind the counter and he can't see what I'm doing.

"We are unable to fill your prescription. But I have a colleague at the University of Colorado Hospital in the Emergency Department and fortuitously he is in today. I briefly spoke with him about your situation and he is ready and able to assist you. The hospital is—"

"I don't *think* I need to see a…" I catch myself and withhold saying *goddamn*. "… physician. I know my condition and what I require to treat it."

"I see. We are *not* going to fill your prescription and the only clear cut way for you to get the help you need to have an evaluation by a physician in our area. I recommend that you see my colleague, Dr. Scott Chandler. He will take good care of you. Here are the directions to the hospital." There's that shit eating smile again. "He is expecting you."

"Is there any way I can sway you to provide the medication without going through an unnecessary ordeal like seeing an emergency medicine physician?"

Enright has a weighty posture. He tilts his head while contemptuously saying, "I am doing you a service by referring you to Dr. Chandler."

"Okay. Enough. I'll go see Dr.…."

"Chandler."

"Right, Dr. Chandler."

"Hang in there."

What's this hang in there bullshit? "Thank you for your help Enright." Fuck 'em.

• • •

"Good afternoon. I am Dr. Coyle. Dr. Chandler is expecting me." I fight back my nervousness, thinking of whom I'm about to see—an emergency medicine physician who has heard every trick to suck drugs out of him. Dread leaches in that I may be humiliated by him in my attempts to get what I need to temporarily patch me up.

The receptionist smiles. She is wearing heart-patterned scrubs with a V-neck that shows her cleavage while she sits and I stand on the other end of the counter. "Are you here to consult on a case?"

"No, I'm here to be treated for pain."

She checks the computer. "I think he just went in with an emergent case. But that will give us some time to take care of your insurance information and get you roomed and your vitals taken."

"I'll pay cash." No paper trail of me being here.

She jerks her head back and blinks. The receptionist looks like she caught off guard that this is a cash deal. "Yes, sir. Please take a seat and a nurse will come to get you."

At this point I feel like strangling the bitch, cleavage or no cleavage. I feign courteousness. "Thank you for your help and I will wait for the nurse." I laugh with a sharp edge.

I look at the wall clock as minutes tick by, feeling shittier and shittier. Five, ten, fifteen and in thirty minutes the nurse calls my name. Her voice sounds sterile, like I'm another bovine being funneled down a cattle chute. The nurse shows me to an exam room and takes my vital signs. She signs onto a computer and records my body temperature, pulse, blood pressure and respiratory rate. I mutter tensely to myself like spitting nails because I'm dope-sick. But I manage a genteel niceness at the epidermal level of my present shit ass existence.

After she has entered my basic patient vitals into the computer, she mechanically says, "So what brings you in today?"

"I am traveling. The airlines lost my luggage which contained my pain medication. I am not only experiencing pain, but I seem to be in withdrawal." My left index finger is twitching. I cover it with my right hand. "By the way, I am a physician." Lassoing my poor judgment crosses my mind, so I don't screw myself anymore than I have already. "I was referred to specifically see Dr. Chandler and he is expecting me."

"You sound like you're in a terrible state, doctor. Dr. Chandler is tied up with a cardiac emergency. But he shouldn't be too much longer. I'll go check." She supportively touches my shoulder on the way out of the room.

Keep you goddamn hands off me. I just need to get what I need. "Thanks for checking."

I wait, pointlessly eying all the emergency medicine supplies in the room. Like what, they're going to leave some Rx opiates lying around. I stand up and sit down, and bite down on my lower lip and force myself to stop it. And then wait to the point of ad absurdum. Screw it. I take a step toward the room's exit, and I hear a tap on the door. Chandler is a clean cut man with wavy dark hair and he looks like he spends a lot of time at the gym working out. "Sorry to keep you waiting so long. A patient came in who had a M.I." Chandler drums his fingers against his thigh and hums. He lifts his hand and gives me a solid firm handshake. And then he has a look on his face like he has a touch on some private understanding. This makes me restless.

Chandler sits on a round-topped stool with rollers. He says. "Peter Enright called and briefly told me about your predicament. I'd like to know directly from you what the situation is."

I'll have turn my cunning into such a sophisticated piece of work that Chandler will have no idea that I am getting over on him. "I am a surgeon from California. My wife and I are visiting. I have chronic back pain caused by radiculopathy and packed my medications in my suitcase. The airlines lost our luggage. Now, without my mediations, I am in pain and opiate withdrawal." I have a jolted feeling in my shoulders and neck that comes from my attempt at deception.

Chandler is examining my eyes, now dilated from being in withdrawal, and the opposite of having pupillary pinpoints when opiates are on board. I see him glance at my gooseflesh forearms. "How long have you been taking pain medication?"

"Three years." I downsize it by two years.

"Who prescribes your medication?"

"Dr....Dr. Kline."

"What would you say to signing a HIPPA compliant release of information so I can call Dr. Kline and coordinate treatment?"

Chandler throws me for a loop, though I back pedal to sound unfazed. A piece of craftiness spins off my tongue without thinking. "That would be fine, but he is traveling in China and unavailable."

"What about someone else in his office?"

"He's in solo practice and closed his office while he is gone to give his office staff a break."

"Isn't someone covering for him?"

"Yes, but the person would not have access to my medical information." I think that Chandler is unflinching and getting the upper hand. I'm starting to feel mired.

"What other treatment have you received for the radiculopathy in addition to medication?"

"Some physical therapy. Core strengthening exercises and stretching."

"And how frequently do you do the physical therapy."

"Daily. I might miss one day here and there."

"Please lean back on the exam table. I want to examine your abdominal muscles."

I lean back. Chandler examines my musculature, while I contract my stomach muscles to make them appear that I do the workout to strengthen them.

He says, "Okay, you can sit up." Chandler watches my mechanics when I get to a sitting position. "What is the signature on your prescription?"

"Eight Vicodin per day."

"What effect does the medication give you? For example, does it sedate you, just take the pain away, narcotize you, or possibly give you a little energy?"

I think Chandler is trying to trap me. "Let's see. It takes the pain away. And I get a little energy from the medication."

"Let me check your reflexes." I imagine Chandler is buying time and I don't see the need for this procedure. "I'd like to discuss my assessment with you and tell you what I think. I need to respectively ask if you are open to this."

"Sure. I need help."

"Okay, and that is what I precisely want to do—help." There's a glint in his eye, like he is carrying some secret with him. "What I have to say is don't bullshit a bullshitter."

I hunch forward. My mouth drops open. The next thing that crosses my mind is that I've been totally had. Then I gather myself up. "What?"

"Don't bullshit a bullshitter, Dr. Coyle."

"I have never heard a professional assessment like that before. Just what are you driving at?"

Chandler reaches in his pocket. He pulls out a bronze colored medallion the size of a silver dollar that has the Roman number XV on it.

I say, "Okay. What's that?"

"It is what is called a *chip*. It recognizes how many years a person has been in recovery. I am a drug addict—a bullshitter of the past—and I can clearly recognize you're addicted and drug seeking. I asked you questions to simply confirm what I smelled the moment I took a look at you."

"Oh, Jesus." I jab my finger toward Chandler's face. It's iffy that I'll pull off this con. "That's way out of whack. I just need help for pain relief."

"May I tell you what I think about your response?"

I wonder if Chandler is going to conciliate, or if he is going to nail me again. "Yeah. Sure. Okay."

"It is hostile and what I would expect from a drug addict who has just been confronted."

"And what about one iota of substantiation?"

"Okay. Enright referred you to me based on his suspicions that you were drug seeking. The excuse of packing medications you depend on in a suitcase is...well...lame. I know of no physician who would do that, particularly one who is so dependent on medications. You attempted to write your own prescription which is extremely suspect. The amount of Vicodin you say you take is completely inconsistent with the degree with withdrawal symptoms you're having." Chandler's penetrating confrontation is done with well-greased ease. "Your information about the prescribing physician did not jibe. And you said that you're doing PT daily, but your abdominal muscles are weak."

My laughter is edgy, feeling utterly exposed. "Is that all?"

Chandler shakes his head back and forth. "No, that's not all. You said that you get energized by the medication. That is the all time litmus paper test for addiction."

Any hope for an appeasement evaporates and I can't stop myself from being antagonistic. "You can't bullshit a bullshitter. Well, I know how to bullshit and I think this is bullshit."

"I have one last piece of bullshit left."

"Yeah? What?"

"Geiger and Enright are friends. Serendipitously, they were speaking on the telephone while you were on the way from Geiger's pharmacy to Enright's pharmacy. You were obviously drug seeking at Geiger's pharmacy with a story about your wife losing her medication and wanting a script for one hundred and twenty tabs, and then the story changed when you arrived at Enright's place."

I bend over and put my head in my hands. "I'm fucked."

Chandler puts his hand on my back. "You are fucked, but we can help you."

His hand on my back feels like a branding iron. I sit upright. Blinking, I say, "How?"

"I recommend that you go for a chemical dependency evaluation at a program that specializes in healthcare professionals."

"A what?"

"An evaluation. There are two places I like to refer to. They aren't the only good places, but the ones that I tend to favor. One is Talbott Recovery Campus in Atlanta. The other is Hazelden-Springbrook outside of Portland, Oregon."

I'm not getting pushed into this. "I can't. I have a full schedule of patients waiting for surgery."

"You can. You mean *you won't*." Chandler moistens his lips. He nods, showing his confidence at handling me. "It's a three-day assessment. You could leave right now to do it."

"I'm just not—"

"What? Ready?"

"I need to talk to my wife about it." I snap back, but actually I'm afraid. My vision is lurid from the opiate withdrawal. I pull the wife trump card out, scrambling for what to say. At first blush, Julie would have relief if I go to treatment, but then I wonder if she could handle all the changes that would be called for—our lives in one giant twist. She has to be getting weary of what me and my compulsive habits.

"If you are in this state of crisis about drug addiction, I imagine that your wife is in a great deal of pain about your drug use and would be very supportive of you going. Am I wrong?"

The idea of change puts me in an anxious bind. The major trepidation is that I don't know if I can get and stay clean. And being in withdrawal now makes it an even murkier proposition. "I'm scared...no call it uncomfortable and cramped. I need to get used to the idea. Is there anything you can do for me now? You know, like a drug taper?" I feel like a savage animal making this request. The likelihood of him going for it is zilch. Give it a try.

"You must know opiate tapers are against medical regulations. The only drugs I can do a taper with are the benzodiazepines because of the likelihood of seizures if there's an abrupt withdrawal. You will not die or have seizures with opiate withdrawal." A questioning look crosses Chandler's face. He pauses, "I can help you, but with certain provisos."

"I'm willing to hear what you have to say."

"Willingness is a good first step. I have a DEA X license which means I can prescribe Suboxone. You are in full withdrawal right now and this is the juncture when it is prescribed. If I prescribe it we will have to monitor your vitals for the rest of the afternoon. The medication is a—"

"I know how it works—agonist-antagonist. It will take away the withdrawal symptoms and if I use any opiates it will sit on the opiate receptor site and I won't get loaded." I'm slightly offended that Chandler presupposes that I don't know how the medication works.

"The medication is a blessing and a curse. Takes away withdrawal. But some people get tied to it forever."

Maybe yes or no that I get tied to a new drug forever. "So what's the proviso?"

"I give you a script for a week. And you go get evaluated."

"Okay."

Chandler steps over to the computer and orders the medication. "Okay, done. There's something else I want you to do."

"And that is—"

"Tonight, I'll pick you up and take you to our caduceus group."

"A what?"

"It's a twelve step meeting for healthcare professionals."

"Which means what?" The tension around my squinting eyes is obvious to me.

"All of the members are addicts or alcoholics who work in the healthcare field. The basic foundation is to share experience, strength and hope about recovery from addiction." He smiles. "Where are you staying?"

I say that I'll go and give him the address of the bed and breakfast place where Julie and I are staying. If I don't go, maybe he will withdraw the Rx for the Suboxone.

Julie is out to dinner with her triathlon girlfriend and she won't be the wiser about what I'm up to this evening. But if she knew, it'd ease her mind. I'm tight waiting for Chandler to pick me up. Maybe I could feign an excuse, or just not be here when he comes. I'm not up for this, but that would be too chicken shit.

Chandler punctually picks me up at seven thirty. He stares in my eyes when I get in the car. He must be measuring if there is any hint of contempt. "You ready for this or are you freaking out?"

"Freaking out? A little. Kind of numb. This is a lot all at once—don't know if I'm ready."

"There's a saying, 'Take the body and the mind will follow.'" Chandler smiles warmly. I know this guy's heart is in the right place. I'm trying to find out what's in my conniving heart.

• • •

We arrive early for the eight o'clock meeting. We walk in the meeting room. The place is pleasant enough and there are upbeat people talking, but strangely I feel out of place. I see Geiger and Enright talking. They smile and come over. Geiger and Enright are reminders that the screws were put to me. They hug Chandler. They shake my hand and welcome me.

Enright's eyes dance. He makes me mad because he is drug-free and seems so goddamn wholesome it makes me want to puke. He says, "God sure has a way."

Geiger has laugh lines around his eyes. "You screwed yourself and that's what everybody seems to do before getting help. In a way, it's a blessing."

My body involuntarily collapses inward and I angle myself away from them. I pull myself up straight. And face them. "Yeah, I pretty much get what you mean."

These guys are warlocks that have forced me in a corner. Yeah, they think they're doing me a favor, but I feel coerced.

I listen to the stories. Chandler was right about the people discussing their devastation and all the work and faith it takes to pull through. I hear them say if you follow the principles of recovery, you can start to trust you might have a better life. And every day is treated like a new day and you live in the moment without living in the future which hasn't happened yet. The meeting is compelling and inspired, but I'm cynical, fearing I can't do what these people have done. And I have a free-floating scared sensation and don't know what I'm afraid of.

Chandler takes me back to the bed and breakfast. He tells me his story along the way. I'm a powder puff in comparison to him. He was in it much deeper. Chandler tells me he injured his hand weightlifting and took some pain meds. He had been depressed for years and with the Rx opiates on board his depression vanished. Chandler didn't have a clue about how depressed he was. All of a sudden he's energized and feels invincible. But then his addiction to the drugs take on a life of their own—it's what is on his mind and it becomes his first priority. His marriage begins to disintegrate and he has an affair. Chandler gets reckless about writing prescriptions to get medications, and he gets caught taking drugs from a patient who comes to the ER with a Rx for opiates. The physician's well being committee and the chief of staff call him in for surprise intervention. He fights with them, but they break through his barriers to get to the heart of his addiction and Chandler agrees to go to treatment at Talbott Recovery Campus in Atlanta. He's supposed to stay three months, but they hold onto him for an extra month because of his depression and needing greater acceptance of his addiction. He has a practice assessment and there is a recommendation he returns to work halftime. He struggled to get his footing and as a result his limited work schedule extended for a period of eight months. Chandler has a worksite monitor to keep tabs on how he does in the clinical setting, and everyday he attends recovery groups. He says today he is more committed to recovery than he ever has been. Part of this is helping people like me which make his recovery stronger.

Chandler puts the question to me about my consequences and the pain that surrounds my addiction.

I stall. It's like digging in heavy sloppy mud. There's trustworthiness about Chandler that lets me talk about what I haven't talked about with anyone. Drugs have been my first priority for a long time. I place them in front of Julie, or anybody. And the piece that makes me numb is my double dealing, the duplicitous manipulations that turn me into a liar, making me feel like an impostor while trying to be the look good doctor.

Chandler glances at me. He puts his eyes back on what's in front of him. "Your recognition lays the groundwork."

"What's next is going for the cure?"

Chandler stops in front of the bed and breakfast place. An outside light from the inn shines on us through the car window. He says, "There's no cure. You only manage your recovery each day the moment you wake up and your eyes open. And you'll fall back into the bag once you think you're cured or get complacent about what you need to do to keep yourself on track."

It's like I've hear this a thousand times before and now it seems like the first time. I get out of the car and while the door is still open, I lean over and thank Chandler.

He says, "By the way, do you really have back pain?"

"No. Some ill-defined pain? Yes, but my problem with opiates gained momentum when I was a trauma surgeon in Iraq." I push the door closed with just enough pressure to make an almost imperceptible sound. In the dim shadowy light Chandler's face looks quizzical, verging on being shocked about me being a trauma surgeon in Iraq. Being a surgeon in Iraq has cut a big slice in my life.

I wake up at four in the morning. Fitful, I twitch and make sure I don't wake Julie. A couple of hours later her eyes blink open. I go to the bathroom and take my dose of Suboxone and stash it in my shaving bag. Taking the medication without telling Julie reminds me that I am still an addict. I hug and kiss her. It's like I should feel relief.

Julie rolls out of bed and slips on her running gear. "I'm going to get in a quick seven miler."

I get out of bed and hold her, feeling like a tight squeeze that's desperate. There's a scrap of anguish in my touch.

My voice is quiet, kind of feeble sounding. "Julie, do you think—" I stop myself short of asking for reassurance.

"What?"

I think of how Julie has enabled my addiction. We have a pact of safety by never saying forbidden words. "Nothing. I just wanted to check in with you about whether you'll be back in time for breakfast."

"Well, sure. Wait for me and we'll shower together." Julie bounces out the door.

I sit, looking out the window and the shock of being exposed and raw from yesterday makes my gut like it's been filleted open. My hands are clammy. My forearms compress inward at my ribs. I'm in woozy, disconnected daze. While she's been gone I've gone over how my father treated me as a kid and my mother's sneaky ways. They had their ways that left me blowing in the wind. I stop from thinking about them. Then I examine the upshot of my sorted ways. The affect on patients has been next to zero. The effects of how I have maneuvered depreciates the way I feel—which is horrible—about myself. Lies and manipulations are never a way to build one's self up. I sucked Julie in, despite her being a willing player.

Julie comes through the door. I turn and my temples feel hot. "Back so soon?"

"I was gone almost an hour. I did a slow eight-minute mile recovery run."

We sit down for breakfast and order. The Suboxone makes me feel neutral. I miss the enhanced drug sensations—like a hunger. Jackie tickles the back of my mind, and it turns into a scratch.

"Glen, are you with me?"

"Sure."

"I'm sorry I was so late getting back last night. Liz and I were famished after the swim." Julie glances to the side and back to me. "So what did you do?" Julie sounds like she making an obligatory remark to check in with me.

"Tooled around and ran into an emergency medicine physician who works at the University of Colorado Hospital and shot the breeze about clinical issues."

Julie looks like she's astonished. "That sounds fortuitous that you hooked up with another doc." She looks askance and I wonder if her the look on her face is about suspicion.

"Yes." I look out the window to the garden. "Julie, there is something I have to clear up with Jackie. I'll be back in two seconds."

I go to the garden and punch in Jackie's cell phone number. She picks up the call. "Sorry to call so early. Were on mountain time."

"I was wake. What's up?"

"Please go down to the office and get ninety tabs of Vicodin and send them to me via next day delivery." I think back to the healthcare professional 12-step meeting. There's remorse that I'm letting Chandler, Geiger and Enright down.

"You sure that's a prudent idea?" I sense she's going along with this very reluctantly.

"Prudent? Maybe yes and maybe no. I don't care. But here's the address. Just send them."

Chapter Four

Being back home gives me the much needed margins to wiggle around in. That Colorado ordeal balled me up, like being in a shriveled desert. And then Jackie rescued me and provided the way to a lush oasis.

Julie is making a clamorous commotion in the bedroom, racing around to unpack our stuff. She can't just chill for two seconds. The pandemonium from the other room unexpectedly stops. I look up from going through the mail, and squint.

Julie calls for me. "Glen! Come here, *right now*." I rush to the bedroom. She's holding the Suboxone. "So, what's this?"

I'm thinking that she is closing in on me. I'd better come up with some ingenious explanation to justify the Suboxone. But my quick witted mind isn't materializing too much.

Julie grimaces. "It says it was prescribed by Dr. Scott Chandler from the University of Colorado Hospital." She shakes her head. "You said you discussed clinical cases with an emergency medicine doc in Boulder. So you were the clinical case?" Julie has a bead on me like nobody else. She catches me all the time, but looks the other way. Not today. Maybe she turned a corner because of the fiasco with her parents in Colorado.

"We yes, sort of. It was a consultation really."

"A consultation? So what is this Suboxone stuff?" Her face draws an intense and unrelenting picture. She's got a hold on me and not going to release me. I'd like to go for a little mercy right now.

My aim is pull something shifty to defuse her conniption—groom a clever line. There're higher stakes with Julie than other people because she has my number down, though she dismisses a lot of stuff I do. "I ran out of my pain medication and tried to get a prescription filled at a pharmacy in Boulder. A very kind pharmacist referred me to Dr. Chandler for an evaluation and consultation. The doc feels I have a mild depression and thinks I am using the pain medication as an antidepressant."

I size her up seeing if I'm getting over on her, playing on her insecurities. I try not to flinch. "He recommended that I get some psychiatric help and be properly treated instead of the misguided use of pain medication for moderate weight malaise. Sometimes when pain medication is stopped abruptly, there can be withdrawal symptoms and he prescribed the Suboxone just in case I might experience some ill effects of coming off of the medication." I keep an even timbre to my voice—and disguise my smile so it doesn't look too fishy.

I don't think I'm getting away with this. She got fed up with what happened in Colorado. She may not be letting me slip though the wide cracks that I've been able to slither through in the past. Julie lowers her head. Her eyes pin me. "Let's see if I have this right. You've been incorrectly using pain medication to self-treat depression. All you have to do for the depression to go away is discontinue the pain medication and get some psychiatric care? Is that right? And this Suboxone stuff is just in case—a cautionary measure—since you might experience some discomfort coming off the pain medication."

I nod, and try to smooth her over, again. I can tell her belief in what I'm saying is up in the air. "That's pretty much it."

Julie puts her hands on her hips. "So let's call a psychiatrist right now and make you an appointment for today."

"Today? Shit, Julie, I don't need to see a goddamn shrink. I'll stop the pain medication and things should settle down."

"Bullshit, Glen. The depression will automatically disappear? You're a mess and I don't think you see it."

Things are going wrong all at once. There's been a lot of people ganging up on me lately. I've got to get her off my back. "So what do you want me to do?"

"See a shrink and see want he or she thinks. And get an appointment today before you can wiggle out of it." I get the picture that she's put up with enough of my bullshit.

"That might be hard to pull off."

"Who is someone good?"

The only way I'm going to be able to appease her is to do the evaluation. Do snow job number ten thousand. I knew how to blow people off in Iraq. And here I go one more time. "I'd like to see Chuck Fitzgerald."

"Chuck Fitzgerald? I met him at a party. Isn't he a little namby pamby? And kind of nutso himself. Are you kidding?" Julie crosses her arms across her chest.

"He may appear that way, but he's a solid guy when it comes to psychiatry."

Julie lets out a breath. And then she picks up the telephone directory. She pages through it. She dials the telephone. "Hold on a second. I have someone here who wants to make an appointment—today if possible." She hands the telephone to me.

I'm exasperated that Julie is being so aggressive for a change and taking control. "Hello, this is Dr. Coyle." I listen. I cower, knowing I'm the patient. "No, not for a patient. For myself." Waiting, I look down. The scheduling person comes back on the line and tells me there's been a late cancellation. Goddamn it, I've had a run of rotten luck lately. Chandler and Geiger and Enright, and then I have the sense that Julie is turning on me. "Today? Well, it's—" I concentrate while she tells me the options. I'll let the con routine go—at least for right now. "Okay, I'll be there at three." I hand the receiver to Julie. She hangs it up. Julie has a jumbled look of trepidation and relief. And I think Julie has crossed a line that she has stayed behind for so long.

● ● ●

I arrive two minutes late and sit down in the waiting room. I'm barely hit the seat and Dr. Fitzgerald opens the door to the inner sanctum. "Hello, Glen. Come in." He shakes my hand and closes the door behind us. Fitzgerald sits in a stuffed wingback chair, and I sink into a sofa. He has a bunch of diplomas and certificates put up like wallpaper. A daunting bookcase filled with psychiatric volumes and hardbacks, making the place look like a library rather than somewhere to do treatment.

"Glen, I am glad you called me to discuss what you need."

"Okay." I contemplate that Fitzgerald is oblivious about how to handle a physician who is an addict.

"Tell me what brings you in. Let's start with the symptoms and some history of what is happening."

I lay out all the excruciating, but really flimflam detail and give a dotted history. One towering omission is the saga of using Rx opiates, and benzodiazepines here and there, and a tad of cocaine when some is left over from doing a rhinoplasty. "Dr. Chandler thought I had a mild depressive disorder. Is that your same conclusion?"

"Well Glen that is certainly one part of it. But given your symptoms, I'd say that you have a bipolar disorder, given the extreme shifts in mood that you're reporting."

Okay. A diagnosis of erratic moods. Good deal. Now I can point to this diagnosis and say I'm stabilized under a physician's care if anyone questions the weird capricious and mercurial shit I do because of drugs. "And what do you suggest?"

Fitzgerald has thinning hair. The colors he's wearing don't match. God awful blue blazer and mud brown slacks, and a bizarre rumpled space cadet tie. And I wonder where on earth he got those weird dorky, boxy shoes. Strange taste. "A couple of more items." I wonder if Fitzgerald is going to come up with something to lower the boom. "Do you have any suicidal ideation? Feel like harming yourself?"

"Well everybody does once in a while, right?"

"Right. And what about any intention."

"I guess the only intention I have is the tendency to shoot myself in the foot once in a while." I think I'm razzing him, but Fitzgerald is too sedate and humorless.

"I see." Fitzgerald clears his throat. "Let's start off with a rather conservative approach. I will prescribe some valproic acid and let's hold off on any antidepressants for the time being, since they may have questionable efficacy in your situation. The next part is that I'd like to hospitalize you for observation and to make sure you're safe."

Who could have guessed this would happen? Payback for fooling around with a shrink. "I think the hospital part is overkill." I pause for a split second. "You know I was kidding with that shoot myself in the foot comment."

"Huh hah." Fitzgerald has a dour look. "Well, Julie called to get you to make the appointment. That is telling in and of itself. She must be very concerned, and by the time a spouse calls there is usually a mental health crisis. I will be forced to do an involuntary hospitalization if you do not cooperate, simply by what you are reporting about your safety."

I didn't pick out that Fitzgerald would be so arduous to deal with. "Come on. I'm not some whacked out psycho."

"I agree." Fitzgerald thumbs his ear, and I think he's giving lip service to agreeing. "We want to provide a pleasant milieu for observation and to monitor firsthand your response to the medication."

And now the juggling act. "And how long of a hospitalization are we talking about?"

"Three days, unless—based on evaluation—the treatment team thinks it should be shorter or longer."

I cross my arms. I'm edgy with being reactive and agitated. And then uncross them, wanting to appear like the model patient. "I need to go to my office first to clear up a few items." I stare at the physician, feeling undone by being hospitalized, particularly since I'm a doc. "What facility are you thinking of?"

"Parkside Residential Services. I am their chief medical consultant, so I will be able to check on your progress."

"I need to go to my office and clear a few things, first. I have some easy cases that would be okay to reschedule." That's bullshit because what I really need is to get a little contraband—no more screwing myself like the Boulder fiasco.

"Okay. Hold on a minute." Fitzgerald picks up the telephone. His face looks like he's all businesslike and with his free hand he drums his fingers on his desk. "Hello, this is Dr. Fitzgerald. You have space for a same day admission, don't you?" He nods. "Okay then." He cups the telephone and asks me if I can be there in two hours. I incline my head to acquiescence— but I should be wringing my hands. "Yes, he can be there in two hours." He hangs up the telephone. "Glen, you've had a TB test in the last year?"

"Yes. It was negative. You want me to take along documentation because it's required in a licensed residential facility. Is that it?"

"Why, yes."

"May I use your phone to call Julie? I think she needs to be included in the mix."

"By all means."

I dial our home telephone. I'm bothered by Julie's rebellion from the status quo and want to call to appease her. And I tell Julie about Fitzgerald's diagnosis and plan.

Julie's voice sounds relieved. "Your moods are up and down like a rollercoaster. The bipolar diagnosis doesn't surprise me."

"We'll see." I hang up.

"What did she say?"

"The diagnosis didn't surprise her. I guess my moods are variable and she's been uneasy about it." I check the clock. It's one minute before the fifty minute hour is over. I grab a modicum of control by winding up with Fitzgerald and getting out of his office. "Thank you and I guess I'll be seeing you at Parkside."

"I'll check in with you tomorrow."

I rise and shake his hand and cordially smile, thinking I've got this guy buffaloed. What a coup to blame my moods on being bipolar.

• • •

I head over to my clinic with the idea of doing a little surreptitious business. Jackie comes in my office to intercept me. "Susan called. She had the second opinion and wanted to speak to you. She demanded to talk to someone since you were out." Jackie folds her arms across her chest for a second. "I was the person who was on tap because you weren't here."

Now what? "How'd it go?"

"She saw Dr. Werner. He gave one hundred percent good marks for the results of your rhinoplasty procedure. Reading between the lines, he must have instantly tuned into her mental difficulties. Susan said Werner counseled her. It was the same thing you told us. He got into her misled idea that the procedure would set the course straight in her life. Werner told her that her rhinoplasty was well-done, but not a cure for all that troubles her. Susan said he made a referral to a psychologist that does dialectical behavioral therapy. She's been to a few sessions and she feels like the therapy is helping."

"Very serendipitous, since Werner used to be a shrink before he retrained in plastics—what a fortuitous stroke of luck. So, she's off my back?"

"That's my read on it."

"You never know when she might come back to bite me."

"Well, if she keeps up what she's doing, maybe not." Jackie drags her hands through her hair along the sides of her head. "I need your—"

"It's about Tom?"

"Yes. And thank you for making a smooth deal for him." She crosses her arms across her chest again and this time angling her hands up to rub her deltoid muscles. "Thanks for doling out the scripts without the pro forma good faith exam."

I warmly cock my head to the side. "Jackie, you are my good faith exam."

"He's a tad low on the Percocet." Her eyes turn cool and her mouth is pitched, telegraphing that her husband is overusing his meds. It's an old newscast that she's covering for him. "Could you please call in another Rx?" Jackie's voice is strained.

I think about the last script I called in—easy to do the arithmetic. He must be in a continual drug haze. Here we go again. Another pharmacy should be used to avoid suspicion. "Sure." I slightly narrow my eyes, while I sound acquiescent. "Don't you think the acetaminophen in the Percocet is hammering his liver?"

Jackie glances away, distracted. A second later she refocuses on me. Jackie is curt and laconically says, "He's fine, no worries." But her clutching her left bicep with her right hand and her eyebrows pulling together tell me a different story, but I yield to what she says. She's irked. I don't imagine she's downplaying this intentionally. Jackie can't help her clinginess with Tom, which might mean she can't help herself with me, either.

"I have a change of subject." I tell Jackie about what happened with Julie and then the upshot of the appointment with Fitzgerald. She takes it in. I see her mind spinning like she figuring how to juggle the practice while I'm away.

● ● ●

In two hours I show up at the residential facility. They do a cursory intake interview. I attend a therapy group with the other patients. Turns out about half of them are also dopers or boozers in addition to being psycho. They call them dual diagnosis patients. Everyone seems nice enough, though they're conflict ridden and spinning around in a lot of turmoil—didn't get there on a whim—messed up and not having any fun is a temperate understatement.

The Suboxone is covering the withdrawal for the moment. My mindset is that I can point to the bipolar diagnosis to deflect getting nailed for being an addict. That's cooler than keeping all my mental systems busy shielding me from being uncovered from my affair with drugs. I'm a little less tense having bipolar to blame.

The next day I meet with a psychiatric nurse in her office for an interview. Nice woman. Janet is her name. "May I call you Glen?"

"Absolutely."

"Tell me the background of how you came to be referred to Parkside."

"Dr Fitzgerald diagnosed me with bipolar disorder and felt I need to be in a psychiatric residential program to have my moods observed, in part, to make sure the medication is providing stabilization. He prescribed valproic acid." I smile. My impression is that the chat with the nurse is pro forma.

"Give me a little more background. What initially motivated you to contact Dr. Fitzgerald?" She has a pleasant look, but unwavering. She has sandy long hair and a thin face. Janet wears funky earth mama clothes. I wonder if she buys her shoes at the same place as Fitzgerald.

I tell her the identical story that I told Julie.

Her eyebrows furrow and crow's feet form at the edges of her eyes. I weigh the explanation isn't flying too well for her. "I hope I have this straight. The physician in Boulder told you that you have been using Rx opiates to self-treat your mood disorder. What you have to do is obtain psychiatric treatment and the opiates will no longer be a problem. Is that it? Sort of Freudian, treat the underlying cause and the opiate abuse symptom with go away? I have it right, don't I?"

"That's exactly right." I compliantly grin.

Janet now seems to be capable of being a stern little tyrant. "I see. And did the physician you saw know anything about drug addiction?"

"Why, yes. In fact he told me he is an addict and has been in recovery for fifteen years."

Janet crosses her legs. She interlaces her fingers and places her hands on her thigh. "I would like to give you my opinion. Please call it a *little feedback* to clear up a few distortions. I need to know if that is okay with you."

I've got to get her off my back. And scoot out this office. Fitzgerald messed up with the misdiagnosis, but it starts to sink in this woman is no pushover. "What do you have to say?"

"Now please try to hear this and not put up too many walls. No matter what reason you started using drugs; substance abuse has a life of its own. No matter what underlying thing we treat, like a mood disorder, addiction a more powerful contender. How about a concrete medical example: if you give an alcoholic with a cirrhotic liver a transplant it won't cure the person of alcoholism, will it? What's the point of giving the person a liver transplant because the person will continue to drink without recovery treatment? I don't mean to offend you, but you may have not correctly heard what the doctor in Boulder said. You have an addiction problem. So even if we manage to erase the mood disorder—if there actually is one—the addiction will continue to exist. That was explained succinctly enough I hope, and I trust you're a quick study, aren't you?"

The bipolar charade isn't going to wash over this chick. "But the psychiatrist—"

"But the psychiatrist what? You've heard the saying, 'If you have a hammer, all you see are nails.' Dr. Fitzgerald is a great shrink, but when it comes to addiction he suffers from the four, two, one syndrome."

"You lost me."

"He spent four years in medical school and had instruction for two hours to try to understand the nation's number one disease—addiction." She moistens her lips. Janet's stern facial expression makes me feel high-strung. "I care. And caring means to do the right thing by you." Janet's eyes widen. "Have you heard of the California Medical Association's physicians' confidential line for docs in trouble?"

"Heard of the CMA line? Yes. I've never called it.'

"Their motto is, 'Doctors are everyday heroes. They are also human."

"I haven't been a hero in a long time." I think about the concentrated moments when life was in the balance and the times when people looked up to me. Iraq was so contorted and warped I can't even sort out if there were moments of hero status there.

"But you're human."

"Sometimes that's a stretch too."

"What happened to your hero status?"

"Well, I went into medicine to—"

"What? Feel good about yourself. You wanted to be something and—"

"Not be a piece of shit."

"That wasn't how I was going to articulate it, but that's what I mean."

"And how'd you come up with that?"

"I know a doc in recovery. Every time I see him, he says, 'If you want to have self-esteem, do esteem-able things.'" Janet dips her head. "He doesn't stop saying it. The guy is at the top of his field and has the corner on doing a certain procedure. He used to race around to get approval from everybody, act grandiose and arrogant. The real story is that his asshole daddy treated him like a piece of shit and reduced him to dirt. So guess what? He becomes a doctor to get the ultimate approval—hero status—but inside he is still a piece of shit, but fakes it. And the double existence gets to be too much. A pill here and there turns into a polypharmacy riot."

Janet has a tie into me. "What are you? Clairvoyant?" She gained access to me and I can't seem to shake her off.

"Not at all."

"What do you mean?"

"I mean you're sitting here with me. Why are you here? Maybe you have a genetic predisposition for addiction, but there's all the tag along bullshit that goes with it, right?"

"I'm fucked."

"And that comes down to what?"

"Having a diagnosis of bipolar disorder would be an explanation for all the erratic things I do. The psych diagnosis would bail me out…like give me an excuse. And my father literally told me I'm a piece of shit."

"And right now—intellectually—you know it is not true, right?" A reflection from the light passing through the window catches a glint in Janet's eye. "Tons of people with bipolar disorder are also have addictions, but an all too common scenario is that bipolar disorder is a mislabel for addiction. Like the families who drag someone in here and say their kid or parent is bipolar and what they are really doing is getting loaded on this or that dope, resulting in wacked out moods."

"Intellectually, I know that I have a lot of after effects to my drug use and I feel like a piece of shit because of that and emotionally…I can't get my fuckin' father out of my head."

"I love you, Glen." Janet is looks accepting.

When she says this, I picture what it would be like to go to bed with Janet. That is the first thing that sifts into my mind. And now the second thing is that I can't recall anyone every saying they love me—maybe someone lied and I filed it and dismissed it from my memory—except for Julie when we were in our courting phase. Maybe my mom said it, too fuzzy to remember now. I think of taking Janet to bed and for God's sake she didn't mean romantic love. This is clear. She meant because I was being upright at this two-second time interval. Patients said they loved their boob jobs or tummy tucks, but they never said they loved me, just the physical improvements and better looks I gave them. Then I ponder is all this racing around to get approval really about wanting to be loved? Being approved of means you're an okay person and being loved is the same thing. At least I Imagine it is. And there is Janet, a stranger—albeit a caring one—saying she loves me and accepts me despite of being a total wreck and because I'm being human. Maybe I can stop pretending.

"Hey Glen? Did I lose you?"

"What you said distracted me for a second. Love me? For what? The piece of shit that I am?"

"No, I don't love pieces of shit. I appreciate you for being honest with me."

"Are you an addict?"

"You can tell?"

"You pinned me. Serendipitously, I went to two pharmacies in Boulder and both the PICs were addicts and then one of them referred me to an addict emergency medicine physician who nailed me. I don't believe it. And now I get you. What's with that?"

"Someone is looking out for you."

"Don't give me any of the God stuff."

"Okay."

"Now what?"

"Now what, nothing."

"Aren't you going to refer me to a treatment center that specializes in treating recalcitrant tough case healthcare professionals?"

"Wouldn't think of it."

"What? I don't get it. You just pinned me and you're not going for the home run?"

"No. Because you're not ready."

"You see I'm scared of change."

"It's normal for where you stand right now."

"Why don't you force me?"

"Okay. Let's start with this. Tell me some reasons to stay the same and keep on using some kind of polypharmacy dope and some reasons that you might be better served by getting into recovery."

"Shit. I don't believe this."

"Believe it."

"Using drugs is like a friend, no, it's more like having a secret lover—like an affair. I trust it. I can count on what happens when I use. I'm I control of it."

Janet nods. "It's in control of you, but go on." She cracks a faint smile.

"If I got in recovery, I might be honest with myself. Stop manipulating my wife and staff. Quit breaking the law and operating under the influence."

"There's more if you got in recovery."

"Not feel like a piece of shit?"

"That is what I was thinking. Two phases. Not feel like a piece of shit because there wouldn't be any more consequences because you'd be doing the right thing. And—"

"Finally sort out what my father did to me and get over it."

"It's not like a breast augmentation where all of a sudden you have big breasts. You make progress at it and eventually get better."

"Ever think of getting a breast augmentation?" I smile. "I'd do a great job for you."

"Come on, Glen. My breasts are just fine, thank you. What's the matter? Is this too intense for you and you're trying to neutralize me?"

"I love you, too."

"Oh?"

"I'm just too obvious to you, right? The way you nail me makes me think you take me seriously and are invested."

"You mean I care about you?"

"Yeah. Other people don't care enough because they let me get away with manipulating them."

"You ready for what you need? The real treatment, not this make believe psychiatric B.S."

"No. It'd be too rough on me." I'm scared. Bare and exposed without my drugs. I can juggle stuff and drug fallout is still manageable. If I stopped? Rearranging myself to become what? Some uncertain piece of quaking Jell-O. And what is it I need—I don't know—and revamping me to find out is—

"Think how rough it is on you now. I guess if you're a piece of shit you don't deserve to get better. You just deserve to be a doctor."

"I'm surprised. That was cold."

"No it wasn't. It was up front and sizzling."

I get Janet's compassion and insight and sensitivity. But I'm walling myself against it. And I can't help it—some sort of automatic pilot reflex. She has her eye on me, like Janet doesn't blink.

She smiles. And I guess this is partly because she tuned into the impact that my father had on me. "Go think about what's the best thing for you and come back this afternoon. We'll talk."

"Shit!"

"Shit is right." Janet clears her throat. "And stop taking that valproic acid. You don't need that crap to stabilize your moods. How about this for a thought. Do what you need to do to get yourself out of this spot."

● ● ●

I leave Janet's office. Her effect is like shellshock. I attend a mandatory treatment group, so distracted that nothing seeps in. I have lunch with the other *inmates*, and then return to my room. The single room is austere and clean and overlooks a lush garden. My mind is in a vacuous state of relief, like the emptiness bizarrely makes me feel full. And then a twitch comes and I don't know what to do with myself and the weird-ass no drug ambiguity builds to a fitful tension. My hidden drugging stuff is a monster that relentlessly screams, putting me in frenzy. That narcotic shit has me in a crippling toehold, and every piece of my protoplasm down to the molecular level. Now it's inescapable. I'm jumping into bed with the monster and let the beast fuck me one more time. I snag my suitcase and pop four Vicodin. I drop some of that crap and the energy surge makes me yell *hooray*. Minutes pass. Now a tap on the door.

"Glen, you didn't make it back to see me."

"I lost track of time." And losing track of time is that I'm terrified by the thought giving in to letting go of the attachment to drugs.

"I see." Janet studies my eyes. "Your pupils look like the head of a pin. You're loaded, aren't you?"

She's no fool. I'm caught. "Just a little energized, is all."

"Telltale sign of you being an addict is that you get energized by taking Rx opiates." Janet shakes her head. "There's not much point in—"

"You're right. I'll pack up." I crane my head, and then bring my eyes back to Janet. "Do you still love me?"

"Well, you're not on an involuntary hold, so if you want to leave against medical advice that's up to you. But let's be clear about something. You need to get straight with yourself, Glen. Then you'll be more loveable. I'll be waiting for you." Janet makes a stiletto jab in the air with her index finger. The effect makes a punctured sensation in my chest. I pretend to laugh.

CHAPTER FIVE

Dreadful sensations pick at me as I make my way to the front door. Partly, I'm trying to get some footing after Janet so easily busting me for taking pills. I grasp the door handle not knowing what to expect once I'm inside the house. She'll be gone. Julie, the obsessed princess of the triathlon, will be grinding out the miles on the road or flipping back and forth doing pool laps or putting miles on her road bike. I signal that I'm home with my signature whistle.

Julie yells from the kitchen, "Glen?" She comes to the entrance of the house. "What are you doing—"

"They let me out early."

"But—" I see the disbelief running through her mind.

"They did a differential diagnosis and found that Fitzgerald misdiagnosed me. I don't have a bipolar disorder."

The squint of her eyes shows disappointment. "What's that mean?"

"I'm okay."

Julie cocks her head and slumps. She uncharacteristically stutters before getting traction with her observation and delivery. "Bull, bull, bull...that's bullshit, Glen." Julie squints with a penetrating stare. And then comes a letdown and foiled and crippled look that's riveted across her face. I realize how much she's been holding back for all these months. "I hoped—"

I say, "Hey, no worries."

"No worries? You're not all right. You're a doctor junkie who's screwing up our lives. I'm unstrung. And there's the strain you've constantly put on me. It's like I'm pushing a wheelbarrow laden with your heavy crap up a sheer precipice." Julie changes her posture and stands like every vertebrae in her backbone is aligned. "Glen, it's time we had a coming to Jesus talk. You got that?"

Julie walks into the bedroom. I reluctantly follow her, not knowing what she's going to say.

I'm getting aggressive because my sense the fallout from her ugly parents is tumbling down on me. "You're going off the deep—"

"No kidding. I feel nuts right now. We need to spit out some honesty." Julie stomps her foot. "Instead of me constantly kissing your drug addict ass all the time."

Julie goes into the walkin closet. She grabs a suitcase. Julie walks back into the bedroom and throws the suitcase on the bed.

"You're talking like a crazy woman…gone bananas."

"Because I am crazy. And you're not getting why."

"What's to get?"

"Be upfront and aboveboard, Glen. That's what. I'm so dejected and doomed—caught in the jaws of your trap. It's been that way for…well… it's been insidiously creeping up on me forever."

Julie tells me, "I'm always second guessing myself and a voice in my head says, 'shut up" and I should be thankful. I have it made and it's not that bad and talking myself out of my perceptions. And all my compensations. First I ran the marathon. Then the ultra-marathon and now I'm gearing up for the Ironman in Hawaii." Julie turns to me, her chin quivering. "Glen, I can't outrun myself anymore. I can't outrun you and what you're doing to yourself and doing to us." Julie's cheek glistens wet, mirroring a ray of spectrum-colored refracted light passing through the window.

"I know I have my moments of distraction."

"Moments of distraction? You talk about it like doing dope is some harmless activity. You're loaded, Mr. Mindfuck." Julie's eyes harshly narrow. While Julie opens a drawer she says, "Glen, you race around to outfox me. I'm sucked into a state of make believe crap with you and I'm about to throw up, I'm so sick of it. It's my fault too, because I've conspired with you, making your game work."

I filter though my mind to attempt to get some footing. "You're leaving me in the dust."

Julie snags running shorts, a singlet, t-shirts, tights, an athletic bra, sweatshirt and socks and hurls them into the open suitcase.

"Leaving you in the dust? Oh, I am? Don't play thick and stupid, Dr.

Genius." Julie puts her hands on her hips and lets out a huge sigh. "You know how I grew up with mom and dad. Or, maybe you really don't get it." Julie says she pictures her super successful parents who looked good on the outside, but at home she didn't know from one minute to the next what could come down the pike. It made her a worried wreck. "I jerked myself in every possible direction to get recognized by them. What I got was zip. And for the first time I'm admitting to myself that I wanted their approval."

She opens another drawer. Julie takes out cycling shorts and knickers, short sleeved and thermal jerseys and cycling socks and throws them in the suitcase without folding them. Julie returns to the walkin closet and gets a couple of pairs of running shoes and cycling shoes with cleats that attach to her bike pedals and pitches them into the case. I'm in disbelief, not knowing if this is all show or the real deal.

"I always felt like I'm a big fat zero in their book and still do. And what a relief to go away to Scripps College. I escaped—or so I thought. And meeting a handsome you—a prince I thought. Stupid me, thinking you would rescue me. At last I thought I'd be safe and be able to trust someone and tell you what was honestly up without feeling like I'd be in some sort of twisted up alcoholic combat zone. Sure, nothing was wrong with us as a couple at the start. But then it started all over again."

Another drawer is opened and Julie takes out three swimsuits and flings them in the case.

"Not alcohol this time. Your trip with drugs crawls under our covers. I turned my back on it, because you still validated me and encouraged me in my athletic pursuits and let me know how smart I am. And I gave you some slack after the Iraq homecoming. And I was so encouraging when you came home because I imagined all that you had gone through. And you trusted me and told me about all the horrific cases you had to do and the procedures and what it was like for you. You're a doc, but had to go through that firefight to save those poor soldiers under fire. I showed you respect for all that you did. It was a one-way street, but I guess that's the way it is with soldiers when they talk about war."

"I'm sorry if I didn't seem more appreciative, but I was."

Something jets into Julie's mind. It must be the accumulation of our history. "You know what? I realized my enthusiasm about physical training is a way to get you out of my hair. The upshot was you could do your thing and sneak around, playing out your addict trip. I helped you hide out. At first I thought you were having an affair, but then I wised up and the picture became clear. You're the same addict as my mom and dad. New day, same fucking story. It's called absence. You're not there."

Julie bends over and puts her head in her hands and cries, escalating to convulsions. Her tears are sadness, but they are mixed with tears of rage.

I put my hand on her back. "I didn't do it on purpose." What a thing to say—worn out, dumb sounding catchphrase. The contrived noise vibrating in my throat is the only sensation I could feel—the rest of me is numb.

"Not on purpose?" She says through her tears. "Doesn't fucking matter. Still adds up to the same final score." Julie looks out the window into the daylight brightness. Drugs are more important to you than I am. And no fancy footwork bullshit is going to undo that, Mr. Smooth Talker."

Julie stands up. She gathers some jeans, skirts, blouses, a sweater and coat—all still on hangers—and lobs them in the suitcase. And then she gets two pair of pricey Italian loafers and chucks them in the case.

Julie has pegged me. I have to do something very urgent so I'm not enveloped by despair and desperation. So far there have been consequences, but I haven't lost much. This is it. "Julie, please stop. Look, we can work this out. Don't turn this into World War Three. I can turn off the spigot and bring drug use to an end right away."

"End it? Get real, Glen. I've been holding this in too long, not saying what I thought or how I felt or not being able to trust I could talk with you. And now the bullshit crescendo has built up, crushing me and I can't hold on any longer."

"Are you sure that you're not taking the pain of your parents out on me?"

"Come on, Glen, stop with the mind fucking and take some responsibility, will you. I mean, Jesus." Julie zips up the suitcase.

"Please, Julie," I sigh. "Don't fight with me."

"It's only a fight if you defy what I'm telling you. I'm saying what's been rattling around in my head. For once and letting it out and trying to express myself for real instead of faking that everything is all nicey, nicey."

I grimace and turn away. My stiff comebacks are too see-through. I better not get any more defensive or I'll be triple screwed. I should have had the foresight that this moment would come and that one day Julie would boil over. I always have a strategy, but now the only tactic I can think of is to be obsequious. "So what do you want me to do?"

"You're the goddamn doctor and you need to ask *me* what to do?" Julie picks up the suitcase and walks toward the front door. "So being intelligent and having degrees is not the same as being smart about how to handle things at home?"

"Where are you going?"

"Tell you when I get there."

I go to Julie and hold her. She's inelastic and wooden to my touch. I try to massage her back as I embrace her to loosen her up. Julie is unyielding.

Wiggling, she struggles and says, "Don't touch me, Glen."

I let go of her. "Okay. Alright already."

"I swear I'll be back. I just need…shit I don't know what. Just to not be around you right now. I want you to think, and think hard. There is a lot on the line right now."

"Is that a threat?"

"A threat? Glen, think about it. You think you can keep it up and I'll just lay down so you can trounce all over me?" Julie cringes. "I'm a big girl now and my little girl pattern is a rerun with you. I'm trying not go through that misuse of me again and again."

I expect Julie's exodus to be like the thunder of a thousand stampeding hooves when she leaves, punctuated by the door slamming behind her. Instead, Julie agitated, but quietly slips the door latch clicks shut. A cool repose falls over me when she decamps the scene. I pant, thinking that maybe I've blown it forever. A tread of a thought comes that Jackie and I could fall in with each other to team up. And then I realize the notion is my mind avoiding what is happening right now. I look out the window and see her attaching her bike to the rack on the car. She slings her bike helmet and pump in the car. She slowly drives away the same way she closed the front door. Her car creeps down the driveway.

And being conscious of my breath unthaws the cover of my addict calloused armature for a second.

● ● ●

A few days pass. I question whether Julie will come back. I go through the motions of faking it at work, like nothing abnormal in my private life is happening. I'm so jagged, having a disjointed sense about me that I'm more amiable and gracious with Jackie. I recognize it's a sideways retreat into safety to cover being unhinged about Julie

I occupy space in my vacant house. My cell phone rings. I expect it to be Julie, but the number display shows it's the clinic. I pick up.

"Glen." I hear Jackie's throat clearing. "Something is up." Her voice wavers. "You need to come to the clinic right away."

"Did I mess up on patient scheduling?"

"No. The slate is clear for today. There are two men here from the DEA. They want to speak with you directly."

"What do they want?" I have a knuckle-white clutch on the phone.

"They...they won't tell me." Jackie struggles to be articulate. "If you don't come right now, they said they'd visit you at your house."

I'm reactively defiant, like I don't want to have to handle one more thing. "Tell them to kiss my ass." My face flushes red.

"Glen, come on."

"Okay, tell them to hang tight, I'll be there." An oppressive pressure rolls my shoulders forward. I'll have to size up the DEA guys and see what they want before concocting a line of attack. I can't help my mind being blank right now. It's the shock of the call from Jackie. My career could vanish into the ether. I have kept this day in abeyance, knowing it would eventually arrive. Now it's here.

One DEA investigator is tapping the arm of the chair with his index finger. He's hairy and his strange face makes him look like a wolf man. Man number two paces back and forth, his eyes blink and fidget. A wimpy looking man, like he's the first man's henchman. They both wear cheap shiny suits that appear as if old sweat had been repeatedly pressed into them. They move towards me, looking grim and dour, covering what I imagine to be twitchy hostility underneath. I extend my hand and introduce myself, showing a formal and obligatory smile. One says he is Kevin Kilgore and the other is Sam Penny. The names sound made up, like some sort of stage moniker so the bad guys can't track them down.

Kilgore leads in, "Dr. Coyle, do you know why we are here?"

I guess he wants me to say because I'm a Rx junky and I'm cooking the books to feed my addiction. "I imagine you are doing a routine review of prescribing practices since I run a small pain clinic in addition to having an in office suite for performing plastic surgery." I try to measure how they are taking this in. Their stone-faced looks make them hard to read. "A lot of medication moves through a clinic of this sort and you must need to attend to the accuracies of the administrative and prescribing procedures."

The investigators glance at each other for a split second. Penny says, "I would say that is a precise and articulate way of framing our visit." His face is marked by serious pretense. "Let's start by evaluating your medication log."

An impulse pushes me that I can't stop. "Now then, is there any other reason you are here that I need to know about that will help direct me in furnishing information you need?" The shooting myself in the foot comment I made to Fitzgerald flashes in my mind.

Kilgore's voice is tight and authoritarian. "Your prescribing for pain medication is beyond the scope of what we would expect for a practice like yours." Kilgore has a dominating and powerful way of coming across. He might as well be my father telling me I'm a piece of shit. "Statistically, you're almost two standard deviations beyond the range of a customary and accepted office practice such as this one."

"I will get the logs for you. There is one kept for the surgical suite and one for the pain clinic." I turn to get a hold of the logs. My hands involuntarily shake. I put them in my pockets, not doing too well at concealing the tremulousness. I have no idea if the logs are going to fly. Except for one thing. The labyrinthine constitution of the logs might twist them up. I must be a total dumb shit if I think that I'll be getting over on them. Most likely they've seen the same dense attempts at being cunning before and the bullshit is transparent. These guys are forensic accounting experts who do their job forty hours a week and have seen it all. There's swelling in my throat.

I walk over to the medication safe and spin the dial to look inside. There's a weighty quantity of opiates inside. Maybe I could waste all of them this second. But my sticky connection to the drugs says don't get rid of them yet. I click the safe shut. I can't help myself, though I know doom is on the horizon and those DEA guys have the power to skewer me.

CHAPTER SIX

The interconnections of what's happened so far in my life seem limitless and nearly impossible to measure. A synergism that grows so big that I have blind spots. But even the eighty to ninety to a hundred billion neurons firing in the brain are finite. Each neuron expands, having ten thousand connections with other neurons. And this is where my history is deeply encoded. Neurons automatically fire and pulsate, and at times drive me beyond my conscious control. The vast fragments in my historical chronicle clutter my mind and make a chatter so loud like cymbals and kettle drums that are troubling to tune it out and forget. When I can't forget on my own, I find other ways to overlook and avoid the self-imposed disgrace in my life.

Wouldn't it be cushy to point to one thing and unequivocally say that's the reason to simply take all the ambiguities out of a bewildering and entangled soul? When I was a kid we moved a lot. Not as much as the enlisted men and their families. But for me it was rough going, followed by rearranging myself to harmonize with all that was new—faking, pretending, fitting in, but always feeling derailed.

Dad is not a bad looking guy, but his military haircut looked too short and odd to me. He's on the thin side and looks okay in a military uniform. The inner circle of his being is a rigid mind. One of these days I'll get him back for abusing me. Mom is the looker. Trim shapely body and she has a nice rotating swing like her hips are greased. It is hard to miss, even for me being her son. And what's noticeable is men observing her. Her blonde hair completes the stunning picture.

I had one buddy. You might even describe him as warmhearted. We were eight years-old. Eddy McGowen was a truly good kid. His favorite subject was talking about his fly-fishing trips with his father that happened every weekend, or at least the experiences were so fresh it seemed that way. He invited me to tag along with them. It was the cocktail hour at our house. "Say, dad, Eddy asked me to go along with his father and him to go fly-fishing. That's okay isn't it?"

Dad springs back with a kind of blustery voice, "Hell, son, I'll take you myself. Go in the garage and dig out our fishing gear."

I spend a frustrating hour rooting through all the unpacked cardboard boxes and then finally find two fishing rods and reels and a tackle box. I take the gear into the house. "Okay, here it is."

Dad is at the kitchen counter pouring himself a drink. "You sure were gone for a long time." Sounds like a soused thing to say.

'Well, there was a lot of stuff to look through."

"You can leave the gear right here and I'll inspect it." I wonder if he's really going to do check the reels.

I nod. "So when are we going to go fly-fishing?"

"This Saturday."

"Eddy says the best time is early in the morning or late in the afternoon."

"We'll take off early." Is that for real, or is dad just saying that?

Saturday rolls around. I'm out of the sack before daybreak. I tiptoe into my parents' room and shake my dad. He grumbles, "I'll be up in a minute."

I wait. And I wait some more. We finally leave the house at eleven o'clock and start the drive. I'm mute at this point. Dad is taciturn and voiceless. Finally, I break the silence. "What are you thinking, dad?"

He begins with a monotonous and humdrum talk about how brilliant he was at the Naval Academy. This is followed by what a good commander he is because of his iron fisted way that me manages personnel he has command over in the Navy. The lasting impression is that he is talking to himself and not to me. And then he says, "I need to make a little stop."

Dad pulls the car into the parking lot of a bar. "You wait here, Glen. I'll be back in a minute."

I'm a little scared being left alone in this seedy bar parking lot and lock the car doors. I look across the street and there's a bank with a clock that displays the time. It's a little after noontime. I wait for a minute that turns into sixty minutes. I gaze at the bank's clock. I think of going in the bar to get dad, and jettison the idea, thinking he will berate me. I look in the backseat and grab the rods and reels and tackle box. I scrutinize the reels. The fishing lines are all fouled up. I try to crank the reel handle and the messed up line spool doesn't budge. I open the tackle box and look for fishing flies. There's a hodgepodge of plastic boxes with fishing hooks and weights. There isn't one fly to be found. I wait. And two hours later my stomach growls. I go in the bar. There's dad talking with two strangers and the bartender. I tug on his sleeve and say I'm hungry. The bartender gives me peanuts and pretzels. "Glen, go back and wait in the car and I'll be there in a sec." My shoulders slump and I shuffle out the door.

After another hour sitting in the car, I move the backseat and curl up. Some drunk guy tries the door and giggles it. He scares the crap out of me. And I don't know exactly what I am feeling, something like fear, intermingled with anger toward my father for putting me in this vulnerable position. The man has a stupid look on his face. And then he goes to the next car and gets in. Stupid drunkard got the wrong car and frightened the hell out of me. He weaves pulling out of the parking lot and another car almost hits him when he pulls onto the street.

Somehow I calm down and fall back to sleep. My eyes peel open when dad gets in the car and turns on the ignition. It's dark outside. He pulls out of the parking lot. I climb into the front seat. He looks like he has his eyes closed. I'm so alarmed that I'm in a panic. I disguise my fear and try to coolly say, "Dad, have your got your eyes shut?" I look at the road in front of us. There's a single line dividing the two sides of the road.

His voice slurs. "No. I just have one eye shut."

My fingers dig into my thighs. "Why is that?"

He mumbles something. And then I finally pull out of him that he's seeing a double dividing line in the road and if he closes one eye he sees one line. Dad comes close to a parked car and knocks off rearview mirror on the driver's side of the car. I subdue myself, but in my mind I and thinking, "Holy shit." He can't drive in a straight line.

Dad manages to get us to a few blocks from our house. The police stop us. They arrest dad. Strangely, I feel rescued by the cops—I felt so unsafe. I see one of the officer's nameplate—Kipfer. He's a rugged looking man that probably doesn't take any guff off of anybody. I butt in, "Officer Kipfer, we're just a few blocks from our house and my mother is home. I could walk home or you could drop me off." I plead for the officers to take care of me.

"We'll drop you off. Good you're mom is home. Otherwise we'd have to take you in and find a temporary foster care. It's extra work for us and paperwork."

I fill mom in on all the sorted details of the day after Kipfer walks me to the door and tells my mother about my dad's arrest. They haul dad away after dropping me off. I was distressed all day and I'm soothed that the cops unburdened me by taking my father into custody.

Mom has a sour look on her face. "You must be starved." She appears undaunted, but I know she's pissed.

"I am."

She goes to the kitchen to make dinner. I hear a racket, pots and pans flying all over the place—confirmation that she's angry at my father.

Just wait until I tell Eddy what kind of big fish the cops caught.

A prominent image in my mind was another move landing us in Coronado. There was a long list of moves caused by my father's lifer career in the Navy. One more goddamn adjustment to another school. I was trooped around all day with a constant fresh smile on my face. My motto to fit in was *let's look good*. The teacher at the school liked me, alright, the pleasant kid who is well-mannered, polite and saying, "Yes, Mrs. What's-Her-Face," to agree with whatever she said. And then there were the kids to fit in with that were like all the rest of my experiences—me grinding a bunch of cogs together, trying and hoping they'd mesh. And I think about the ten thousandth time my father has put me in an awkward position.

Like this time in Coronado, new elementary schools were a special challenge. The new kid was supposed to be beaten up on the playground. My advantage was always being the biggest kid in the class. The kids had a type of kangaroo election of some guy to take me on. I pitied the boy who feigned supernatural fighting prowess by assuming a karate stance, since all it took was one tap on the chest and the boy was on his butt. But what I learned early on with daunting opponents: I had to win the fight in less than thirty seconds or, as the saying goes, my ass was grass. My ass was never grass.

By high school my father's career in the Navy settled down and I moved in to one school and stayed there until graduation. By this point my new kid strategy smoothed out. I'd sit in the back of schoolroom and blended into the class fabric, except for one thing. I aced every test and every assignment. The other kids got the picture about my crafty street smarts, but otherwise I didn't call attention to myself. The best grades were my newfound way to pretend I was okay. Besides—and I found this out serendipitously—being the test and assignment ace was like camouflage over all the rawness underneath. So my father told me I was a piece of shit, but at school I angled toward classroom stardom. It was like life became a series of compartmental compensations to protect myself.

One Saturday dad comes into my room while I'm pouring over a Spanish text preparing for a test. "Glen, your hair is looking pretty damn long." Dad being a commander had well-groomed hair that was short on the sides. Mine had a beach boy look. He's going to pull something and I want him off my back. "I heard about a good barber in Tijuana. I'll take you down there for a haircut." An alarmed sensation grows into being scared. He has endlessly abused me, so that I don't know what he's going to do next based on his fickle and sometimes volatile moods.

"I have a huge Spanish final to study for."

"You have all day tomorrow. Let's go." He doesn't say so, but I know he has an agenda other than me getting a haircut.

He tells my mother we are heading south. She looks askance. We jump in the car and leave Coronado and motor down the Silver Strand toward Mexico. Dad is more talkative than usual. "So how is school going?"

"Okay." I decide to take a chance. "All the moving around because of the military makes it tough to always fit in."

"Yeah."

"Dad, don't you have any to say other thing to say besides 'yeah.'" I'm afraid he is going to scream at me for my backtalk.

"Moving around because of the military is unavoidable. Not something to whine about. Just buck up, Glen, and make do." I bristle at the harshness of his tone.

I mistakenly put my hand out to dad one more time, but shit, the same old thing. I'm let down again and discouraged.

"Glen, you sure got quiet."

"End of subject, I guess."

"Well, there's something I want to discuss with you."

"Oh?"

"I've got a deployment coming up. I want you to look after your mother and make sure she's okay."

I think how insecure my father is. He's suspicious that she'll be sleeping around while he's gone. "She's a big girl and can look after herself."

"While I'm not here, you have to be the man of the house and make sure she's alright."

I think for a second and recognize he's on shaky ground when he is away and mom is on her own. I could give a shit less about what mom does. "Man of the house? Okay and I'll look after mom."

We cross the border. Dad parks off of *Avenida Revolución*. We find the barbershop. I wonder if it's any old barbershop or if he actually had this specific one in mind. I sit in the chair. "Glen, I'm going to explore around while you get a haircut." At this point in my sparse years of life I know what this is code for. I'm sick of his bullshit ways of conniving to do his thing with John Barleycorn.

The guy cutting my hair is nice enough. A chance to give some of my Spanish a workout. *"Corte un poco aquí en el lado y atrás. No mucho en al coronilla, por favor."* I tell him to cut a little off. I still like the beach boy look and I don't want to have a military look like dad. He finishes the haircut and I'm amazed how good it looks. I step down out of the chair and pay the portly barber. I sit in one of the chairs for waiting in the barbershop and read magazines in Spanish. Time passes.

Hunger sets in. I ask the barber, *"Voy a conseguir tacos. ¿Le gustaría unos tacos?"*

"Sí, por supuesto." I go next door and get two chicken tacos for the barber and two for me. I return to the barber shop. We eat together. He chats about his kids. I think he's a religious man who is tied to his family. His loving way toward his family has a calming effect on me.

The barber says, *"¿Donde está su padre?"*

I tell him, *"El está tomando."* I don't make an excuse and I say that dad is drinking. After two hours he stumbles into the barbershop to collect me.

"Glen, I have an idea. Come on." Dad having ideas immediately make me apprehensive. We go out into the street. There is a live burro that has painted black and white stripes to look like a zebra, but it really doesn't look like a zebra. The animal still looks like a painted up burro. Dad has me mount the animal. The Mexican guy who is running the silly business with the burro gives me a huge sombrero to put on. I feel absolutely ridiculous. And I'm so uncomfortable that dad puts me in these positions. "Okay,

Glen, smile so the man can take your picture." I feel dour, but fake a smile that I know doesn't look real.

The Border Patrolman when we cross the international boundary line asks my father what we purchased in Tijuana. My father tells him I got a haircut. The Border Patrolman points up the road. "You see that café? Please stop there and get a cup of coffee before your proceed in your car." My father says he will do that. I know in advance that he is too agreeable.

We stop at the café. They serve beer and my father has two. And then we drive home to Coronado. As we drive up the Silver Strand with the San Diego bay on the east and the Pacific Ocean on the west I think of how picturesque the azure waters are and the white sand has a dreamy look in the simmering daylight. I pull down the visor that has a mirror. I see what a good haircut the Mexican barber gave me. And then I think of the welcoming and loving way that he conversed with me about his family. I look to the left and see my soundless and hushed father whose eyes are practically at half mast, like he occupies his own numbed-out secret world. I take a breath and the cab of the car smells of tequila and beer. A familiar feeling of disgust washes over me. "Dad, do you mind if I roll down the window? I'd like some fresh air."

There are the unforgettable and remarkable days that tie my life together. One was the first day of high school and the first day of a biology class. That was my first exposure with Mr. Krebs. He has a full head of long brown hair. His white shirt is a little oversized and not tucked in his pants too well. He's slick and cool and has the charisma to entertain a class of kids all day long. Mr. Krebs asked, "Which came first, the chicken or the egg?" Now I knew this was a biology class, not a philosophy class or a class on riddles. A couple of kids answered, thinking Krebs was warming the class up with a teaser game. He shook his head. I raised my hand and he called on me.

"I've been doing some reading on Darwin and getting familiar with his concepts on evolution. The egg came first, because, biologically and in terms of Darwin's theory of evolution, other species on earth had eggs well before birds. And chickens are a type of bird, so the egg came before the chicken." The answer seemed easy enough.

Krebs's mouth fell open. He got a little giddy. My hunch was he didn't anticipate anyone getting the answer right, other than by a guess. My second hunch was he was going to use the chicken and egg punch line as a springboard to engage the class in biological theory. Even so, he used the biological riddle to start a lecture on Darwin.

The other Darwinian tidbit I took on was it isn't necessarily the strong that survive; it's the ability to adapt that ups your chances for survival. Undoubtedly, being strong is secured in second place.

Krebs held me after class. We chitchatted about biology and joked. As a result, I caught he had a pulse on the workings of life and knew how to sway students by being clever and smart. He effortlessly and naturally carried enormous authority in the classroom and with each student. In retrospect I unconsciously compared my father's emotional insecurity to Kreb's self-assurance and confidence and sense of personal freedom. We weren't real friends because he was the teacher and I was the student, but we had a teacher-student type of friendship. Whenever he had time I'd hang around and we'd talk seriously about science and make wisecracks and clown around. With him I felt like a rose and not a cow patty. Or closer to it, I felt like the rose growing out of the fertile nutrients of the cow patty.

My father, Frank Coyle, CDR, got all puffed up to the point of penetrating me with his ego when he crowed about his appointment and graduating with honors from the U.S. Naval Academy at Annapolis. But his military education didn't add up to his highest rank, despite going on and getting a master of arts in national security and strategic studies at the Naval War College. Dad was a Navy career man who hit the rank of commander, but who kept getting passed over when any glimmer of being promoted to captain floated on the horizon. He was stalled. Being a military kid I had the occasion to meet men who graduated from the academy. They were at least captains, and there was a smattering of admirals. Dad was schooled in being a gentleman, but he said the wrong things to people to whom he should have been doing a lot of ass kissing. He was supposed ooze genuine leadership and military bearing. Instead, he was exacting and firm and ironhanded.

There's one thing I noticed about many Navy types bathed in the power of the military structure. There were many unfulfilled missing pieces in their lives that were filled in by having serious parties. But dad was to the extreme when it came to being serious about parties. And most of his serious parties he had all alone. Being post-party ragged the next day didn't help his career because he was likely to snap at people until the cocktail hour when relief would come by, taking the edge off with his first drink. He said a lot of stupid stuff. A normal person would have had remorse. Not dad. He would come up with some puffed up reason why he was in the right and have some flimsy or well-constructed intellectual justification, even though he had said something foolish. But he'd be dead wrong. His brain occupied an unwavering rigid place, not being able to yield to the possibility of imperfection, or see other possibilities. For such an intelligent guy this foible made him dumb. And what made him dumber is that he didn't know his failings, like upright Commander Tight Sphincter who shits red, white and blue the diameter of a piece of twine.

Mom was a good military wife, socialized with the other Navy wives and kept a spotless house and always acted like everything was okay. The way mom dressed in her outfits and pumps always looked like she was in uniform. Mom's name is Gladys. I secretly renamed her, "Glad Ass," because of how she contrived a happy face when I knew she wasn't happy.

Mom was a different person during my father's deployments. Relaxed and not in uniform and her little socialite agenda with the Navy wives slacked off. She would make me dinner or give me money to eat out. And then she would go somewhere and fabricate an excuse for where she was going. Sometimes she wouldn't come home at all and slip in the backdoor before daylight and feign she had been at home all night.

One morning when darkness developed gradually into the twilight dawn, I waited for her in the kitchen. She quietly slithered in the back door. "Hi, mom."

The look of bombshell astonishment zoomed over her face. "Ah, ah, good morning Glen."

"Did you have a nice night?"

"A nice night? I woke up early and couldn't go back to sleep. So I decided to take a walk on the beach."

"You're dressed kind of snazzy for a walk on the beach."

"I just threw on what was laying around. Plus, you never know who you're going to run into."

I'm not too schooled on the subject quite yet, but I could tell that she had that freshly fucked look. "Sure, mom." Her shoes are on and there isn't a speck of sand anywhere.

"Now, Glen—"

"Hold on a sec. I promise to never interfere with your early morning walks on the beach. Everyone deserves time alone, no matter what time of the day it is."

Mom has a sorted mix of tension and being discovered, combined with relief. She looks like she's enlisted me as a coconspirator since she knows the ill will my father's abuse and unpredictability has provoked in me. "I'm nonstop thinking things will be different with dad, and then he does the same disappointing bullshit." I must appear pained, but the look in mom's eyes tells me it's the same pathetic and shot down way for her.

"While your dad is away I need a lot of walks on the beach."

After that moment I never said anything about her sub rosa flurries that made her happy while my father was deployed. In my mind there was hazy sense of retribution that she could get over on my father—and the letters she wrote him were a work of chicanery and genius. She left a few letters on her desk before mailing them. I was a bit of a sneak, too, and read them. Jesus, that woman was smooth as glass. Her smoothly greased crafty letters read like Better Homes and Gardens domestic tranquility. I was a student of observation, though now the stakes are higher for me.

I eavesdropped on their conversations when he returned from being deployed. There was his questioning—not driven by anything he observed or she had said, but by the fact he was gone and being driven by his insecurities and he wasn't around to protect the goods. Mom had long blonde hair and completely stunning looks. I thought men must have strained themselves the way they rubbernecked when she sashayed that tight body of hers down the street. The way she moved was unmistakable, even for me to notice as her son. Most kids wouldn't think this about their mothers. I did. But the duality of her life was like two seemingly disconnected, but superimposed and intertwined compartments.

Fate gave me a break and beamed good fortune. Her name was Connie. She was a handsome girl who was solidly budding into womanhood. And she was smart and did not let on to the other kids about her straight "A" record. Her parents weren't military, but she was messed up by her alcoholic father who drove the haphazard kinetics of her family. We spent hours and hours commiserating and being each others' confidant. The relief we gave each other showed the way to other things. That led to hours and hours commiserating in the sack which made us a genuine item. The subject of a what we were up to turned into a guessing game for the students in school, leading to farcical gossip that was more dramatic than what we were actually doing. But I thought it was a kick to be glamorized.

Connie and I also studied together. And we took SAT practice tests and studied and prepared to the point of saturation. I loved taking the momentary breaks by looking into her lupine blue eyes for a few seconds of distraction. Connie and I analyzed academics to death and rewarded ourselves by stealthily slithering between the sheets. I knew she was smart, and I didn't think I was that smart, but I worked my ass off. By graduation we both had the grades and SATs that paved a road in different directions. She went to Brown University and stayed in California and went to Pomona.

I recognize I've become the very thing I hated. The catastrophe of the DEA agents being in my office tells me it has been a long twisty road to get to where I am today. Did my dad do it to me? His genes deposited in my addict body are one thing and not the whole show. I could have been like him or not. At least I'm not abusive, but his abuse made it his fault that I unwittingly had to medicate with drugs and turned into an addict.

CHAPTER SEVEN

I'm a fraud and an imposter. The pretense and masquerade are old and well-worn deceptions. I'm not going to let the Kilgore and Penny demonic duo make me their pigeon despite the curse I've inflicted on myself.

I haul the logs back into my office and place them in Kilgore's outstretched hands. Penny says, "What space can we use to review the logs?"

I obsequiously clear a few items off my desk. I can hardly breathe and when I do breathe my breaths are shallow. I uneasily pull a second chair to the desk. I sweat, getting pissed these two bozos are taking my power away from me.

Kilgore coolly speaks, "Thanks for letting us use your office. Now, Dr. Coyle, please standby somewhere in the clinic in the event we need clarification. After the investigation we will need to talk with you."

I look at the wall clock and the doorway, and then back at them. "How much time do you need?"

Penny says, "It depends."

Kilgore chimes in, "Shouldn't take long." His eyes have a burning penetration—well-practiced at making the target of his incisive look feel uncomfortable. He smiles when he sees how uneasy I am.

I begin to shut the door behind me. Penny's voice screeches. "Leave it open."

I glance back. They're glaring at me, and then crack open the log books.

Kilgore and Penny undoubtedly wanted the door open to eavesdrop on conversations going on in the clinic. I grab Jackie and we sit on the stoop in front of the clinic. I'm shaken causing blank spaces in my mind. I need Jackie to bolster me. "Jackie, I'm horrified by what they're likely to find. I'm already starting to feel screwed."

"There's a lot at stake. Not only for you, and your medical license and career. My job could vanish." I feel her connection and the sweetness she has toward me. "And I don't want you to vanish, either."

"Let's think this through." But I'm so jacked up; I'm at a loss to contemplate what to do.

Jackie voices, "Okay." Jackie and I both know the logs have been made to look good. The surgical logs are not egregiously inaccurate, but the pain clinic logs are where they're going to nail us.

Jackie takes charge. I'm clear that's a major reason she works for me. "I've got it. Look, let's acquiesce to the fact that the logs are sloppy and the handling of the patients has been less than conventional for a pain management practice. And then we offer up a remedial plan. As a matter of fact, let's tell them we've been working on revising the office practice and have engaged in extensive conversations to remediate what we feel has not been working very effectively." There's release in her face, coming up with ingenious idea to sidetrack the DEA agents.

"Righteous devious plan." I pay homage to her since it takes a conniving guy to see her tricky scheme. "My brain is so jammed at this second I can't think. Go one down because we know we're screwed, and then volunteer a proposition to fix it."

For the next forty minutes Jackie and I sip high octane coffee and fire back and forth the particulars of the counteractive plan. It's like a dress rehearsal. The receptionist comes out to the stoop to tell me it's time.

I enter my office, greeted by Kilgore and Penny's cheerless expressions. Kilgore starts, "A thorough review has revealed a few things."

"I can imagine."

"You can imagine? What do you mean?"

"Go ahead with your analysis, and then I'll have some ideas to discuss with you."

"Dr. Coyle, are you diverting drugs for your personal use?"

I feel over reactive. "No. Why? Do I look like a drug addict?" I realize I'm not too keen on authority figures questioning me.

"Drug addicts do not look any particular way. Some sleazy guy off the street or a sparkling guy in a classy clinic practice. Addiction is an equal opportunity problem." Kilgore puts his hands together to form a temple. "Your logs are consistent with other logs we have analyzed where the physician is diverting medication for self-use."

"It could look that way, but that's not the case. In fact, I have been engaged in extensive conversations with my clinic staff about developing prescribing policies that are more consistent with the standard of practice, particularly with the limited pain management clinic that I operate." I'm carefully watching Kilgore and Penny. "Admittedly, I do not have a very robust pain management contract for patients and we have been discussing the revisions that are needed. Two other major difficulties I have faced have been my leniency with respect to giving new prescriptions when medications have been reportedly lost or contaminated." I bite the inside of my cheek. "The second one is giving in to prescribing when early refills are requested due to the patient's report that pain has increased and more medication had been taken." I think the explanation is starting to fly. "Another issue is the overemphasis on using opiate pain medication and we are in the process of reevaluating alternative medications to treat pain, such as gabapentin, or the use of nortriptyline or amitriptyline for the treatment of neuropathic pain. We are particularly concerned about the patients diagnosed with fibromyalgia where the diffuse symptoms seem like a moving target, and over time pain medication seems to have decreased value." I look Kilgore directly in the eye, and then Penny. "In addition, those patients who have long term use of Rx opiates seem to experience decreased effectiveness using the medication and we will be reevaluating those patients and possibly titrating over to other medications which are not in the opiate class of medications. But the bottom line is this, and I hope this is what I want you to hear." My voice is firmer the more I speak. "We will be developing a very stringent pain management contract and we will be stridently adhering to it. The contract will be—in patient terms that are understandable—the above that I have described to you and more. If you lose your medication or it gets contaminated: tough. If you use too much: tough, absolutely no early refills. Patient will be advised that non-opiate medications will be emphasized as the first line of treatment and that extended use of opiate pain medication has decreased effectiveness over time. We will be referring to cognitive behavioral therapists who specialize in pain management so that patients become more functional, despite their pain and we will also prescribe physical exercise programs so that they get their bodies working." I have blasted them out of the water— hopefully—and if that doesn't work, I know I'm really fucked.

Penny says, "Would you please step out of the room for a minute and this time you can close the door."

They call me back into the office. Kilgore questions, "So why weren't these standards already put in place?"

"A colleague was on medical leave and asked me to temporarily fill in for him. When he came back a few of the patients wanted to transfer to me. And then a small pain management practice insidiously grew. I attended continuing medical education programs concerning pain management and how to orchestrate them, but frankly my practice is dedicated to plastic surgical procedures and the pain management sideline has not gotten my total concentrated attention. Your visit today has changed that and I am appreciative that you have inspired me to pull together the missing elements of the pain management practice. Alternatively, I could close it completely and refer the patients. If you have any advice in the subject, it would be welcomed." This has got to win a prize for ass kissing. Not as good as my mom's bullshitting my dad, but close.

Penny says, "You're sure there's no drug diversion?"

"I'm sure. I said no once and I mean no." I look back and forth at them, thinking I have been triumphant at fooling them. "How does the remedial plan fly with you?"

Kilgore inflexibly replies, "Let's call it probation. You pull the administrative structure of your practice together and without notice we will come back to visit you to further assess your progress. And doctor, if you have a drug problem, well—"

"Thanks. I don't."

"Your practice looks like a lot of the patients are dependent on narcotics. What do you plan on doing about that?"

"The pain management contract should flesh out the drug dependent patients. I will refer them for evaluation and treatment of substance abuse. Possibly, I'll go through the training needed for the DEA X license so I can prescribe buprenorphine, Subutex or Suboxone for the patients who need to go that route."

Kilgore says, "Dr. Coyle, be careful. We have our eyes peeled and wide open." Without any cordiality they don't say another word and leave.

Jackie comes in my office and closes the door. "I eavesdropped. They went for it for now. But you know something, Glen, they don't believe you."

"You sure?"

"No kidding, I'm sure." Jackie comes close and gives me a hug.

I absolutely melt, blending into her receptivity following the surly back and forth with Kilgore and Penny. She doesn't see, but my eyes moisten. I whisper in her ear, "I don't know what to do."

She pulls back. Jackie has a threatened look on her face, like her mind is spinning a million miles an hour. She vaguely reminds me of how Julie looked when she was throwing all her stuff in the suitcase. "I do."

I'm scared about what Jackie is going to say. "What?"

"Close the practice for awhile and get treatment. The time lost we can make up later when you get yourself on track. I'm scared. Afraid I'll lose you completely to drugs. And horrified that my job with you will slip away."

I shift to a place that probably is not too realistic. "A lot is at stake between us. I know I can quit drugs on my own." I embrace Jackie as a diversion—for her and for me.

"Tom always tells me that, too. He never does stop. Or if you do stop, it's like the Mark Twain saying, 'It's easy to quit smoking. I've done it hundreds of times.' Glen, it's not about stopping, it's about staying stopped."

"Watch me."

Jackie looks resigned. And I sense this is larger than me. She's also married to delusional Tom. "Okay. I'll watch."

• • •

I sit in my office feeling a freakish sense of calm and I let out a soft moan after a torrential storm made an oozy sweat over my body. And there are the hideous after currents, thinking about the volleys between me and the menacing faced Kilgore with his gravelly voice and pasty sordid looking Penny who chirps when he speaks. It's deeper than trying to smooth them over to get the surly DEA investigators off my back with some plausible story so I don't cook myself and my medical license. They say their mission is to protect the public and for patient safety. But they must get their jollies out of screwing guys like me.

A blinding glare reflects off my desk making my eyes ache, and I reflexively squint against its penetrating light. A box with my address on it dulls one patch of brightness on the tabletop. I look at the jerking second hand of the wall clock and it lurches along at half the count as the pulsating spasms in my chest.

There is something I fight against. I turn at an angle and flip my hair in annoyance. All my turbulence is caused by just one thing—the control opiates have over my world. I hide from what creeps in the shadows ready to ambush me, but I always keep it in abeyance, held in suspension on the most tenuous tread that's ready to snap. Now my self-loathing is center stage, illuminated by an incisive laser light.

I pick up the box sitting in the glare of my desk and look at the return address. It is from a patient I operated on when I still had the wherewithal to do reconstructive hand surgery. It's been awhile since I've done a complicated hand procedure. Another grievous loss. It's one more unwanted conclusion from being saturated with mind twisted by dope. And I remember having a sweeping involvement with this patient to get him back to where he wanted to be. A good guy and we got this athlete back to the rigor of his sports.

I open the box. It contains a wooden carved sculpture of a hand with all digits attached. The wood is hard and exotic. There is a letter from Chip Inman. The patient writes he carved the hand for me, now that his own hand is fully functional. The patient cut off his finger using a power tool. The message also says thank you, thank you, thank you and he feels like his digit had never been severed because he has recaptured his life. He says he has surfed at Mavericks when the waves were fifty feet and he has done some double century bicycle rides. And he writes it still freaks him that I used blood sucking aquatic animals—medical leeches—to suck off the pooled blood from the skin grafted area, allowing for continuous blood circulation since the veins were not working to draw off the excess blood. And the little creatures infused anticoagulants—blood thinning—to avoid clotting.

I look at the hand sculpture and the letter sitting in front of me. There's a swelling in my chest.

It's still fills a hole in me to do breast reconstructive surgery since it horribly affects a woman's psyche to lose a breast. But reattaching a dismembered finger gives a person's physical function back. The small venous capillaries grow back and circulation is restored to the finger. The person feels whole again. And I feel…I don't know. It's been too long. I loved it. All I remember is the wondrous human connections I had with patients when severed digits were restored and they were rehabilitated to a semblance of more than normalcy. It was like their lives were better than before since they recovered a loss that gave them a new a deeper sense of themselves in the world. And one guy said to me, "I love you buddy." And everyone made some variant of the same statement. It wasn't like a doctor-patient relationship. It was human to human and I miss that feeling. You just don't get that connection with a breast augmentation or a tummy tuck.

I pick up the telephone to call the patient who carved the hand and wrote the letter, and then hang up, my voice suddenly feeling weak. I take a piece of stationery out of my desk drawer. I write him a letter thanking the patient for the sculpture and note. The words say helping him may have as much meaning for him has it does for me, though in different ways. The letter is a little vague. I leave it indistinct.

• • •

Jackie reappears. "Glen, today has been like a goddamn string that's been pulled too taut. Thank god we didn't snap. Are you spent from the DEA fiasco? Dumb question. You must be." At this instant I'm drawn in by a distraction. Jackie's sweet phermonal scent steals my olfactory senses. It doesn't take too much to drop into envisioning our pasts. I start to be a little frisky. "Yeah, spent, but with you around I'm a little jacked up."

Jackie's lips press tightly together. I get the message today is not the day. I downplay the spark I feel and change the subject.

"I'm sitting here in my office. But it's strange. I don't feel like I am anywhere, like there's no place on the face of the earth or in paradise or nirvana where I'd feel at home or comfortable or okay." My jaw makes a singular gnawing motion, but there's nothing in my mouth to chew on. "Have you ever felt that way?"

Jackie angles her head to the side. "I feel that way all the time with Tom…leaves me lost, like I'm occupying space and just going through life's motions. I feel kind of disconnected. But then I come to work and feel like I'm alive again. Like life is coherent again because I have a slot here at the clinic." Jackie warms to a nurturing smile. "Is it something similar?"

Jackie's soft looks absorb me into a soothing evanescent rescue. "Similar. I'm just surviving right now. It's freeing to lay eyes on you because of all the confusion today."

"How else should you feel?" Jackie moves next to me and puts her hand on my shoulder. I melt into her touch. "Look Glen, there's nothing to do at the clinic today. Go home."

I'd like to anticipate Julie will be home when I get there. Her fire finally burned out because of my drug addict ways. The likelihood of her presence is as remote as running into her in the middle of a godforsaken desert. The most I could hope for is a mirage.

I'm on the road heading home. The lush multicolored green stands of gnarly oak trees—valley, black and live oaks—and the bays and willows line La Laguna de Santa Rosa, laden with snowy white egrets and blue herons and kites and red tail hawks, and passerine starlings that pirouette through the sky in formation. Some days you'll come across a bald eagle or an osprey or an American white pelican if you're lucky. I'm immersed by the picturesque panorama. It sweeps me up to the point that my mind manufactures the impassioned Tchaikovsky violin concerto in D major. Scarcely any violinists have mastered the thorny and demanding intricacies of the crescendos. For the briefest moment I'm spared, like a pardon and have a sensation of being out of the snare of a trap.

I visually retrace a winter night walking along a laguna trail under the deciduous stands of oaks. Aromatic herbaceous smells waft up from the earth moistened by dew. A full moon and the illumination cast shadows from the barren spiny branches onto the area surrounding the path. The peaceful moonlit shadows aroused the earth and brought the landscape to an imaginary animation in the still of the night. As I traipsed along the terrain something emerged from the scene's inactivity, and I became stirred and emotionally awakened. The shadows moved as I moved. The dimness transformed into an animated pulsation, turning the fixed stillness into life.

Rounding a serpentine angle of the trail, a merlin stood on a four foot high stump, bared in full view in the incandescent moonlight. The small falcon's chest stood out like military chevrons on a soldiers arm. The bird of prey's head moved left and right waiting for a victim, feral game to ferociously grasp in its talons. I stood motionless for fifteen minutes, and then there was the moment of wild assault and the merlin plunged into grass and sunk into its prey, flying away with the indistinct outline of something in its clutches.

● ● ●

DEA investigators' coarse bitterness puts me right next to my latent shame. Now it's inescapable. If you feel shame, you can't see or experience beauty, except for possibly a split second until it disappears through your fingers like grains of sand, or like fine dust being blown away by explosive gale force winds. Today, the countryside driving home is an opaque monochromatic and motionless landscape with no passionate musical notes. Shame is where I'm stuck in my head. I'm caught and embarrassed and look into my worthless self brought on by the disgrace. Was I really meant to be a doctor? There's constant struggle of feeling like I'm an imposture while I thrash about on the inside to look good to the world.

The convergence of pressures weighs on me, making breathing tight. And right now I want to die rather than face the twisted pain of my drug use, or vanish and get lost somewhere and never come back. I want to beg someone for everything to be alright, but I don't know who to beg. I'm starting to feel chills and diarrhea of drug withdrawal coming on. But it's not as bad as the lies I believe in, pleading that my self-deception will give me some hope. Or the high strung spasms in my mind, and self-hatred that right now is bigger, overriding the opiate withdrawal. I'm a mess trying to escape myself. Like I'm the guy who's propelled at a hundred miles an hour inside my body trying to outrun myself, but now I'm at a zero standstill as if manacles are squeezed tight, painfully baring down on my wrists. The shadows of my dungeon envelop any remaining passion, except the drive to do drugs. I come up to the house and sink coinciding with feeling bolstered with seeing Julie's car in the driveway.

My hand grabs the front door handle like the grasp is disconnected from the rest of my body. Her suitcase in the hallway. She's so neat and tidy I wonder if she is keeping her suitcase on tap to make another escape. "You're back. You didn't make any calls to me. Where'd you stay?"

"I held up in a place in Napa Valley that had a lap pool and plenty of roads to run and ride my bike on. I wore it out after a couple of days and decided to come home."

Julie is sitting in the living room, sunken in a cushy chair, surrounded by books on triathlon training and exercise physiology. Her head rises from her reading and she refocuses on me. I have a pasted-on grin. I say, "What are you up to with the gobs of books?"

"I'm boning up. I've decided to start a women's coaching program for the triathlon, marathon and ultra-marathon. I'm going to start up a training program." She smells fresh, like being dusted with baby powder after a hot bath. There's no hint to point to where her stirred up edginess evaporated to. Except for the proposition that she wants to fend for herself by initiating a training business.

"Honestly, I can't think of anyone who would be as spot on than you. You have the brains and talent and patience to do it." A thought flits through my mind that this may be a recompense because we have spun our wheels and don't have children. And the absence of kids is a setback because of my self-centered dope distraction and knowing I'd be a shitty parent. And if I got clean, I fear that I couldn't stay that way. Going back and forth between recovery and relapse would ravage a child who needs to be the first priority.

"I didn't think of that…just automatically came to me." Julie looks quizzical. "Where you been? Out thinking things over?"

I tell her about Jackie calling me to the office, and the DEA investigators. The plan Jackie and I fashioned will hopefully get some space between the DEA agents and me. "I told Jackie I'd stop using drugs."

"Just like that?" Julie's expression blanches. "My parents said that all the time. They've never skipped a beat when it came to drinking. They just kept jacking their jaws and didn't do shit except pour another drink or say, 'Hey, how about another nightcap.'" She shakes her head. "You need help. It's not a solo ride to clean up."

Her mistrust of me is like an indelible stain.

I'm always able to do something for everything. A patient comes in with a problem and I fix it. I can control outcomes. "Julie, I'm having a little bit of an emergency." I run to the bathroom and shit my guts out, like an anal Vesuvius erupting into the ceramic thrown. God, there's a horrible gurgling gaseous churn in my intestinal tract. I rummage around and find the Suboxone. I open the window air-out the bathroom and leave.

I must look like hell, being washed over by a clammy sweat. "Julie, I can handle this. I can quit on my own."

"This is going to turn into an argument that isn't going to go anywhere. You quit on your own?" She pushes her sleeves back and solidly stands up straight with her shoulders back, with a look of disbelief that I don't have any credibility. "But you have to agree to enter treatment if you use. And I mean use only one time. No bullshit excuses." Julie's eyes narrow. "Or the other piece is if you quit and you're a total asshole to live with because you're in a foul mood because you don't have your fix, you go into treatment then, too."

"That's a tight leash. You mean I can never be in a bad mood like a regular human being?"

"Human being? Yes. Asshole because you want to get loaded, but are dry? No."

"This is sounding like an ultimatum."

"An ultimatum? No. What'd I just say? It's an agreement. Julie moves closer to me. Her voice is low pitched. "Agree or no agreement?"

"Okay." My voice is just above a whisper.

"Okay, what?"

"I agree that if I use, I'll go into treatment. The asshole part is a little sketchy because I can be an asshole without using." I sound like a tape recording. Then I think I can put together an undisclosed escape clause that she won't be able to detect.

There's a sliver of an unexpected flirtatious look and then she gets serious again. I'd like to have a pass at her rather being put to the task. "Okay, Mr. Tiptoe Artist, don't have a go at getting over on me."

My eyebrows curve upward. "But Julie, if I change, doesn't that mean that you'll have to change, too?" I shrug. I twist my left wrist to gesticulate with an outstretched open palm. I'm regretting making such a flat commitment and I'm figuring how to weasel an escape hatch.

"Bullshit, and forget the sidestepping number. As far as you're concerned I've got my life sewn-up. Me changing? That's not at stake." Julie waves me off. She emphatically says, "No! You're the one tied up in a Gordian knot. Don't try to put it on me and suck me into your squirmy convolutions."

I shake my head. Duress sets in. "But—"

Julie short-sheets me. "But nothing."

"So Julie, have you heard the saying by Goethe, 'Love is an ideal thing, marriage a real thing; a confusion of the real with the ideal never goes unpunished.'"

"Glen, you're messing with me. You make me nutso enough with all of your mumbo jumbo crap without citing an old German writer to justify how you screw with my mind."

I walk to the window and look out. The promise I made Julie has major consequences and I don't know if I can do it. I've always been able to do something about everything, but this agreement is too elusive for me to grasp. I think about whether I'll fail or don't have the constitution to pull it off.

CHAPTER EIGHT

Five days trailing my promises to Julie and Jackie, I'm finishing up an uncomplicated standard rhinoplasty. The nose job looks like a good result. This woman is a good candidate for the procedure and has realistic expectations. It's a relief that she has reasonable thoughts going on in her mind, unlike the torment that Susan put me through. A faint distress signal fires in my mind that Susan could come back at me again.

I watch Jackie waste the unused clear drug left in the syringe into the wastepaper basket. She looks up and squints at me like a stiletto piercing my skin. A wash of chagrin wraps around me, feeling caught by her doubting eyes. She knows I crave the dope.

The receptionist taps on the door to the surgical suite. "Dr. Coyle, the men from the DEA, Mr. Kilgore and Penny are here."

"Tell them to hold on in my office. I'm wrapping up a surgical procedure." I turn to Jackie. "You'll take care of rest? And move the patient to the recovery room."

The receptionist dizzily blinks. She's breathing heavily.

Jackie's face is taut and ashen. And she appears threatened, like maybe I'm history. I suppose my clinic staff are thinking their sustenance depends on me, the iffy guy.

I still have my scrubs on, minus the ugly looking head covers we wear, and enter the office. My hands are in a knot, but I pry them open, feigning being relaxed, despite knowing for certain that I'm going to be hit by a second volley of artillery. "Good afternoon, gentlemen." My voice is firm, but blandly neutral. "Did you come to do some follow up on the progress of our practice remedies?"

Kilgore takes the lead. "We can start with that." I think Kilgore could go to a costume party as a werewolf with just an iota of makeup. He's a vitriolic type cop and I bet his daddy did some bad shit to him. He has an Irish name. Just maybe his father was an alcoholic, and Kilgore's job is a way of getting back after being worked over as a kid. And somehow being an investigator gives him a sense of immunity.

I twist my neck as if it's sore, knowing they could give a shit less about what we're doing to transform the pain management clinic. "We are in the final draft of a patient pain management contract. It clearly identifies and states all the points I made to you during your last visit." My voice has the modulation of a prerecorded message. "The draft should be finalized tomorrow or the next day, and we will be sending it out to all of the patients for their agreement and signature. It will include a cover letter to outline that we need a more accountable pain treatment program. The document should appear reasonable and make sense. The staff and I are clear on the boundaries the contract establishes and everyone the clinic is comfortable with it."

Kilgore's face is coolly flat and expressionless. Kilgore sighs and critically eyes Penny, unveiling he had screwed up. "But we—"

Penny breaks in, "We inadvertently left our testing gear at the office the last time we were here."

Kilgore muscles in, "Okay. Dr. Coyle, we should have done this during our last visit to rule out any doubt. We want a urine sample from you for a drug screen. Are you amenable to this?"

I take half a second to calculate the last time I used hydrocodone. It was about the time I had a run in with Julie. I know there is an eighty-five percent chance the drug screen will come back negative. The fentanyl use was four days back. I doubt that they'll be able to catch a positive with the levels left in my system. And if they include Suboxone in the screen I'll be screwed. "Sure. I've been in surgery for a while and need to piss anyway."

Kilgore makes a curt nod. His feet are planted in a wide stance, like he's ready to do a quick draw in a western movie's gunfight. "Mr. Penny will go to the bathroom with you and observe you urinating into the cup. He must see the flow of urine go from the urethra into the cup to insure this is a forensic quality urine test." Kilgore moistens his lips. "Have you used any substances recently which might make this a positive test?" Penny seems to be a candy ass henchman, like he has to act like a bad guy because he hangs out in Kilgore's shadow.

"No." The stakes are higher with Kilgore and Penny, not like the illusion I forge when I bamboozle Julie about my drug use. "The UA should be clean as a whistle." And one slipstream frame blinks though my mind. I ought to have checked myself by getting a drug screen while I was at the lab a couple of days ago having my testosterone levels taken for the ten thousandth time.

Penny and I enter the bathroom. It's a big area, a ten by twelve foot room set-up to meet ADA specs in case I'm operating on a patient who is in a wheelchair. I move toward the toilet. He stands two feet away which makes me dreadfully ill at ease, kind of a prickly sensation, particularly relative to amount of space in the room and the twit in a position of power standing so close. Penny pulls out a pair of latex gloves from his jacket pocket and dons them. And then he reaches into another pocket and produces a cup and another container that's composed of two cylinders-shaped compartments integrated within it. Penny says, "Here, urinate into this cup."

"So what's the deal with the container with the two cylinders in it?" Not knowing the underlying motivation makes me antsy.

"We do split samples." Penny's posture is stiff. He comes off cold, his affect is all business. "If one sample comes back positive we send the other sample to another lab, and a medical review officer—an MRO—reviews the results to determine and authenticate the accuracy of the testing."

I unzip my pants. I'm not pee shy, but I'm keyed up with this guy standing almost on top of me. "Mr. Penny, would you please backup to not be so close so I can relax and pee."

And then the jerk moves back one foot. "Just think waterfalls, breath normally and let go." Given his edgy voice he might as well have said, "Take a piss, asshole and quit whining."

I look at a dot on the wall, shutting Penny out of my mind. I focus on my breath like I'm meditating, trying to release. I feel the urine coming. Penny twitches and I tighten up. I tell Penny, "Say, I need a little more space to loosen up. You will still be able to see the flow from the urethra into the cup. So please move back three feet." He actually does it. I look at the dot on the wall. My bladder is so full that my abdomen is distended. I push on my abdomen and ease enough to fill the cup to the brim. I hand it to Penny, and some spills on his hand. "Oh, sorry about that." And I am thinking fuck 'em. Penny pours the urine into the split sample cylinders in the container. "Are we done?"

"I need you to sign and verify this is your urine. I'll fill in the collection documentation data. And just so you know, we have a chain of custody process that tracks the sample, so there are absolutely no slipups in terms of keeping track of your specimen. This is what you call forensic quality drug testing."

"Good to know you have high standards. What else do you want from me? Let's go over the revised office policy and patient pain management contracts."

"I can tell you that right now Kilgore and I have little interest in what you have reworked for the office." Penny's voice has a merciless, grating echo. "We are trying to establish whether you're diverting drugs for self-use." The corners of his mouth curl down. "We'll be in touch when we get the test results from the lab." I'm certain the drug screen will be clean, but I don't know what they'll pull next. Penny says, "And we'll be on you like white on rice if it's a positive drug screen."

We walk back to my office. Kilgore looks at the sample in Penny's hand. "Dr. Coyle, we're done here for today." The two of them march to the door. No goodbye. Just a curt impersonal brush off departure. When they are out of range I voice a retaliatory, "Fuck you, too."

• • •

I'm swimming in a sea of ambiguity considering what to expect next. I'm hyper-alert, working double time to hold all my combatants in suspension—Julie, Jackie, and the two pencil-necked buffoons who just left my clinic. I'm calculating how many milligrams of opiates I'd have to take to override the Suboxone, because those DEA agents will not be revisiting me for awhile and I can slip in some drug use before they retest me or maybe they won't retest me at all.

"Glen?" Jackie sashays into my office. "What happened with those guys?" She's on edge. "What'd they do?"

My cheeks feel hot. I tell Jackie that they made me piss in a cup for a drug screen, while twit shit Penny observed me urinate. I say I haven't used for several days and I'm fairly certain that I'm outside the window of drug detection. The only caveat is whether their drug screen includes Suboxone, which I doubt. "And if it does—"

"They'll know you're addicted to opiates and using the Suboxone to stave off withdrawal...if buprenorphine is on the drug panel to capture the property that Suboxone and Subutex share." Jackie states the obvious. But in deference to her I nonetheless bow my head to agree with her.

Jackie rubs her hand back and forth across the back of her neck. And then she changes to curling a lock of hair around her index finger and tilts her head. I weigh the percentage of the time I feel unglued with attraction when Jackie is near. The times of heat between us maybe one conspiratorial ingredient that keeps her mouth shut about my drug use. Our pull can happen at unsuspected times, like when I'm worked up and a lot is going on. It something about her long hair she wears in a swishy ponytail. She's an eyeful. What shakes me up is the way her well-proportioned body moves when her hip bones swivel in their sockets when she sashays and glides around the clinic. The way she naturally smells makes my nostrils flare—she could make millions if she could bottle that scent. And then and I remember what I try to forget— faithlessness, the heavily dotted punctuation points when we went astray.

"The lab made a mistake and faxed your testosterone results.".

My brain skids into the thoughts of opiate's mechanisms that depress testosterone levels…my mind goes clinical thinking how the drug inhibits the hypothalamic-pituitary-luteinizing hormone which causes a lowering and inhibiting LH-dependent testicular steroidogenesis. The result: testosterone degradation. "Did you see the results?"

"Yes." She struggles for what to say next, grimacing and rubbing her right temple. "The lab made a mistake by sending the results via fax and I made a mistake by looking at them. I'm sorry, Glen."

"So, tell me." I shove my hands in my pants pockets, and my shoulders nearly touch my ears.

Jackie's face opens up. "Good numbers. Five hundred and sixty nanograms/deciliter."

"I haven't knocked myself off, yet."

"That's a *yet*," she says straight-faced.

"What do you mean?" I pull my head back and squint.

"*Yets* are about things to come that haven't happened *yet*."

"Do the numbers mean something?"

"Don't play with me." Jackie pins me. "Look, Glen, the past thing with you was an irrational slipup in judgment, okay, blowing it a couple of times. Tom was out of it and I was hurting. Emotional. Vulnerable. It's as much my fault as—"

I think Jackie is taking too much on and I want to let her off. "Look,

Jackie, at this point blaming you or me or anybody is a dead end we can forget about. Let go of that one. It was too good to regret. But at the same time I see eye to eye with you. A misstep that sparked fallout…the conflict of loving it. Let's just guard our sweet secret of the past. Sure, we happen to hit each other when we were both having a tough time. You were exposed because of the turmoil with Tom and I was having a distant patch with Julie." I draw in a breath and slowly let it go. "I keep what happened tucked away in a little box."

She shrugs. "I know. Regrets or blaming anybody is a no win game. I do the same as you, keep it secreted away someplace. But I also take that little box out sometimes and have a look inside. I kind of like doing that."

The corners of my mouth curl upwards. "I do, too. There are times when my mind is idle and I picture you. Or I see you move in a certain way and I can't help but let my imagination go for a second." My eyes fall for a second. I look back in Jackie's eyes. "What do you want now?"

Jackie rolls her shoulders up and lets them fall. "How about to make the tension go away."

I catch which way the wind is blowing. Tom isn't going away anytime soon. Jackie's emptiness with him could lead up to enticing her with more sex. "My tension probably won't go away. What do you say to being awake to what's happened and not doing something about it again?"

Jackie nods. "That's probably more realistic." A disappointed look crosses her face.

A thought makes my face turn to stone for a second. "You're probably not going to like what I'm going to say. But in some ways I just like Tom. In my own way I'm a loser. But I get away with it because I'm a doctor and can pull off looking good. Tom just hides out and does his thing with drugs."

"Well, at least your testosterone is five hundred and sixty." Jackie cracks a smile.

"Spiteful?" My voice ticks up at the last syllable.

"Yeah. I've always been caught in the loop. My dad was alcoholic and I swore that would be the end of relationships with substance abusers." I catch on to the parallel childhoods that Jackie and Julie share. "And look who I married—Tom. That's me…snagged by the same cycle. I work for you and at the start had absolutely no clue. I must have some little psycho unconscious sonar device in my guts that draws me in one direction. It makes me question, who's sicker? The addict or the person who gets in relationships with addicts over and over again." Jackie shakes her head. "I think it's me who's the sicko."

"Come on, Jackie." I can't help slipping in a flirty look. "That's pretty harsh and unforgiving, how about you—"

"Hold it, Glen. Look, the DEA guys are probably going to nail you. The office will be history. There's not much more time before everything goes away. Come on, let's do it one more time and then we bury the little secret box so deep even we won't find where it is." Jackie turns and closes the office door.

Fuck it. I tell myself. I need an out—to breakout and vanish and sidestep all that's coming down on me. Sliding into it with Jackie one more time will add to the other two notches, and then we'll stop.

• • •

I inch my ramshackle car up the driveway. Julie's car is in front of the house like a monument to her presence. What happened with Jackie was reckless. I cheated on Julie when I was clean. Jackie is like using a drug that takes my distress away. Being with her is like switching addictions

I'm showing up to a woman who quick-minded and graduated magna cum laude. She's tripled her inheritance portfolio and has not spent a cent of it. Her obsessive focus turned her into a consummate athlete. Physically, Julie is muscled from all her athleticism, making her exceedingly attractive with whatever she wears or without a stitch on. Jackie is softer, endowed with striking good looks and figure that she uses to the max. They don't outshine each other. They have their own special gorgeous ways about them.

I didn't expect her to be at home and the alarm feeds into a sensation of dread. I turn off the car's ignition. And I sit motionless and dazed. Julie comes to the window. She waves, and then motions for me to come into the house.

"I expected that you'd be out doing your training—surprised to see you." A humiliating sensation churns up from my stomach and I feel frothiness at the back of my throat.

"I swam earlier, but I have some hamstring tenderness from speed work on the track and I don't want it to turn into an injury, so I'm chilling out, stretching out and taking anti-inflammatory meds." Her look softens and warms. "I was waiting for you so we could...you know...snuggle." Julie lifts one eyebrow and cocks her head. "Glen, you don't look quite right."

"I'm baffled. You split and ditch me. Then you show up and want to snuggle."

"Well, I'm mixed up and kind of disoriented. I really don't know what I want. I could feel your skin and change my mind and kick you out of bed. We separated and then I get all confused about love and hate. It makes me feel like taking you back in, but also spitting you back out again."

I'm thinking, crap, of all the days to want to have some puzzling push-pull about sex. I backpedal into a diversion. "Two agents from the DEA came to my office today and they took a urine sample for a drug screen, suspecting me of diverting pain medication for self-use. It should come back clean, since I haven't used for awhile."

"It sure took long enough for those bureaucrats to get you on their radar screen. What now? Your medical license is toast?" Julie hesitates and I can see her head is spinning. "You scare the shit out of me, Glen." She tells me despite everything, we have a lot of assets. The house is paid for and we own the clinic outright. Our way of life isn't about blowing money. She buys a new pair of running shoes every six weeks, and my time is spent working my butt off. Julie says her personal assets are rock solid.

She defensively calculates, "Let's say you had a sizable hiatus from your practice. We'd be able to maintain the house and the clinic even if we had to close it for a period."

I step into Julie's invention of false optimism. "Even if my DEA permit was revoked, Jackie is a nurse practitioner and she could prescribe if I could get another doctor to supervise her."

"There's ways to finagle." I feel like a heel after being with Jackie and now Julie is scheming to cover up for me. "It's not a done deal, yet."

"The urine sample should come back clean, since I'm several days out from my last use."

"You're unhinged, baby. What do you think about my nuzzling proposal? Maybe we could team up to make it all better. At least it's a possibility."

On the inside I groan, edging on wanting to avoid Julie. "I got all worked up today and feel scummy. Let me take a hot soapy shower first." My duplicitous secret ways with Jackie makes a filthy sensation crawl over my skin.

CHAPTER NINE

I pick up the phone in my office and the receptionist tells me Dr. Miles Dietrick is on the line. I put together right away why Miles is calling. He'll be more of the torment that's been raining down on me.

"Hello, Miles. I hear your practice is hectic. How's it going with keeping up the pace?"

"Night and day. There's Jack and me covering the cardiothoracic on-call and that's it. We're getting hammered. I'm forced to use a locum tenens doc if I want to take time off."

I can't stand the apprehension, inciting me to say, "What's up? Do you have a surgical reconstruction case you want me to do?"

I'm hoping against the possibility of hope. Miles is the head of the Physicians' Well Being Committee and I know I'm about to be called on the carpet.

"No. I'm calling about something else."

No shit he's calling about something else. "Okay." I look at my medical degree and medical license hanging on the wall like they are about to disintegrate.

"The WBC wants to see you this Wednesday at six o'clock."

"Hold on, I need to consult my calendar." I stall for a minute. "I'm tied up then." I'm tied up in a knot right now and then.

Miles's voice shifts from collegial to ominously formal. "Please make arrangements to be there. Your hospital privileges could possibly be affected if you don't appear."

I keep pretending I don't know what's up, looking for an angle. "And what's this about?"

"This is not a matter that would be appropriately addressed by telephone. It would be best done in person."

"I'm in trouble?"

Miles's voice comes across as decorous. "It depends on what you have to say and your response to our queries."

"Do I need an attorney?"

"No. Not with the WBC. If you get bumped up to the hospital's Medical Executive Committee that in all likelihood would be a different process than with us, and you might opt for representation. But you are getting way ahead of yourself. For the time being, I'd like you to solely take care of business with the WBC."

My knee is bouncing. I can't stop a tic on the upper part of my cheek. And then I clear my throat, surprising myself by leveling with Miles, "What you're saying is making me very nervous."

"Do you understand the role of the WBC?"

A generally known fact in the medical community is that the WBC is in place to assist and help physicians who have emotional or behavioral or chemical dependency problems or whose abilities have declined due to a cognitive problem. But these days I also understand the medical-political climate has changed and that the WBC also answers to the Med Exec Committee. I can't sit at my desk any longer and I stand up. "You primarily help impaired physicians. But your role has changed over the past several years because of the hospital's increased concern over medical liability, and you have sorted obligations to the Med Exec Committee."

There isn't any slippage to Dietrick's voice, and it has a sonorous and anchored sound, as if he wants to shore me up. "All of that is true. But we do not come from a punitive position. After all, we are clinicians in the practice of helping human beings."

Dietrick is reassuring, but no amount of uplifting encouragement would be enough to sway the trepidation making me unsettled. "I am afraid that if my hospital privileges get suspended the hospital will file an 805 report to the Medical Board of California which will trigger an investigation by the MBC."

"Remember what I said about the disposition of your situation. It depends on what you have to say and your response to our queries. We could do nothing, put you on medical leave, or…" Dietrick's voice eases. "Let's give this a rest right now, and then pursue our concerns when we meet with you on Wednesday. Fair enough?"

I reluctantly acquiesce, without sounding like an obsequious supplicant. "Okay. I'll be there." All the color has blanched out of my face.

• • •

Six o'clock, Wednesday. I'm on time and wait outside the conference room at Memorial Hospital. At five minutes after six Miles cracks open the conference room door. He has a job to do, but at the same time Miles extends his hand to me. We shake hands and forged smiles flip back and forth between us, signaling a polite cover for the strain that's about to happen. Miles ushers me into the conference room. He indicates where I'm to sit—prominently at the head of the table—*the guest of dishonor* who is about to lose face. The conference table is flanked on both sides by a total of ten physicians. Miles sits opposite to me at the far end of the rectangular table, looking forbidding and austere, shielded by permeable compassion. I scan the cast of characters on the WBC. Almost all of the docs are known in the medical community for being addicts with long-term comebacks from the misadventures with drugs and alcohol. And I suspect they redeem themselves by guiding others from addiction's vise. Two of them are internists who are known to be board certified in addiction medicine by the American Society of Addiction Medicine. And I'm rattled knowing I'm not going to be able to dance fast enough to delude these two docs.

I make out how Julie and Jackie are hardwired and grasp how to work over their vulnerabilities. But today I'm going to be dead meat, since the physicians occupying this room have a bead right on the middle of my forehead.

I imagine they've heard every scrap of bullshit and are bulletproof when it comes to maneuvers and schemes rigged by addicted doctors. They've heard it all, and I'm the neophyte that's up against the men who know the well-worn path. I have the sensation of being screwed before we begin.

Miles says, "Glen do you know why we have invited you to meet with us?"

I have to dig down deep to stop myself from twitching in my seat. "You have concerns. The function of the WBC is to assist physicians who have impairment and you want to determine whether I am impaired." No bullshit to begin with is a cunning opening move. But I can't sustain anything like the craftiness I'd need to outmaneuver these guys.

"We're off to a good start. Most physicians are unable or unwilling to acknowledge, or reject the purpose of the meeting. And, yes, we have a number of concerns. I will address each one separately and would like you to respond."

Miles looks down at papers lying on the table in front of him. All the physicians are looking at him. They sit with their fingers interlaced in front of them. Some more white-knuckled than the rest.

Miles raises his head. "First, we have documentation of two episodes when you were rounding on patients in the hospital, where you had performed mastectomy reconstructive surgery. The hospital staff indicated that you appeared impaired, and also noted that your pupils seemed tightly constricted which would be suggestive of opiate use."

Oh Jesus, here we go. "It is unclear what you mean by 'impaired.' I recall the two episodes. I was having extremely bad days and my mood was foul. I may have not been as polite as I'd like to be. Unfortunately, in these circumstances I tend to hold emotions inside and not bother others with them. The downside is that they may come out sideways in regrettable ways. Possibly, this is what the staff was seeing."

They'll never buy this bullshit, I'm thinking. "In terms of my constricted pupils, I made my rounds at night at and the patients were recuperating in brightly lighted rooms which would cause anyone's pupils to contract. Of course, not every constricted pupil is the result of opiate use."

My voice's edgy coarseness is a little too antagonistic. I'd better watch it, put on the brakes and chill. "As a side note, all of these reconstructive patients have said in their own words that they felt their lives were at an end, but through the surgery they got their lives back. These are hardly comments that patients would say if I was impaired." I look at the opaque sidelights on either side of the conference room door and see the human forms of shadowy figures outside walking back and forth. Two episodes? Shit, that's all they noticed. A glance at the wall clock shows it ticking along at a sluggish uphill pace.

Miles's face forms into a pinched expression. "Okay, one down and we have some other items we would like you to address. We have gotten an uptick in a number of patient complaints. These complaints are from your private practice, but nonetheless, they were lodged with the hospital and made their way to Executive Committee and were referred to us to address with you at today's meeting. One concern was the number of postoperative infections." Miles gives me a glassy stare. "But the alarming part was that you informed patients to consult their PCP, despite the fact that you were the treating physician. And in the four cases we have documented, the PCP deferred to you since you had done the surgeries. Afterward, you had your nurse practitioner follow-up with the cases and you sidestepped the continuing care of the patient." The words rolling off his tongue are sharp and testy. "We determined that this would be considered to be compromised clinical practice, and specifically a problem with professional judiciousness. And explicitly, this, in my mind, could be interpreted as a sign of physician impairment, since you seemed to lack discretion."

"Your concern is understandable, particularly since the cases resulted in patient complaints. I am concerned too, as is my staff. The increase of postoperative infections seems to be a blip on the screen and I do not see it as a trend—a statistical outlier, if you will. Our office policy is to provide the patient with written instructions and this is followed by self-care counseling with my nurse practitioner." I'm blasting them with my rapid fire talk. I slow it down. "In the cases you cited, they had long-term relationships with their PCPs and I thought the primary care physician would be in a better position to handle the case. My nurse practitioner—who I pay handsomely—supervised and prescribed antibiotics when the patients were referred back to our clinic. This is part of her job description and prescribing antibiotics for inflection is within the purview of her capabilities."

I rub the back of my neck, noticing the pinched fixed eyes around the table pinning me. "Believe me; I was not dismissive of the patients. In retrospect, the patients probably wanted direct physician contact and felt slighted that they were handed off to my adept and skilled nurse practitioner."

A couple of the docs have their lips tightly pressed together. I tap the table with my index finger, and then twist my wedding ring around my finger, while my gaze darts on all sides of the room. "In my view, these complaints are a function of patient-doctor politics, rather than a transgression of good clinical practice. Please don't misinterpret what I'm going to say next." I cross my arms. "Nonetheless, the patients were advised on home postoperative self-care and must have mismanaged themselves which resulted in the infections. One woman, for example, went into a bacteria-laden hot tub three days after her surgery and this was the source of her infection. And another who lied to me about her smoking which diminished her healing that caused secondary infection. The potential risks and circumstances for infection were addressed in detail prior to surgery, and post-surgery. They complained about me, where the onus of the responsibility was solidly in their court. I'm not blaming them, I'm just saying—"

I look at Miles. His alabaster his face is wraithlike and expressionless, as if he's holding his foreboding cards close to his vest. And then I check the members of the WBC and the majority of them have raised eyebrows. Miles steals a look at this watch. I have the sense that I'm digging myself into a deeper hole.

Miles breaks in, "We have information on good authority that you were visited by DEA agents. You have to know that none of your office staff informed us, but it was rather a serendipitous discovery. Please tell us about their motivations for contacting you."

One of the committee members is pulling his earlobe. I moisten my lips—despite my dry mouth—while I'm gathering myself up to push through the next installment. "They were mainly concerned about the orchestration of the pain management clinic. As you might know, I temporarily covered another physician's pain practice while he was on medical leave. That was Dr. Henning. When he returned a number of patients wanted to remain with me." Under the table I'm running my hands back and forth on my thighs. "The pain practice took off on its own, and it was not by my design and I had never intended to make this addition to my plastic surgery clinic. Nonetheless, it took form without my stringent attention to the details of patient contracts. I have to admit that I have been altogether too forgiving of patients who request early refills, or who have lost or contaminated their prescriptions. This has resulted in being somewhat too liberal with my prescribing practices."

Two committee members shake their heads, like I'm miserable at lying "This was the DEA agents' concern. I negotiated with them to revise my office policies and develop highly structured patient contracts which would call for no early refills or replacement of lost or contaminated pain medications." I look at the exist. "Additionally, if it was discovered that anyone of my patients were abusing pain medications they would be referred for evaluation, and if necessary, treatment by a specialist in that area. The DEA agents revisited me and were advised of the progress that my staff and I had made with making the revisions in the office policies." I expel a small breath of air.

One of the addiction medicine physicians, Dr. Hickman, lowers looks over the top of his glasses. "Did they have concerns that you were diverting pain medication for self-use?"

I turn toward Hickman and blink. "There was mention of this issue. They said it was a routine question, since many practices where the policies are poorly structured were associated with drug diversion."

Hickman purses his lips and says, "And what did you tell them?"

I look down at the imitation wood grain on the tabletop and lift my head to meet Hickman's eyes. "I indicated that the practice may have the appearance of diverting medication, but in fact my plastic surgery practice was my first priority which has caused me to not be as vigorously attentive to pain management side of the clinic. In retrospect, I can obviously see how they had their suspicions."

Hickman squints, "And did they ask you for a urine sample for a drug screen?"

"They did. And I complied. One of the investigators, Mr. Penny, observed me while I produced the specimen. He indicated it is part of the forensic-quality process they use to obtain samples."

Hickman's voice is pointed. "Have the investigators advised you of the results?"

I shake my head. "Not to date." I follow with a nod. "But the results will be negative."

Hickman slightly jerks his head up and narrows his eyes. "What makes you so sure?"

I curl the corners of my mouth up to make a playful, yet painfully uncomfortable smile. "Well, you have to use drugs to get a positive result and I didn't use drugs."

Miles says to Hickman, "Can we move onto the next item, or do you want to pursue this more?"

Hickman's face is deadpan when he responds to Miles. "Let's move on and we can come back to it if necessary."

Miles scratches his cheek and continues. "The next concern is sensitive, so please bear with us. Dr. Fitzgerald advised us that you sought treatment with him and you were briefly a patient in a psychiatric residential facility. Is that right?"

I jerk back. "He's violated my patient-doctor confidentiality."

Miles frowns. "It may seem that way to you, but there are exceptions to confidentiality. Namely, if there is danger to self or others. His concern was about your transient suicidal ideation. And he was more concerned about you being impaired and there is the potential for danger in terms of your ability to practice surgery." He sniffs. "Let me give you some background. He consulted two psychiatric colleagues and an attorney before contacting the WBC." Miles's voice gathers momentum. "He felt working through the issue with the WBC would be the most prudent way to intervene, and he also had the options of informing law enforcement or reporting you to the enforcement arm of the Medical Board of California. So, you should consider yourself fortunate that he contacted us, rather than enforcement agencies." He leans back in his chair.

"What did he say?"

Mile's speech goes bland and more factual. "He had misdiagnosed you as having a bipolar disorder. This diagnosis was made on the premise of significant mood variability. He admits to not being an expert in sniffing out chemical dependency." I have an uneasy sensation that Miles is about to deliver a blow. "He indicated that one of the staff at the psychiatric facility was quite alert to problems with chemical dependency and determined that you were chemically dependent and the bipolar disorder was a misnomer. The staff member informed Dr. Fitzgerald that she recommended chemical dependency treatment by a program that specializes in healthcare professionals. She asked you to consider this recommendation and return to see her, which you did not do. She went to your room to seek you out, and apparently you had contraband and were under the influence of opiates. At that point you left the facility and did not go through with her recommendation." The tension in the room is taut as a snare drum.

I am fighting to maintain a cooperative composure. "I am upset that my confidentiality was violated." I sound flat, with zero substance behind my words.

Miles's voice is unrelenting. "As I said, Dr. Fitzgerald seems to have responded responsibly since you are a surgeon and have a history of drug dependence. So either you operate under the influence of drugs or in a state of withdrawal and in either case it causes impairment for the patients undergoing surgery." He pauses for half a second. "And you are held to a higher standard than the general public." He lets out a weighted sigh. "To repeat, he had two consultations with other psychiatrists and sought legal help in making the determination whether to come forward. And you must understand that you are extremely lucky that he contacted us rather than the medical board or some other legal regulatory agency."

I splay my hand across my chest. "You can put your concerns to rest, since you will find that I am not using drugs. If you wish to do a drug test right now, I would be happy to furnish you a sample."

The other addiction medicine physician, Dr. Moffitt, says, "So you've stopped using drugs?"

I recoil, being bated. "I want to say that I am clean of psychoactive drugs, yes." Fuck 'em, they don't need to know that I'm self-treating with Suboxone.

Moffitt grimaces. "And your plan is to stay that way?"

"Not use them." I shrug.

"Maybe you've heard the Mark Twain saying, 'To promise not to do a thing is the surest way in the world to make a body want to go and do that very thing.'"

"Sounds familiar." I'm getting sick of this shit. "Twain died in 1910 and things have changed since then."

Moffitt has a smug, knowing look. "There is a major difference between stopping and staying stopped." A familiar line I've heard before.

"I imagine there is, but I have stopped, stopped." I have the sensation of the jaws of a trap just sprung and snared my ankle.

Moffitt nods. "Good that you acknowledge the use of opiates." They sure herded me down the cattle chute and sucked that piece out of me. "Look around the room. There are a lot of experienced people sitting at this table. Let me tell you what I think. There is being dry. But being dry without a solid program of recovery leads in two directions. One is obvious. Relapse." His eyes widen. "The other is being dry and being miserable since there are no mechanisms in place to support having meaning in life without the use of drugs."

My shoulders roll forward. "You all have experience. But how does that size-up when it comes to a specific individual who may or may not be like the norm?"

Miles steps in, "Thank you for saying that, because it leads to what we want you to do."

There's stepping into a trap and then there's jumping into one. "And what is that?"

His voice vibrates with smooth confidence. "The docs who participate on the WBC have the wherewithal to funnel you in the appropriate direction and we may have our ideas about what you need, but we depend on the independent assessment for treatment recommendations and disposition. We want you to go a chemical dependency program that specializes in healthcare professionals and be evaluated for treatment. Maybe they'll say you don't need treatment. Or you need outpatient treatment. Or inpatient treatment. Let them be the judge since that's what they are in the business to do."

This is bullshit, since they already know the outcome. They're simply trying to get me to land someplace for treatment. "But I have cases scheduled." I stupidly blink. "Lots of them."

Miles give me an easy nod. "We want you to suspend your clinic and hospital practices until you are evaluated and follow the recommendations."

"And if I don't?"

Miles's face looks like chiseled stone. "We will have to advise the Med Exec Committee and they will suspend your hospital privileges which will generate a mandatory 805 report to the medical board. But this, in a sense, will be a redundancy, since we will have already reported you to the board. The 805 will just add another piece showing your hospital privileges have been suspended."

I'm emotionally choked. "In other words, I am screwed like being forked in a game of chess. I don't have any choices about how to move next."

Miles clears this throat. "Let's reframe this. Look, by following our lead it will help you to stop screwing yourself. I hope you get that. Our worry is patient care. I'm going to dip into something else that's not our territory, but I have to put it out there. The WBC's experience is by the time a physician lands at out meeting things at home are a real mess. And my hunch is that you are cutoff and living in a solitary affair with drugs. One thing about treatment is that you will start to feel not so alone in your addiction and you'll be able put your relationships more on track." Miles rolls up his sleeves to mid-forearm. "All the healthcare professional treatment programs we use include the significant other in treatment. You need to know that."

"Well…except…but—"

Miles drops his head and raises his eyebrows. "Before you put up any opposition, just tell me what you're thinking."

"I'm too overwhelmed to say what I'm specifically thinking."

Miles compassionately smiles. "That's what we would expect at this point."

Dr. Hickman clears this throat and says, "There is a basic saying in the Twelve-Step programs that is, 'One day at a time.' There is a reason for the saying's widespread use. Addicts and alcoholics tend to jump into the future and attach fears to what is going to happen. The *one day at a time* approach keeps you anchored in the moment and increases your ability to handle things as they come up and decreases being overwhelmed by things in the future that you can't control today. Get it?"

"I get it."

Miles comes back onboard, "We want you to go to one of the healthcare professional programs soon, like tomorrow or the next day. There are several, but the closest and many of our docs have gone to is Hazelden-Springbook and—"

A pressure tells me to show a willingness to be compliant. I take out my cell phone and get the number of Hazelden-Springbrook off the internet feature. I dial it. "Hello, this is Dr. Glen Coyle. I want to come to your facility for an evaluation." The person on the other end of the line says that I will be contacted in the morning for a screening over the phone and arrangements will be made. I hang-up and report what was said to the WBC.

Miles says, "We're done for the moment. Glen, call me tomorrow and advise me of the details."

"Hey Glen, I've got a final question for you." Moffitt's eyebrows knit together in a probing expression. "Your residency in plastic reconstructive surgical procedures included the subspecialty in hand surgery. And you're board certified. I used to hear all the time about people cutting or chopping off their fingers and you'd be on the spot instantly to reattach the severed digit. But I haven't heard about you performing these operations for a long time. What's up with that?"

I slump in my chair. All eyes are on me. I want to get out of that door this instant. A sensation of degradation makes a vacuous feel in my stomach. "For right now, let's just say I lost my edge." That's a bullshit euphemism and they totally know why I haven't done the procedures for awhile. "You've worked me over pretty thoroughly already. Normally I have a lot of tenacity, but could we give it a rest?"

Moffitt straightens up and smirks. "Son, best you learn to fly before you fuck with a bunch of falcons."

● ● ●

One lone parking lot light casts a cone-shaped illumination on my old wreck of a vehicle. I sit in my car, crossing my arms on the steering wheel to cradle my forehead. I'm too defenseless. My eyes water and wetness covers my cheeks. So much shame has floated to the top…being the respected doctor who people count on and regarded, but I'm really an imposter. A fake who deceives the world around me. And the upshot is I'm kept helplessly tethered to the drug that's controlling me. And at the moment there's an unexpected inkling of relief because they didn't let me hide.

I think about the times I'd pocket drugs at the clinic with the intension of using them when I got home. But then I would use them in the clinic parking lot. Or pull over to the side of the road to do my affair with the drug as if it was a noxious lover. I just couldn't wait, being drug-dumb and sick detached from everything else.

The WBC made up of recovering drug addict physicians told me it's time to get clean. They've done it. But the truth is that I don't know if I can get clean, much less stay that way. I'm scared. I'm scared of myself. I'm scared of my deceit and my cunning and my self-destructive ways and the way I hurt people and manipulate them. I'm scared because it's so automatic I can't conceive how I can unravel those behaviors. I'm helpless. I don't know how to do it. And this feels like being naked and it's all new and unfamiliar and untried—because I've always found a fix for everything

CHAPTER TEN

My gait is hesitant, moving into the living room. Julie's body forms a half moon yoga pose, her right leg horizontal to the floor and left leg perfectly straight supporting her body. Her left arm is straight with her hand is on the floor. Her right arm is in the air and perpendicular with her outstretched right leg. She's wearing loose short shorts and a running bra—hair tightly pulled back in a ponytail. Her svelte, muscled limber body is easy to look at. "Hey, Julie, I'm home."

She stands. "I put in a lot of miles today. Let me stretch the other side." Julie switches to the opposite position. She must be into her exercise obsession again as a distraction, forgetting about our skewered relationship and about me. And then a bewitching thought comes. The image comes when we'd run five to eight quick miles through the lush rolling countryside around our home, being awake with sweat when we got home and slithering with each other like we got a moist second wind. And afterward we take a shower together and laugh, acting goofy. Nothing else mattered. She was fun like it was never going to end.

Julie stands. She arches her back. "Julie, excuse me for a minute. I need to go to the bedroom."

"Okay, I have to finish a few more yoga poses and stretches."

I head to the bedroom and pullout a suitcase. I methodically start packing with the thought that I'll be in rehab for an extended period and need layers of clothes for the Oregon weather. Despite the stress of the day, I manage to automatically put together what I need. It's like I go into a robotic mode. I think back to the emotional upheaval and how Julie haphazardly threw what she needed into the suitcase when she took off. My emotions are constrained as I think of every this and that for who knows how long I'll be away.

Julie enters the bedroom. "What the hell are you doing?" And her eyes quizzically narrow. "What the hell are you doing with the suitcase out?

What's up?" She's jumpy seeing me meticulously backing up. "I'm sick of all of the surprises."

I lift and drop my shoulders. "I had a mandatory meeting with the Physicians' Well-Being Committee. They worked pushed me into a corner about getting treatment."

She lets out a quick breath and speaks in a jabbing voice. "You've totally messed up this time, haven't you? Glen, I'm relieved and feel threatened at the same time that the Well Being Committee jumped in to help you."

"Messed up? I'm totally fucked actually. They nailed me. They want me to go to a place in Oregon called Hazelden-Springbrook and have a chemical dependency evaluation. I'll be there three days and they will determine how botched up I am and tell me what hoops I need to squeeze through."

"No shit?" Julie blinks, and opens her eyes wide. "It'll be a huge impact closing the clinic down because no doubt they'll hold onto you. Even though it's tense sometimes having you around, the house will be empty without you. Well—"

I close my eyes halfway and lower my eyelids. "Well what?

Julie steps towards me and she's limber in the elastic way she hooks her thumb in my belt and pulls me closer. Her lustrous and flawless skin has a glowing sheen. And my nostrils flare smelling her cleansed sweetened honeysuckle fragrant skin. I edge on being flirty alongside her even though I'm in big trouble. "Okay buster, this shit between us is going to stop." She puts her hands on her hips. "And no goo-goo eyes when I'm pissed off at you."

"Well, there was that little tug on the belt loop. What'd you expect?"

"Forget I gave you a tug and get serious." Julie pinches her lips together making face go tight.

"They will expect you be part of the treatment, too. One of the programs is actually for you—to see how you've fed into my problems and assess our setup for when I get out. You're part of the deal."

Julie twirls her tongue around her lips. "I'll do it. But I resent you for putting me in this position. You fucker." Most of the time when Julie cusses she is somewhere between incensed to furious. But "you fucker" means the top of the anger scale.

"Well fuck it if you can't take a joke."

Julie stomps her foot. "Don't say that to me. I mean you just said you loved me. Glen, don't pull that cavalier bullshit with me. It isn't fair. I want you to think of me for a change."

"The joke thing was stupid to say. It's just that I'm really, really nervous and blurted it out."

Julie takes a bead on me and stares. "Well, what are you going to do for me?"

"You labeled it. Get better and not be so narcissistically self-involved."

"I'll wait for that. Here we go. Goddamn it, I'm putting you on probation again." Julie crosses her arms and looks away and postures. "Another thing. I found—"

"What?"

"Your Army uniform in the trash." She pulls in a breath and lets it go. "And at the bottom of the bin I came across your oak leaf rank and two Commendation Medals and your tarnished lapel caduceus insignias." Julie moistens her lips. "Why did you throw all that away after—"

"I had to get rid of it...just taking up space."

"Bullshit, Glen. What happened?"

"A couple of days ago the war came over me like a blood bath. Just sick of thinking about how some days in Iraq I'd be up to my elbows in blood and all the smells and sounds of the OR. Not even close to cutesy stateside plastic surgery. Oh yeah, those guys with maxillofacial injuries were a mess—shocking to look at when they landed on my doorstep. But we really did well for those guys patching them up and putting them back together. And being a doc and getting caught up in that god awful firefight. I just wanted the memories to go away. So I got my Army gear and threw it out."

Julie is still, contemplating what I said. "So throwing out your Army stuff is going to make the memories go away? Glen, you're an incredibly smart man, but Jesus, you sure can do some dumb stuff sometimes." Her eyes widen. "Those memories aren't going away. You just proved it by what you told me."

"I know. I get it in spades over and over again about how smart people do very dumb stuff."

"Well, I sent your uniform to the cleaners. Polished up your oak leaf and medals and Medical Corps insignia. I'll pack up everything and store it."

"I want to be rid of that stuff."

"There are some things you can't get rid of. Those tokens of the past are keepsakes of what you went through."

I weigh up that Julie is trying to get me to mull over my war experience. "Look, I ruminate about Iraq enough without having my old uniform and other Army stuff around."

"Ruminate? So you need to make more headway, rather than having a piece of your mind dominated about it."

"I'm considering what's in front of me, going to Oregon. Let's drop the Iraq situation, okay?"

"Okay at this point, but there's no wiping it out."

● ● ●

I call Hazelden-Springbrook and speak to the intake worker who adeptly goes over some rudimentary elements of my drug history. She covers the uncertainties of my need for detoxification, and determines at this point that detox will not be a necessary part of the chemical dependency evaluation. I leave out the fact that I am taking Suboxone and getting down to the end of my supply. I don't plan on renewing the Rx with an addiction medicine doc before going to the program, assuming using the agonist-antagonist drug to prevent withdrawal is part of their treatment regimen. We arrange for me to arrive the next day. I call Horizon Airlines and make a direct flight reservation from the Santa Rosa Airport to Portland. I re-contact the worker and advise her of my arrival time and there will be a driver to meet me. I follow through with Miles.

The idea of switching my life is daunting. A pressure builds in my chest, tension squeezes so bad in my jaw it feels like a molar is about to snap for the thousandth time.

The next day I go to the trim and easy access airport. Two flights are leaving in close proximity of each other. One to Portland and the other to Los Angeles International Airport—LAX. I picture the WBC physicians gathered around the conference table, and pressing me into a hole with no possibility of getting away. They had me and I can't stand being had. But now I'm in transient and nobody has got me tethered to a pole. There's a reckless jumpiness in my chest, a tingling at my fingertips. What if…no I can't do that. Do what? Say fuck 'em and just split. But maybe I can just enter a kind of no man's land for awhile. Lie low and take cover.

My knee starts to bounce. I get up and walk to the window and see the two airplanes. One is going north where I am supposed to be and the other is heading south. And LAX could be a jumping off place for somewhere else. And now my thinking starts to get inventive—romancing a whimsical vision. I sit back down and unbutton the top button of my shirt to let a little air in. And then I bounce back and forth in my seat a couple of times. I'm at the window again checking the airplanes, looking at one and then the other.

I dance my way across the little airport. I say to the airline counterperson, "I have a flight planned today to Portland, and I'd like to change it to Los Angeles. Can you get me on the L.A. flight?"

She runs though screens on her computer. "I'm sorry sir, but…oh, wait a minute. Yes, there is one more seat on the flight for L.A. You want me to rebook you?"

"Please." I have a relieved smug feeling. Same dumb thing I told Julie. Fuck 'em if they can't take a joke. "Horizon is operated by Alaska Airlines. You fly to Mexico. Would you please book me a flight to Cabo San Lucas?"

"Do you have your passport?"

I never took it out of my suitcase. "Yeah."

The counter person checks though the flights. "Your connection to Mexico is going to be tight." She fleetingly scrutinizes her watch, and concentrates on the arrival time of the plane to LAX. "You can make it."

And a shadow casts over me. I don't know what is wrong with my mind that I can blot-out the impact that my escape to Mexico is going to have on Julie. The odds are…I imagine she'll be better off without me being around, since I don't give her anything worthwhile to hang onto. She pretends to depend on me when she de facto has to depend on herself. It just like I'm a ghost that she can see once in awhile and then I vanish again. Maybe I'll worm my way into a rift in the Mexican earth and die. Or get swept up in wandering about the country, existing in delirious illusion of being lost and never come back.

I feel like I'm taking control back.

I'll run out of Suboxone, but undaunted me will thread the drug needle one more time. Then it occurs to me that I'd better not screw myself. I call Hazelden-Springbrook and get the intake workers voicemail, leaving a message which says I've been delayed a week. I dial Miles's office and leave the same bullshit line with the receptionist to relay to Miles. And what runs through my mind is that I will be back in a week…maybe never. Minutes later my cell phone displays Miles's office phone. I ignore it. A call comes in with the Portland area code. It's dismissed too. What to do about Julie? What to do about everybody? Fuck 'em. And I realize I'm actually making a mistake, but I don't care.

I call the doc I filled in for, Tom Henning, and talk with him about covering the pain management practice. He sounds obligated since I took over his practice when he was out. He admits he had a sudden recent down tick in his practice and would oblige me by taking on the extra work. I'm relieved to continue to say screw you to the world, feeling a glimmer stir in the background that this won't last forever.

I land in San José del Cabo Airport, still feeling iconoclastic. I snag a car from a rental agency, with the plan of heading north to Punta Pescadero. There's a beautiful hotel there perched on a cliff that overlooks a rock-studded beach and a heavenly paradise beach with the aquamarine-azure sea. And on top of that it's located at the end of a ten kilometer lonely and semi-wicked dirt road running up and down the steep cliff paralleling the ocean. Who will find me? Nobody.

I pass through a turista fishing village named Los Barriles, the naming came from the rugged mountain geological formations that look like barrels behind the village. A *farmacia* has a sign out front advertizing Viagra, antidepressants, and muscle relaxants. I stop. I chat with the guy at the counter. He's flush with what I need. I get euphoric in anticipation of getting loaded again.

Some gringo wearing a faded oversized tee shirt to cover up his bulging paunch stumbles through the door. He thinks nothing of reaching up to rest his forearm on my shoulder to hang on me. He's wearing a ratty old ball cap with a blue marlin stenciled across the front, and sandy-white hair puffs out from underneath the hat. He has the stale smell of booze oozing out of his pores. "Hey bud, come on down the street with me and let me buy you a double or a triple at my favorite watering hole, Smokey's." His voice has the coarse sound of walking on gavel. "You look like a good hombre to stomp around with," he says tanked and stumbling over his words. He's bent over at the shoulders, making the protoplasm of his short squatty body look like a sack stuffed with dirty old socks.

My face tightens, guessing this guy must have burned out his drinking buddies. I'm quick and biting. "Sorry, I'm pressed for time to get up the coast before it gets dark."

He slurs. "Shit, you've got time for a couple. It'll make that goddamn ride a lot easier."

Irked, I've got to get this drunken gringo asshole away from me. "Could you take your arm off my shoulder?"

The drunken guy takes one step back, lifting his weight off me. "Come on." He obnoxiously punches his index finger in my chest. His drunken oblivion forms droopy sacks under his eyes. "I need a good buddy to tie one on with."

I laugh. "Looks like you're already there, dude." And I think that I can't remember the last time I ever called some guy dude, maybe I never have.

His nose is bulbous. There're broken capillaries in his cheeks. "Shit, you ain't seen anything, bud. You just wait until we pull some stools up to the bar and I give you a lesson or two or three about how to drink *ta' kill ya*."

I step back a foot. "Drink what?"

His bloodshot eyes widen. "Tequila. Where you been man? Don't you know nothin'? Tequila, which translates into *ta' kill ya* in English."

I glance at the mystified store keep. "Now I have the official translation. Thanks all the same."

He drapes his arm on my shoulder again. I take my hand and lift it off. He says, "Okay, you ready? We'll amble on down the block and do a good one at old Smokey's place."

I head for the door. The store keep says, *"¿Señor, no necesita sus drogas?"*

Feeling disgusted and turned off, I look at the shopkeeper, and then shake my head as a sign that I don't want any drugs. The ataxic gringo tries to follow me as I bolt out the door, but I outpace him in his greased stumbling state. The pixilated guy disappears in the distance. But he makes an indelible mark on my mind. I don't want to be like that guy.

I drive up the dry vegetation flanked sinuous mountain road and descend through the curves. I turn off the road to the dirt washboard leading to Punta Pescadero. The growth along the road is in shades of green and the dry vegetation doesn't seem that should be alive, but it is. The gnarly weather-stressed trees are survivors, punished while keeping a grip on life. The hot colored changing crepuscular sky fades into snippets of darkness while I negotiate the sketchy road.

I look out the east to see the changing lighting effects on the sea. And my gaze is caught in a paralysis for a moment while I'm overcome with images in my mind of the loathsome and repugnant besotted boozer that cornered me at the drug store. For a split second repugnance about attachment to intoxicants sickens me. The gravel road is unsteady. I put my eyes back on the dark road and I hadn't anticipated a curve to the left. I scream, "Oh shit, I'm about to go off the edge of the cliff." I grip the steering wheel, seeing the immediate danger is in front of me that erases my fixation. I slam on the brakes, but it is too late. The right front wheel of the car is over the cliff, though I've come to a stop. The care is teetering at an angle like vehicle could plummet down the cliff.

My heart throbs in my throat. Jump out the driver side door? I put the car in reverse. The wheels spin in the dirt trying to get traction. I'm taking too much of a risk. And now I hear the pulsation of my heart in my ears. I have no time to think, but I'm thinking of everything: Julie, Iraq, my father, my mother, how I feel too much and not enough, how I think about this all the time, and the huge missing middle section filled up with drugs. The tires catch. The car pulls back. All four tires are solidly on the dirt road. I sit in the motionless car, panting. And then I cross my arms and lean on the steering wheel with my forehead on my wrists. I could have been a dead man. Maybe I should have been.

I arrive at what seems to be the nearly deserted hotel. There doesn't seem to be many guests so I'm banking on there being room for me. I had no foresight to get reservations and I make my way to the reception desk. It's occupied by a lone woman with her black shiny hair severely pulled back in a tight bun that exposes her radiant sharp-featured and fresh face. Her delicately sculptured cheekbones show her Amerindian ancestry. The woman's supple figure gives her a wash of seeming friendly and welcoming. Her nameplate says Lucia. I say, "*Buenas tardes, señora, Lucia. ¿Tienen una habitación? No veo otros huéspedes, entonces debe de tener espacio.*"

When she speaks to me, it is obvious that my accent has betrayed me. She smiles politely. "You are correct, we are not filled. We have a room for you." Lucia looks down, flipping through some pages to see what rooms are left. "We have a quiet room overlooking the ocean, *perfecto.*" I have a reminiscence of staying here before. Its peacefulness soaked in and the dread of my life momentarily slipped away. "And how long will be staying with us?"

"*Quizás una semana, más o menos.* I guess about a week."

"Okay." Lucia sweetly beams. She gives me the registration form and asks me to fill it out. She picks up the telephone and tells a man named Enrique to come to reception desk. A boney and spare looking man with a blousy white shirt that offsets his dark reddish-brown face appears at reception.

Enrique and I walk to the rental car to get my bag. "*¿De dónde es usted, Enrique?*" I make small talk.

"*Soy de La Ribera, cerca de aquí. ¿Y usted?*"

"*Soy estadounidense y vivo en la parte norte de California, cerca de San Francisco en el campo de viñedos.*" A minute after the chitchat about where we are from, Enrique slips the key in the door. I didn't suspect such a lovely layout and décor. He puts my suitcase on a luggage rack and I discretely slip him twenty bucks, knowing he is not making too much because of the scarcity of guests. He submissively bows his head and departs.

I open my carryon and take out the Suboxone. Keep it, or pitch it? Go back to the pharmacy and get the opiates that I turned down? Put myself into withdrawal and get all the opiates and Suboxone out if my system for good? End my life and stop the struggle? I take the remaining medication in my hand. I open the door and walk to the cliff and throw the drug down the hillside, among the grainy dirt and rocks and cacti. I whisper, "Fuck me."

CHAPTER ELEVEN

Starving, I head to the dining room. There is a couple at one table and a man sitting alone. They all turn when I enter the room and smile. The couple is handsome and blonde, probably scuba divers. The lone man is pasty and thin. A slightly overweight hostess dressed in a white embroidered peasant blouse comes to me. She must be in her early forties, but she looks cherubic. Her nameplate says Marta. She is sunny-faced. "*Buenas noches*. You will be dining with us?" I grin and nod. She shows me to a table near the window and hands me a menu. "Something to drink?"

I order a carbonated mineral water. Marta disappears. The couple's voices are low and I can't make out what they are saying. The woman laughs and her clean-cut looks become vivacious. The alone man appears like he is contemplating the world. I'm mostly disconnected and a sensation of isolation runs through me.

I study the menu. And then I look up. After a second to reflect I know I've laid the way for the pain of opiate withdrawal. But how bad is it going to be? And then there's the drugs waiting on the shelf in Los Barriles. Maybe yes. And maybe no to going back there. The blotto gringo might spot me and I'd have to push him away one more goddamn time. I was preoccupied with the thought of him that almost plummeted me over the cliff.

Marta returns with my drink. I order the fish cooked in the Veracruz style. She vanishes into the kitchen. The couple gets up to leave. They catch my eye and come to my table. They have been scuba diving in the area around Punta Pescadero, they tell me, and have spent a day diving the area south, off of Cabo Pulmo and have gone as far north as Isla Cerralvo. They let me in on seeing a hammerhead shark and huge manta rays and a whale shark, and then name off several smaller fish and nudibranchs they have seen. Their fascination and excitement is infectious, and I think about how in a day or two I am going to be slammed by withdrawal symptoms and feel like I'll be seized in Davy Jones's locker, while they will be blissfully floating along taking in the underwater sights of the Sea of Cortez. Their easy stride makes them appear to skip out of the dining room.

Drug hunger grew while at dinner. I return to my room and go to the place where I threw the Suboxone over the cliff. I feel myself getting self-destructive and rash. I imagine appearing like an accidental fatality. Someone who took a misstep and plunged down to a sprawling mess on the rocks below. The well-meaning WBC members lighten across my mind. The fuck you to them is misplaced. The fuck you should be toward my father, but not in self-damaging ways, but to fight against him calling me a piece of shit. The next move is to put my life in order. That has never existed before. My conflict with authority made me be deviant in the military, but I made it work for me to thread the system.

The sun rises out of the ocean, Punta Pescadero being located on the east side of Baja Sur. At first light is breathtaking and then the thin layer of clouds high above the ocean are illuminated into a spectacular show of deeply chromatic oranges and pinks, making showy reflective ribbons of hot colors across the glassy ocean.

I have no sensation of withdrawal. The stuff—Suboxone—must have a long half-life. All day long I'm like I've never used a drug in my life and I'm on an ill-deserved reprieve.

I go to the homespun landing strip, reserved for local use. There's a sexy eight-seat private airplane. I take a picture of it sitting perpendicular to the runway. And then I study the dozen homes on the cliff. All of them are high end beautiful and well-designed and must be used only occasionally. Am I killing time? Or am I in a fantasy that I should escape here fulltime? I merge into the landscape scenes. The rugged jagged staggered mountainous terrain in the distance that is like layered fingers with blue hazy spaces in between giving dramatic views lining the sweeping half disk-shape coast running south.

The next day I awake on the edge physical sensations, not withdrawal, but prodromal symptoms. I should have tapered the Suboxone. Am I a physician or a dumb fuck? Probably a good measure of both. I look at the landscape. Today it doesn't have that euphoric oneness. The beauty is there, but I can't see it. There's the cravings, some tremulousness, nausea, I'm feeling a little panic, my nose is runny and my skin feels clammy.

The next day arrives with what comes to mind as an eloquent clinical term to describe the sensations in my body. *I feel like shit.* My stomach is in a twist and my muscles are beginning to feel cramped.

I feign being okay when I interact with the wanting to please hospitable hotel and dining room staff. I look out over the sea reflecting the sky like a glassy mirror. The amiable and companionable Lucia comes to my table and asks me if I would like to go out with another man to go fishing or scuba dive with the couple. Her fine featured face is doll-like in the morning light. I'd get decompression sickness if I dived in this condition. Maybe fishing would get my mind off how I feel. I'm down at the boat in twenty minutes. If I'm going to feel horrible I might as well be fishing and feeling awful, rather than curled up on a hotel room. We get out on the glassy ocean in a small fishing panga.

Two days have passed. The other guest who seemed dour at dinner and contemplating is now a joker. He and the boat captain spoofing, they're friendly and I try the best I can to chime in.

I say to the captain, "*Me llamo Glen. ¿Y usted?*"

"Joaquín."

The captain has deep lines in his face and is dark from the years of being on the sea and in the sun. His cap is bleached from the elements, and well-washed chino pants are indelibly stained with what seems to be years of fish blood and the rigors of running a boat and cleaning motor oil from his hands by rubbing them onto his *pantalones.*

The guest whose thin face is the color of white linen, wears expensive high tech sun exposure clothes, keeping his skin lily white. He is the lone diner from the night before. And his fishing shirt and pants hang on his bony skeletal frame. His fishing gear is the expensive quality of a true aficionado. I shake his hand and say my name is Glen Coyle. He nods, "I'm Jim Lucas. And a civil engineer from Colorado."

"I'm from northern California and I practice medicine there."

"Sorry I wasn't into socializing in the dining room, but I was totally beat from a day out on the ocean." He shrugs.

"We all have our days." I forgivingly smile. And I think that I am sure having mine today. I'm a little sweaty and my breath is shallow.

The sea is placidly still like plate glass and reflecting shades of an azure and cobalt sky. The boat is an eighteen-foot cyan blue-green panga with a six-foot beam and white interior. Aluminum tubing supports a lapis colored canvas cover for sun protection. It's powered by a single hefty hundred and fifteen horsepower four stroke Mercury engine that nicely glides the panga through the mirrored water. I fall into a confident rhythm, knowing Joaquín's touch senses the force of how sea works. He makes me feel assured, since he has a grasp on what he is doing. And he must live as if the ocean is one his own internal organs. He doesn't even have to think about it—the ocean seems like a self-contained part of him that has an extraordinary vital function. What comes back to me is a Spanish idiomatic saying used by men of the sea, *el lobo del mar,* the wolf of the sea. Seeing his mastery and sureness at helming the panga, Joaquín has to be *un lobo del mar.*

It's a push, so much so I realize how harebrained it was to agree to go out on the boat. I fight being in a torpid and dazed and stupefied state. The feel of detoxifying off the Suboxone stretches out and withstanding the sensations is more daunting and bottomless, a worse cessation than coming off the Rx opiates. Despite the creepiness crawling over my skin I hookup with a bruiser of a fish—early morning combat on a serenely vast sea that reaches to the east making a threadlike translucent ultramarine opulent blue line with the horizon. Joaquín keeps an eye on the sport of the struggle. He yells out, "dorado." I work the dorado and it works me, overshadowed by feeling like crap on top of feeling like crap. The fish comes to the surface, iridescent and blue on the dorsal side, down its body fading to green and then yellow to silvery-white on the underside. It's baffling why the fish is called a dorado—*golden*—since it is so opalescent and multicolored.

We get the blunt nosed, four and a half foot long fish onboard. Wet, the dorado's luminous colors glisten and change coloration with how it is positioned in the sunlight. When it starts to dry in the warmth of the sun, the fish's radiant colors fade into muted grayish nothingness. Captain Joaquín throws ice from the cooler on the fine catch. He's excited and says, "*Está alegre de su pez. ¿Verdad, Señor Glen?*" I nod and smile and then Joaquín grasps my shoulder like he is my brother. It's a comfort since physically I'm not doing too well.

Jim hooks-up. Señor sixth sense howls, "Roosterfish." Joaquín knows the type of fish by the fight. The roosterfish gives Jim one hell of a workout battle. The rod is bent in the shape of a horse shoe. He looks like mister technical fisherman. Jim is calculated. He plays the fish and moderately pulling the rod and strategically working the reel. Pound for pound—the fish versus the fight—it closely matches up to a battling bone fish. Jim is skillful, technical like the engineer he is, and pulls the roosterfish onboard.

He's jacked up with excitement and talks and talks about working the fish. Last night he was retired and unassuming and now he's exhilarated to the max. Jim's animated fervency infects Joaquín and me with an electric and stirred sensation. Jim turns into a fishing buddy. And these moments string together to holdout against the angst of my fight against withdrawal that's a torment ravishing my body and soul.

The morning grows on. The wind picks up, sending ruffles across the surface of the ocean, disturbing its smoothness and tranquility. The Sea of Cortez had been so glass-like that at moments the space between the horizon and sky seemed to disappear and the horizontal plane merges as one. That goes away. The reflected heavens change. Now the windswept swells are blue-gray and the air blows a blush of white caps at the top of the rollers. I buck up and try not to have the symptoms affect me.

Jim has another strike and is laid-back maneuvering a yellowtail onboard. Joaquín surveys the sea conditions and says, *"Ya acabamos de pescar."* He turns to Jim, "We're finished fishing, Señor Jim."

Joaquín navigates the panga to hit the ocean swells straight on with the bow, keeping the boat perpendicular to them so we don't capsize. Joaquín skillfully guns and pulls back on the engine throttle to guide the boat up and down the waves.

Jim eyes me. "Say, Glen, are you feeling alright? Are you seasick or something, kind of shaky?"

"I'm queasy, but it feels like it's going to pass."

That night at the hotel the staff filet the dorado and grill the fish serving it with garlic. It's gastronomically in another intoxicating culinary dimension, but I strain to squeak out enjoying it. And this is foreshadowed by the staff turning the hard fighting roosterfish into a raw fish dish— ceviche. The ceviche is followed by a platter of the yellowtail cut paper thin to make sashimi, served with spicy green wasabi paste. The sashimi vanishes like a vacuum glided over it. Jim says the cook is an old hand at various ways of preparing fish dishes—no surprise for being on the Sea of Cortez. And then mister detail man, Jim, says that in Japanese yellowtail sashimi is called, *hamachi.* It doesn't get better than this. The evening is so mixed up for me, wonderful food, people and ambiance. I want to put on a good show to look good. But here I am feigning not being a wreck, wrestling to grasp an elusive inner compass. I tussle with the continued withdrawal symptoms. I feel sweaty and my bowels are loose and I have some gooseflesh skin.

The handsome couple and Jim and I share the same table, and the blue water's munificence from a day on the Sea of Cortez. I was dazed when I first saw the couple and did not catch their names, and now everybody has the first names down—Maggie and Chad. I have gooseflesh and chills and intestinal churning, but I fake the withdrawal isn't happening.

The cook says he'll freeze the rest of the fish so we can cart it back to the States in coolers. Instead, Jim and I offer up the rest of the catch to the hotel staff. Their faces glow, since we are openhanded and it means their families will have more food.

And the next few days I just gut-out feeling waves of horrible to terrible to dreadful. The cramping is worse, and sweats, gooseflesh, I feel hypertensive and my appetite is shot. And what rivets through my head is how I could have gone out fishing, since now it's an impossibility. The withdrawal symptoms keep on coming, like sinking down a precipitous descent with no possibility to put on the brakes. What's added is the opiate withdrawal dysphoric depression that is amalgamated with being so anxiously uptight that the old hackneyed saying I feel like climbing the walls comes to my mind. The sensations are on the periphery of a dark gruesome feel that I try to hold myself back from deteriorating into, but it's no use. Without thinking my mind's cravings instinctively pull me to the little pharmacy shop in Los Barriles. I'm white-knuckled, and I jerk myself back one second at a time to sever the tie with the drug connection. My sleep is unstrung and I'm oppressed and saddened and sucked down into a shadowy ugly vortex. And all my senses are uneasily juxtaposed with the Punta Pescadero paradise while I struggle to align myself with fragments of normalcy. It's no use. I can't dodge or circumvent what I'd like to evade.

I think back to the enormous tolerance to opiates that I developed and how if a nonuser took as much as I did the respiratory functions would stop and the person would croak. The amount I needed to get high would make an otherwise upright person drop dead. I had a smattering of a half-life after throwing the Suboxone of the cliff, the time the bodily organs take to eliminate Suboxone and clear it from blood or plasma. The steady-state of the drug being in my system has vanished, since the work of my renal glands have flushed the stuff out. I'm Jonesing, making for a drug hunger while I put myself in a semi remote place that's heaven in Baja Sur that's turned into hell. If some opiates were in front of me I would have the overpowering impulse to use—not logical or rational because my cravings right now are so fierce and intemperate. A voice screams in my head to do drugs. Maybe one of the guests has some pain pills or a staff person. I could disguise my withdrawal and be sly and scheming and calculating to root out who might have some drugs. I think about how my use is a constant intrusive thought that has dominance over my guilt and shame about being a doctor-addict. And I plot out again the one second at a time rule to stop myself from drug seeking.

Engulfed by an internal harassment of drug cessation physical pain erupts, added to my gastrointestinal upheaval and shitting my brains out. I begin a hacking cough. A faucet has been turned on in my nose. I look in the mirror and my pupils are the size of saucers. I feel a muscle twitch, making for a crawling sensation across my skin. And the pain goes deeper into my bones and there's joint pain and my lower back hurts like hell. I have to leave my room or I'll go nuts.

I step out along the railing that separates the patio from the cliff. I pace back and forth. Being antsy is out of control. Enrique sees me and walks toward me. He gazes at me with an intense focus. A concerned look on his face says that he senses my agitation. *"¿Puedo ayudarle, señor?"*

"Sí, tiene…" I stop the impulse to ask him if he has any drugs. What, this Mexican guy has a pocket full of dope? *"No necesito ayuda…solamente aire fresco. Estoy bien, gracias."*

Enrique's eyebrows arch up, knowing that I'm making up a distorted fabrication to hide the torment that is oozing out of my body. *"En mi opinión…"* Enrique drops his head and then obsequiously regains eye contact with me. *"Si combie su mente, estoy de sus ordenes."* This man is kind, knowing full well that I'm in a retching and compromised state of existence.

"Gracias Enrique, su aplomo es muy servicial." After I tell him his presence of mind is helpful, he nods and turns to walk away.

I try to hide the noisy sniffling from my running nose. And then I have a crawling sensation covering my entire body, followed by abdominal cramping.

Day one, two, three, four, five pass and the withdrawal symptoms become a reduced load that has weighted my being. I look out on the eastern horizon and see the sun peek over the curvature of the earth, illuminating the sky with the colors of hot end of the color spectrum. And for once in days I am able to absorb the splendor of the sunrise reflected in the magnificence of the Sea of Cortéz, surrounded by the rugged exquisite Baja Sur. The easing and release from being handcuffed to the withdrawal symptoms counters having to be on cue second by second to wiggle through the wretched persecution that I have instilled in myself. And now that I feel a semblance of being functional it's time to take care of business.

I stop. Realizing that Julie must feel abandoned not knowing where I am. It's like I did liposuction on myself and got down to muscle and bone. The amiable woman with soft, smooth facial skin at the reception desk puts in a call to Julie. We talk.

Julie's breathing is harsh. I tell her what's happened. Julie's voice is up and down. She sounds moderate and then her voice is loud with sharp anger. "You needed to let me know right away. I didn't know if you were alive or dead or had vanished forever. Glen, you have to stop doing this to me. I've been lonely to begin with, though we're married and now you pull this goddamn stunt."

I tighten my grip on the receiver.

"You're no longer on probation, buster. You have to do jail time. Get your act together and keep me in the loop."

And I wonder—like a thought's encore—if she'd be better off without me. She would be. Or would she unwittingly trip and fall into another relationship with some disaster case like me.

"There's nothing I can say to justify not telling you. I wanted to escape and use again before the evaluation and treatment. I changed my mind and went through withdrawal."

"You've got the picture about letting me know?" She doesn't sound convinced.

Julie won't believe me if I say yes. "I will work on it."

"Okay for now. Get up to the program in Portland." Julie hangs up. The receiver has force behind it when it hits the cradle.

I gently hang up the phone on my end. I turn and look at the eastern horizon of the Sea of Cortez, an image in my mind that may be permanent or fade away.

CHAPTER TWELVE

Relief comes over me on the flight to Oregon that I've made the decision to attend the program. Yet, there is still trepidation about all of what is to come will entail. After I collect my bag from the Portland Airport carrousel a driver from a limousine service meets me. He's dressed in dark clothes. His hair is a white mop. His name is Dick. Dick mutely drives me southwest in his black Lincoln Towncar. There a cloud covering the inside the limo, like Dick is uncomfortable and having a setback about what to say.

The ride takes us along a highway and through green and tree studded rolling rural areas. We get off the main roadway and a western bluebird and a mountain quail and an osprey and a wedge tailed eagle all freely wing through the air. And then a turkey vulture is off the side of the road cleaning up the remains of a raccoon carcass. The vulture's head is deeply buried in the guts of the nocturnal animal's victuals.

The limo rolls up to the facility built of wood and stone and surrounded by extensive grassy areas and trees. I tip Dick. The limo's taillights disappear round a corner and he's gone. I'm unsure and nervous. I stand there, bag in hand, wanting to go in the building and wanting to be like a thin layer of ground fog that is blasted by the sun and vaporizes. A dazed moistness fills the bottom of my eyelids. Most of the time I can handle whatever comes my way. With the exception of the vulnerability made by my father, there's only been a few times in my life where I've lacked protection, whether real or contrived. And I feel see-through as I stand there, yet no exchange with the program has transpired.

A skinny staff member in a red plaid flannel shirt and baggy jeans appears. He acknowledges me by name. The first thing he asks me is what drugs I'm on. I tell him zero and it has been that way for a week. There's the unsaid addendum is that my guts and skin and head are still in rotten shape. He's says my treatment person is expecting me.

The therapist's face is wrinkled by his pushed together eyebrows and crow's feet squint at the corners of his eyes. "I heard about your voicemail message that you'd postponed coming here for a week. We had your wife and referring physician calling. They were unhinged, not knowing where you had vanished to. Actually, your wife was frantic, until she let us know you called her." Despite starting off with rigorous, stringent notes, his voice is cushiony, showing not one iota of condemnation. "So—"

I ambivalently gather myself up to satisfy some level of accountability and to resemble being a willing patient, still knowing that being *willing* is actually not the same as *doing* anything. Everybody knows what lousy patients doctors are. "You want the realities of what happened, or—"

"No. Just the bullshit and lies that keep you sick to cover your ass." His voice still has a spongy feel. "Glen? May I call you Glen, or is it Dr. Coyle." The walls of Dr. Rod Nevin's office are loaded with snow skiing photographs, showing shots in steep mountainous terrain where he must have been flown in by helicopter to do the ski runs. The high windows let in natural daylight and leave out being observed from the outside. We occupy two of four chairs in a semicircle. I glance at his desk in the corner. It's orderly in a disorganized way; papers stacked on top of papers in his in box. Needless little trinkets lined up in a straight line, like a figurine of a frog riding a bicycle.

Rod is an old hand at maneuvering the clueless. "It has to be Glen if I'm interacting with a chemical dependency therapist. Wouldn't you say?" I'm stumbling around, trying to make my backbone straight and wrestling my natural impulse to manipulate the situation. "Kind of like I'm the patient, and not the doctor."

"That's what I'd say. You got it." Rod Nevin sighs. "Okay, what was going on with you? Beginning to end." Sketchy question, like the psychologist is waiting to see how I'll choose to fill in the blanks. An image of the turkey vulture feeding on the carrion passes through my mind. And the image comes to me while I starring at a bare, unornamented portion of his wall. The vultures sink their featherless heads deep into carcasses and their barren smooth-skinned but wrinkled crowns keep them free from collecting bacteria.

"It started out as a big 'fuck you.'" I catch myself slipping up and sounding contemptuous. "I was waiting at the airport in Santa Rosa to come to Portland, and figured I needed a little more time to sort things out before coming here. I took a little detour to a place in Baja California called Punta Pescadero. I had a little something to take care of down there that preempted me from coming directly here. I went through a village and stopped to score some opiates, since I was running out of Suboxone. But I blew it off."

"You were taking Suboxone? We didn't know that. And we don't use it here. We're one hundred percent chemically free…unless you need non-addicting psych meds." Rod inclines his head slightly as a sign for me to press on. "But go ahead."

I cough to clear my throat. I'd like to spit on the floor just to be audacious and brazen, but I hold back the foolhardy twinge. "So, I'm in this shady Mexican pharmacy and was arranging to get a boatload of meds when this and that happened. I had a change of heart and tossed out my remaining Suboxone. And two days later—holy shit."

Rod is straight faced, a humorless bent to his voice. "The withdrawal from buprenorphine—Suboxone—is worse than opiates." He moistens his lips. "Even people tapering off the medication do okay until they get down to one or two milligrams and then hell breaks loose."

"No shit, you're telling me. I knew that before I threw the Suboxone away. My ass was twisted up in a knot. I couldn't sleep and got really depressed, while fighting it off in paradise."

"And now?"

I rub my left shoulder with my right hand. "I'm still sleep deprived and like a depressed sack of shit."

"When did you d/c the Suboxone." Rod has a clinical resonance in his voice.

"A week ago."

"You're still in the thick of it, aren't you? Listen, our addiction medicine doc could possibly give you some blood pressure medication and a low potency, long-acting benzodiazepine for the next three days to help things along. It could temporarily decrease some of your symptoms."

The scenario in Mexico to get of drugs was horrific. I don't want to take anything else that will hook me. "Fuck it. Plus, the benzos are addicting and I thought you don't use addicting meds."

"It's a short term minor exception. Okay. Nonetheless, let's place you in our detox program for the next three days to keep an eye on you. We'll keep talking to solidify the evaluation. And you can start attending the health pro groups with addicted healthcare professionals for support and see how well you'll identify with the physicians and pharmacists and dentists and others in the group."

"You think you need to negotiate a lot of extensive evaluation to determine whether I am in fact an addict?"

Rod's eyebrows arch upward. His mouth is a straight line. "You want my candid impression?"

The corners of my mouth curl downward. "Like you said, no, bullshit me."

"Your physician well being committee provided the details about your visit with the DEA investigators and your brief run with residential psychiatric treatment where the therapist determined you were addicted to opiates. But more compelling was the two-step shuffle you did on the way here and that says to me that you are an addict that is trying to be controlling. One other piece is the numerous phone calls we got from your wife. The way she was frantic and telling us what we needed to do says to me that she is very imbedded with your disease of addiction."

I lift my shoulders. "So this is a done deal before the evaluation has already started?"

"Glen, the evaluation started a very long time ago."

"At least thank you for—"

"Not bullshitting you?"

"Yes."

"We are above board here. We may articulate feedback in ways that you can hear, but no holding back. We can't, otherwise, there's no way that you can be helped. Get it?"

"In spades."

Nevins wrinkles his face. "My timing may not be the best—a little too soon, but let me give it a go. Julie said that she found your Army uniform in the trash, along with your lieutenant colonel and caduceus insignias and medals. What was that about?"

"Tied of having that crap around."

"What crap?"

He must not be listening. "The military crap."

"Remind you of something?"

"Something I'd rather overlook."

"Does that mean something you'd like to stop thinking about?" Nevin looks down. I don't answer. He looks up to catch my eye. I'd rather avoid getting into Iraq, but Nevin has it right here in front of me to look at. "How did you manage to move up through the ranks so fast?"

I'm contemptuous toward myself because maybe I didn't deserve the rank, despite all that I did. "I wasn't in the military that long. I happened to move up in rank quickly because of the surgery specialty. Really simple as that—war zone surgeon. If I had been another type of doc I wouldn't have been wearing that oak leaf cluster."

"And the medals?"

"The same. Meritorious service in the OR. That's it. No combat heroism to really speak of."

"No heroism? I see." His breath has a hitch to it. "You have any nightmares or flashbacks about what happened in Iraq?"

"You're asking if I have PTSD?" Being a doc in Iraq I was thoroughly familiar with the diagnostic criteria for PTSD. "I don't know. But working in the OR in a war zone like that one is totally fucked up."

"I only have a glimmer of how it must have been for you..." Nevin is concentrated, anticipating me saying more.

"Major wounds from IEDs. Big numbers of soldiers who died where killed by IEDs. Sewing people up. Amputations, mostly done by the orthopedists. Seeing a container in the corner with legs or feet or arms in it from multiple people. The fucking stink in the OR and the constant goddamn sound of the anesthesia machine."

"And—"

"When a medical specialist wasn't around I had to evaluate soldiers with TBIs."

"I don't know too much about TBIs. They worked you into a multi-specialist."

"Yes. The key is to improvise when there are gaps to be filled."

"I'm curious, how does it—"

"Let's say there's an IED. The concussion from the blast of a roadside bomb plummets the person to the ground and his or her head is smashed into the dirt or against a fixed object. The brain is encased in what's called the *dura mater*—Latin for *tough mother*—which is a thick membrane and the brain floats in cerebrospinal fluid. But the force is so great it either rotates the brain or slaps it against the skull. The results are a TBI. The brain rotations are the worst because of the tissue stretching and tearing. There may be a loss of consciousness from a few minutes to twenty-four hours. When the person returns to consciousness there's a severe headache and cognitively feeling in a fog. Maybe amnesia. The amount of time of lost consciousness—five minutes to a day—is diagnostic of the severity. But the scary part is when the person opens his or her eyes and one pupil is dilated and the other is contracted. Unequal pupils are a sure sign of brain damage." I look at a ray of light streaming in from the high window, and back at Rod. He is diligently taking in what I am saying. "I am sorry to go on and on about the clinical this and that about TBIs."

"There's the clinical part. But I'm more concerned with the force behind what you are saying."

"What do you mean?"

"The most important piece of our connection is where the heat is. You speak clinically like a doctor, but the way you tell me has juice behind it. You're not just relating what happened, but what happened to you. There's more there. You know what I saying, don't you?"

"It's still a bump in the night for me?"

"Yes." Rod nods approvingly, moving his glistening lower lip over his upper lip. "We have plenty of time. It's okay to give it a rest for now." He's unbothered and pushes his shoulders back and smiles. "Our program works with treating addiction and trauma, should you have PTSD to some degree. I have to say that a significant percentage of regular everyday noncombat trauma surgeons who practice Stateside have PTSD."

"Well, I'm in a safe zone now since doing plastics is fairly straightforward

"I hear the words, Glen, and there is something there. I could be right or wrong, though my hunch is something is missing." Rod's face goes neutral like he is waiting for the unfilled space to be colored in.

"I used to do entangled complex hand procedures in my private practice, but lost my edge to do them."

"How did your drug use affect your abilities?"

"I used to reattach severed digits and lost the surgical elegance required to perform the procedure." I look away, losing concentration.

"There's another element, isn't there?"

"A certain amount of detachment is involved with being a surgeon. But with the hand patients I became extremely involved to the degree that connections seemed like good buddy friendships. It was a place in my life where I felt the strongest tie, taking the patient through the surgery and managing the recovery. But the drugs made me numb and distant and I couldn't emotionally do it anymore, irrespective of the surgical piece." I cradle my face in my hands for a second and look back at Rod, dry-eyed.

"I'm glad you said that. It's a remarkable insight."

I sigh. And then look around the office.

Rod clears his throat. "Just one more thing before we close up for now. Did your opiate use get switched on when you were in Iraq?"

"It did. The meds gave me energy. I was in cahoots with another doc and we teamed up to divert drugs and never got snared in a drug screen or caught."

"You know that—"

"Right, if opiates give you energy that's a sign you're an addict, and if you get narcotized it's a sign that you have a lower probability of being an addict."

"And Iraq was the genesis of your addiction?"

"The genesis? No. My father was an alcoholic. He was a commander in the Navy and I'm almost certain that he got passed over being promoted caused by misjudgments because of his alcoholism, despite being an Annapolis graduate and attending a war college. Maybe I have a genetic predisposition. I drank heavily in high school and kept it from my girlfriend whose father was also an alcoholic—and we had teamed up because we both had alcoholic parents."

"Have you had enough for now?"

"Definitely. I had enough almost before we started."

"Well, thanks for being more approachable as our conversation progressed." He nods. "We're off to a good start."

Rod looks at his watch. "I want you take you to detox and have the addiction medicine doc evaluate you. Mostly as a failsafe measure to make sure you're okay. That shouldn't take enormously long. After that we'll go to the health pro group so you can begin to see how it works."

"You obviously think I need treatment. How long?"

"Treatment? Yes. We typically recommend ninety days for physicians, and the length will vary depending on evaluation of your progress."

"Sometimes less? Sometimes more?"

"At times, sometimes more, depending on your status and improvement and readiness to leave."

"I thought these programs were for a month.'

"You might be referring to cookie cutter programs. Ours is based totally on evaluation. With docs you are so smart that your brain can out-fox honesty. To be straightforward, it can take a while. But the other critical issue is that there is a lot at stake with a physician. You have a high degree of responsibility in contrast to John Q. Public. If you screw-up there are major consequences. You may know that we do a practice assessment toward the end of treatment that will define your reentry into clinical practice."

I'm simultaneously conflicted and wanting to accept what he's saying. "That's a fuck of a long time."

"Tell you what. Take it one day at a time."

"Seems like I've already heard that." The initial session put on the pressure to face myself. Nevin lays it out like he's on my side. He's no bullshit, which makes it tough, though I'm safe with the man. We'll see if this plays out the way I think.

● ● ●

An anesthesiologist leads off the health pro group. He shrewdly diverted drugs for years and was undetected. What he does is to appear to waste his unused anesthesia medications when he was actually shooting water into the wastepaper basket. Dr. Shrewd here, never getting snagged doing that, but then the next twist in his checkered story. One of his colleagues went into the bathroom and found him after he had shot up and had overdosed. The anesthesiologist's wife knew about his addiction and saw his deterioration. Oddly, she didn't insist that he get help, fearing that exposing his addiction would ruin his career. But his career that was teetering on the abyss and he guy almost died. And all the lying and sneaking and diverting drugs and not being able to wait until he got home to shoot up was like he was telling my story. He shook me.

The others in the group share scraps of addictive behaviors that drove tons of underhanded maneuvers. One doc says he reduced himself to being mean spirited at times to control people and get them off his back—pushes them away with anger. Each person tells a fragment of recounting past events and horrors and their sagas. It opens me up to not hide. I identify with these docs. Their histories shove my story in a mirror for me to look at. And it's scary and a relief. A release. It's painful, placed side by side with being soothed. And there is the irreverent laughing at the absurdity of our drug-related transgressions and our bullshit ways to get over on people to protect our active addictions. Hearing the docs' stories I start to be more buoyant, not so lonesome and isolated.

● ● ●

"I'm sorry. I know—"

"I suspected what you were doing, but I didn't know where the hell you were doing it." I look at the clock on the wall and watch the second hand jerking with each tick "Did you take anybody with you?" Her voice is riddled with suspicion.

She suspects...and the mental picture of Jackie darts through my mind. "Yeah, I took Glen with the idea of shoveling a boatload of drugs in him, but then we had a chat that led to an epiphany." I'm supposed to be starting recovery, and here I am again in my good old misled ways and wiggling out of things with deflection.

"Oh, yeah? A moment of insight?" Her voice is dour with skepticism. "It took a while, you leaving me high and dry, but most of all I was out of my mind, not knowing where you were—alive or dead. You, Mr. Master Communicator." Julie pulsates across the line in a flurry, punctuated by a jabbing and scathing voice.

"Come on, don't be that way?"

"What way should I be? Brain dead so you can do whatever the fuck you want?" She blows a strong lungful of air into her telephone mouthpiece that sounds like a monster wave breaking in the earpiece on my end.

"That would be..." Don't be a dumb shit and dig yourself deeper. "... not such a good idea. You're totally right. I should be more accountable. My slippery mind was doing the talking that landed me in Mexico. At least I unearthed the clue to give me more evidence when I was there. Does that absolve me in any way with you?"

And Julie has given me the communiqué. What's happened have been my preoccupations. A narcissistic horror show driven by self-gratification at the expense of her. Julie is burnt by everything always being about me.

"I told you once and twice and a million times that I'm sick of the abandonment…first by my parents and then I traded them in for you." She's the one that did the trading, but I'm the one who continued the betrayal. I have a premonition that Julie must be wondering—maybe hoping—if the remedy will have an effect. What will it take to patch me up to turn me into a regular human being that isn't going to incessantly screw her over? "So, how long will the program in Oregon take?"

"I've spoken to my staffer here about my evaluation for care. He said the evaluation was just about done before I got here. The docs stay ninety days. But the time can be extended if the way they are mediating with me isn't seeping in. Mainly if I'm being too headstrong or they need to give me more of a hand."

"It shows how sick you are." The curt quip smarts. She's so irate it doesn't faze her to be hurtful.

I take a breath to stop myself from defensively striking back. "They balance care with needs. So yes, we're sick. And all the people here are similarly sick—some worse than others. The team holds the docs to a higher standard because of the level of responsibility we have for others." I tap my foot a few times. "The therapist is uneasy, thinking I might have PTSD from the war. They're going to sort that out." I lose focus for a second. "The war made an indelible mark and that's for sure, and I know I have some of the classic signs of PTSD, but not enough for a cohesive diagnosis."

"I can help, but I'm in a stirred up tizzy." Julie blows her nose. A huge honk. "My allergies are kicking up from running this time of year. Let me think."

Silence grows into thirty seconds. Julie lays it out. She says I carry war experience around like an anvil strapped on my back. She recites how I've told her about the messy, messy humans were wretched bloody wrecks, or thrown into changeless disabilities or had sketchy prognoses. And Julie enumerates the cadre of those who helplessly slipped away. She's at a loss at how to describe it—I was there, she wasn't—but Julie knows it will never be undone for me. Julie makes the exception that my perception about what happened might change with more time and distance. And Julie comes across with *her* perception which is a sliver of how I view the war has changed in the time I've been back. She tells me to hold on a sec. Julie has to catch her breath. Julie is a star athlete and she's never said she has to catch her breath. And then she says that war is trauma, but it is a matter of degree. Her thought is the work I did was traumatic and I have been deeply affected, but Julie I doesn't see me as a hopelessly traumatized guy, unless I've been too snowed by drugs to show it.

Julie changes the subject to business and hits me sideways, "So, we have to pay the costs of the clinic, plus put the staff on hold for three months and pay their salaries." My head jerks back a few inches from the abrupt shift. "We can't fire them and tell them to collect unemployment insurance because that would not be fair and we're vulnerable since they could seek legal remedies." I'm shocked that she goes into the fix-it mode.

"True. A lot of funds are going to get sucked down a rat hole. A huge bite." I swallow, making a gulping sound. "Look, Julie, I know you don't trust me, and you won't for a long time. But I want to say that I am sorry for putting us in a precarious position. Fortunately, being in the pits of my poor judgment didn't extend too much into the financial zone, other than I could have had a more successful practice. The drug use actually tied me more to work to have access to meds and we didn't blow a lot of dough on vacations. I drive a shitty car and don't compensate for I feel about myself by tooling around in a jazzy Porsche."

"Guess what? There is something brand new sitting in the driveway and it's mine and not yours. Oooh, it's a handsome piece of metal, flashy blue with sexy leather interior."

I know she indulged herself to get revenge. "You're putting me on."

"Got your iPhone? I'll send you a picture of the little darling hot to trot Porsche."

"You know they don't let us use cell phones."

"Well, chucks, you miss out. Maybe for the family week I'll put the pedal to the metal and speed up Interstate-5 so you can lay your big baby blues on it."

"So you're going to do whatever you want and leave me out of it."

"Maybe yes and maybe no—depends on what you do, doper big shot who fucks his wife over." She makes a raspberries sputtering sound over the phone. "Your probation changed into jail time, remember? It used to be I'd listen to what you'd say and not go by what you did. And you watched what I did and operated around that. So Mr. Master Manipulator you can forget that now. Oh, I know it was the drugs doing the talking, but you were the guy doing the acting and you're not off the hook. So now I don't care what you say. I'm watching to see what you do. Trust? We'll see, because it's going to be a long probationary period when you get out of jail, Mr. Smooth Dog."

I've got to get her to back off. "You've been doing a lot of reasoning."

"Ah, a little empathy for once, huh?"

"Look, I'm at this doc doper rehab place. Progress? Yes, I can imagine standing in your shoes. But I swear to God, I don't want to be here. And, sure, it's all the goddamn consequences for messing up." I sigh. "Any chance for a little support?"

"Here's the deal, Glen. I'll work as hard as you do at getting things together. Not harder than you to cover the bases like I got sucked into doing in the past."

I don't know if she's actually being evenhanded or if Julie is punishing me, but I'd better take a one down posture. I've already given up my rights, so what's the difference. "I'm working hard up here and it's going to get harder."

"So when am I supposed to come for the family week? I'm dying for a long ride in the new sex machine Porsche." I'm floored that tight fisted Julie pooh-poohed me and blew a big chunk of dough on the car. Reciprocating with a big slice of vengeance—being showy that she reins her big bucks and I'm enervated when it comes to her monetary horsepower.

"I don't know yet."

"I really want to come to get some stuff straight with you while someone else mediates."

My hand holding the receiver tightly constricts. My palm moistened. "I guess that will be part of it, but the main agenda is for you to look at how you've had a hand in the husband-wife unspoken and spoken contract." My grip relaxes.

"So I'm the bad guy?" Julie's voice hits a harsh higher octave. "I'm sick of everything being put on me, especially by default when you're the one fucking up."

"That's not what I said. It is supposed to help you, and in turn, us when I get out of here."

"I get it. But look, it's not up to me for you to get your shit together, buster. So for me to come is supposed to help me so I can help you. For god's sake, all this is still all about you."

"Julie—"

"No more insight. No more about you being the center of attention. I just want you to do what you're supposed to do so we can have a damn good life for once. Insight doesn't mean shit, unless you do something about it. Like going to the market and seeing luscious things, but it doesn't do any good unless you buy them and take them home and cook the food and then eat it. Just standing their contemplating your navel while you look at the food and doing nothing is like…I don't know. You're just twisting in the wind. Put force behind action, rather than just thinking about stuff." Julie waits a second. "I've had it. I want to get off the phone."

She gets off the line. I stand, looking blankly. Pessimism washes over me.

CHAPTER THIRTEEN

The beginnings of acceptance coax me through the first two weeks as the screws are being tightened down. My mind is provoked and prompted to reveal what's masked, blowing off what has been batten down like a ship's hatch covers. This place and its newness spin into a weighty stimulus overload. I'm disoriented, trying to find my footing in loose mental gravel. Yet I catch an opening connection on what's now an ill-defined and elusive path. I need to reach for what's real. It will take a while, or most likely an infinite series of stages that will last forever.

I'm sitting in a health pro group. There is a doc in his mid-fifties with sandy hair and rugged good looks and he looks to be a few inches over six feet. He took a stab at some inconsequential treatment in the past. He managed to stay clean for a few years. This doc gradually deteriorated, ending in a somersaulting relapse. He said he had looked solely at being hooked, avoiding a dominant background issue of coming from a well-educated family—his father an engineer and his mother had an advanced college degree—and being emotionally and physically abused by his alcoholic father. His alcoholic mother stood by and provided no protection, only to tip another glass of bourbon. His father castigated him for something imagined, which was confusing and unwarranted. This caused panic because the doc as a kid didn't know what was going to happen next. He didn't know if he'd be safe or not safe and this made for a lot of angst. Family life was like living inside a random barbarous pinball machine.

This doc makes me think of my alcoholic father and placating mother who slept around when he had been at sea. He knew what she did. Dad drank, struggling to cover it up, but he couldn't cover up what seeped out. And he was powerless at home caused by empty attempts at handling my mother. And the man never came close to meeting my mother head-on. What did he do? He berated me. He took it out on me. And, yes, I remember three times that he hit me when it was meant for my mother. A spur-of-the-moment mechanism that snapped. I had submerged this memory for years, and then today it all came back sitting in this group listing to this doc who was relentlessly abused.

I remember when I stopped thinking about it. I was fourteen years old. I got my physical genetics from my mother. The men in her family were athletes and played college football. I had a hormonal surge igniting a huge growth spurt. I filled out and was the biggest kid in my class. My father was jacked on spirits and came at me after he had returned from a deployment. He knew my mother had her fleshy ways while he was gone. He stood in front of me with his arm cocked. And I hit him so hard with my right fist on the left side of his jaw that I decked him in two seconds. I wasn't sorry, an absence of remorse and need for retribution. There were no pangs of conscience for what I did. No more transferring his conflicts with mom by taking them out on me. I mostly put it out of my mind until right now in this group, with the doc baring his guts to us all. And I get the shades of how the group works. It holds up a kind of brace to exchange someone's life story for your own—identification with the story to open you up. And the group buttresses the layers of shit you have to face to stay clean.

● ● ●

The staff pounds the gavel. They are a cast of characters from different walks of life, some large, some petite, some thin and some with a little extra weight, some good looking, some so so, and the thing that connects us is that they care. But one thing in common is their commitment to the principles of recovery and how they keep their own lives together. This in turn helps us.

They say the right of admission to getting clean hinges on embracing powerlessness and unmanageability. The cradle that holds the fervor to make it happen is humility. Accepting powerlessness depends on the guts to embody boatloads of humbleness. I remember a fragment by Philip Rieff, "The most complex analyses grow beautifully simple…" But simple doesn't translate to easy. The gavel pounding tells us if we don't get where we're powerless, and take on humility, our lives will continue to be a mess.

That is a tough one for a guy like me who has been so controlling and feels like he is the master of the universe, while underneath feeling like I am the shameful scum of the earth. The next part is believing in a God or a higher power that will return you to sanity. I don't think I've ever been really sane in the first place. Then comes the leap of faith: turning your will over to a God as you understand him. Yikes. Him? Is God male or female or some amorphous spirit floating around out there? Or is God the manifestation of grace or a trickster coyote? A relief comes when the staff tells us that the majority—over fifty percent—of people that come through the doors of recovery have no conception of God and they are agnostics or atheists or have been so screwed over by religious fanaticism as kids that they reject God-like conceptualizations and are nonbelievers.

Now Rod knows how to earn his keep with docs who are so smart that it paradoxically makes them too stupid to be open to the idea they might be powerless or there may be something in their lives they can't work around. He sparks me to catch onto one thing—an out of control substance abuser. That's the central place where I'm powerless. But then he adds a huge caveat. That I can't control outcomes, at least with respect to doing drugs and a lot of other instances in life. I can only do what I can do to affect an outcome, and that's about it. I have to have to turn the other things over to a God that I have not yet come to fathom, much less accept. And then he says that unmanageability is the same as the consequences of my addiction. Okay. And then he says I have a disease. What did I do? Catch it? This leaves him an opening to say, yep.

Rod is a smart guy who knows how to appeal to the heady clinician types. And this is how he starts. He tells me that addiction is mediated by neuroadaptation in the mesolimbic dopamine system. He says that if you throw drugs on the brain that the ventral tegmental area residing in the midbrain goes through changes. And yes, you can catch addiction with no genetic predisposition because of the changes the brain goes through because of drug use. But then he says this extends to the stimulating sites in the nucleus accumbens up towards the basal forebrain. So, after using drugs for some time your brain changes into an addict brain. And the other tidbit is that the prefrontal cortex which spells out making judgments and decision making is compromised when it comes to drugs and that you do really dumb shit things. He says, in other words you are powerless over drugs. You take one drug and there's a chain reaction to do more. If you take a drug that is not your main drug it also stimulates this neuropathway and you'll either go back to your drug of choice or get loaded on something else. Rod transforms the nebulous disease concept of addiction into something unmistakably concrete.

He convinced me that I am powerless, which of course I knew anyway, but dug in my heels to avoid admitting it. They didn't teach this neuroscience stuff in med school and they sure didn't in my plastics and hand surgery residency. It's like what Janet said about the four, two, one syndrome in med school. Rod flips and reorganizes my way of thinking.

I get that Rod has me on a trajectory to lead me on a pathway to accept God. What he says is that you have to rely on something outside yourself if you are powerless to keep you clean, because your willfulness is not going to do it. Your brain is shot in this department. Powerless, yes. Rely on God, well…

● ● ●

The nameplate alongside the door says Joseph Coombs, M.D. I knock on the door. He howls through the closed entrance, "Come in." Coombs stands and turns from his desk. He's in his mid-fifties. The man's paunch tells me he sits too much. Coombs has a pleasant and inviting face and he has wavy dark hair. He's not a tall man. Coombs has a strong sense of presence. He appears to be a genteel person. Maybe the doc yelling at me to come in is an exception to his refinement. Dr. Coombs extends his hand, "You are Dr. Glen Coyle?"

I take a two second glance at the office. The desk is stacked with journals. He has a miniature foot-high Alaskan totem. And on the walls there're photos of star constellations and a supernova at its zenith of brightness and a spectacular shot of the aurora borealis. "You have some astonishing photos."

"I had a premed and astrophysics double major as an undergraduate and have always kept up an interest in universes." Joe has an easy style, and looks me directly in the eyes. "I want to make sure the signals are straight. What is your understanding why Dr. Nevin has asked you to see me?"

"I was in the Medical Corps in the Iraq War and was a surgeon who dealt with a lot of action in the OR." I tilt my head and have a trifling frown. "He wants you to find out one thing which may have many parts to it. Did the war shape who I am today?"

"Let's sit down." There are chairs arranged separately from the psychiatrist's desk area for consultations with patients. "The diagnostic criteria for PTSD were well-established after the Vietnam War and my understanding that the dynamics of stress responses were no secret in Iraq. And being a physician you must have been acutely aware of stress reactions." Joe crosses his legs and folds his hands in his lap.

"Yes, very much so. The diagnostic criteria I know backwards and forwards. When I was over in Iraq I started knowing by intuition whether a GI had PTSD or not. You could just sense it without asking." I marginally shake my head. "But getting the GIs to talk about their stress reactions could be tough. I'd like to talk with you about what happened to sort out the ways it's blazed on my memory…being a doc I can see PTSD in others. But in myself…well that's why I'm here to see you." I think the war is like a branding iron. "Some minor things in life aren't worth remembering, but what happened in the war is fixed in my mind. That's not to say it's constantly in my thoughts, though the memories are irrepressible. I think about it when I want to and don't think about it when I don't want to." And what flickers in my mind is the artillery attack and what ensued afterward. My buddy and I are on a building's flat roof near the surgical unit and see the two of the enemy forces, having pinned down and on the verge of killing four of our men and my buddy and I blast the shit out of the enemy.

"Okay, that's a good backdrop. We're off to a good start." Joe nods. "The reason I want to acknowledge your background is that some of my questions may seem rudimentary to you, but are directed at getting a baseline understanding of your exposure to trauma and its sequelae. But first, give me the idea of your duties."

"I worked in an OR and the majority of the cases were traumatic wounds. We did immediate stabilization and did medevac as soon as possible to Germany where the patients could receive more sophisticated continued acute care. At times there could be internal injuries to be treated and debridement of necrotic tissue. We had limb loss, but in some cases there were reattachments and digit reattachments, but the hard part was there was no follow-up. I didn't know if the case was successful once the soldier arrived in Germany or was further transported back to the States." I mark time for a few seconds. "Initially, there was the novelty of the clinical situations that kept me perpetually focused. And there was the stress of cases. But I would say that the stress of dealing with the combat wounds was accumulative."

"Tell me more about what you experienced."

"There was the challenge of the massively difficult cases and I had to instinctively invent surgical interventions on the spur of the moment. You wouldn't know when it would happen, but there was the onslaught of cases where it seemed like chopper after chopper would arrive where you couldn't fuck up assessing the severity of the cases to do triage. And there were the TBI patients I had to assess since in some instances a specialist in that area wasn't present. The surgical team was like a family. Another doc and I were diverting some drugs, but none of the personnel knew about it. Or at least, I don't think so. They could have put me so high on a pedestal that they looked the other way, though I don't think that was the case. We were very sly. The military makes you that way."

"That's what you did, and—"

"The impact on me? There was the tedium when we had an onset of too many cases, followed by downtime. You're either switched on or off. I already mentioned this to Rod, but knowing there were limbs in the bio-waste bin from different human beings twisted me up in an emotional knot, despite my clinical detachment. And the constant tic tic tic of the anesthesia machine got to me."

"What happened inside you?"

"At the time it was horrific. And the intense apprehension that I would not be able to get the job done because of the pressure of doing seemingly hundreds of things at once. And a sense of helplessness because at times things were so out of control." I stop for a second. "You know, Joe, I've never thought of it like this before. I just always kept my head down and kept on charging forward. And then there were the times I was diverting opiates."

"So you tuned out what was happening?"

"How do you mean?"

"Well, like you were detached and went numb to turn off your feelings."

"There certainly was some of that. Well, maybe a lot of that. At times I was in a daze and what was happening seemed unreal to a degree. Sometimes the patients didn't seem like real human beings, but they were."

"How about your memories now about what happened? What I'm getting at is whether you have blacked out portions of what had happened."

"To some degree. There are a few things that are fuzzy because of the overwhelming pace that things happened. But when you have an experience like that, mostly you don't forget it. It was war. And those memories can creep in. I'll never forget what happened and I think it will always be a part of me." A mental switch flips, and I think of what Julie said. "My wife had the observation, or maybe intuition, to say that my memories would last, but my perception of the memories might change with time. She has something there."

"So you've confided in her. She sounds like a sharp woman." Joe's eyes narrow.

"I used drugs here and there. I think it was kicked off during the war, but didn't blossom into a full on addiction until I was in private practice." I look away for a moment, and then back at Joe. "Now that I think of it, I didn't use opiates when I got home because of PTSD. I just got sucked into getting loaded."

"Let's check something out here. I have an observation. The surgical duties in a combat war zone were horrific. We know that by your history. But we also know it because of what war entails. Please let me make a jump. Were you self-medicating because of everything that was stirred up in you?"

"Yes, but it was more about the effects of the drugs and the fact that they energized me."

"Okay. Let's take a shift to now." Joe's eyebrows push together amidst his well-scrubbed face. "For example, is what happened still kindled in you, like recollections about what happened at war come up and you have no control over them? The memories act on you?"

"If you have the fierce experience of war, you don't lose sight of it." No amount of clinical training prepared me to totally handle the emotions of treating the torn-up men and women at war. "But I can't say that I am blindsided by memories of what happened. At times I was high-strung and affected by the poignant medical situations I was thrown into. I do mull it over and will continue to ponder what happened because it cannot be forgotten." I blink twice. "I trust you're cognizant about what I'm saying."

"Yes—I catch on." Joe gives me an accepting, psychiatric-type nod. He's genuine, not a pro forma kind of shrink. Joe says, "I've read all the politics about the Iraq war and destruction. Probably most people know that an IED is an improvised explosive device. But for the life of me I'm clueless about how the medical system worked. Except, I read about troops being medically evacuated to Germany. Tell you what; explain to me about the frame and setup of how trauma medicine works." He looks at his watch. "We have plenty of time. I want the details of the medical system, since it will give me a frame of what you went through. And then let's talk about some of the cases so you can tell me what you were up against. It may not sound very psychiatric to you, but by the process of you telling me about the war will help me piece things together for the evaluation. Now tell me, are you okay with that?"

Joe is an interested and inquiring person, a curious character. And more so, he's a physician, who most likely is laying the groundwork to help me. "I really want to tell you about the war experience, because when I do, it's telling you about me. When I lay out the facts I am giving you the circumstances under which I operated."

"Okay, let's start. Tell me about the conditions, situations, atmosphere, moods and character of what happened."

I say that Operation Iraqi Freedom—OIF—had advanced medical intervention over previous wars. I line-up for Joe the priorities and the trauma system motto, "Get the right patient to the right hospital in the right amount of time." But the Iraq war wasn't like other wars. The soldiers had state of the art body and trunk protection. The Kevlar helmets were substantial shields for the head. And then the protective eye gear.

I visualize a scene where there was complex orthopedic trauma to limbs. And then I flash on another one where there was massive oral-maxillofacial damage. Both of these men had damage stemming from the soldiers' unprotected areas. I paint the picture for Joe of a man with amputated leg and damage to the other leg that was saved. And this leads me to tell Joe this war was unlike past wars where about a third of the deaths occurred caused by trunk injuries. Yes, soldiers died of wounds, or DOW, after they arrived to the surgical units, but a lot of the time if a soldier died, he or she died instantly or quickly in the field before they ever saw the entrance of a surgical unit.

We ran the numbers through the war theater trauma registry. Almost a third of the cases we treated were oral-maxillofacial cases. Many of the cases were from IED detonation of one form or another. A soldier next to the epicenter of a bomb blast would be affected by the heat—burn casualties—complex injuries that were hard to control and having the likelihood of death. The farther from the blast would be ballistic wounding. With many of the IED maxillofacial injuries there were open wounds and debris impregnated in the face, or facial lacerations or major injuries requiring reconstruction. There'd be major mandible fractures or missing bone structural pieces because of high-velocity gunshot wounds or other high-energy weapon facial damage.

I recognize that I got off on a tangent and didn't answer Joe's question. I pick up by telling Joe how the military labeled the progressive levels of treatment, called echelons. There were four echelons we coordinated with. Level I was the battalion aid station or combat medic level. The troops received first-aid training, and had improved and more sophisticated medical devices over other wars. Self-rescue was like nothing ever seen before. And possibilities for care from buddies in the field had been broadened to step up survival rates. A boon was the use of field topical hemostatic applications and state of the art medical tourniquets to prevent blood loss, and stop total exsanguinations and hemorrhaging. And the training for medics had bumped up. For instance, the medics could initially manage lung tears resulting in a pneumothorax. I'm amazed at how elegantly the field medics intervened to handle airway control.

I clue Joe in. The first docs on hand were at Level II, the second echelon. This was named the forward surgical team or FST. You may be aware of the fact that the military always uses tons of brevity codes like FST. Those docs—including me during one brief stint—worked out of what looked like surgical tents. The main concern encompassed lifesaving resuscitation and emergent flashpoint surgery.

It was near the end of my deployment that I worked in one of these units, since at one transient point a FST had a sudden and desperate shortage of docs. My general surgery background slipped me into temporarily filling that position. A new in-country doc who was boarded in plastics took over for me at the Army combat support hospital so I could fill-in at the FST. Having three general surgeons was the setup protocol for the FST. Plus, there was a much needed orthopedic surgeon because combat protection covered the torso and head, but left limbs defenseless against wounding.

Ideally, the medical staff was fleshed out with a couple of nurse anesthetists and a critical care nurse, and technicians who were on their toes.

"I can picture one case where there was a penetrating injury to a soldier's ankle. A blast literally blew off the bottom of eighth of his foot that extended up to his ankle. Fortunately, there was very little missing bone, but we had some fracturing to contend with. It was an ugly mess and I considered amputating the man's foot. We resected the necrotic tissue and we were blessed this wasn't too severe. There are about a hundred and twenty bones in the foot. So it was quite a patch job. Very intricate, but I was able to transfer some of the facial bone techniques to the foot area, especially with the consultation of an orthopedic surgeon who was there but dealing with a couple of more complicated cases. That orthopedic guy really propped me up. We shipped the soldier out to the next echelon level ASAP. We heard back that with some added procedures he would have some resolution and be able to resume walking. Those IED traumas were horrific."

We had more crisis and drama at the FSTs than at the next echelon in the nexus. I remember times when troops would drag in their wounded buddies. The troops' adrenaline ran their high emotional tensions. They'd scream to get help for a buddy. But then they wanted to stick around. We had two patients. One was the wounded patient. And the other was the buddy who brought in the wounded soldier. This made for a lot of pandemonium. We'd have to judiciously calm down the buddies before getting them out the FST. The buddies were not only in the way of the staff getting our jobs done and contributed to the chaos, but they potentially compromised the maintenance and integrity of the sterile medical environment. We were scrubbed. They just came in from being exposed to who knows what adulterants from field duty.

At the FST echelon we only worked at first-line stabilization. There wasn't much in the way of holding capacity. As a matter of fact, next to none. We did rapid air evacuation. We'd move the wounded soldier to the next level of care ASAP if that was required and it was called for most of the time. But there were the minor wounds, where we were able to return the soldier to duty. Since there was few staff—and we were tightly connected—I was shadowy and clandestine about diverting drugs. It was tough, but doable.

The location of the FST was more vulnerable than other posts, since it was not enormously central to our military defenses. At one critical moment we had a mortar attack. Hell had ruptured without warning. What was the plan? What's said in the military is when the first shot is fired, and then you make the plan. Luckily, we had no urgent patients, and not up to our elbows in blood. The mortar rounds died down, but enemy forces were in the immediate area. The surgical team evacuated the MASH-type surgery suite. We grabbed weapons and went to a nearby Iraqi structure. We occupied the building's flat roof surrounded by a four-foot high wall that protected us from enemy fire until the combat blew over.

I tell Joe about the some of the upfront main clinical concerns, above all with the soldiers that were gravely injured. The urgency with the medical team was to jump on the lethal triad. If body heat dropped, the maimed troop developed hypothermia. Next up was metabolic acidosis, where upsets in the homeostatic system caused the blood pH to go out of whack, which made blood more acid than alkaline. The blood pH has a narrow range and we didn't want it to slip below 7.35 on the acid to alkaline scale. Things became dicey if it did get under that level. There could be a decrease in oxygen diffusion from arterial blood to the tissues, resulting in cell impairment and irremediable tissue damage. The last of the triad was coagulopathy. The blood's ability to clot was weakened that could cause microvascular bleeding. The medical-military clinical catch phrase for treating the triad was *damage control resuscitation.*

The dangerous life-and-death imperatives strongly encompassed making absolutely sure that the airway was good to go—especially in the oral-maxillofacial cases—and we took the necessary measures if the airway was not clear. The other piece of the crisis juggling act addressed initial debris clearing by irrigation if there was contamination. Predictably, there were miscellaneous this and that rubble imbedded in the soldier caused by explosive detonations. Part of the endless attention was to reestablish blood flow. The soldier-patient would get a compartment syndrome if there's a build-up of pressure caused by insufficient blood flow. This was mainly focused on the extremities where muscles and nerves were affected.

I say to Joe that the docs had to be very conscientious about the capabilities at a particular echelon. All medical interventions were a coordinated strategy among the echelon levels. And if cases required the next level of care, we always bumped up to the next echelon, and used immediate and typically extremely effective air transport. As I said, we were very conscious that there was little, next to no holding capacity at the FST.

For most of my deployment—because of my specialty—I was assigned to the third level. The exception was at the tail end of being in the Iraq war theater. Staffing problems pushed me into the FST. The third echelon was the Army combat support hospital, or the brevity code of CSH. Here we rolled up our sleeves even more. There was more surgical capacity. In this frame of the sequence, damage control and triage and resuscitation were center stage. But we had the resources to do surgeries and the team work to get the patient's medical treatment in a definitive—and hopefully stabilized—direction.

A key piece at the CSH was blood. There were effective transfusions. This included the use of equal parts of thawed plasma and red blood cells and platelets. There was a common term, *the walking blood banks*. These were the in country soldier donors. The CSH physical structure was a modular setup. It had loads of resources. The majority of the time we had a full complement of medical specialties for combat wound treatment and surgery. There was even a shrink.

We had a very unusual occurrence. Unexpectedly there was a momentary two-day glitch where we had no orthopedists. I had never heard of this happening before or afterward—a sudden manpower management irregularity. A soldier's shattered leg required bone screws and plating and stabilization before medevac to level IV at Landstuhl Regional Medical Center—LRMC another brevity code—in Germany. Thank God or dumb luck there weren't any joint issues and only a few screws required for the fibula—basically we attended to the large bones, the tibia and femur. And since I had been doing mandible bone reconstructions the commander told me to scrub and get to work. We had high-speed communication and e-mail and I got consultations with a genius orthopedist at Walter Reed. This was a young soldier who had a college track scholarship. Quite a person. His surgery worked out because of all the tight communication lines. We had good results before the medevac to LRMC. This is an example of how we stretched ourselves, since you had to use the resources that were available. Do what you can do, and do the best you can do. And this usually worked because of the consultations from Germany and the

U.S. And if it didn't work, we'd improvise like crazy. I was totally amazed at what life-saving ingenious interventions our docs came up with. This was particularly the case when a situation presented itself that you'd never seen before. And you couldn't flip to the exact page of a textbook to show you what procedure to perform.

Joe breaks in. I recognize that I'm longwinded about the descriptions. Underneath I'm edgy, stirred by my exposure to the medical system and touched by what we did. "I have an impression that I want to pass by you. And I have to reveal a little something. I am not an advocate of war. But the services and the help you gave the wounded GIs in Iraq are very commendable. Now I say this knowing about you self-medicating at times. But the level of responsibility you took is striking."

"I appreciate you saying that. I always think of Iraq as a dirty mess that happened. I've had the idea that it was life changing to put the GIs back together, but I never really touched on it being life changing for me to help them. But now, sitting here with you I recognize the impact it had one me...and in positive ways."

"Good. That's the way our talk is supposed to work."

"I hope this doesn't feel abrupt, but I'd like to move on to something else."

"Sure. Could we do something first? Okay, Glen, I got the general survey of the systems. And you touched on some cases. But I want to get into the life of Glen Coyle in a day at the OIF CSH. Let me know what it was like for in the trenches and the cases you had to shoulder."

Something snaps and a have the sensation of being a deciduous tree that has lost all its leaves, exposing its bare branches for every passerby to see. "We had six OR surgical tables and the medical staff and I used them for the majority of time in a twenty-four hour period."

"Tell me about various crisis levels of cases you had, so I understand what you were up against."

"Is some background okay?"

"Sure, if it will help me make sense of what you had to tangle with."

"It will. I'll pick up the thread." I'm whipped up going through all I was up against. I'll give Joe an encapsulation.

About forty to sixty percent of the wounding was from IEDs. And there was what we called the *high velocity wounds* that caused tissue loss through *high energy transfer*. I've already explained the soldier's proximity to a bomb blast which results in burns or ballistic injury. But the modern munitions velocity is astonishing. The high-velocity of projectiles is determined by kinetics. When a bullet hits tissue there is about twenty percent of kinetic energy transfer, but it doesn't stop there. Now we know this from a physician who did extensive research in this area. That was a famous woman named Janice Mendelson, who was keenly known in military medical circles for her extraordinary work. Here is a sketch of what she exquisitely detailed and exactingly recorded in the medical literature, and we found by experience to be true. Bullets can break-up creating blast fragments which increases the kinetic energy and damage, and forty percent larger wounds. And you have to factor in ricocheting and fragmenting and deforming of the projectile as it is passing through tissue. And then there is the heterogeneity of tissue, like skin and fat and muscle and organs of assorted degrees of compactness and bone. So, there is the projectile, what it does when it hits tissue, and what tissue it hits that determines the degree of wounding.

"Glen are you—"

"Dancing around the cases I dealt with? No. It's necessary to understand the ballistics to comprehend the wounding."

"That makes sense." Joe has a knowing expression.

"You want the worst cases first?" I may sound clinical, but I'm running hard on inside because of the love for what I did, combined with the recollections of the second to second fear of handling all that was happening, or the scared anticipation of not knowing what would happen next.

"Whatever works for you. The worst cases are okay to start with."

I describe to Joe a case of facial wounding caused by an IED. The soldier looked as if he wore a mask of debris. Foreign material was so mashed into his facial skin that the saturation steeped in to soften and compromise the soundness of his skin. This man looked like he was wearing dirt and sand and small rocks on his face, since they so fully permeated his facial skin, caused by the force of the exploding IED. We dealt with the debris contamination through painstaking removal and irrigation. We needed to do debridement to remove necrotic tissue, while applying layered tissue wound closure to approximate the man's preexisting facial features. I have to say this time consuming work took an enormous amount of concentration and sustained focus. And it may be obvious that we had to saturate him with antibiotics since the risk of infection was in the danger zone. Fortunately, these wounds are not lethal, though they look absolutely dreadful on first presentation. He was moved onto Germany and then the States for further treatment. I suspect he had a good cosmetic outcome, despite how horrible he looked at first blush.

"This seems like a good case, what about—"

"A god-awful one? Okay."

I remind Joe about the effectiveness of the Kevlar helmet to protect the head, yet there is facial exposure. This case required major reconstruction. I have to underscore there was complication upon complication, caused by a gunshot wound to the right side of the face. The major surgical issue was facial soft-tissue damage and facial bones being pulverized and splattered into small parts. The first business was a tracheotomy since there was no way that we would be able to intubate the man because of all the oral and mandible damage. We did all the SOP damage control measures, as well. We did imaging and had the results read. We had severe maxillary and mandibular fractures to contend with, in addition to the soft tissue damage and missing bone. The duct damage caused impairment to the production of saliva, in addition to facial nerve damage.

"I'm picturing the case. You said it was god-awful and that means a good result unattainable?'

"No, god-awful means tedious work and you work your butt off."

We expected some facial nerve regeneration, but kept hopes in abeyance. I did major debridement for removal of foreign matter and dead tissue and bone fragments. We also used a pulsating lavage to decontaminate the dirt that had entered the wound. We used arch bars to secure the fragmented bones, followed by maxillomadibular fixation using titanium plating and screws. But the *tour de force* was partially harvesting ribs to put in place where there were gaps in the mandible. This one was a great team approach and again I suspect this soldier had a good outcome with his further care at the LRMC and in the States.

"Are there any other cases you want to discuss?"

"No. These two cases give you an idea of what the surgical work was about."

"And now the undeniable question. What was the impact on you? All the Army doc info laid the background for me to ask this question, didn't it?"

"I guess so. Right. First of all, we were extremely task oriented. At the CSH and the FST it was a medical team experience and that cohesion helped prop each other up. Initially seeing the facial and bone injuries and debris and skin impregnated dirt and rocks and other contaminating fragments was a shock—in some cases up to a quarter or more of the person's face blown off. And then came the second thought. What are we going to do? Not what am I going to do, but what is the team going to do? We talked and cussed and listened to each other. We weren't alone, except for the times we were alone with our own stomachs churning." I've been so rapid fire that I have to pause and collect myself and get clear to concentrate. "Yes, I was stressed to the max as was everybody else. But the screaming in our minds had to transmute itself to focus to get the work done. Some of the docs could have done some whining, but I never heard it. The docs signed up for military duty and there was anticipation what they would be getting into. Another thing is that we knew our place in the system, and that further help for the soldier was going to happen at the next echelon of care…like being a rock climber and knowing you're on belay. The drugs mitigated the stress, but I'd say that when I was on duty it was all systems busy. This was constant. Because you'd finish a case and say to yourself, 'okay, what's going to happen next?' So, most of the time you were on ready alert expecting what unexpected thing was going to happen next."

"It's a little awkward to make a transition here, and I hope you're okay with it." Joe says, "Okay, this is a similar question, but let me ask you something first. Rod said that you used to reattach severed digits. I assume that meant Stateside. Is that right?"

"Yes, but I haven't done the procedures for a while in private practice." I make a fist with my hand, my thumb sticking out. I gesture my thumb over my right shoulder, pointing east. "I did the operations in Iraq." I pause for a second. "They weren't that frequent, because if there was severe damage to a finger it was usually amputated by a blast and there was nothing left to reattach."

Joe is straight-faced, his voice weighty. "Well, let's say during those procedures here or other types of surgical operations, do you ever flash on what happened in the OR in Iraq?"

"Think about it, yes." My voice's inflection has an uptick. "But if you mean like a flashback, no." I shake my head. "I think about being filled with apprehensions at war and trepidations, and I am amazed that my feelings don't act on me, like flashbacks."

Joe grimaces and turns his head at an angle. "So you don't have the feeling that what happened in the war is reoccurring during various surgeries?"

"No. I did at times in the past when I was doing hand surgeries." I bite my lower lip. "The reminder was there with a severed finger. But doing plastics are so…it's not life-threatening." I purse my lips for an instant. "Even the disfigurements we work with in reconstructive surgeries don't bring anything back."

"What about nightmares?"

The tempo of my voice quickens. I bring to memory two bloody nightmares. "I've had several dreams." My speech eases back. "But I wouldn't say that they were frightening like nightmares and I've slept through the dreams and remembered them the next day." I think that not being besieged by nightmares is striking, given all that I had to contend with. "I've had two nightmare since my return from Iraq. Same scenario. Twice a doc asked me to assist him when a case was going south. In a flurry I did. The injuries were devastating. One soldier had trunk trauma because he was not wearing Kevlar protection. The other had two amputated legs from an IED blast and the blood loss looked hopeless by the time he made it to medical care. I tried to have hope, but at a lower place in my soul I knew there wasn't a chance. These were the only two nightmares and after having them they stayed with me for a couple of days."

"So what I'm getting is that you choose to think about what happened in the war and don't necessarily block it out?" Joe touches his temple with his index finger.

My jaw has firmly set sensation. "That's right. It's on my mind. I think about it." My voice warms. "I talk about it with my wife, Julie. And we were married when I was in Iraq and she knows a lot of details of what happened through our discussions. I talked to her about the two nightmares."

Joe leans back in his chair. "One last question. What about outbursts of anger at times that surprises you?"

I let out a breath. "Well, I do get angry at times, but it's situation specific." My fingers press heavily, running up and down my thigh. "And I am angry at myself for letting my addiction insidiously get away from me. I can get frustrated with hospital politics. Normally, I'm fairly unflappable. The DEA numbskulls pissed me off." Antagonized by the thought of the DEA investigators, I angrily jab my index finger in the air.

"You've given me enough to go on." I practically see a glint in his eye, like an inner light. "Oh, one more thing—"

I lift my eyebrows. "How was it when I got home?"

"Right."

"Not quite on the level of being in a war, but the homecoming was a trauma in itself." My face wrinkles and distorts. I glance at Joe's northern horizon photographic shot of the aurora borealis. "It wasn't a surprise beforehand, but it was a surprise when it actually happened. You probably imagine the entire goings on in a combat-related operating room. Whacked out music. Disgusting jokes. Everyone had filthy mouths. A guy says, 'Here we're doing all this heavy surgical shit and what the fuck is it going to be like when we're back in stateside doing all that non-trauma Pollyanna Ville pussy surgeon stuff.' I remember a doc saying something like this, flicking his latex-gloved hand and blood flying through the air. So there was the frontend loading about returning home."

"And when you arrived back home, how was it?" Joe has a deadpan neutral look.

"What I anticipated." I shake my head again. "But there is anticipation and then there is living it." My cheek lifts up. I felt like I was in another war zone, but it wasn't a war zone. "I hate to sound trite, but it felt like severe culture shock. Guys talking about their goddamn golf handicaps and appendectomies and taking out gallbladders and for a while the only docs I could relate to were the trauma surgeons." My lips tighten. "But what was worse was the estrangement—feeling detached from everyone— like a pariah. Everybody had a lilywhite like existence and it was like I still had icky blood on my hands and washing wouldn't get it off. I was sullen and withdrawn and it took me about three months before I started to have some openings and I built on that."

"Let me ask you if you've ever articulated your return from Iraq in this way?"

"I always seemed kind of out of it. Like irritated with people whose lives were so smooth. But by you and I talking about it now, I realize how estranged I was and the difficulty returning from a dry war-torn desert environment to green lush northern California with stores that had everything you could possibly want and more." I stop for a minute. "There was a piece I happened to see on TV of a GI returning from war, wearing his desert camouflage fatigues. He gets of his transport and walks through the city. There's no one there. He's alone. I haven't told anyone this before. But poignant alienation the piece expressed made me cry." I pause again. "Joe, discussing this with you is leading the way for me to tie up the loose ends that I've just let dangle."

"You're getting it."

"I guess I am."

"What about Julie."

"Julie?" My voice firms-up. "She was like Rosie the Riveter while I was away, chiming out the saying, '*We can do it.*' She was one tough lady when it came to finances, and keyed into research and managing her portfolio. At the time people were losing money in the stock market, she saw the opportunities and scored. She focused on training for the marathon and triathlons." My speech raises an octave. "And I'm pretty sure she didn't screw anyone while I was gone."

"Screw anyone?" Joe's words race. "Where did that come from?"

I sink into familiar, but unspoken and concealed thoughts. "My father was a commander in the Navy. And I was angry thinking that my svelte and well-built butt-swinging mother was a man magnet during his deployments. People don't think of or characterized their mothers that way, but I do because of what she did. I knew it; being pissed off, but for the most part overlooked it. My father was lame when it came to dealing with my mother and he took it out on me." I sound let down. "He was alcoholic and drank to cover up what happened."

"For the '*most part*' you overlooked it?" Joe's emphasis pulls me into focus.

"I had anger at times about what went on." My cheeks have a reddened hot sensation. "I did some reconnaissance and found out who one man was. It was winter, early in the evening but dark. I went over to his house and his gorgeous sexy Porsche stood in his driveway. I approached the car with the idea of taking out my anger towards my mother by sabotaging the car in some way, but the man came out of his house. He had a place on the smaller side, but an architecturally well-designed home in good taste." I rub my index finger under the bottom of my nose. "Without any overt suspicion he asked me if I liked his car. I said it's a beautiful piece of machinery. The man said he planned to go out for a bite to eat and would I like to go for a ride and join him. I did. He must have recognized me from a picture my mother had shown him. We exchanged names. I didn't disguise mine. Pete didn't let on that he knew who I was, but he did. It became a mutual unspoken secret—who he was and who I was. He was a man's man and treated me with respect, unlike my whippy and self-doubting boozing father. It's a guess, but he must have known about my emptiness because of the lack of fatherly direction I had. I loved talking to him, and it surprised me. The most amazing goddamn thing is that he invited me to do things, kind of like I was the kid he didn't have."

"Your mother knew?"

"Well, I never told her." I lift my shoulders and shrug. "I think that Pete must have told her because she never questioned my whereabouts when Pete and I were together."

"What kinds of things did you do?" Joe bends forward. I wonder if Joe needed a guy like Pete in his life to constitute some strength in his backbone—every male does.

"He had a sloop slipped where we lived in Coronado." Warm memories soften my face. "She was a beautiful thirty-eight foot classic sailboat and all teak down below in the cabin, galley, V-birth at the bow and head. We sailed a lot. Sailed in the bay and open ocean." I take a breath, expanding my chest. "He taught me to be one hell of a sailor. Guess the boat's name. On the transom at the stern it had the lettering, *Shootin' the Breeze*. And that's what we did. Talk and talk. And more talk. He actually bought me a surfboard that he kept in his garage and we'd surf in Coronado or if the waves were crappy, we'd go up the coast. We'd run on the Silver Strand, starting out at short distances and he'd run at my pace and Pete built me up to over five miles and I stretched myself out until I could comfortably run at his pace." I moisten my dry lips. "And I kept running until I went to Iraq. That could have been another hole I filled with drugs."

Joe's wrinkled face makes him look curious. "That's a lot of time together and you talked about—"

"Pete was a real Renaissance man." I tilt my head and casually nod. "You name the subject and he could knowledgeably talk about it: sailing, surfing, exercise physiology, art, science, engineering, architecture, medicine, and what you want to talk about would be something he knew about."

Joe's body posture perks up. "Medicine? Was he a physician?"

"Yes, an otolaryngologist."

He makes a humming sound. "An ear, nose and throat man, huh? He influenced you to go into medicine?"

My eyes widen. "Yes and influenced me about nearly everything. Pete was quite confident. I even got my undergraduate degree where he went to school—Pomona." I think about it for a moment. My father showed me very little that was constructive, but Pete was like a mentor. "With certainty, you could say that he gave me so much to go on that in some ways he pulled some core pieces of my life together."

"You know, Glen, I hear a disappointment looming." Joe squints.

I raise and drop my shoulders. "That my mother didn't kick my dad to the curb and she didn't hook up permanently with Pete?"

"And that was because—"

"I mapped Pete out as this perfect guy. He wasn't perfect. I think he must have had a strong connection with my mother. And he certainly did with me. But I think in some ways there had to be an element of glue missing in his personality where he could not take the commitment leap with women. To this day I don't know why—despite his confident ways. He didn't get married. Maybe he was just a free spirit who needed connection, but also needed a lot of alone time." I shake my head. "My guess he is the one who dropped my mother."

"I may or not be correct, but Pete had to have given you a lot of backbone and strength that you missed out on with your father. And that says that I sense you have substance, regardless of your problems with chemical dependency."

"I'd say that's very close to the truth." I heavily exhale. "And Julie and I have connected in ways that I didn't get from my parents or Pete...we found each other like a port in a storm."

"Due to the fact that you both grew up in alcoholic families?" Joe's pointed tongue touches his upper lip.

I frown which is more like an upside-down smile. "That's exactly right."

"I have to say that your history with Pete...well, is very compelling and I think as a result of his sway with you, you became buffered from a lot in life, where you otherwise would have been more at risk." I hear Joe and his shrink's point of view, that Pete gave me a good turn.

"Yes. He happened to be there at the right moment. He molded me, but I still dragged that crap around from my parents. In ways he toughened me up, and at the same time the weight he carried made me expansive. I've never discussed the impact that Pete had on my life until now. I see what he did for me, despite his imperfections and the clandestine connection with my mother." I exhale. "So, what is your evaluation? I mean, in terms of diagnosis and need for additional treatment aside from the chemical dependency?"

"Sure." Joe's looks down at his open hand and takes a short-lived glance at his palm like the truths about the mysteries of life are written on that patch of his skin. And then his eyes meet mine. "I want to give you some feedback. First of all, I don't think you have a classic form of PTSD, though elements of PTSD are distinctly present. But I think at the time you spent in Iraq you had an acute stress disorder that has laid down some enduring and lasting memories." He curls his lower lip over his upper lip for a second. "And to be specific about your question whether your war experience should be a part of your treatment? The answer to that is a definite yes. That is, because it is a significant piece of your history. I don't think you need to enter our trauma program, but you do need to be working with Rod on it and if and when it feels comfortable, possibly in the health pro groups."

"I responded as accurately as possible," I put both feet flat on the floor, placing my hands on my thighs and squeezing tightly, "and there is one thing I'd like to tell you."

Joe minutely lowers his head while keeping eye contact. "And what's that?"

"In fact, my military duty was surgery." Pressure builds in my chest, making a throbbing sensation in my neck and I fleetingly hear a blast of wind rushing like white noise. "But one day there was a mortar attack and where we were under siege by the enemy. The artillery died down and the staff from the OR grabbed automatic weapons and went on top of an Iraqi building near our FST. We had cover because there was a four-foot wall surrounding the flat roof of the building. I already mentioned this piece to you, but there is more." I conjure up the smell of zero humidity dry air and the fetidness of rot. "I saw in full view two of the enemy. They had cover, so four of our soldiers—a PFC and a specialist and a sergeant and a first lieutenant—couldn't fire on them and take them out. The enemy had our soldiers pinned down and our soldiers' shield was sketchy. Our guys were totally exposed, actually. Our men would have been dead meat in about thirty seconds. My physician buddy and I looked at each other and nodded and took in a breath and we blasted the shit out of the enemy, laying them out."

Joe's eyes widen as if he is caught off guard, while he preserves his clinical decorum. "How do you feel about what happened?" I wonder if he didn't know what else to say.

"I'll tell you." I commit my words like stickpins. "It happened in the weeks ending our deployment. We had seen a countless number of wounded and dead and irreparably injured soldiers in our OR. I hated the enemy for what happened to our troops—a bitter anger about the enemy and war in general. It was a reprisal for evil done to our men and my doc buddy felt the same way. Fuck 'em is the way we felt. One, we had no problem doing it because of all the men we had operated on, and second the four men who had been pinned down shipped out and went home safe and sound to their families—not like the patients we had in the OR where I felt like calling their families and saying we did the best we could." I frown. "And in a lot of cases the best wasn't good enough. Most of my cases turned out well, but a lot of the other docs who had different specialties couldn't say the same. We depended on God and that person on the table to make it. A lot of times they didn't make it or I imagined they had poor outcomes after they left our OR."

Joe takes in a breath and exhales, "It was war."

"It *was* war." I swallow. "My duty is to save lives and of course not take them. And I felt remorse for what we did, but I forgave myself, given the circumstances and being in the place to save our men. I didn't want it to happen. It happened and the four soldiers have a life. Thanks for listening. I've told Julie and other veterans who have seen combat. I've been very selective about where I discuss what happened."

"Well, thank you. I'm not a military person, though from where I am sitting it certainly sounds like you did the right thing. Those four GIs must think your buddy and you were heaven sent—they have their lives and you to thank. I appreciate that you felt comfortable enough to discuss it with me." Joe relaxes into his chair. I get uncomfortable the way he is staring at me. He leans forward. "What you have explained has given me an idea of what preoccupies you about the war. But, Glen, give me more of the idea. What was the OR like for you, I mean really. You did tell me, but what about the daily grind when casualties came in, and you were at the peak of prioritizing what you had to do."

I fully open my eyes and exhale at the same time. And then I have a collapsing sensation. I already told him enough to get the idea. And it wasn't enough. And I let Rod in on what happened. Still not enough. At first blush I wonder if Joe hadn't been listening. And then I recognize this man isn't a surgeon. He is a physician who talks to people to get them straight and prescribe meds. He doesn't hold a scalpel or make physical incisions. Only mental ones.

I give him more enumeration of what it was like. I tell him when duty started. I had to be on tap all day, every day. And all day means all night. The CSH surgical unit had sophistication and it wasn't like I did procedures in some goddamn foxhole. And there was my stint at the FST where at times there were the horrific realities of being up to my elbows in blood with a GI, knowing his wounds were beyond what I or anybody else could tackle to bring back. Only a sliver of life was left, but the meat grinding wounds overtook the possibility of being a survivor. The futility drove angst deep into my chest. I raced, knowing the recovery goal wouldn't be realized—the death march of the OR. But I had to try. What was I to say, "Oh, that guy is a goner. Don't waste time. I need to move onto the next slot." No, every case was a case that had merit. And despite being covered in some bastard's blood, I had a sense, a craving and a longing that was almost a dream when a casualty had a chance for recovery, no matter what that recovery meant. A full recovery, or a lifelong disability or a protracted recovery or some god awful disfigurement. I wanted to do enough at the FST to get the GI to the next level of definitive care at the CSH.

I'm suddenly conscious that I'm squeezing the crap out of my thigh. There happened to be the guys who screamed for me to either to help them or kill them, begging for an overdose of morphine. I was merely a witness to what was happening in the OR, like someone channeled to do the work and I was only a minor player in the scheme of life. I knew what to do, but I have to admit that I was so out of control that the drugs paradoxically gave me the illusion of having control.

Almost all of the soldiers were so young. And I am rethinking for the ten thousandth time when I was at the FST that I wanted to call their families and say that I did everything possible to save your kid, and I *did* do everything possible. And it was never enough. I never had the confidence that what we did was enough. I thought the chaos would never stop. At the FST we sometimes had complex abdominal vascular injuries when body armor wasn't enough or the GI wasn't wearing protection. And you want to know what complex means? It means that I had to improvise without the time or space to think, just be a surgeon on automatic instincts—zero reaction time. What was in my brain had pulsated directly to muscle memory in my arms and hands. But there were the times that I looked at the scalpel and said to myself, "Remember, sharp side down."

There was so much debridement. So many transfusions. And then at the FST a GI might slip into shock or cardiopulmonary arrest—disappear—before getting him or her to the CSH. And with many of the guys who lived, there were multiple injuries. Legs ripped off by IEDs leaving gapping bloody wounds and hoping there was enough skin flap to make a closure. But those men with part of their jaw bone blasted off by high velocity weapons was a dreadful bloody sight. I'd question myself. Had I missed something before the GI got to the CSH or later medevac transport to Germany. Did I miss something? Did he or she lose a limb or die because I fucked up?

And there is something lodged in my brain, like being stuck in the lining of my nose. The smell of the OR at times. Burned flesh, wounds, dirty feet, stale tobacco, Betadine solution and body fluids—urine and feces—from extreme sympathetic stress reactions. The smells fermented by heat and mixed with antiseptics, disinfectants and alcohol. The weirdest thing was the smell of sweat and the pus and the blood from my patients mixed with a good cigar after dealing with the onslaught.

And in contrast to my whitewashed outpatient plastics practice, I can't get the stink of war out of my head, but that wasn't the worst part for me. It's the constant tick, tick and whining sound of the anesthetic machine.

I recall one kid, the orthopedic case I mentioned before that I was forced to do because of the absence of orthopedic surgeons at the time. He had been a track star in high school and his first two years in college until he dropped out and joined the Army. His name was PFC Daniels.

I remember Daniels as being a thin, but muscular and handsome young man. The bones in his left leg had been shattered during a firefight and there was a significant amount of muscle mutilation. He was one of the soldiers who screamed at me in terror, fearing that we would have to amputate his leg and begging for a lethal dose of morphine. There was a renowned orthopedic surgeon at Walter Reed Army Medical Center in Washington D.C. I called him and he walked me through putting multiple pins in Daniels' leg. The orthopedist advised me on constructing a halo around the leg that ran the length of Daniels' appendage.

We heavily medicated Daniels, but the day after the surgery his mental status had enough clarity that he comprehended what I said. I told him he would make it. Now, when guys are on the brink of death, terrified fellow GIs tell a guy he will make it and to hang in there. But it's a lie, and they know damn well the guy is short for this world. And I said to Daniels that this was no bullshit line. I felt confident that he would be able to rehab his leg. The bad news was that he would no longer be able to run a sub-four thirty minute mile and I didn't know if he would have a limp. I didn't give GI patients my telephone number. Daniels was the exception. He first went to Germany and then to Walter Reed. The orthopedist I had consulted with followed up with Daniels and managed his continued rehabilitation.

The orthopedist told me what exactly to do and I did it. This was one of the complicated cases where the procedure had to be done immediately and couldn't wait for a medevac. Daniels kept in contact with me. He had inspired motivation to fully recovery and he came close. He healed. He strengthened his muscles. This guy did the work. Daniels called me and said he had gotten back on the track. No longer a track star, but grateful that he had two appendages he could run on. He finished college and went to physical therapy graduate school and specialized in sports medicine. Quite a guy.

Joe asks me about how frequently I got connected to people like Daniels. I tell him that the medical unit was about triage and trauma surgery and stabilization before people were shipped out. There wasn't much time for connection because of the lack of follow-up and further treatment. And with the patients whose physically wounded lives had been spent, god forbid that there would be connection. If that happened, you'd probably end up killing yourself because you could never process all the grief. And when I said all kinds of crazy shit happened Joe asked what kind of crazy shit.

I tell Joe the nurses and medics looked to me to help them deal with the enormity of everything that happened within a second or a minute or a day. Hell, I was too busy trying to stop some guy's bleeding or establish an airway and put his face back together before I had to move onto the next guy. A couple of times I got so frustrated and pissed off that I threw a scalpel across the OR. And was I the only doc who did that? No. But during the down time I was able to extend myself and give support to the OR staff. There were the techs like Parsons and Franz. These guys were from good and humble backgrounds, honest and caring. Good guys and traumatized by the onslaught of all the cases. But I think the discussions we had helped them get some perspective and see the war situation for what it was. And then a med-surg nurse named Mitchell joined in. She was tough and seen it all before. But even tough people get taxed to the max. She was a captain in her thirties. Attractive, and had stunning attributes in all the right places. There was glue between the four of us because of the work and no bullshit about rank. The techs were enlisted men. One thing I can say about all of them is that they had intestinal fortitude magnified beyond the scope of what the average guy on the street could imagine. My respect for them felt like love because of Mitchell and Parsons and Franz's selflessness and dedication to be over the top present in the worst situations you can imagine. They leaned on me canonizing my position and rank, but in reality we all leaned on each other. What happened in the OR turned any sense of narcissism into humility. No bullshit.

The four of us had a unique tie. I think it was a protective factor that kept enduring traumatization in abeyance. That wasn't the case for others. There was one female nurse, Brenda, who acted out her trauma by sexualizing it. And she easily sucked others into it because of everyone's vulnerability to maxed out stress we were under. Brenda strutted around like she was making a trophy of one of the clergymen that she was screwing. A real piece of work, but oddly in craziness of what was dumped on us, we knew what she was up to, but nobody laid too much judgment down. You turned the other way and gave her a pass. And this is just one example of the crazy shit that happened.

The session with Joe seems like it has lasted for hours and hours. I'm a strange combination of exhausted and energized. He asks me if I need to go into more of the military OR color and stories that occurred in the Iraq war theater. I tell him there is always more. And there will always be more. But now he has enough to be able to make sense the importance of how we survived. And yes, the war contributed to my drug use, but getting loaded had stirred before the war and took off later when I got home.

Joe looks away for a second and then back at me. "My timing may be off, but are you ready to move on to something else which may or may not be related?"

I shrug. "Sure. But first let me tell you something. Many of the things we talked about today have shown what's unfinished in my life. Thanks for giving me a safe sphere to not only talk about it, but to pull pieces together."

"Like I mentioned before, that's what we want to do. This may seem out of context to you, but in terms of prioritizing the most the most critical issues in your life to be resolved, what would they be? What you told me about the military might be part of it."

"Not surprisingly, I need to be connected with recovery and have a plan to stay that way." I rock my head left and right. Even after talking about the war, I know my addiction is the first priority. "But there is something that is bugging me that I can't shake. I had sex three times with the nurse that works for me." I press my lips tightly together, and then carry on with what I need to say. "She is empty and vulnerable because of the addict she happens to be married to—and I think we took advantage of each other's vulnerabilities. I think I can get resolved with her, but the deceit with Julie plagues me, like I walk around with an arrow in my side that I can't or won't pull out. I have a sense that Julie knows something is up. Second, I need to do my part as a physician to be reintegrated into my medical community. And then the war? Never dismiss it like it never happened, because it did happen. I know this was an assessment of PTSD today, but it was larger than that. Glimmers of light bled through. And I thank you for that, Joe. But my biggest unresolved issue, second to my recovery, is getting square with Julie."

CHAPTER FOURTEEN

Intuitively—verging on involuntarily—I am pulled to the anesthesiologist who told his story the first day I arrived. Dave Singleton has been here for three weeks longer than me. He has become buddies with another doc in the program, an internist named Mike Lyke. Dave and I spend a voluminous amount of time talking. Eventually Mike joins in. We work into a trio. Amazingly bright men who maneuvered the system in similar ways as I did to keep their addictions tied in a tight knot until it choked them. Just spending time with Dave and Mike comforts me.

The *pièce de résistance* is a big chunk that sticks us together. Their uncontrollable faithless charm with women ended up in a freefall disaster. We're three points of a cohesive triangle built on talking. We all have wives who unwittingly enable our addictions. All three wives were emotionally hurt, like we impaled them with a nasty instrument of destruction— ourselves. I tell them about making myself unhappy and empty, with all of the perplexities of my past being drown in substances. And then reaching outside myself for a steamy fix. That misdirected fix was Jackie. Their eyes are concentrated. There's a lot of head nodding.

Even whiz kids have their blind spots. Dave is fifty-three and became absorbed with a woman at his athletic club who was twenty years younger. He said she had some kind of troubled daddy-doll connection with her father and Dave easily became sucked into the quintessence of a father figure. But it gets nastier. He had a sexual-emotional bind with her. She puffed up his ego with her good looks and the sway of her body. Dave didn't catch onto he was about to step on a disastrous landmine. He found himself in an illusion, obliterated by his inflated ego. Dave is terribly edgy about her picking up the phone and telling his wife. He's sure this move would torpedo his marriage. Dave's little Miss Fix It turned into a thick slice of toxic danger who was not going to let loose of her sticky grip on him.

Mike's slips in discretion were closer to mine. He acted in the position of a hospitalist, where he became friendly with a pretty redheaded and blue eyed nurse working on the hospital floors. Friendliness burned into flirtation. Flirtation turned into going out for a drink. Drinks tuned into kissing. He didn't add any sordid details after this, other than to say her father was an alcoholic and she had quite a history with alcoholic and drug addict men. Unlike Dave, Mike doesn't have too many fears of the nurse's reprisal. The nurse Mike slipped between the sheets with was put together with a few sick ingredients, but she wasn't scary dangerous. Mike linked one of her downfalls to her being nurturing to a fault—selflessly giving herself up in the process.

Our program has ironclad boundaries about the fraternizing between female and male patients. Some alcoholics and addicts in early recovery can switch addictions to sex as easily as rolling over in bed. No chitchat. No flirtation. Don't talk. Men are not even allowed to open a door for a woman, which goes against my inbred grain of polite society etiquette. Looking at the women is something that has to be stepped back from, but is a relief. And what I found that the clear gender contact delineation helps. The other note—it seems to increase the trio talking about conflict with women which draws us closer together.

I have the sensation that I'm in the safety of a lifeboat in an unsteady sea when I'm with Dave and Mike. All three of us know we're botched up. No hiding it. And our good-buddy private handshake unites a knot, a freedom to be loose with each other. With so much shame that we discuss, we have an abiding acceptance because we all make sense of each other. And there's survival dependence among us and our strong friendships grow. When there are three friends together, there seems to be one odd man out. This has never been the case with Dave and Mike and me.

I read over the eighth and ninth steps of the twelve step program. Dave and Mike and I are having a *tête-à-tête* get together. I say, "I've read the eighth step about making an amends list, and then the ninth which is making direct amends to people you have harmed, unless making the amends would harm them further." The Jackie film clip runs unrestrained in my mind.

Unhesitatingly Dave clinks in, "We're talking about you making an amends to Julie about Jackie?" His head tilts back. Dave erupts in a booming laugh.

"That's it. And making an amends to Jackie, too." I lean forward, with my elbows on my knees and cradle my head in my hands. I pull myself up and look back and forth between Mike and Dave. "It could be a nightmare, but my hunch is that she would be more receptive than Julie."

Mike says, "What do you think is at stake?"

"Several possibilities. A nasty divorce. Julie might make me fire Jackie, which I'd dread. Julie's distrust would give me zero to stand on. There'd likely be pain on both sides that will last for a longtime."

Mike purses and then moistens his lips. I'm edgy, leaning forward, waiting to hear what he's codified in his mind. I sense from Mike that being totally open with Julie would be a disaster. "Glen, you being completely open with Julie will cause a lot of irreparable damage. How about coming up with something different? Let's say, from this day forward you are completely honest with Julie about your connection and struggles with her." He blows out a short blast of air. "That'd be a mission, like a piece of business you'd grasp each day, rather than make reparation that will destroy you."

"Isn't that like a lie of omission?"

The corners of Dave's mouth curl down. "Focus on the hurt aspect of it. One way to make restitution to Julie is to never go outside the marriage again. I'm stung so badly by that poisonous sex pot who glommed onto me; I'm not going to fuck up like that again. And second, to work on rebuilding the damage from the past. All I have to do is picture that Velcro chick that sticks to me and my wife is looking pretty damn good."

Mike scratches the back of his head. "Dave is onto something here. There are many ways to make atonements without hurting Julie more." Mike briefly widens his eyes. "Wait until you get to that step. Get a damn good sponsor and spend some time working it out. Until then, don't do anything about your affair with Jackie."

I turn my hands, palms up, like I have the sense they are focusing too much on me. "What are you guys going to do?"

Dave's voice sounds sharply punctuated. "Fuck if I know."

Mike rolls his shoulders forward. "Beats the shit out of me."

"As far as Jackie goes, I not only abused my power as a boss, but also took advantage of her since I knew she was in a vulnerable position with her husband." I shake my head. "She wanted me, but I should have taken a higher road. Mike, your scene resembles mine. Come on, what's your hit on this?"

"For me it'll be one-sided. I'm definitely going to get clean with the nurse." Mike's face has an affirming look. "I'll probably be the first guy who has ever done that with her."

My look shifts to my other buddy. "And what are you going to do, Dave?"

Dave goes gray. "Oh, that woman is too dangerously vitriolic and it would turn out to be more of a disaster if I said boo to her." His face tenses. "There's risk and and then there's stepping on a landmine on purpose."

"As far as our wives go, just hang tight for now; pull back from doing anything that's hasty." My stomach churns. "But I'm still messed up."

Dave says, "Get your feet on the ground more and don't fuck yourself up by being too anxiously impetuous. I don't want to sound too banal and pedestrian, but things have a way of working themselves out if you're tuned in about repairing the past—you know the past—when you weren't so mindful because you were too loaded."

● ● ●

Eventually I opt for sharing my story in the health pro group about the abusiveness of my alcoholic father. The key piece I've been dragging around is how he deposited his rage about my mother by punching me. And then I decked him. He never raised a hand to me again.

I'm cognizant of the attentive and penetrating eyes of one of the group members, a man about sixty years old, thin, with a concave chest and a noticeable paunch. His stomach and body looked like a martini olive on a toothpick. I feel old hat thinking it, but he reminded me of the guy in grade school and high school who the team captains never picked and he had to be on a team by default because he was never chosen. The second— an almost eerie piece—was his jaundice jags of observing the Mike, Dave and Glen trio. This physician's name was Lester Gamba. He had two weeks left in the program and I had the premonition that he knew what to tell the staff to give the impression he was ready to complete treatment. You see, he was a psychiatrist, and a gamey one. He had a long-term history of benzodiazepine addiction and alcoholism.

After my share he made a move to talk to me. He told me about being a psychiatrist. It took me back to medical school where the medical students predicted who would be the ones to go into psychiatry and we were almost one hundred percent right. Maybe, it was because there was something a little off about the person, or something unexplained. Lester said that he appreciated what I had shared. I asked him if he could relate to it. He got fuzzy at that point. A common question to ask is what ultimately brought you into treatment, which I asked Lester. He said an adult patient came to see him for an urgent appointment and the patient was accompanied by his mother and father. The parents had concerns about the patient being suicidal. Lester didn't hospitalize the patient, but instead increased the dosage of his medications and added a short-acting, high potency benzodiazepine, Ativan. He told the parents to take the patient to the emergency room if he worsened and to keep an eye on him. The next day the patient killed himself. The parents found him hanging with his neck in a noose. The parents reported Lester to the medical board, and included that he reeked of alcohol. That was the event that landed him in treatment.

Lester told me the program did a rapid benzodiazepine taper over one month, and put him on gabapentin to help with his anxiety resulting from the continued withdrawal. He also told me that his stress tolerance was shot because of the continued aftermath of the benzo withdrawal and he reasoned that the addiction medicine doc should have more gradually decreased the benzodiazepine before totally taking him off of it.

Agreement existed among the patients, from beginning to end, that Lester was an odd duck. He said that he never married. He dated a few women, but they all turned out to be depressed or anxious and he never had any traction with them. He tried to connect with me, and at the same time put up walls. He just didn't know how to be a buddy. A peculiar guy, yes.

Two weeks passed and he was discharged. A week later we heard that he relapsed on alcohol soon after he was discharged. And then the chilling news. He committed suicide via a drug overdose. We already knew that psychiatrists lead the pack among physicians in terms of suicide. The treatment team told us that if someone relapses in the period shortly after discharge there's a significantly higher likelihood of suicide. That isn't just at our program, but also reported at other programs that specialize in the treatment of addicted physicians and it's due to the steep demoralization and hopelessness that comes with a relapsing doc.

Later I talked with Rod about having an inkling about Lester. Lester returned to emptiness and problems with the medical board, nothing in his life but a void and troubles. I don't think Rod broke any confidentiality, but he said the staff worried before discharging Lester, but he didn't accept their recommendations to stay longer. Rod gave me some detail about Lester's potential for killing himself. He said the right things to get the treatment staff off his back. Rod said Lester probably had already made the decision to kill himself before he left treatment.

Lester was a casualty, but in a way he helped us all. I began to believe in treatment as a transformational and spiritual experience.

I seek out Dave and Mike. There's the shock about Lester and this is counterbalanced that it's also not a surprise. I have to say to them, "I started to suppose that we are simply beaten to shit by the realities of this addiction disease. And then what to do—recover."

Dave is stunned by Lester's suicide, which makes him sound slightly detached. "Recovery must be a codified arrangement of being beaten to the point of happening upon transformation, and then finding personal enlightenment. For Lester he had less than a slippery grasp. He said what the staff wanted to hear. One some level we must have all known he was giving lip service, he never really connected with any of us."

Then I work at having perspective to find my bearings. "Lester never got it, and he never had the promise to get it, no matter what treatment he received—like the collateral damage of the addiction war."

Chapter Fifteen

I'm not what you'd call a religious person, but what springs into my mind is a line from Matthew in *The New Testament*: "It is easier for a camel to go through the eye of a needle, than for a rich man to enter into the kingdom of God." I'm not rich, though I transpose richness to mean I'm the guy who has advantage and who is so smart that I'm made dumb by the drive of my compulsive habits. I need to be a person who I have never known. The onus is on me to not avoid what I have to face to become that human being. It has me saying, "yeah!" and, "oh, shit!" at the same time.

I begin with a quote from the Bible and end with internal scary rumblings causing me consternation for a good reason. The staff is mainly composed of people who have spiraled down and made it back from hell. They want us to sit down and go through our histories of compulsive ways with substances and give cases in point that show our powerlessness. The essence: what made us deteriorate.

And the idea brings up a legend about natives who want to capture a giant boa constrictor. In a clearing they construct a large circular picket fence with openings just wide enough for a giant nocturnal boa to enter. In the center they put a small piglet. The boa slips in at night, constricts the piglet preparing it to eat, and the lump in the boa's slithery body makes it impossible to escape through the narrowly placed pickets until the piglet is digested which takes days. The natives don't have to rush to get back. They can patiently wait to retrieve the captured boa. And that's how I feel, like the boa that has a lot to digest. And the drums are beating, while the savage dancing natives are my enslavement waiting to consume me while I'm caught with a huge lump in my stomach. I have to believe on a daily basis is there the possibility of staying clean. I've previously undervalued being honest with myself and everyone else, that was driven by trickery to keep my secret agendas undisclosed. The result made me feel isolated while I struggled for an elusive connection that at best was fake. That's not living.

My eyes narrow. "Where's Mike?"

"Went to do a little individual work," Dave says.

I'm uneasy about revealing my story in front of the group. "You've already done the drill about working on powerlessness and being out of control—"

"More stuff comes up all the time." Dave pushes up his shirt sleeves. "But before I started to go through the powerlessness piece I was just skimming in the program. The work on powerlessness and being out of control is —without a doubt—the most meaningful process I have ever engaged with in my life…to restore some sense of equilibrium and equanimity. And it's my stake at being honest how I've made my life a mess. You see, I could tell myself that doing drugs was misguided, but as soon as there was the opportunity to divert drugs, they were in my pocket. I'd slip in the OR bathroom and shoot up. If the opportunity to divert came up, I'd do it without thinking, like an uncontrollable reflex. But in retrospect, I actually came up with all those opportunities." Dave's eyes pin me. "And you know exactly what I'm talking about, Glen."

One corner of my mouth curls upward. "Finally, there's the eye-opener of making the connection between being powerless and the related consequences."

"When we're using, the feedback loop between drugs and consequences gets disconnected."

I can't help but frown. "For us, maybe there was never a feedback connection in the first place."

"Now you're getting it."

"I'm a skimmer, yes." I'm hesitant. "How much should I get into the powerlessness with the group?"

"All the way." Dave's voice is forceful. "Throw yourself into it." Dave squeezes my shoulder. "They've told us you need to nail-down powerlessness perfectly and remember it each day when you wake up, or you aren't going to stay clean. And particularly because our kind of mind is a devious place. Everything else is developmental work that takes time. I believe it. Obviously, I'm no expert, just a couple of weeks in front of you. It seems to make common sense to me, but as Voltaire said, 'Common sense is not so common.'"

"Smart guy, that Voltaire." I pause for a second, rethinking how this saying came up recently. "Maybe he was an addict or had a friend who was an addict. And I remember another one by him and you'll know why I remember it. 'Men use thought only to justify their wrongdoings, and speech only to conceal their thoughts.'"

"No shit. Get on your story that shows powerless, write down the whole kit and caboodle and detail the consequences. You'll see what I mean when you reveal the work to the group."

"You're a good man, Dave."

"Good to hear that from you. I'm trying to believe that. It's still tough.

• • •

I feel in control when it comes to patients. The exception is when I was in the blood bath in Iraq. Anything that comes up I can put together a remedy. I focus on outcomes and design the plans for them. And now I'm touching the fringes of my piss-ant M.D. grandiosity—the tricky deception of control over what my outcomes will be. I hope I know how prospects will turn out, but I don't. Who does? I'll bet even God stands back and watches the randomness in the universe unfold. So I stupidly get competitive with the other people in treatment about constructing the work on powerlessness. It has to be the best, and it's really about being seen, rather than doing a good job. But it's for me, not directly for anybody else…just the leftover of being competitive in medical school and my residency and internship. I tell myself, "Stop it. Be real, not some prick trying to be the best."

I feel energized. I have the sensation of vivacity that comes from the absence of a drug hangover. The greater part is being significantly past the sleeplessness and depression of withdrawal. Today is about being exposed. Suddenly I feel like I have no protective barriers, as if I'm totally exposed. So far, a lot of the docs in my groups have been enthusiastic about recovery and some reserved, kind of like a statistical bimodal distribution—two bumps on a line making a couple of bell-shaped curves. The staff would place me in the enthusiastic bump. I don't know what to expect—what's the right answer? There is none. Just occupy a little ambiguity for the moment. The group leader is Tad Weiss. He gives a warm up preamble to lead off, but we know what today is going to be about. He asks me to go first.

I feel a kind of choking in my throat. It's time to be real. "When I was ten my parents had a party. My dad was an alcoholic. When the guests left there were glasses on the coffee table, some half-filled, others with various amounts of alcohol left in them. I cleaned up the remaining booze by drinking it all. And then got so loaded, I must have turned green and threw my guts up and passed out."

Tad says, "Did you have any inkling that you were out of control of alcohol at that point."

"No, I just thought I couldn't handle it because I was a kid and all I had to do was get older." I nervously look down at my notes. "When I was about sixteen I entered a bicycle race. There were six stops that had to be made, and at each stop you had to drink a beer as fast as you could and then start peddling again. After beer five I rounded a corner and hit some gravel and went down, getting the worst road rash from my hip to my knee and there was blood streaming down my leg. I got back on the bike and made my way to the last stop to drink beer number six. I won the race. After all the fun hoots and hollers and people eyeing my bloodied leg, I rode my bike home. I went into a refrigerator my family had in the garage and rooted out another six-pack and drank it. I didn't clean myself up. Instead, I sat on a chair and started calling up a bunch of girls. Some were charmed because I was funny, others disgusted. My mother came home and started screaming at me because I ruined the cloth upholstery of the chair I was sitting on—I didn't realize what I was doing—blood all over the place. She was pissed. Yelling at me that I was a drunk, just like my father. I just dismissed her. This was just good old teenage fun. My favorite saying was, 'What's the matter, can't you take a joke.' This was my first cover for minimizing that I might have a problem."

One of the group members says, "And your mother wasn't able to do anything to stop you?"

"No. I just got more secretive. She told my father, who gave me an obligatory talking to which was hypocrisy at its finest—or worst—depending on your perceptual spin on hypocrisy. There were numerous bouts of heavy drinking in high school, but I had not yet crossed the invisible line into addiction and despite my ways. I was a straight "A" student and scored high on the SAT. Frankly, I was half-assed, but did well in school anyway, by effortlessly seeing how to get the job done, doing it, and not making school complicated. I was going steady with a girl whose family was alcoholic and that is what bonded us because I also had an alcoholic father. I even concealed my drinking from her. Really messed up betrayal and deceit, engineered by the two sides of me. Glen number one who loves her and Glen number two who was into the sauce."

I take a drink of water and moisten my lips to move onto the next part. I look around the group room and everybody is waiting. "At Pomona College pot and cocaine were thrown into the mix. I got so loaded once, I missed a test. I begged and lied to the professor that I had gotten food poisoning and he let me take the test a day later.

"I was at a party and offered this gorgeous young woman some cocaine. She was the girlfriend of an acquaintance who was out of town. The woman got so loaded on coke that she came onto me. Any allegiance to her boyfriend quickly circled the drain, followed by a roll in the hay with her.

"I'd get loaded and not study, and half an hour before the test I'd read a friend's notes and walk in and max the test. This was my party hardy mentality. And I rationalized what I did by telling my whacked out mind that there was no fallout that I had to account for." I look around the room. "And I was a runner and I was able to continue to run, so I thought I must not have a problem."

One of the group members said, "You're telling my story." I saw a couple of others nod.

"This continued until medical school. I seemed to pull back the first two years, but was still drinking alcohol and using pot and cocaine, here and there, but everything in miniscule amounts. And then I started to question myself. Anxieties came up about medical school. Should I be a doctor, or is this just some sort of act? Still, at that point, I don't think that I had gone over the line into addiction. In the last two years of medical school I drank occasionally and microscopic quantities, and the pot and cocaine dropped off to zero. Honestly, I have to say this had to do with my insecurities about being a physician. I'd meet people who were not in medical school, or talk with family members, and be asked about this or that ailment and what to do for it. I hadn't even gotten my degree and they thought I should be giving them medical advice. This made me feel more hesitant and unsure about myself. And I started working harder the last two years of medical school."

One of the group members says, "And you weren't using at that point?"

"Some alcohol at parties, yes, but not much."

He says, shaking his head back and forth, "I just can't believe it—a carbon copy of my story."

"Except for one thing. I convinced myself I didn't have a problem like my father. I was the master of control, and an omnipotent son of a bitch. Then came my residency. The illicit drugs had already fallen off the map. I had exposure to pharmaceutical grade opiates. I'd take a little here and there. They didn't dope me up, they gave me energy—the stamp of being an addict. But still, my mind was switched off to the fact that diverting drugs was wrong and somehow I had the right." About a third of the group is nodding their heads by now, which makes telling my story easier. I still feel threatened and exposed, but like I'm in good company doing it.

"Then I was a trauma surgeon in the Army in Iraq. I had similar pattern of drugs use, diverting but not using incessantly, or nonstop. In part, I must have been self-medicating because of the acute stress, but also to give me energy after a major battle or onslaughts from a Humvee hitting a bomb booby-trap or soldiers being in the vicinity of exploding IEDs, and if there was an overwhelming number of wounded soldiers to treat. The whack, whack, whack of incoming helicopters—knowing bad shit was onboard but not knowing what exactly was onboard—gave an adrenaline surge, but the sustained focus of sorting out stabilization and trauma surgery and whether to medevac the soldier took prolonged energy. The opiates helped." I glance around the circle. Everyone's concentration is pinned on my unfolding story. "I serendipitously discovered another doc who diverted drugs because he was copping meds at the same time I sneaked my fix. We became a tag team to get drugs, working out a system to cover each other to get over on the military. I had a tight four person support system and I felt like crap that I was copping drugs behind their backs."

Tad raises his eyebrows. He's probably wondering when I passed over the invisible line into addiction. I start to get a little hyper and then reel myself in, thinking about the thrill of diverting opiates. Because if you divert them it means one thing—you use them. I'd actually got a high from diverting and then the second high was actually using the drugs. I imagine how a little dopamine gets released just thinking about getting a fix. But once I had the shit scared out of me when an Army nurse practitioner caught me, and I made some flimflam excuse about giving some opiates to a patient. She believed it, but I always felt afterward that she looked at me with suspicion. I really don't know if my imagination about her doubts and mistrust occupied reality or not. The thrill of diverting was taken out of my *modus operandi* and I was always on guard not to get snagged again by anyone.

I crossed the line when I came back to the States. I had always been good with deadlines and I gave myself deadlines to quit. The deadlines floated by and my grasp on them loosened, and the hold of the Rx drugs tightened. And sometimes—in a fit—I'd impulsively say stop out loud, but I'd automatically keep on using. Like a part of my brain automatically took over control. I know now that the automatic pull of my midbrain was now in control do to the neural changes caused by the habituating effects of drugs, and the reasoning functions of my prefrontal cortex was someplace in the ether. From that point on I became more secretive and cunning and clever to avoid detection."

I tell the group how I went into plastic surgery and my motives for a private practice surgical suite were purely driven by my addiction, so I could have access. And the chronic pain subspecialty fell out of the heavens—or came up from hell—when I covered for a physician who was on medical leave.

My notes fall on the floor. I don't pick them up, and continue. "I'd take drugs from my clinic with the intention of using them at home, but then I'd use in the clinic parking lot or pull off the road and use on the way to my house. And there was the diversion of drugs at the hospital while doing major reconstructive surgeries—it became a pattern that I wouldn't make it out the door before a detour into the bathroom to shoot up." I reflect on my hyper-alertness to avoid people watching me, while at the same time feeling the tension of my desperation to get what I needed. "I took enough drugs home for my days off, and almost always I would have to go back to the clinic during off hours to get more." I let the men sitting in the circle know about going to Colorado and stealing drugs from my in-laws, followed by the fiasco with the two pharmacists and having Chandler confront me and his try to help, but I get my co-conspirator Jackie to send me drugs by express delivery.

I look around at my company, like we're boy scouts sitting around a campfire. But we're the kind of boy scouts who earned our merit badges through cunning and trickery to hide our affairs with drugs. "My take was it's not okay to be an addict. But I knew I was an addict—just couldn't accept it." I pause. I feel my innards are bared to the stinging breeze. But I know I have to tell my bigger secrets if my stay here is going to work.

I tell the men about the most significant event. In college and medical school Julie's attraction to me was a blueprint carved in her from having alcoholic parents, but she wasn't aware of it. She found a familiarity with me that mirrored her past. It was like Julie was at home in a place that was partially inhospitable. She made me comfortable by looking the other way because our relationship fit like an old shoe of her past. I tell the group about Jackie, and me writing scripts for her addict husband and the dance where she enables me. And then comes being dogged by the DEA. And the WBC elegantly sniffed me out.

The docs sit attentively perched in their chairs as I wind down. "If I told this story to someone in the street, the person would be flabbergasted. But here it's like carving out a niche that everyone is acquainted with. My story has so many likenesses to the ones I have heard from you." There's more head nodding around the circle. And it's peculiar and novel and unfamiliar to be so validated by being so messed up. The groups recognition and the similarities between us backs my acceptance of my addiction.

And my acceptance of addiction is the turning point. Airing out the accumulative chaos where opiates drugs were the agent of my debacle makes me stop escaping the actuality and truth and facts and nature of how I tricked myself into disbelief of what I was doing.

CHAPTER SIXTEEN

I pick up the residents' phone and punch in her cell number, the digits irreversibly scorched in my memory. "Jackie, can you talk?"

"Glen!" I hear an anguished exhale. "Hold on." There's the echo of her footsteps, and a door that squeaks open and the click as it slips shut. "Okay, I have privacy." Jackie pulls in a breath. "Good God. You're been sticking out in my mind. A lot's happened."

My hold on the phone receiver forms moistness in my palm. "Tell me."

"I'm getting help. When the WBC physicians descended on you, it was like they also spoke to me." She hesitates, like she's collecting herself. "I have zero boundaries around men. I do the same bullshit with you that I do with Tom. Run around controlling everything, thinking I'm all powerful. But really I'm grasping at this and that to fill what feels so empty. It's like I'm a lunatic reaching for an illusion that doesn't exist. I try to think of a time it hasn't been that way and I end up being more unsettled when nothing comes up."

My hand cramps, clutching the receiver. "Jackie?" I didn't imagine the call would start out this way.

"Please, Glen, let me say my piece." I get frightened about what Jackie is going to say next. "I've been building up for a long time." She clicks her tongue. "You may have thought you sexually took advantage of me. But I used you just as much as you used me. I may have used you more. And I'm sorry for it. I was needy and became aggressive, wanting to be touched because Tom was completely whacked-out."

I collect myself. "This is why I am calling."

"What's that mean?"

"Now I'm what you might call conscience-stricken." I look at the texture of wall in front of me and rub my hand over it, feeling the grainy finish. "Regretful for my sordid part in it. You can't dissolve the past, though I like to call up some new ways of linking up with you that isn't going to lead to another goddamn disaster."

"Oh yeah, what would that look like?"

"Have a healthy tie with you…keep things above board."

"Clue me in, because I'm too stupid to figure that one. No, really closer to the truth is my reasoning is so bizarre that it makes me too nutso to figure things out."

Mike walks by the residents' phone and puts his hand on my shoulder. He whispers, "You look pretty serious there, guy."

I cup the phone speaker. "I'm talking with Jackie." He nods and gives me a thumbs up.

"I don't know how much longer I'm going to be here." The feeling of being high-strung begins to abate. "They'll do a practice assessment and develop a reentry plan for me. I'm sure the recommendation will be to discontinue the chronic pain clinic, or have it heavily supervised. I'll likely come back to work at a reduced schedule."

"Sure, okay. What about Julie?" Jackie poignantly pauses. "Are you going to tell her about the sex scene between us?"

"I don't know yet. My guess is she already has doubts about us. If I tell her, she might want a divorce, or she'll hold onto it, forever blemishing our marriage. As they say in the practice of law, if you ring a bell you can't un-ring it."

"Maybe the three of us could have a talk."

I glaze over, looking straight ahead at the blank wall. My posture stiffens, feeling threatened by what would come out. I would be the one to get the pounding. "You're kidding."

"I'm not kidding. That way she could see that I no longer pose a threat to her. Maybe forgive you. See it as a past indiscretion. And I could redeem myself."

I try to envision if the three of meeting would be civilized or a hornet's nest. Civilized? How could it be? "That would be a pretty gutsy move. I've got a lot to consider, and work out with you before I come home." I look left and right, feeling overwhelming commotion in my guts. "Julie still has to come to the family week to dig into her codependency, and see what's needed to adapt to being a clean and sober couple. God, I'm just thinking what it will be like for her to come with you hanging in background…or actually, you'd be right up front in the foreground."

"Don't have me hanging. I can't stand that. I'll fly up and we can work it out while you're still in treatment." Jackie is even, resolute. "It'll be the safest way to do it."

I can't speak for a second, staggered with trepidation. I wipe my forehead with the back of my hand. I find my voice again. "The idea of it scares me shitless."

"Well, you weren't you scared shitless when we had sex." There's an edginess shadowing her words.

"And that means—"

"No more duplicity with Julie because it oppresses me. I'm the other woman. Be upfront. I'm not into sharing, Glen, so she can have you back one hundred percent." Jackie blows into the mouthpiece. "Clean it up with her and no whitewashing it."

Jackie has unwavering self-possession, but I look at her stance as another version of being swept down in a self-destructive vortex. I'm not there, yet. And I don't know if I ever well be.

"Jackie, I'm not being a chicken shit, so don't misread me, but I'd like to go over this with my therapist here and then make a decision. Being in treatment, I think that's the thing to do. Does that work for you?"

"Sure. And if the therapist needs to give me a call…I'm good with that. Maybe it would even help me, too."

I want to change the subject to something neutral. "Let's be done. What else are you doing?"

"I'm going on tons of horseback trail rides at Five Brooks Ranch out at Point Reyes. It's a respite from all that I'm contending with. Being out there I drop into a blissful zone."

I think back to Point Reyes as like another world. I ran there all the time when I was training for the marathon. Do an out and back on Bear Valley Trail to Arch Rock on the coast. When they still had the fallow deer out there I saw one when I ran through Meadow Divide at daybreak. It stood mid-body in tule fog. "The Point Reyes scene is dusted in magic."

"Yeah, the place is like that. You come across miraculous and enchanting stuff all the time. Last time I came upon the silhouette of a golden eagle in the distance. The powerful form of the bird was like a presence when

I got closer and it came more intimately into view. The golden eagle took off and was huge. There were light colored feathers under its wings. And later I checked in a birding book and the light color showed it was actually a juvenile—astonishing how big it was."

"Lucky you had that sighting. I've seen a couple of those rare birds when I was on the trails at La Laguna de Santa Rosa. I know what you mean about how striking they are. Another run I'd do would be going out the Bear Valley Trail to Arch Rock and then taking the Coast Trail all the way to Limantour Beach, and then turn around and come back—a twenty-miler. You'd see all kinds of things, like bobcats. Amazing to hear them scream, and sometimes catch the echo off the walls of Bear Valley canyon."

"You sure have a lot of memories from Point Reyes."

"Yeah, it's a release to have those recollections. I'm caged here. Institutionalized. I love the wilderness. Take some good horseback rides for me, would yeah."

"Sure, will do." Jackie hesitates for a few seconds. "Glen there's a couple of other things you need to know. I don't want to be caught by unsuspected fallout."

"Looking for other work?"

"Yes."

"I don't fault you for taking care of yourself."

"Thanks. The other thing is that I am considering dumping Tom… no decision yet."

"Keep horseback riding."

"I know what you mean."

● ● ●

I close the door and sigh, then roll my eyes.

"What's up? Looks like some kind of dilemma."

"Yeah. Here's the story. I have a nurse anesthetist who works with me. I called her to make an amends with the anticipation of doing a preemptive measure before I go home."

"Ah huh, was she pretty good in the sack?" The pitch of Rod's voice has a twist to it, like asking me if it was worth putting my marriage at risk.

"Better than pretty good." I've already recognized that my thrill seeking with Jackie and took too many risks that finally pushed me over the brink.

"How'd it go?"

I give Rod the details of our conversation.

"No kidding. Coming up here to face things with Julie is a quite a gutsy position to take."

"Gutsy? That's exactly what I said to Jackie. She wants to redeem herself and repair the damage from the past. And the reason is most likely obvious to a guy like you—not to make herself sick anymore by living in secrecy."

"There are other ways of being honest, without being destructive."

"I know. I've been talking about that exact same thing with Dave and Mike. I'm afraid Jackie might be overboard."

"Do you think she is doing this for your connection at the clinic, or just to cleanse herself?"

I nod. "Both, really."

"Well, I agree that it could have a devastating effect for your marriage. In fact, it will."

"So don't do it." I'm relieved Rod is giving me an out.

"I didn't say that. How deep into it were you with—"

"Jackie." It's risky telling Rod my secrets, but I'm ready. "We had sex three times. It wasn't like a torrid affair. She is pretty on all accounts. You name it, she's got it. Jackie was another one of my missteps. She was empty. I mean, she wanted me, too, to fill something that couldn't be filled. Two misdirected hurting people having sex, pitiful and desperate."

"Do you think you could gain comfort with Julie, given what's happened with Jackie?"

"Julie said she wants to work out what's stacked up over the years. Julie's parents are alcoholic and guess who she marries. She wants to stop the pattern." That sounds coherent, but I'm so confused my head hurts. "So there's the possibility gaining a semblance of honesty with Julie…but the deal with Jackie is still undone."

"I get what you are saying. In terms of Jackie, you could make amends with Julie by never having sex with Jackie again. Stop yourself from jumping in the sack with her another time." Rod looks to the side for a second, then back at me. The pause gives me time to realize I'm going to end it with Jackie. "Having Jackie come could go either way, so I am not going to advise you, but I will support your decision whatever it is. And I am willing to mediate a session or sessions with the three of you, if it comes to that."

"So Rod, what's your take on secrets."

"Your secrets have immense power. Think of it. How you kept everything underground about your addiction. And what happened? You destructed. And how you collapsed was caused by the malignancy of your secrets. And you did this, hidden in the shadows of a dark imploding ruin. And my guess is that you were disassociated with the degree of what you were doing to yourself."

I lean forward. "You mean me, the secret keeper, hurtfully undid myself because I became my secret?" …my backhanded way of acknowledging Rod is right.

"That's how denial works." Rod sits straight. "You shut out what's real and your level of self-awareness is like a shroud of black opaque mist that you can't see through."

"I have to say, Rod, you're a bit poetic, but you *are* talking about me."

"Listen. Get out of all that self-absorbed bullshit and get with program. Lester Gamba was Dr. Bullshit Artist Extraordinaire. So good at it that he pushes the self-destruct button big time. And the others that live in secrecy end up relapsing. Some OD and flat out die. That's the nature of it all and you'd better get it." Rod looks to the side. "Okay, you want to shift? Take it from secrets in negative and destructive direction and look at the flipside."

"Okay, shoot."

"Now this hypothetical and about Julie and you." Rod says this conjecturally, but I have the sense he's laying down a version of the law. "And I'm not recommending that you do this, but the premise has multiple applications and we see it demonstrated in your return to work and other situations. You do not need to be a bleeding heart about your condition. You simply need to be honest with how you go through your life, and do not have to masochistically reveal yourself to every person you come in contact with. Now let's look at the power of keeping your three time flings with Jackie a secret. Suppose that Julie will be irretrievably demolished with your admission about Jackie. Let's say you hold back, and use the power of the secret to infuse your marriage with reparative conviction.

Now, I say this because I understand that you fear divorce or irreparable problems with trust if you tell her. And the secret can swell in you to motivate you to empower yourself to consistently do the right thing in your marriage."

The tenor of my voice softly smoothed out. "You're a good therapist, Rod."

"And what makes you say that?"

"I'm going to tell her." I drop my shoulders.

"That's what I figured you'd do."

Chapter Seventeen

On the flight home I reckon that I don't have to understand every fine point of how redeeming myself works. I just have to follow the principles of self-rescue to make it happen. And this inception launches something that has been most cases nonexistent: faith.

Most of the docs in the program stay ninety days, but Rod estimated I might relapse because the Julie-Jackie drama was unsettled. They didn't discharge me until I had been in treatment for one hundred and eleven days.

I'm no superman who is immune to doubts in life. But I've come to believe in the weight of my doubts. They tell me about the division of adventures and misadventures. Be awake and alive, or occupy a shadowy place.

The residential program sows the start of generating a new life. They say there's no cure for my affliction. Now I believe it. What's at stake is managing oneself. And that's unending if I'm to stay well. I was protected from myself while in residence. Now comes the next part: returning to the real world. I let go of one grip and latch onto another. Perhaps all the sizable details of what I face stepping back into my community will be disheartening, or maybe a boon to restoring me. Facing my existence will be tough and I recognize that is what will rebuild me.

The first stage was the residential program. And then there's a new design and fabric I will weave into. Stage two is a healthcare professional monitoring program in my community. I will attend a monitoring recovery group twice a week and have four to five or more random forensic quality urine tests per month. A case manager will keep track of me, in addition to the leader of professionals' group. And what I do is communicated to the WBC.

The practice assessment maps out that I erase the chronic pain portion of my clinic practice, since my interest in the pain clinic had been totally driven by drug seeking. It wasn't motivated by the benevolence of treating patients.

Surgery and rounding at the hospital will require a worksite monitor to keep an eye on that I'm fit to practice and see that I'm not diverting drugs.

And now the kicker. A worksite monitor for the clinic is mandatory. It's not going to be Jackie because of our history. It will be my scrub nurse. Secondarily, Dr. Kranzler, the dermatologist from next door, agreed to pop in at least twice a week to validate that I'm not impaired. The scrub nurse and Dr. Kranzler agreed to provide monthly written reports to the monitoring program case manager. In my relay around the comeback track, I've let go of residential baton while solidly grasping onto a new baton back home.

I hate the trite term, but I'm on a short leash. That is connected to a choke chain that can be pulled tight at any second. That's what my recalcitrant self says. My healing self says it's the setup I need to stay clean and give me back up to say I'm okay to be a doc. The WBC will meet with me this week. We'll have check-in meetings as frequently as they see fit.

• • •

The twin prop passenger airplane from Portland lands at the Santa Rosa Airport. I feel a racing sensation in my chest, anticipating meeting Julie. There's all my professional payback that I face so that the medical community knows I can be a doc. Though what presses on my mind, like I'm a tin soldier relentlessly beating a little toy drum, is Julie and how I have to square things with her. She has an upturned face, filled with laugh lines. She wraps her body around me in a hand in glove hug. "Welcome home, honey." But she sounds contrived, like a counterfeit imitation of her past self when we were first an item.

"I feel a little institutionalized." My face must be ashen gray. I look around. Everything is so familiar and simultaneously foreign and disconnected at the same time. I kiss Julie. And then I collect my bags. We head to the car. And then I see it. "No shit, you did buy a Porsche—too gorgeous—going to let me drive it?"

"When you're out of jail, and off probation, mister." The welcome home piece was short-lived.

She sits in the driver's seat and puts the key in the ignition, but stares out the windshield into the distance, not seeming focused on anything. "Julie?"

She doesn't flinch. Her voice is flat, mechanical and deadpan. "What?" But she's transparently irritable, testy.

I lean into her. "Where'd you go?" And then I recognize that even a momentary reprieve from Julie isn't going to happen. For her there's no overlooking the slicing pain I've done to her. Jackie will be the opposite, since she gets what this journey is about. And I'm more willing than Tom who is terminally inculcated with drugs, leading his mind into oblivion. The disparity between the two women is like opaqueness and light. Julie is in the darkness of not forgiving.

Julie sways back and forth looking like she's struggling with what to say. "The family week opened up a lot for me. You're a fucking asshole, do you know that?"

"I know. I feel miserable about…sorry." I rub her neck where her taut trapezius muscle runs down to her shoulder. I work at having a soothing voice. "I know it started way back with your folks."

"Get your paws off me." She pulls away. "Don't placate me with that mom and pop bullshit." Julie's breathing runs shallow. She blinks a couple of times like film clips are running through her mind. "And your loose goose faithlessness drove it deeper." She wraps one hand around the steering wheel, turning her knuckles a shade of fleshy white. "Did you also stick a cucumber in her cunt like a dildo to get her off?"

"Julie—"

"Shut the fuck up, Mr. Rubber Band Man, snapping the shit out of me." Her cheeks glow red and heated moisture makes her skin glisten. "It's all mixed up and I don't see how it's going to be undone. I knew there was something fishy with Jackie and you. I didn't know how extensive it was. And yes, the sessions fleshed it out during family week. In my head I understand about your drug-influenced shitty judgment. There's an itsy bitsy iota of relief finding out you messed up only three times and it wasn't some fiery, sultry every five minutes sex up against the wall thing. But you fucking up is a done deal, buster. Yes, the sessions were emotional. And there was intellectual understanding about the two of you being engaged in your precious cutesy respective recoveries and working on boundaries. But I don't give a shit." Julie makes a fist and hits the top portion of the steering wheel. "It's just getting some traction about trust. I don't know if it's going to happen. And the fact that you want to keep her in the clinic…frankly it's painful…no reassurances that you aren't going to lay her between cases. You think that's going to work? Get your shit together, Mr. Flimflam."

I draw in a breath and let it go. I may get screwed for this, but I'm going to try to slow it down. "This may not make any difference to you because in a sense it's more of the same. About the egotistical me and not about you. You have your emotions, but please let me try something." My voice feels like it's thickening. "So—"

"Glen, I don't want to hear any more about you. You're pathetic. And you can take your paltry self and shove it." Julie lets out a gushing breath. "Just give it a rest."

"But—"

"Insight, insight, insight—who cares? When a woman's husband does it with another woman it's like you get deeply impaled in the chest. That's me. I want to protect myself from being hurt again." Julie's red cheeks fade to a cloudy glum look. "I'd like to believe what you're saying, but remember what I told you before you went into treatment. I don't care what you say. All I care about is what you do. The blah, blah, blah I don't give a shit about."

"Well I—"

"I don't give a flying fuck if you are new to recovery, if you expect me to tiptoe around and treat you like you're fragile. Your recovery program is up to you and you better work it. And part of it is undoing how you screwed me over."

"You don't come across as supportive."

"What'd I said? Definitely supportive. I'm not taking any shit off of you and that's doing you a favor." Julie turns on the car ignition and puts the shift lever in reverse. She looks in the rearview mirror. And then she pushes the down the accelerator. A couple doesn't see her backup lights and step in the car's path. Julie slams on the brakes. "Goddamn it, why can people watch what the fuck they're doing""

• • •

We drive down country back roads to get home. Julie accelerates through the curves, showing off the agility of her new hot machine. My head has a doughy sensation. I slow down my mind, and wander, feeling my first drug craving in a month. Being home is a trigger. Despite the tension of Julie crawling all over me, there's one conclusion in my mind. All I have to do is get through today without using. And this expands to settling something else in my mind that evaporates any ambiguity. Either you use or you don't use. The resolution in my mind is to not use, but it is larger. I have to face my triggers, and not avoid them, like a crisis that makes me take action to maintain a shelter and sanctuary within myself. I habituated parts of my brain by using over and over again, leading to losing authority over myself. And now I'll habituate my brain by facing my triggers over and over again until my mind is a safe haven that is predictable.

"Julie, the program taught us we have to live in the moment in order to stay clean and not jump into the future."

"Oh, so you can't give me any assurances that you will stay clean."

"I can give you assurances that I will be clean for today."

"That's ducky."

"What do you mean?"

"I need a lot more security than just for today."

"But that's not how it works."

"Leave me alone."

She's shutting me out, accelerating and braking, gaining control over the serpentine road. And a central part of the recovery treatment is having patience, not demanding what you want on your terms and having it right now. So, that's what I'll do. Practice patience. My words said to Julie were bald claps of thunder. What do I have to do? Wait for her desire. I'll be on the hook for a long time. With Julie. With the medical community. And with myself, and that contemptuous voice at the back of my mind that still tells me I'm a fraud. Maybe there's no completely getting over those self-critical thoughts talking in my brain. I've already given up the idea of perfection. And instead of being the power wielding omnipotent doctor, I'll be a real person who is capable of humility.

We're not heading toward our house. Julie turns onto a narrow country lane called Oakwild that is lined on the west side with valley oaks and black oaks and liquid amber trees on the east side. She pulls the car over to the side of the constricted lane. "Okay Glen, I thought that I'd give it a shot, but I can't stand to be around you. I'm not ready and I don't know when I will be ready. I had the premonition that I should get the locks changed and now I'm glad I did. You're not going home with me. Where do you want me to drop you off? A hotel? Somebody's house?"

I move my hand towards her shoulder.

"Don't even come close to touching me." She shakes her head. "Tell me where you want go, or get the fuck out of the car."

"You're teasing me, or is that what you honestly want?"

"Are you stupid or what? Look at me and what do you think?"

"Okay, I get it. You're laying down the law." My mind spins into a jumbled mess. But no doubt I'm blacklisted.

"No shit, Sherlock."

"Just a second." I take out my cell phone. "Hello Miles, this is Glen. I just got back." I listen. "Not so good. Julie changed the locks on the doors and doesn't want me to come home. We are parked along the side of the road and she wants to drop me off somewhere." I go mute for a second and make an effort to hear. "Are you sure? I'm not imposing?" I go silent. "Thanks for the help and support and—" I pause to hear. "She'll drop me off and I'll wait for you to get home." Miles speaks again. "Oh, she is? Okay."

● ● ●

Miles and his wife, Carla, and I are having dinner. They exude much needed kindness while I recover from Julie's pronouncement, causing my reverberating shell shock. They have an abundance of room in their house since their three kids have successfully launched and have their own lives. They'll have me out back in the cottage where Mile's mother stayed before she died. Miles and Carla have a stately old house in the McDonald historic district, where Hitchcock's *Shadow of a Doubt* with Joseph Cotton was shot, and *Scream* and Disney's *Pollyanna*. Nice to be in a homey place where all the houses have a hospitable and substantial look with traditional appearing spruced up landscapes.

The phone rings and Carla picks it up. I think that Miles might need to go to the emergency room, though I don't imagine he's on-call tonight. Carla comes back to the table. "Glen it's for you. Julie gave the man our number. It's a detective. A surge of adrenaline saturates my nerve endings, and my adrenaline is thinking it's the DEA.

I go to the phone. I have to be purposeful to hold the handset loosely. "Hello, this is Dr. Coyle." The voice on the other end says it's the police department.

"Dr. Coyle this is Detective Nace." I let out a breath, because it isn't

Kilgore or Penny on the other end of the line. "I have some extremely bad news for you."

"Okay?"

"Your clinic has burned down."

I grimace and the corners of my mouth turn down. I was looking forward to coming back to by practice and now I'm coming back to nothing. "How bad is it?"

"It burned down to the ground. It's a pile of rubble. The contents are demolished."

"None of the contents survived?"

"No." The first thing I think of when Nace says nothing survived is the hand sculpture with all fingers attached that my patient carved for me. A keepsake that has more value than the building or the thousands and thousands of dollars of medical equipment or things of lesser memories.

"A question. Why are you calling me and not the fire department?"

"Well that's the other piece. You know the fire department is close to your office, but they couldn't save it because of the nature of the fire."

"And that translates to…what do you mean?"

"It was a criminal event. An act of sabotage where flammables were completely doused throughout your building and ignited. They found melted plastic three-gallon gas containers and a couple of metal gas cans."

"You mean—"

"Yes, it was arson." Detective Nace clears his throat. "Do you know of anybody that could be responsible for this?"

My head is swimming. "Right off, I'd say no. But you really dropped a bomb on me and it's hard to add two and two right now." The shock makes my nerves swing between being electric and numb.

"Can you come down to the station so we can talk?"

"At the moment I'm out of a car."

"Can I come over and talk with you?"

"Hold on." I cup the phone and tell Miles and Carla what's happening. They say it's okay for the detective to come over. "My hosts say it's fine." I give the officer the address.

"You're close. I'll be there in ten or fifteen minutes."

The last bite of dinner is finished. I take my plate to the high ceiling kitchen that has a huge antique white Wedgewood stove and white tiled counters and a seemingly endless number of cabinets. I thank Carla and head to the porch out front to wait for the detective. I sit on a cushioned white wicker chair. In five minutes an unmarked black cruiser glides up to the front of the house. The detective gets out of the car. I guess I expected a man who looked like he played football for the 49ers, but this man was under six feet and medium build. He climbs to the top of the stairs and we shake hands. He has sharp-featured face, though it's jowly. There's only one light illuminating the porch, though I can see his hair is coal black. We go into the parlor. Miles comes in and introduces himself. I ask the detective is it's okay if Miles joins us. I want Miles to help shore things up.

"Detective Nace, isn't there special investigation units for suspected arson?"

"There are. But in this case it was so obvious to the firefighters that they immediately called us. The site will be studied more for conformation. But this case is kind of a slam dunk." The detective takes out a notepad. "Do you have fire insurance?"

"Yes."

"Are you over insured?"

"My wife handles our insurance. But I know the insurance agent visited the clinic and provided an evaluation and recommended the policy limits."

"Okay. By the way, are you just having dinner here tonight?"

"I was out of town for an extended period of time. I returned today and my wife and I had a falling out because of a conflict and we are separated for the time being. Dr. Dietrick has graciously taken me in until I either move home or make other arrangements."

"You said 'conflict.' What are we talking about?"

"While I was away she found out I had a friendly relationship with the nurse practitioner that works with me at the clinic. She seemed calm when she picked me up at the Charles Schulz Airport, but things rapidly heated up. She said that she had changed the locks at the house and was not ready to be with me. Frankly, I'm unsure how this is going to go."

"Do you think that she could have been vindictive and committed the sabotage on your office?"

"She is quite pissed off right now. I wouldn't be surprised if she wanted to get back at me in some way. But doing something like this is not her style. She's a very smart cookie. Nah, she wouldn't do something like destroy the clinic."

"Does she happen to have her own money? Or—pardon the expression—is she a trophy wife?"

"Well, kind of both." What seeps in is how Julie is very good looking and fit because she is a top tri-athlete. She received an inheritance and has been extremely shrewd about investing her money.

"So, she really doesn't need you to support her?"

"But I do. She's actually quite frugal, except for buying expensive running shoes. And I was gone so long that I think she got reactive and bought a brand new Porsche with her own money. I saw it for the first time today—pretty sexy looking."

"I see."

"Are you thinking she is a suspect?"

"Yes."

"Well, I know her. She is furious with me, but again this wouldn't be something that she would do. Her brain just isn't wired that way."

"I'll consider what you've said. You never know during times of high conflict with couples." Detective Nace makes several notes. "Okay, let's move on. What about the nurse you were *friendly* with?"

"We clearly have some tensions we have to work out. It's not her character to do something like this."

"She's married?"

"Yeah. And I'd like to volunteer the fact that her husband doesn't know about us."

"How do you know that?"

"She told me."

"Any way he could have found out?"

"It's doubtful. He's kind of caught up in his own orbit."

"I see."

"Does that mean you see several possibilities?"

"Well, yes. So far there are numerous possibilities to check out." Nace makes more notes. "What is your practice?"

"Plastic surgery at the clinic. I used to manage chronic pain, but I am giving that part of the practice up. And I do some reconstructive surgery at the hospital."

"Any disgruntled patients? You may remember that one patient who murdered a plastic surgeon in Petaluma." I think of Susan berating me, but settling down when Werner referred her for psychological treatment.

"I remember that murder. But my patients are happy with their results." I've never botched a case. "And I doubt that some husband would be pissed off enough to burn down the clinic because I made his wife's boobs too big."

Nace lets loose a smile and then gathers himself back up into a serious detective front. "Any of your employees have a grudge?"

"I closed the clinic down and we paid their salaries while I was gone as an act of goodwill. Doing anything to the building would kill their jobs. Everybody was onboard with our plans to reopen the clinic."

"I think that's enough for now. Please give me your cell phone number for easy access to get a hold of you. And please keep it with you while we are doing our investigation."

I give Nace the number. The three of us stand. Miles and I walk him to the door. Nace says, "Thanks for being so candid with me." He reaches into his breast pocket and pulls out a business card to hand to me. It has the Santa Rosa Police Department emblem embossed on the card. "Oh, just a minute." He takes the card back and writes something on it. He says that he included his cell phone number and for this case he has twenty-four/seven availability. I don't know what other information I can provide Nace. I tell him that. He says I'd be surprised at what things come to people's minds in cases like this one.

"I want to help. I just don't know what I am going to do about my practice. Rebuilding will take months."

A neighborhood streetlight glows over his dark unmarked cruiser. He's dimly lit walking down the steps and along the stone pathway to the street. And his shadowy figure becomes a bluish silhouette as he nears his car. Then a warm faintly luminous light brings him back into focus. He opens the car door and dome light comes on. He sits. The car goes dark when he closes the door. Nace turns on the dome light and takes out his notepad. We see him making more notes. Miles and I close the front door. We sit in the parlor and consider the interrogation. From the quiet street we hear Nace's car start and the sound of his engine as he accelerates down the street. I look at my wristwatch. He was in front of the house for seven minutes completing his interview notes.

Miles moves a little closer to me. "The clinic news is a shocker. It's a lot to handle your first day back…with Julie also dropping a big bomb. But, look Glen, you can stay with us as long as you like. You'll have privacy in the cottage out back and you know we'll always be here."

"Thanks, Miles. The arson could be an opportunity to build a more state of the art surgery suite." My mind drifts to a metaphor. The clinic burning down is like the phoenix firebird that crashes in flames and is reborn from the ashes. I remember a saying from Joan of Arc that the crash of the phoenix is a way to be released from prison.

I anticipate restless sleep. After ten minutes of fitful thoughts I rollover and the world around me moves to a distant place. It's mostly exhaustion, but also giving into Julie's decision and knowing there is nothing I can do about the clinic, except rebuild it.

The first light has not come yet when I awake. I turn on the bedside lamp and walk out of the backyard cottage and through the backdoor to kitchen. I move through the house and turn on the porch light. I pick up the *Press Democrat* on the front stoop. On the cover page is a picture of the clinic in ashes. The photo jolts me. The article says arson is *suspected*. I love the way newspapers put in these caveats when in actuality they don't exist.

I look up from the paper, caught off guard to see my old piece of junk car parked across the street. I walk over and put my hand on the hood of the engine. It's warm. Julie must have driven the heap here and run over fifteen miles home. A regular person wouldn't have done this, but her? Her chance to get rid of my car and an excuse to get a workout in. I tightly twist the newspaper, thinking she will use the Joe Rodota Trail as a conduit to get home. Homeless people camp off the trail near town. She can outrun anything, but that doesn't sound like a failsafe plan. I move up to the porch and open the mailbox. The car key is inside.

• • •

I'm ushered into the meeting room. The members of the WBC are sitting in the same seats. It reminds me of Desmond Morris's *territorial imperative* where ground is staked out and kept as a matter of possession. Miles leads off. "You look a thousand percent healthier than when we last saw you, regardless of what's happening."

I can barely focus. And then I look Miles in the eye to pull myself together. "As the hackneyed saying goes, it's a work in progress. My experience in treatment was...it woke me up to the realities of what I have to fess up to and face, leaving my farcical history in the dust, while keeping it in mind while I move on."

"Well Jesus, that's a little different than the last time we saw you." Miles shows a welcoming expression. "Let me lay out a few things before we get started. You were put on medical leave status with your hospital privileges. You were not suspended, which would have generated an 805 report to the medical board. So, as far as we know, the medical board hasn't been informed about you. And we haven't heard anything from the DEA investigators. Now, the hospital is operating under a different administrative structure and we answer to the Medical Exec Committee which, as you know, are the top dogs when it comes to medical privileges."

"The medical board part is a relief. And I hope it goes well with the Medical Exec Committee. The DEA people made contact with my office during my absence and they were advised that the clinic was simply closed down for a period, with zero explanation...the DEA...one of my loose ends." I scratch an annoying itch on my chest. "My hope is to strike a bit of luck and they vanish as quickly as they appeared."

Miles says, "We received the practice assessment. What's your take on it?"

I give a glance around the meeting table and at all the WBC members. "The assessment is well-defined and I will comply with it." I'm pleased I can say this to my peers. Now I'm establishing a foothold to gain their respect someday. An acquiescent smile runs across my face. "Did they tell you about the five-year monitoring I have to engage in and my participation in community self-help meetings?"

"Yes. And we would have mandated this if they hadn't." Miles has a business-like expression. "We have to rely on the physician monitoring program, since well being committees are not in the position to provide day-to-day monitoring, other than making sure that your practice at the hospital is okay. We will periodically meet with you and get the reports from the monitoring program."

"That makes sense." I nod. "I assume that most of you saw the piece in the *Press Democrat* about the arson at my clinic."

There's head nodding around the table and a few WBC members say, "Yes." Having my clinic burn down is such a loss and setback. There's a sense of defeat. But strangely the adversity makes me feel unstuck. I think about what I told Miles that it could be an opportunity to have a better clinic.

Miles gets the committee back to what we were discussing. "So, Glen, let's finish with the plan."

"The plan? Well, I feel like I'm doing well with respect to drug use, and I don't necessarily think the onsite monitoring is needed. But I also think it is a part of providing assurances that I continue to not be impaired and demonstrate to the professional community that I'm fit to practice. They also recommended that I terminate the chronic pain clinic, since my motivation to have it in the first place was to divert drugs for self-use." My hands are clasped in front of me on the table. I lean back in my chair and run my hand across my chest. "I'm completely onboard with this recommendation because their assessment about the clinic hinged on my drug seeking behavior. I don't need to put myself in harm's way."

All the members of the WBC nod.

Dr. Hickman raises his bushy eyebrows. "Glen, I'd like to look beyond your professional practice related to addiction. You staying clean depends on many elements. In addition to the healthcare professional monitoring group and twelve-step groups, what else do you plan to do?"

I lean forward. "I'll connect with the healthcare professional twelve-step group."

"So, see you there." Hickman narrows his eyes. "I think it's fair game to ask you about the personal scene. Is your wife on board with your recovery?" He interlaces the fingers of both hands and rests his forearms on the table. "I've been in recovery for over twenty years. Remembering when I returned treatment...well, my wife and I had one hell of an adjustment. I expected the world around me would be automatically forgiving. But it was like I hit a brick wall. The major thing I learned is that it's easier for the addict to occupy a place in recovery than the world around him to be forgiving. If I was five minutes late getting home, I must have been using. There was her suspiciousness and looking for the telltale signs of use, like giving me a kiss so she could check out whether my eyes were pinpoint from opiate use." Hickman tilts his body toward me. "How is it going with Julie?"

It's like a monster is whispering in my ear wanting to tell Hickman to get fucked. I recognize I'm reactive. He's not an ogre. And I'm thinking about the difference between honesty and openness. How much to put out here? "I was gone for over three months," and I explain what happened. When I stop the room is silent. I dig my fingers into my thighs. "At this point I don't know if she'll reconcile. She doesn't trust me. In fact, she initially said that I'm on probation, but now it's like I'm six feet under the surface with her, and without any possibility of coming back topside."

Hickman says, "Is that putting at any risk for—"

"No. I had been tense a long time because of my marital offenses. But, yeah, all hell broke loose when she found out about me violating the limits of where we stood together. I'd like to point to some justification to fault her. Nothing legitimizes the damage I've done. Right now I'm sucking it up and I wish I could spit it out, but I can't and keep on swallowing. Miles and his wife have been very kind and have taken me in until I can make other arrangements."

Miles cocks his head down and sideways. I expect he'll be sympathetic. "If there is something that is beyond the scope of the WBC that you have to personally have to work out with Julie, you do not need to tell us, but we will ask you to find the appropriate venue to take care of your business. Unfinished business festers, and festering can create a life of its own that leads to relapse." Miles nods once. "That makes sense to you, doesn't it?"

I suck in a quick breath and let it go. "It does."

Hickman pushes it. "When I was using, I was a flirtatious rake. Lines that were drawn by someone didn't exist for me. I dismissed everything, taking what I wanted. That's what I'm hearing you say right now. And I agree with Miles. We do not need to know the specifics. We do need to know that you will progress with your recovery, otherwise there isn't recovery."

I shift in my chair, knowing Hickman wants me to be accountable. "What's clear is that I'm powerless with respect to using psychoactive substances. But I have the power to take action in the rest of my life."

Hickman stretches his shoulders back. "And you need to make a moral inventory as part of your step work? This is my recommendation. Don't make an immoral inventory of how you have messed up. Make it more dynamic. Outline what your morals are or what you would like them to be, and show how the consequences of your drug use have compromised your morals or put in conflict the morals that you're inspired to have. This includes a relationship inventory. This will also help fuel the work on the steps dealing with character defects and your amends work. Take this to heart. It will deepen your recovery work." I hadn't heard this spin on the moral inventory. It's simple, but brilliant.

"I didn't expect this today. I expected to be slapped around about how I will be watched when I am at the hospital and what arrangements have been made for onsite monitoring for my clinic work."

Miles says, "We already have that worked out. We want to know what your plans are when your clinic pulls through. I'll be your worksite monitor here at the hospital and in the operating suite. And I'll expect people to report to me any unusual occurrences. We will coordinate with the monitoring program and they will give us updates on your progress." Miles squints. "We know your marriage is iffy. And we expect you to focus on all aspects of your recovery, including your personal and professional lives."

Hickman says. "The clinic made quite a front page splash. What's the impact?"

"I'm still in shock. I own the property, though getting money from the insurance company for the rebuild is still fuzzy. In the meantime, I'll try to hook up with someone's practice, or work at the surgery center and the hospital."

Hickman says, "You're riddled with transition. Newly home, your marriage and a practice that's up in the air. Call me anytime, and I don't care what time it is. The article said they suspect arson. Have they turned up who might have done it?"

"Newspapers seem to use those ambiguous words like *suspect*. I spoke with a detective and he said that it was arson for sure. You understand that when a building completely burns down and the fire department is just a few blocks away. The firefighters instantly knew it was arson."

"Let's hope for the best."

The members of the WBC stand. I rise out my seat. And then the unexpected. Miles comes to me and gives me a hug. Hickman does the same. These are the people who will be looking over my shoulder. The people I am responsible to. They aren't cops. They're real people who didn't give up on me.

Hickman says, "Glen, do you know what the best monitoring is and what makes the work of the WBC most effective?"

"Being compliant?"

"No. You working a damn good recovery program. Because if you're doing that, you'll do the right things."

● ● ●

I leave the hospital and sit motionless in my crappy beat out car. I thought I'd be judged. Prosecuted. My body feels fuller, and curiously it feels hollow. My eyes water. I want to do the right things. And I'm afraid of myself.

CHAPTER EIGHTEEN

I call a colleague, Stu Fogerty, who has slowed down to a snail's pace at his plastics surgical suite. He knows about the clinic being in ashes, as does everyone in the doc community. When we meet, I tell him about the sorted minutiae of my life. He nods his thick platinum haired head—a forgiving wise old soul. Or maybe he just needs someone to help with the clinic overhead so he isn't so financially zapped. My mandated reduced reentry schedule dovetails with his. We shake on the deal.

I fear that my surgical skills have become stale rusty. At one uncertain moment I imagine my ability to operate has evaporated all together. The practice assessment permits me to go back to work, my reduced schedule makes being clean a prominent force

An unanticipated revelation emerges, like light beam through dense murky clouds. I need time to reacclimatize in my home territory before stepping into the clinical theater.

The absence of running since before Iraq makes me feel kind of flimsy. I need to reclaim my physical self. I stretch out all those taut muscles to prepare for a run. I run two eight-minute miles. That feels like a marathon, but it will get easier. And then the post-run muscle stretch.

The physical movement gave me perspective, considering getting back to what I was trained to do. And having an advantage now—being healthier and having consciousness of the world around me. I need to accept the staff's reactions to me when I return to the hospital and at the clinic. I can't control people's responses to my reentry to work. The only guy whose behavior I can put into balance is me. I have to own myself. Claiming myself is claiming the part of me that still wants to use drugs. The part of me that wants to be dishonest and manipulate. The part of me that slips into fantasies of philandering and turns fantasy into an actuality.

I'm sick of myself-indulgent insights and preoccupations. I wish I didn't have to do it. But keeping conscious is one of the necessities of keeping my patchwork self-sewn together.

I don't want to have a goddamn shadow. Who does? But it's there. The shadow is permanently sewn onto the underbelly human being existence. And people who aren't concerned about their shadow side, douse persons around them with evil doings, either unwittingly or by commission.

And the larger part of the overarching shadow side operates unconsciously and gains momentum until I sabotage myself. Erase it, pretend it doesn't exist, cut it off like an appendage? All that will do will allow it to breathe, while I close my mind off to its power of survival and that it will ultimately prevail if I don't acknowledge the menacing hold it has on me. A lucid revelation comes to me. Don't try to throw the shadow away. Own it. Work with it on a daily basis. It's not going away. And realizing its power takes its power away.

● ● ●

Jackie picks up my call on her cell phone. "You've heard—"

"Who hasn't?" Jackie is perpetually clued in to what is going on, but what she does about it is a different thing.

"By the way, hello."

"I was waiting for that." There's anticipation and relief in her voice.

"You remember Stu Fogerty?"

"Sure. Kindly old gentleman."

"He's slowed down, opening up a space for me at his place until the clinic can be rebuilt. It's welcomed to help with his overhead." I cough to clear my throat. "Did you pick up another job?"

"Nope." I wonder if Jackie has been on hold, waiting for me.

"You up for a trial run?"

"A trial run of what?"

She must be on the fence. A throb briefly shoots in my neck. I take a breath. "Working in the surgery suite. Anything extracurricular is a past done deal."

"I heard through the grapevine about—"

"Julie?"

"Yeah. Temporary or permanent?" The message comes through her voice that we could possibly be a match.

"No way of knowing. Things are distant right now. I want to ask you something. Did the police talk to you about the clinic burning down?"

"Yeah, a Detective Nace. He treated me as a suspect. That dispelled after about ten minutes of talking to me. He got the picture."

"Good. That's how I expected it to go."

"I heard about you. Did you hear about me?"

Something is about to explode. "I'm not as tuned into the grapevine as you."

"I gave Tom the boot. He isn't living here anymore."

"Where'd he go?"

"He's staying with his frail old mommy who doesn't know shit from Shinola. Tom is sleeping in a little box of a room at her place in a white trash trailer park. I've been there before. It's a cluttered old lady's place. Smells of long-lived sickness."

"What went on between Tom and you?"

"Told him I couldn't live with his doper life anymore. He said that he promised to cut down. What bullshit. That was it. I said his raggedy ass was out of there."

"Did anything come up about—"

"Us? Verbatim he asked if, 'I'd fucked you.'" Jackie pauses for a split second. "I said, 'You bet your booty baby. He's a lot better fuck than you with that limp worthless member.'"

"His reaction?"

"At first he smoldered, was restless and agitated. And then he blew up and threw stuff around the house. He came at me and grabbed my throat. I punched him in the stomach knocking the wind out of him and the twit doubled over. I called 911. The police arrested him for domestic violence. I went down to the courthouse and filed a restraining order. It's now in effect." Jackie has residual taut sound, but also comes across as relieved.

"Did the police talk to him about the arson at the clinic?"

"I don't know. He isn't allowed to call or see me."

I shudder. "Do you think—"

"Glen, Tom is unpredictable." This lets me know what's running through her mind.

"And what about giving it go to work together again?"

"I've got something in the hopper. But there's a good likelihood that we could get back into the work saddle again. Okay if I let you know in a couple of days?"

"That'll work."

• • •

I attend a twelve-step meeting that isn't listed in the directory. It is the healthcare professional twelve-step meeting which is attend by physicians and dentists and pharmacists and nurses and a smattering of others linked to healthcare. No last names, I'm just Glen. Hickman gives me a tie to the group. I look around at who's attending the meeting. There are faces I expected to see, and then a few surprises.

They ask me to speak, which shocks me because I'm a newcomer. I tell a sketch of my story, and it is somewhat ubiquitous for an addict-doctor. And I take a risk. I relate my insight about recovery and the shadow. And I see a lot of head nodding, like this is a key to grasp in the early phase of pulling life together after years living as a dark character.

Several people come to me after the meeting. Some shake my hand, others hug me. And I feel welcome—the familiarity of what we share in common.

Hickman sticks around. "Is there anything else I can do for you, Glen? I mean, aside from the WBC." He takes out his card and writes his cell phone number on it and gives me the card.

"I appreciated what you had to say at the WBC. Would you consider being my sponsor, at least on a temporary basis?"

"Sure. I can have two roles. The WBC checks on how you're functioning as a physician. Being your sponsor—temporary or permanent—will be more personal. And if there is ever a conflict between the two roles, we will have to give up one or the other. Does that fit for you?"

"Sure. And thanks."

"I'm available anytime by telephone. And let's meet face-to-face weekly."

I have a secure sensation making the changeover from treatment to becoming involved with recovery where I live. I'm slightly undone that Hickman has so graciously stepped forward. "You're a good guy, Hickman."

"Good to hear gratitude come from you—a key piece of the work you'll have to do." Hickman purses his lips for a second, then says, "I know you have completed this already, but I'd like you to redo the first step and share it with me next week to establish a basis for our relationship. And let something new come up."

"Okay. That sounds like the place to start." We make nuts-and-bolts arrangements about time a place to meet. And we say goodnight.

I slip into the seat of my car. I think about the exchanges with Hickman. Just maybe I'll start to get shaped up, whether Julie is in or out of the picture. It's like a sensitivity I've never had, and now I feel textures and surfaces, and see shades and vividness of color.

● ● ●

Dawn's earliest golden-yellow light pours through the east window of the cottage. I slip out the door, onto the street—a three-mile run at a seven minute and forty-five second pace. I cleanup and go into the kitchen. Carla says the coffee is freshly brewed. We drink a cup together. And she tells me what her tuition was at Cal Berkeley, in comparison to the monster amount they paid for their kids' university costs. And then the conversation swings around to the clinic. She hints that I'm dodging seeing the damage first hand. Carla offers to go to the site with me. I think it's time. Her observation tipped the balance.

I choose to make a solitary trip to where the clinic used to stand. A mass of scorched rubble. And the yellow police tape stops me from tromping through the remains of what I once knew. I have a sinking sensation when I spot the carcass of my thirty-five thousand dollar operating table. And then I imagine my keepsake hand sculpture being torched to ash. And I visualize the patient that carved it for me, Chip Inman, and think of what a guy he is and the memory of our connection.

My cell phone rings. I think it is going to be Nace or Hickman. I push the answer mode on the phone's screen. It's Julie. There's something startling in her voice. She sounds sweet. She asks me to come to the house. Driving over to the house the two sides of my ambivalent mind are like a tennis ball being slapped back and forth across the net. Is she going to beat me up more or negotiate for reconciliation?

I put my hand on to doorknob to open the front door. And then I stop and knock. Julie is standing on the other side, posed. My skin tingles. Feeling dumbstruck after over a hundred days of celibacy I say, "Sweet

Jesus, that outfit is so see-through, did you consider using Saran Wrap instead so it'd be more diaphanous?"

This has to be a message that she wants me back. Julie's teddy exposes everything that's delicious. Julie slips her hands over my shoulders and pulls me in. The room's light catches in the gloss of her lips. I'm caught up. We fall into the luscious immediacy of the moment.

"Julie, I've never seen you so aggressive."

"What happened just happened. Emotions flooded together into a blur. The dam broke."

"Does this mean—"

"It doesn't mean anything, other than I needed a release."

"Just a little incomparable to how you were when you picked me up at the airport."

"Same fire, different airing."

"You puzzle me."

"Think about how unglued and lost I am and everything seems so muddy right now."

"What can I do?"

"Get the fuck out and don't come back."

"What?"

"Call it a swansong or you being on the other end of a yoyo string. See you later...sometime...maybe never." I never knew this about Julie. She is capable of revenge sex.

CHAPTER NINETEEN

I drive into the parking lot and slip my less than ritzy car in the space with the new painted sign marked, "Dr. Coyle." We don't have any cases scheduled today at Stu Fogerty's clinic. Only Jackie and the receptionist are there. For almost four months I haven't set foot in a clinic where I'm the clinician. I sit in my vehicle for a few minutes, gathering myself up to go inside.

Jackie and the receptionist are gossiping about something I don't catch because I'm distracted. They turn toward me. Their eyes brighten and they smile. Jackie comes and gives me a hug. It feels too good, which makes me feel rotten.

It's different with Stu not being there. I check around the place. It smells musty, with an overlay of antiseptic fetidness and Betadine. Stu's office has pockets of clutter, like old issues of medical journals that haven't been read and stacks of unfilled hard copy charts, since it appears that he has not converted over to electronic charting. A lot of old guys can't shift to the electronic mode. Thank god the operating suite and waiting room sparkle. But the faded old Audubon bird prints give the place a stodgy feeling.

The receptionist says, "Hey there, welcome back stranger." She has a tittering chuckle. She's nervous and seems to want to blend in to me returning to the office. "You had tons of mail. No worries now. Up in smoke. So there's no carting in the wheelbarrows full of the stuff you have to go through."

"Good to see you again, too." And then the key question because of the fire. "What about recovering the accounts receivable?"

"All the plastics cases are square." She squints. "And there are some outstanding reconstructive cases, but I can recreate those accounts through the hospital since they still have a record of your surgeries there." She frowns. "The chronic pain patients...well—"

"Forget 'em." I take in and expel a breath. It's like it would be bad news to have to still have connections with those patients. And I'll just suck up the loss of revenue. "I've already called Tom Ferguson. He'll continue to manage the chronic pain patients. We'll send them a tidy little form letter saying they are permanently transferred to him because I am closing the chronic pain part of my practice."

Jackie's eyes are fixed on the receptionist. "It's going to take some swimming upstream to get used to these temporary digs. I've already navigated around the surgical suite and it pretty much looks like a snap. Glen, I'll bet you need a chance to land." She looks at me. "Have I got that right?"

Jackie can still be in the caretaker mode with me. "It feels foreign being back in a clinic and double that because it's Stu's place."

Jackie walks ahead of me to Stu's office. I don't remember the intensity of her butt's smooth sexy sway. Was I too loaded? Or is she doing it right now for my benefit? I sit at the desk. Jackie stands in front of it, the flat palms of her hands on her hips with her fingers pointing downward. She arches her back, jutting her chest out. I don't remember her doing that either.

She says, "For now we don't have to worry about changing the security codes for the safe. It's just sitting over there in the ashes and the dial has probably melted off. I had already gone through the medications and wasted the excess ones that you were using. So if the usable contents for the clinic are still intact the chore of wasting the overflow surplus drugs has been taken care of. For future reference does that give you any reassurances?" I get that she mixes being flirty with the set-up for me to be safe.

"Sure. Thanks for taking sewing that one up. I should have asked you make those changes while I was away."

"Good." Jackie looks over my head. She sighs, and then reengages me with her eyes. "How do you feel about being back in a clinic, Glen, even if it isn't actually yours?"

"Frankly, I feel triggered to use drugs, since the medical setting is the scene of the crime."

"Surprised?"

"No, I anticipated it. And I have the out of leaving anytime I need to. Today is the first day back. I predicted feeling triggered to use drugs by being here. Just need to get desensitized. I had decided that triggers are part of coming back and I'd work at living with it, expecting the pressure to lessen."

"How is it for you?"

"Good to be here. And with you again. Jackie is still for a second. "Glen, could we—"

The receptionist rings me, "Dr. Glen, your old buddy Susan is on the phone."

I tense-up, thinking now what? I push the flashing light button on the phone. "Hello, Susan."

"I read the in the paper about your clinic burning down." I wonder if she is a suspect. "Reading the article gave me a jump on what I've been putting off. Dr. Werner made a good referral for the DBT treatment. After a few months of work in therapy, I recognize my hostilities toward you and the rhinoplasty were misplaced and I had things confused."

"I'm pleased you see that." I try to be as neutral as possible so I don't kick start riling her up again.

"Plus, I'm starting to understand the affect my tirades have on people."

"I don't suffer from being faint of heart, but I'll tell you that our conversation rattled me." I downplay how talking to her actually capsized my emotions.

"I know. That's why I'm calling. To clean things up." Susan is silent for a second. "My nose looks just right, and now I'm working on how to handle things in my life."

"Good to hear about your progress, Susan."

"Thank you, Dr. Coyle. Goodbye." Good she kept it short, otherwise she might have unraveled.

The receptionist comes to my office and raps on the door. "Dr. Glen, those DEA guys are back."

"You're shitting me."

"*No. They're here.*"

"Show Kilgore and Penny in. Let's get this over with."

I stand when they enter the office. "Haven't seen you two for a while. Have a seat." I lower my head to signal that fun is not on their agenda. "What remains unresolved in your investigation?" My eyes widen. "Oh, by the way, you never contacted me about the results of the drug screen. All negative, right?"

Kilgore says, "Correct, Dr. Coyle, it was negative."

"You obviously caught wind of my clinic burning down. So, you knew where I was by the message on my voicemail?"

Kilgore says, "Yes, I heard about it, and then looked up the newspaper article online. So it was arson. Did the police turn up the culprit who committed the crime?"

"They've interrogated a couple of people who were false leads. Nothing has turned up yet."

The two of them being here is a clue that I am going to get fucked today. "Back to my question. What do we have to conclude since the drug screen was negative?"

Kilgore continues, "You just happened to not use for a few days and it came up clean." Kilgore dismisses my question. "We understand that you were on medical leave for over three months. What was that about?"

"What was it about? It was about medical leave. And under the technical mandates of HIPPA the nature of medical leave is protected, and the only exceptions to the confidentiality around it is if I would be a danger to anyone or to myself. And frankly, my medical leave doesn't fall in either category. So, you can read that my medical leave is my business and not subject to the inquiry of your investigation." I feel cool and smooth as a slick piece of ice. If I told those guys were I was, it would be a masochistic knife that I would drive straight into my own chest.

"Were you in treatment for chemical dependency?"

I cross my arms across my chest. "Mr. Kilgore and Mr. Penny, I don't believe that you heard me. My rights to medical treatment are under the sanctions of HIPPA which supersedes your investigative authority, but I am sure you are informed about the mandates of these regulations."

"Do you think you need to get legal counsel?"

I sigh, knowing they are trying to intimidate me. "The regulations are clearly spelled out, but I'll get back to you on that one. Legal counsel? I doubt it, if you have heard what I've said. But you can give me your card should I need to contact you." I know damn well that I'm not going to call them.

Penny takes a card from the inside breast pocket of his shiny bargain basement sports coat, stands and hands it to me and returns to his seat.

Kilgore's face is a blank screen. At night he probably practices his scary penetrating stare. I'm not going to be unnerved. "Are there any other concerns you have that I can help you with?" I swallow. "I just returned to the office and have a lot of business to cover."

Kilgore says, "So, what is the progress with the management of your pain clinic?"

"Over the past couple of months I've had the opportunity to think about the priorities of my medical practice. The pain clinic has become more of a nuisance than satisfying clinical work, at least for me. Others might find it more fulfilling. I have decided to work strictly in surgery, doing reconstructive surgery at the hospital or cosmetic surgery here in the clinic. The pain patients have been referred to another physician, Dr. Henning. He's the physician who I covered when he was on medical leave, covered me while I was gone and the patients transferred to his practice. Easy transition and nothing problematic."

"What medications will you have on hand in the clinic?"

"The primary medications will be for anesthesia and a limited number of pain medications for postoperative care until the patient can fill his or her prescription. We will also have some benzodiazepines for preoperative anxiety on the day of the procedure. Our medication supply has already been thinned out to what we need by the nurse practitioner who works here. But that's academic because they are in a safe buried in the rubble of my old clinic. It's hard to know if the safe's heat tolerance kept the medications intact or not. My guess is that they are history."

"We would like to verify that."

I stand and go to the door. Jackie is in the hallway and I ask her to come in the office. I tell Jackie what transpired with Kilgore and Penny, then say the DEA investigators want her to confirm it.

Kilgore looks at Jackie, "Is that accurate?"

"Yes. I knew prior to Dr. Coyle's return that the clinic practice would be revised to handle only surgery. And I took the initiative to review the medications and waste the excess ones that will no longer be needed. As an aside, I am happy with Dr. Coyle's decision because for me the pain clinic was a taxing part of my position here and frankly empty for me personally, since it has never been in my interest area. In other words, I feel relieved that we will no longer be treating pain patients and surgery will be the sole identity of the clinic."

"And you are under no threat of employment retaliation to be telling us this?"

"Are you kidding? No. Many of the pain patients were bothering us with wanting early refills or saying they lost their scripts and it was weary dealing with their manipulative behavior. Granted, most of the pain patients were aboveboard, but the few drug seekers made life miserable." Jackie politely smiles. "The change is welcomed."

I alternate looking at Kilgore and Penny directly in the eye, trying to determine if they're buying what we're saying. "The pain clinic, in fact, was quite fragmenting for the clinic and made for a lot of confusion." I take a couple of easy breaths, and think no shit it was fragmenting and made for a lot of confusion. "The staff and I are looking forward to having a unified vision for the services we provide." Now this is judicious bullshit at its finest.

Kilgore remains deadpan, "Alright for now. I will need to consult with my supervisor about these developments." He readjusts his bodily posture. "We'll be in touch if we need to pursue this further."

I straighten my tie. "Please let us know if there's any other information we can provide you. Hopefully we're done. Now if you'll please excuse us, we have to shape up the office." And then I extend a business-like handshake and forge a formal smile, all the while I am thinking, fuck you.

Jackie's body has the presence of a curtsy, and her beguiling expressive smile has to neutralize Kilgore and Penny, and if not, their testosterone level must be at subzero. She waves her arm past her body, pointing her hand and extended fingers toward the open office door. Jackie ushers them to the front door to deposit them on the street in front of the office.

She comes back to my office. "Well?"

"Did you mean what you said, or were you pacifying them?"

"I meant what I said *and* I was pacifying them." Jackie leans forward, her lips part. "Like before, I was eavesdropping. Jesus, you really went toe-to-toe with them."

"I was shooting from the hip. It was a bluff. I have no idea whether DEA agents who suspect drug diversion have access through legal means to chemical dependency treatment records."

"Are you going to get legal advice?" Jackie makes it obvious that she's still threatened.

"Well, what I said worked. Or it seemed to...I'll wait."

"What's going through your head right now?"

"First day back at work. Back in what feels like my old drug-using stomping grounds. Triggered to the max. Then those assholes arrive on the doorstep, and that's after Susan calls and she is contrite because of how she worked me over. Standing up to them? Well, it was standing up for myself. Jackie, you really caught onto this. At base, I'm working at not feeling crappy about myself. Today? There was the glimmer of not being the piece of shit I've always thought myself to be. Backing those guys down was part of it. And you were a champ by what you said to them."

"Me, too. We're both up against a lot, just in our own ways."

"Jackie before the assholes came, you asked, 'If we could...' but you didn't have the chance to finish. What was is it?'

"Let's have one more go at it. I'd like to call it goodbye sex."

"You know what I think? It'd be hello sex." I can't help but smile at her. "Would I like to have sex with you? Totally. But we'd fall into to blurring things between us again. It would be absolutely the worst thing for both of us, right?"

"Too right. And you saying it'd be hello sex puts my head in a new direction. I'm surprised because I have the sense of being closer to you right now, like hands off is the decent thing to do."

"I love working with you and don't want to mess that up. It means that much to me."

"I get it. Don't mix things up like we did before."

"You got Tom out of the house. And you got the message that you can't bank on me. Say, have you thought of another man? Not somebody you have to take care of, but somebody who will take care of you, instead."

"It passed through in a flash. I guess I'm not ready, yet. Seems too unfamiliar."

● ● ●

I call Hickman. We discuss the first moments back in the clinic and my drug cravings kicking up. He thought I did well with the DEA agents. The item about Jackie was brand new. I gave him the backstory. Today Jackie and I tested boundaries. He reminds me about our meeting to go over powerlessness and unmanageability—fitting for today. Hickman says that just because you're powerless over drugs, you don't have to roll over and play dead when you are up against big stakes, like having the DEA breathing down your neck. He thought my fuck you attitude saved me.

And then his question: do I deserve more or less, and more or less of what? I'm baffled by the question's fuzziness and have to think it over.

I pick up the phone again and give calls to Dave Singleton and then to Mike Lyke. We talk about Jackie's bid for goodbye sex, and my saying it would be the start of new chancy twists and turns in our lives. And for me her touch would angle me toward teetering on a dangerous precipice. And worse I might step into the cataclysmic illusion of looking good again. My sleight of hand thinking can hoodwink me. But by talking with these buddies I'm helped with honestly putting one foot solidly in front of the other.

CHAPTER TWENTY

Being stalled by the insurance underwriter gets to me. It's complicated. The clock ticks and ticks and there's no insurance payout.

I knew a nurse at the hospital whose house burned down. I listened to her devastation of losing everything and all her family pictures—not having anything except a few threads on her back. A lifetime of possessions gone, turned into cinders.

The clinic has a different sentimentality. Despite it being the prison of my past because of my drug use, there're all the clinic's life-changing transformational surgeries. The memories are close, and they are detached because of the absence—my own old turf jerked away. One more ambiguous transition that dictates uncertainty.

I do research. I call the insurance adjuster. There's nothing stated in the policy that rescinds insurance coverage if there is arson. He tells me fraud is rampant in commercial property when arson is involved. I say okay. My wife and I are named on the policy. We have both spoken to Detective Nace who cleared us of being suspects. The adjuster spells out that the insurance company has its own investigation process. Talk, talk and more talk, and he finally budges that he sees that I will inevitably be awarded a settlement. He adds a tagline. The arsonist isn't found in the majority of cases.

I swivel my chair around and look out the window at a shaded flowering white rhododendron. A name comes to mind, Silas Dawson. He is a San Francisco architect who specializes in designing hospitals and surgical suites—a mix of upscale modern architecture and the latest medical technology. The telephone company information line connects me to his office. I'm put through to him. The specifics about the clinic burning down are gone over in about two minutes. He tells me of two clients that had similar situations that finally settled after twisty insurance company negotiations. We set a date to go over the building site and to discuss preliminary plans. Silas says he would do some initial AutoCAD architectural renderings after he checks the site to stimulate some design ideas. I put the receiver in the cradle. There's a burst of enthusiasm that maybe life is more settled, regardless of all the pockets of uncertainty.

● ● ●

Jackie and the receptionist are busy scurrying around setting up the office and surgical suite for our style of practice. Stu had given the okay to change the setup to suit my work. I motion to Jackie to come into the office. I close the door behind us. "You know the arsonist hasn't been apprehended, yet. Do you think—"

"What?"

"You know."

"That it could be—"

"That's what I've been thinking."

We speak in code, paralleling what's on our minds. Jackie puts her hands on her hips. "Well, I don't think there's any hard evidence. Just supposition. At most an inference."

"I think it's more solid than that…don't you think?"

Jackie lets out a breath. "If we shook-up ideas and guesses in a bottle and spilled them out on the desktop, what do you think we'd have?"

"The answer."

"I'm scared."

"Of what?"

"What will happen?"

"The complications with the insurance company might get smoothed out. You think he might retaliate against you?"

"That's why I'm scared."

"Sure. Take your time. But do me a favor. Don't take forever."

"Alright, that's fair." Jackie turns to walk out of the office. She stops and pivots on her heels. "I decided. Well, maybe I had already decided, but I needed the shove to get moving. It's not in me to call the police and fink on Tom. You do it. I dread having to talk with the police, but guaranteed I will be forced to do it." Jackie's last statement has a grating and sour note. She leaves the office and closes the door behind her.

I take the card out of my breast pocket and lay it in the desk. I pick up the receiver and dial the phone number. He answers. I say, "Hello, Detective Nace. This is Dr. Glen Coyle. Do you have a minute?"

CHAPTER TWENTY-ONE

The receptionist shows Debbie Brunner to my office. I stand and motion for her to take a seat in front of my desk. Her hands fidget and she's clumsy sitting down. Debbie's face has a fragile, an about to crumble look—lines drawn across her forehead and her eyebrows arched up in the center, and an uneasy twitchiness around her eyes.

After a career of countless surgeries, my four-month layoff digs under the skin of my confidence. Can I still do it? This morning I see a woman for a pre-surgical consultation for a mastectomy reconstruction procedure.

In past preoperative consultations, I dismissed the patient's edginess, while I'm thinking about the surgical outcome. But I always gave the patient a realistic appraisal of what to expect. Today is new. I don't hide behind my doctor's guise, and protect myself by putting up the barrier my desk. Something comes over me. I move to the chair next to Debbie.

"May I call you Debbie, or would you prefer Mrs. Brunner?"

"Oh, please call me Debbie." The twitchiness around her eyes settles down.

"I've reviewed your chart and the extent of the margins required for your mastectomy. The tumors were significant, but I must say that the surgeon's work seems effectively done, as far as I can tell."

Debbie grabs the top of my forearm. Her chin trembles. "Dr. Coyle, I'm scared." Debbie's voice quakes. She stutters getting through the few words she says.

"I'd say what you've been through so far is near the top of the list of scary things for a woman. It makes you question life. It makes you question womanhood. And if you've kissed life in the past, you wonder if you should be kissing life goodbye. But based on what I've seen in the chart, your prognosis looks good and I think you could work more on being optimistic." I cautiously smile, not knowing this woman.

"Other women who have gone through the operation understand." She lowers and shakes her head. "You're the only other person who seems to get it. Not my husband, though he's been nice, not my kids. Nobody." Debbie slides her hand down my forearm and wraps her fingers around the top of my hand. I turn my hand over, and our palms touch.

"Thank you for saying that. I'll tell you what, Debbie, I'll do my best. I'd like to say that I can make you brand new." The nervousness comes back imagining the scalpel in my hand after being away from surgery so long. "But my hope is that the improvement you experience will help pull you back to your life as you knew it. And a big part of that is what you do to have the life you want. It will be different. And just possibly it could be better." I'm connected with Debbie and it's fresh, after being so distant with patients in the past. "You see, you've been through something tragic and survived. That gives you a different perspective on life. And just possibly you could be emotionally richer, depending on how you come out on the other side."

Debbie's taut face softens. There's a hint of a glow. And she looks as if having deeper meaning in life because of being a cancer survivor is a possibility.

We stand. She hugs me and I hold her. "I'll do the best I can. That's a promise. And let's hope for the best. The rest is up to you."

"Thank you, Dr. Coyle. I'm glad you're the person doing the surgery. I promise to do my part, too." Debbie pauses. "Well, to be honest, let's say I'll work on it."

Debbie leaves, and somehow her presence is still in the room. I return to the desk. I've been such an egotistical and arrogant bastard in the past. And only now do I realize how I've disregarded the angst patients go through. I guess I gave myself permission, because I wasn't that much different than a lot of other surgeons. And there were the empathic times in Iraq when I was emotionally engaged when part of a soldier's face was shot off. We have to be full of ourselves to have the guts to do what we do for people. I can see that now, but in these times I can add a greater degree of humanness to more completely treat the patient. That means one thing. To be more invested. And it's emotionally riskier.

I pick up the phone and call Hickman. "Sorry to bug you two days in a row."

"It's okay with me. In fact, I'd like you to call me every day for the next thirty days, and at least leave me a message if I don't answer. That way I'll know that you're invested with me and then I can invest in you."

Investment is the word of the day. I recount the consultation appointment with Debbie—and how I astonished myself by becoming in tune with her fear

Hickman says, "Good to hear. And you're in for the ride. That's one kick I've gotten out of physicians in your position."

Suddenly there's pressure. Because of some sort of mandate to be tuned into the nuances of patients' needs. Being the old self-centered way was easier than connecting with the patient.

"Hey Glen, you got quiet on me."

"There was kind of a strain, like needing to be the constantly tuned-in clinician."

Hickman laughs and he seems to be laughing at me. "God, chill out. Glen, we don't do perfect, so give it a rest. Watch what happens. I'll see you later on. My next patient arrived."

• • •

Today is my first reappearance at the hospital operating room. I review the procedural plan for Debbie. Can I still do surgery? Then the angst about reentry. I question whether the docs and nurses and support staff want me back. I struggle with the shame. I want to pull back from it because if I get too swamped I'll dose myself. I calculate what I have to do to get each individual person comfortable with me. To get back to the OR, I need to be aboveboard and free of deceit.

• • •

I sit in front of the hospital parked in a space designated for physicians. And I beginning to hate my pattern of thinking in my car. I think of canceling the case with Debbie. And I stop myself, anticipating the anesthesiologist is already preparing her. I look at my wristwatch. I'd better go. All eyes will be on me. I walk through the front door. There are familiar support staff who nod and smile. I make my way to change to a surgical gown and head cover. There are other physicians getting organized for surgery.

One doc, Frank Rhoads, who I've known for years says, "Hi Glen, haven't seen you for a while. We must have missed or you've been too tied up at the clinic. Jesus, I've got one hell of a case today. A resection that's going to take forever. They've been working my butt off and you would not believe the on-call and having to operate the next day with major sleep deprivation." He throws on his scrubs. "Shit, sometimes I can hardly focus. We have two docs down on the on-call service and I've been getting slammed." Frank puts on his head covering and moves toward the door to scrub for surgery. "Good running into you, Glen."

"I hope you slow down before you get fried."

Frank laughs as he scoots out the door.

I scrub and enter the surgical theater. The anesthesiologist is at the patient's head, the anesthesia machine operating. The scrub nurse is hustling getting the room ready. The surgical nurse is setting up the instruments. Both the nurses turn and smile when I enter the room. The surgical nurse says, "Hey, where you been, Dr. Glen—on a long fishing trip?" The scrub nurse and the surgical nurse laugh while they continue setting up.

"Oh yeah, I was doing a lot of deep sea fishing."

The anesthesiologist, Chick Halverson, eyes me. "Was it catch and release, or play and fillet?"

"It was a little bit of both and I'm better for it." He knows. I fashion a shift. "This woman is quite fearful about the outcome and she will need a lot of support when she comes out of the anesthesia. And I will follow-up with her." I look at the nursing team, and turn to Chick. "Are we good to go?"

Chick says, "We're there." He gives a go ahead nod.

We're mid-surgery and there's the table talk chitchat about food, workout routines and the friendly this and that of safe topics to keep us entertained and to work as a team during the operation. The surgical nurse discusses a great restaurant to get an authentic margarita. I feel Chick staring at me. I look up at him and smile and wink. He smiles back and shrugs. For a second time Chick acknowledges that he knows. A momentary sensation of shame passes through me. I lose concentration. I stop for a second. The abruptness sends a hush over the OR. For a brief moment the only sound is the vital sign monitor and the whirling of the anesthesia machine. I say, "They have anything else that's going to get you more loaded than margaritas?" Chick and I laugh, the nurses look confused.

• • •

I go to my locker to change into my street clothes. As a matter of habit I check my cell phone. There's a call from Detective Nace. I get out of my scrubs and go to my car for privacy to call him. Nace says they didn't know Tom's residence until I briefed them. He's puzzled why his now estranged wife didn't let him know during his interrogation with her. I tell him she passed on it out of fear of Tom striking back and settling the score by taking revenge.

Nace says when they arrived at the trailer park Tom was blotto with drugs. I asked who had written the scripts, if anyone. I wondered if it was Henning, knowing that Tom would not still have the meds left that I had prescribed before leaving for treatment. Nace says the drugs were from a prescription mill in Miami, and Nace was surprised since he thought all the nefariously-driven operations in Florida had been exposed and were out of business. Tom was too loaded to interrogate but they took him in until he evened out. The doc at the jail has experience with addiction medicine and treated Tom's withdrawal symptoms. The detective indicated Tom put up barriers, but the investigators did a marathon tag team, weakening Tom's defenses. They prevailed and he confessed. He also said he was irate and enraged, making him savage and wild. Tom had been being placed on a restraining order because of domestic violence, but he also told the detective that I had been having sex with his wife, and she humiliated him. Nace asked me about that. I said it was true, but limited to three times. And then I reminded him that I already told him about being friendly with Jackie. I also asked Nace if that justifies arson, and he said of course not, and I laughed at the teasing in the question. He went on to say Tom had been booked and a conviction was a certainty.

After hanging up, I feel weary with the back and forth letters and phone calls with the insurance carrier. And the arson feels like Tom assaulted me. I drive over to the insurance agent's office and he's in. I advise him of the arrest, confession and the detective's certainty about a conviction. He agrees a payout should be forthcoming. But he points to higher administrative processes which further a sense of my immediate frustration, though the agent's agreement brings optimism about the eventual outcome.

After leaving the agent's office I sit in my car and use my cell phone to call Silas Dawson. I tell him about what had transpired. The arsonist arrest could have an impact on the availability of the insurance funds. He says he has come up with some artistic plans. And he wants to send me an electronic attachment of a prefatory rendering. We discuss solidifying the architectural plans. But Silas says to wait and see the visual image he had transcribed from our discussions into drawings. He mentions ideas for contractors. I slow things down since this move would have to wait until after the settlement. Sure, we've gotten jaded and it's been monotonous due to the workings of the insurance conundrum. He'll send the architectural design in one second. I pull up the attachment on the cell phone screen. And there it is. The striking angular reliefs of the upper part of the structure—perpendicular to the vertical axis—set off the whole building. And windows rising up to the angular roof are dramatic. I'm dazzled by the sophisticated architectural design. I ease back. I'm glad that old place spiraled up in smoke to lay the path for what's to come. It coincides with the changes I'm making in myself.

A boy on the sidewalk is staring at me. He's wearing an oversized gray sweatshirt and has a massive thick mop of amber-colored hair. There's eye contact. I get out of the car. I ask him what's up and he says nothing. I look across the street at chic delicatessen and then back at him. I tell him he looks a little hungry, whatever that looks like. I point to the delicatessen and ask him if he'd like a sandwich. He swallows like he's salivating and gives me a wide-eyed nod. He reads the choices on the menu board and wants a roast beef sandwich. We order and sit down. He's eleven years old. I ask him what he is doing out of school today. He tells me that he ditched school. He stops there, though I kind of push it. He says that he doesn't feel part of things, like he's an outsider which makes him feel uneasy and awkward around the other kids. And he is more carefree when he takes a detour on his way to school. I see the link when he says that his father up and left when he was almost five, and boy's struggle to make connections have been a result. No reason given, his father vanished, and that was the last time he had seen him. Our sandwiches are ready. He must have been hungry; given the rate he began to devour the food. I say the only way to be part of things is to press yourself and take the gamble to be part of things. I ask him if there is anything he is good at, and he says soccer and baseball. I ask him to envision the classroom and groups of kids being like the soccer and baseball fields. He squints and says that he never thinks of it that way. He leaned back in his chair, thoughts rolling through his head. He sits still in the chair for a few minutes and his eyes shift back and forth.

I say my name is Glen. He leans forward and tells me his is Jack. Jack wants to know what all my business on the cell phone was about. I tell him about the clinic and it burned down because of arson and now I'm making design arrangements with the architect.

I ask Jack what his mother does for a living. He says she is a paralegal and plays the cello for the Santa Rosa Symphony. I ask him if he's been caught for ditching school and he says he has. I ask him how his mother feels about it. He says she gets pissed off, but he counters by putting up the argument that he's a straight "A" student. Jack says it lessens the tension, though his debate tactic really doesn't fly to win her over.

He asks me what I do for a living and tell him that I'm a physician specializing in plastic surgery. He says his mother doesn't need that and I ask why he says that, because everyone could look better. He says there is no way she could look better. I study Jack and he's a handsome kid. I ask him how he is such a good student if he doesn't feel connected with the kids at school. He says he focus on academics is his way of hiding out. I start to sense I'm talking to an adult rather than an eleven year-old kid.

I look at my watch and tell Jack I have to get back to the office. We get up and walk out of the delicatessen and across the street. We stand on the sidewalk for a second and he politely thanks me for the sandwich. I start to turn and he asks me to wait. Jack asks if he can have my phone number. I take out a card and write my cell phone number on it and tell him it is the best number to use. He puts out his hand and gives me a firm handshake. As I get into my car Jack yells out that he will go back to school for the afternoon classes.

I'm amazed at the unforeseen connection with Jack and his receptivity. There was a pull I fell into that was brand new. I felt fatherly.

● ● ●

I'm back to the office for two minutes when the receptionist comes to the door. "Dr. Glen there's a patient on the line who wants to talk with you."

I joke with a grin on my face, "You're keeping me suspense."

"It's Chip Inman." She softly smiles. "I remember him as being one of your all-time favorite patients."

I see the phone's blinking hold light, and push the button. "Hi Chip. How's the man who surfs the mega waves at Mavericks and does two hundred miler bike rides? I hope to hell all your fingers are still intact." I squeeze out a laugh."

"I'm A-Okay, plus all my fingers are good to go, thank god. I'm still getting in the water and pushing those pedals pretty damn hard." He pauses for a second. "Say Dr. Glen, the reason I'm calling is that I saw in the paper that your office burned down to the ground, and arson was suspected."

"Yeah, a devastating blow. I was out of town for a period of time and the clinic was leveled the exact day I got back. But I think a new building is shaping up that might actually be a much cooler spin on the old one."

"Well, the other reason for the call is—"

"You want to know if the hand sculpture you carved for me burned up in the fire?"

"Yes."

"It did. I have to say, Chip, it was a keepsake that was extraordinarily important to me…more so than my medical equipment, or really anything else. It's because I got a lot out of helping you to get back into one piece. Now, I don't want to get all soft on you, but I was touched when I received the hand sculpture."

"Well, good deal, because that's the idea."

"What's that?"

"I enjoyed carving the first hand sculpture so much that I will make you number two."

I splay my hand across my chest. "Touched once, and then touched twice. Is that the idea?"

"Sure is. We're getting a lot of mileage out of doing a repeat because of the clinic burning down."

"Thanks Chip. You're the man of the hour. And I'm super thankful of you thinking of giving me a call to check in."

"Thanks for being a good doc. And god only knows I love having my hand back in one piece."

"Take care, Chip."

"Likewise."

Jack filters back into my mind and the unexpected tie. I can help patients. This was all brand new feeling I could influence Jack to do better for himself, something he deserves. He's a smart, good looking boy that makes me wonder what his mother is like. I was really partial to being around him.

CHAPTER TWENTY-TWO

I'd already started the healthcare professionals' monitoring program. A key piece is initiating the forensic quality urine testing program. I also had a hair follicle test this week which tracks whether or not there has been any drug use for the past ninety days. Some people might think this kind of surveillance is like cops looking over your shoulder. But for me this is no question. It the assurance that I'm not using drugs. If there's any random accusation or someday I'm in a shitty mood and someone makes a denunciation that I must be using drugs, I have my backup drug screen documentation that I'm clean. I assume that if you're an addict doctor, you can't be in a bad mood because that must mean you've been getting loaded or hung-over.

I had my apprehensions about getting back into the hubbub of the medical community and practice when I was in treatment. Visualizing what it would be like, and who would say what and being the center of attention. Today I see people running here and there doing their business and I am just one part of many cogs getting the job done. I'm not the focal point, though I am certainly on various persons' radar. Chick and I speak after the procedure is over. He asks how treatment went for me. He's neutral and objective and interested. The first blush of acceptance from a colleague is a piece of serendipitous luck. Chick helps me feel connected. But I know this is not the zeitgeist of what is to come.

The biological testing is the objective part of the physician monitoring. The next part scares me since it seems more subjective—the healthcare professional support group. And I understood the leader of the group assesses my progress in recovery and determines relapse warning signs. Basically, in terms of recovery and emotionally the question is, am I okay to practice? This seems daunting. My idea of the group puts me back in the mode of trying to look good and measuring what I say. I fight with myself in the dilemma of honesty being the key to getting better, versus knowing a lot is at stake and the power that is over me that could interfere with my ability to practice.

I call the leader of the group, Rick Fulbright. He's been leading the group for thirty years, implying he has heard it all. I tell the brief version of my story. He sounds accepting, but I don't trust it yet. He lets me know the logistics of the group. But then he says I have already been through very grounding primary treatment and I should consider the group a secondary commitment for sewing my life together and on-going recovery.

Alarm rings in my head when drive to the location of the group meeting. And I arrive punctually and save myself from the awkwardness of interacting with the other group members before the group has gotten underway. I look at Rick's name on the door and his name is followed with a doctoral degree letters. He welcomes me and has me write down my all my contact information and needs to know how to get a hold of me anytime, day or night. He gives me his card and I see his board certification in addiction treatment. Rick is an old hand at the group, and I imagine well-seasoned. He's broad in the shoulders and narrow at the waist and his age is hard to tell. My arithmetic calculates he's older than dirt, but not too worse for the wear. The guy is cordial, but I still don't trust what the monitoring process is about to entail.

Rick starts the group. There are other docs and dentists and pharmacists. Rick asks them to relate their stories to me. I'm relieved that I don't have to tell my story first—get the lay of the land, and see what the culture holds for this group of pros. Everyone is forthcoming. And I almost suspiciously think they are props to get me to reveal myself. And this is a crazy thought. The group sits in a circle and we go around, each person sketching out their story and treatment experience and current recovery and the complexities of reentry to work and graining trust from family members and colleagues.

I'm initially shut down. But by the time the group circles around to me what comes out is like on automatic pilot. My father's abuse and the escalation of addiction and interludes with Jackie and my wife enabling my addiction and treatment and feeling like my reentry to medicine is like walking through a mine field. And I think, shit I said too much. Too exposed.

But then the group members ask this and that question. A couple of them give me responses how they handled their misadventures with women when they were still using drugs, and the fallout with their wives.

Many say what they do on a daily basis to stay clean and sober. And how they navigated the dicey medical-political and trust and acceptance paths of reentering professional venues. Feeling that I bared too much goes away. And there's more to go into on another day.

They complain about the inconvenience and cost of the urine testing and the other monitoring fees. One doc concedes that nonetheless it's part of the process to get your life back. The recovery rates for the group are prodigious. The upshot of the program and the culmination of the motivation is to maintain medical licenses. And another doc submits that interacting with the other group members and hearing their stories has reduced his overwhelming shame to an almost nonexistent sliver. Rick sits and listens, like he's heard the urine testing and financial complaints a million times before and isn't fazed by it. They acquiesce that it's a piece of the burden to insure they're okay to practice.

Then there is the post-meeting meeting in the parking lot. They tell me Rick's agenda is to help us to be successful with our recovery and walk the sinuous lines of dealing with medical staff and hospitals. Even after what has happened this evening, I don't trust the system, yet. It's like I'm going to be unexpectedly broadsided.

● ● ●

I slip into my car. There's on my cell phone that I left on the seat. It's an unfamiliar number. I listen to the voicemail message. Jack invites to his house. I ask him if he passed this by his mother. He says yes.

I pull up to the cottage that's in the Santa Rosa college district. Jack answers when I knock. The living room is tastefully furnished. Fine art is on the walls. I see his mother's cello case. Jack shakes my hand and closes the door. His mother walks in the room. She is barefooted, wearing a t-shirt and jeans. What he said about his mother not needing plastic surgery is an understatement. Her hair falls beyond her shoulders. She has a beguiling smile. There are women who can wear anything and look gorgeous. She's one of them.

She has already heard my name and says hers is Lisa Baxman. And she asks me about Jack and what I said to get him to attend class. I tell her about the experiment. She laughs, like some stranger does something clever that she couldn't pull off. And then I tell her I recall seeing her name on the program at the Santa Rosa Symphony and remember her playing the cello. There's that smile again.

Lisa tells me her father was a dermatologist. Maybe that explains her glamorously smooth and silky skin. She offers me a glass of chardonnay. I tell her I have an alcohol and drug addiction history and have sworn off using anything that is mind altering. I don't tell that her looks are mind altering. Lisa says her husband was a substance abuser and it led to the demise of their marriage. I look at Jack. His face is blank, a shocked look like he had never heard this before. Lisa says that she got home late from work and just finished making dinner. She invites me to stay. I see Jack nodding.

Chapter Twenty-Three

I arrive at my new digs, still having gratitude for the span of time that Miles and Carla put me up. The place has a lodge feel to it. It has a huge kitchen that's the center of the house, with an adjoining living room, a bedroom and a place I call my office. I love the quaintness of the place, surrounded by countryside on a beautiful road in the rural western county. The cell phone rings. It's my mother. There's an apprehensive gust in my chest. I clear my throat to say how it's nice to hear from her.

My parents and I speak infrequently. There hasn't been much thought about why—just an automatic occurrence since leaving home to go to Pomona. I picture my father's abuse of me. A visceral sensation shutters in my body like an uncontrollable icy rawness. The disturbing leftovers make me not want to put my hand on the red-hot stove one more time and fry my hand to a cinder. Instead a protective wall wraps around me, but nothing can be totally dismissed, only minimized.

Mom says, "How are things?"

My legs feel like electricity is moving through them. She doesn't know about my drug addiction. Mom is proud that I became a physician, vindicating her from the twisted shit from the past. But I have felt unsafe with her, still trapped in my childhood and her lack of protective guardianship. And her cunning misadventures while my father was deployed stick with me, because of the fallout that rained on me instead of her when he returned.

I'm not open with her, and I question if I'm lying by omission by not telling her about the fallout I've gone through and reconstituting myself. I settle with myself that lack of safety with her is why I keep myself bolted closed—at least for now. "I am actually doing well. There are always the challenges of life, but things seem to be falling into place." But she's not calling to talk about me. She never has. "What's up?"

"It's about your father." Her voice sounds nondescript, yet the tenor has an ominous dark overlay. She wavers and her voice shakes at the end of "father."

"What is it about him?"

"He had a heart attack." Mom weakly trails off.

"Severe?"

"Yes."

"Mom?"

"Yes?"

"What's his condition?"

"He's dead, Glen." Her affect is spiritless.

"And—"

"He died three days ago."

"But why—"

"Oh, I was jumbled. Too distracted with what to do that I didn't call. I'm calling now." She sniffs. "Hold on a second."

"Are you crying?"

"No. Just collecting myself."

"Okay. Whenever you're ready."

Thirty seconds pass. "It's about the arrangements. Your father was very specific in his planning for death. No military burial or fanfare. He simply wanted to be cremated." Mom stops and coughs, as if there is a snag in her throat. "He wanted his ashes spread at the entrance of the harbor because that was the last point where he was connected with home before his ship plotted its direction for various deployments."

Topside, mom's explanation is prosaic. "That seems sentimental." All I bring up at the moment is dad being clouded in distress and anger. My nostalgia for him is remote. "What was on his mind, mom?"

"I'm not sure."

I pull back for a moment, followed by, "When is the memorial service?" I briefly think of the cases to be cancelled and the arrangements I'll have to make with the physician monitoring program.

"Your father specifically left instructions that he did not want a memorial service."

"Are you going to have some form of remembrance, anyway?" There's a strong uptick at the end of my question.

"No. Glen, please…"

"Please what?"

"I just want to follow your father's wishes…it was his life."

And I think of how my father found himself vanquished by my mother's secrets that swam below the surface. That's what gave a twisted insecure meaning to his life. I back pedal. "This is a shock to hear. You must be feeling—"

"We'll you'd think I might be overcome by losing him. But the fact of the matter is that I have so much to do that I can't hardly think or feel anything." She lingers for two seconds. "I'm running around making sure the details are taken care of."

"You want me to come to help?"

"No. You stay put. I want to handle it on my own."

"What do you have to do?"

She tells me he has already been cremated. And the Neptune people are making arrangements to spread his ashes at the harbor's entrance. Dad had already thinned out his things. Mom donated all of his clothes. She says there isn't that much. Mom needs to sort through his personal memorabilia. And she says she'll take her time to do it.

"There must be something I can do."

"Yes, there is. You can just hear that your father has died. And know it. That's all."

"I'd like to lend a hand. Make it easier for you in some way."

"Not now. I'll let you know." She exhales so I can hear it.

"Okay, I'll be in touch." This is a familiar feeling—helpless to rally round her in any way that will carry some weight. I whisper, "Shit."

"What was that?"

"Oh, a little stymied that I can't step in."

"There isn't much you can do, really. And going through his things will take some time. I don't want to rush it." There's an awkward moment, where she doesn't leave me room to say anything. "Glen, I'd better be going."

"I understand. Please promise that we'll be in touch."

"Okay." Mom says goodbye and hangs up.

I put the receiver in its cradle. I sit in my desk chair, looking vacantly out the window. Growing up and until now I always felt like an orphan. Like I didn't have a father. And my mother was so inaccessible, it made her invisible. I imagine when a parent dies people feel like orphans, particularly if both parents die. But I've always felt like an orphan in the past and now that my father has died, I don't feel like some orphan kid whose parents are dead. It's a strange incongruity and enigma that puts a warp on things. I'm not vacuous any more. It's a relief.

● ● ●

I arrive at the office and wire flowers to my mother. A gracious white floral design, dotted with sanguine red blooms. And the card enclosure: roses are red and violets are blue. Dad was an asshole and so are you. This is just the imagination of the impulsive, agonized and five year-old kid in me. What it says is that my father's death is shrouded in unfinished business. Other men my age are sad and feel loss and get used to the death over-time—a handshake goodbye, but always feel the lasting touch. And all I see are misty clouds making the foreground hazy. Through the obscurity, faint illuminated cracks reveal details in the distance. There's relief. I don't feel like an orphan. And there's the tattered residual heartache of what he left behind. I send my mother the actual enclosure card, "Please take care of yourself. I am available to help you anytime. Your son, Glen."

● ● ●

The few times I've spent with Lisa, I didn't hold back about my family and the sinuous direction of my life. She took it in. And she didn't hold back, either. She is a good soul and I call her about my father's death. She's been through it, a woman seasoned with walking the course of grief. We talk about loss and the mix that complicated grief can bring. An intimacy between us loosens a snarled knot. Lisa asks me to come over. I drive back to Santa Rosa from the west county.

I get Hickman on the phone for our daily check-in. I tell him about my father's death and the conversation with my mother. He says it's an entangled bereavement that could cause some serious snags for me. Hickman references the steps and discusses a fearless moral inventory to root out my resentments. And that I need to look at my character defects. Hickman editorializes that this segment is in the sphere of the progress and is not done thoroughly enough by a large share of people. He won't let me languish when we come to these steps. He says making an amends with my father is doable, despite him being dead—it has the possibilities of being safer and more expansive, but he keeps it vague, so I don't get too ahead of myself. Overlaying this framework gives me some mechanisms to shape what I'm going to do. And then he says I have to lay it on the line with my mother about my addiction and stop being withholding. Thank god for Hickman. He says I might need grief therapy, but we'll wait and see.

I hang up the phone and breathe. After talking with Hickman it's like a spell is broken. I'm uplifted. I'd be a fool to not know it's temporary. And then comes the elucidation and capacity to make sense that I feed into what I'm going to I feel.

● ● ●

"Hello, mom. I'm getting back in touch with you because of an omission when we spoke."

"You want to know if you will be receiving any inheritance from your father's estate?"

I'm not surprised she thinks I'm a self-centered hawk going after the family blood. "No, that's not it. You see, there was one aspect of father that was carved in me. He was an alcoholic. I developed a pretty severe opiate addiction when I returned from Iraq."

"And it's your father's fault."

"I'm not saying that. I could or could not of developed a problem. But I do think that his alcoholism and his abuse of me were key factors, among many others."

"You're practicing medicine while on drugs?"

"No. I've been to treatment and I am working on developing a drug-free lifestyle. The treatment was important and has helped to continue to be clean."

"Well, son, I can say it's not exactly a total bolt out of the blue."

"Anything you'd like to know?"

"I'm glad you're taking care of it."

CHAPTER TWENTY-FOUR

Hickman and I prepare ourselves for the work to come by indulging in first class on our flight to Guatemala. The booze flows like a cascading Roman fountain. The passengers traveling in our section are mostly well-behaved. I'd be out of it I was sloshing down all that ethanol. The food delicacies make up for our non-drinking sobriety status quo. One passenger says dumb things to his silent wife and makes an ass of himself. He confirms I'm not even tempted to split the main brace. "Split the main brace" is an old nautical term I like, meaning heavy drinking after getting into port following a day of sailing.

We are three hours from landing in Guatemala City. Hickman's taking a snooze. I hear his heavy slow breathing, just shy of a snore. I'm facing forward, my mind is adrift. One prime detail is Julie. There're all the residual marital bits and pieces for me. And I've come to realize that if I am feeling something about someone, it's likely they also have something going on about me. But another thought interrupts her being on my mind.

I center my thoughts on my mother. I finally told her about my addiction. Most everything exposed to view, while the key ingredients weren't held back. Her response was deadpan, but then a spike of emotion sparked up when she told me I was like my father and must have come from the same gene pool. She shamed me, but for once I amazingly didn't feel ashamed. Mothers have a lot of power, even if they're lunatics.

I mull over that I must be getting better since she didn't get to me, to the point of being unhinged. It wasn't that I simply dismissed her credibility, but I let her self-possessed elucidation pass by without a modicum of sticky glue to attach it to me. And the grand message is revisited. When there's scarcely any expectations, disappointments are sparse, far and few between.

My mind filters back to where the scorching heat is, and that's Julie. In truth I knew what was coming. Foolish me thought we might improve. There's disavowing being hooked on dope, but then there's living in fantasyland about women. My dreamy chimera about women has yet to totally devour me. I flitter my thoughts away about the ideal woman that doesn't exist, and imagine some woman do the same about men.

I was stupefied by the delivery of the divorce papers. It's like I being a post driven into the ground by a pile driver. Yet maybe the news wasn't really such a bombshell after all.

Julie's resiliency about the three passes with Jackie made trust a non-recoverable possibility. But more damning was that I couldn't give her one hundred percent certainty that I would never use drugs again. That's how the recovery scheme works when you live just for today. This made her so anxious that she had to take flight. Julie gave lip service to supporting me. But this turned out to be a fabrication she manufactured to avoid conflict. I was a willing partner for marital metamorphosis. She avoided her own conflict. So the reason we were drawn together in the first place—our vacuous lives because of our childhood history—was what drove us apart. I changed. She didn't.

When the word came about divorce, the shakeup became roughly textured with a betrayed feeling. A hurtful stabbing wound for me. And second, her withholding about her plans brought about my resentment toward her. I called Hickman about what led up to the resentment. He made a recommendation. I should pray for her. I am absolutely not a prayer person. I gave it a try, wishing her hope and piecing together forgiveness on my part. I went into some dimension that brought the forces of negative and positive together that mitigated the charge on the resentment. I reported back to Hickman.

Fortunately for me—to some degree—Julie has her own money. Her only extravagances being her expensive running shoes and her acquisition of a racy Porsche while I was in treatment. She finally spent a big chunk of her change. I saw it as a misdirected act of compensatory desperation. The rules say the base amount of her inherited assets I couldn't have access to, but the increased valuation of her portfolio turns out to be community property. It's cliché, since most men say they were taken to the cleaners when they get divorced. We added up and divided by two. I thought the best deal was to give her the house and she liked that idea. There was some financial cleaning, but the solvent wasn't so strong that it totally dissolved me.

Julie immediately put the house on the market when it shifted into her name. The house must have been like a piece of scum she had to wash off her body. The place wasn't a palace, but artfully constructed with a stunning view and a green rolling hills setting in the west of the county. She sold it in one day at an attractive price. And then she's gone.

Julie moves to Santa Barbara to swim in fresh and salt water, and run the paths, and bike the flats and hills. And then what? She's a magnet who draws in a man against her own best interests. Later, I get the blush from her without the sorted details. While still recovering from divorce shock, she ricochets into a new relationship. Her new connection is with an attorney who also has an MBA and lives in a Montecito mansion that is ten times the size of what he needs. Depending on his mood, he either drives a Maserati Quattroporte S Q4 when he's feeling sedate, or a Lamborghini Aventador LP 700-4 when his juices flow. Julie must have been swept away by the skin-deep appeal. But the guy is another out of control person who limitlessly gets blasted using alcohol. She didn't see it coming. I don't know for certain what goes on in her mind, but maybe she didn't want to perceive his problem and trouble in the making. She was clouded over by the man's opulent appearances and affluent facade. At this point, she needs to figure it out herself. I have to step to the side.

Julie calls me. Disillusion is in her voice. Deeper is desperation that trickles to the surface. She wants me back. I tell her I still love her. And I tell her we're done, realizing our dance, and likely I won't stay clean if we are together. She's familiar. We have history. There is still my love for her. The tug is strong. Yet I know that if I take her back, one of us would eventually spit the other out again. And I'll continue to have the pain caused by the destructive residue from the marriage. But the real cause of our dissolution was the rules of the game changed because I got clean. Nonetheless, there's no escaping the lasting pain and ache of splitting up. She not the cardboard cutout she thinks she is. I know she has a good soul. I miss her. And now I also know our marriage will not work.

A fantasy encroaches on what is stirring about Julie. Jackie left Tom. I think of the possibilities—Jackie and me being an item. And I think of the potential tragedy. There's the heat that drew us together, a lustful passion, crammed with our unwell warped selves. A dream that something healthy and wonderful could spring between us? Too many old and unknown new hitches. And I am not ready yet because I'm still too off center with women for anything else but a prodigious goddamn drama packed with torment. The Jackie fantasy dies a high-speed death. I'm going slowly with Lisa. And with Lisa I haven't kept it a secret why. There's a penetrating sense that her patience will have its nourishing rewards.

● ● ●

The airplane captain comes across the loudspeaker. We are landing in thirty minutes. Hickman opens his groggy eyes. He wipes his hand across his face. "Almost there, huh? I went down for the count." He lifts the window shade and peers out—nothing much to see except cottony cumulous clouds. "What have you been doing while I was out?"

"Thinking."

"That can be dangerous."

"About Julie."

"Keep praying."

We both smile, knowing I must have been thinking crazy thoughts. A lamentation salts my voice, "At times the ways we live our lives are laughable."

The physicians' monitoring program doesn't mind me coming to Guatemala because I'm with Hickman. I'm still fairly early in recovery, and on a good trajectory. And by luck, the two places we are going to, Antigua and Río Dulce, are the only places in the country that have English speaking recovery meetings. With my language ability I could fit me into the Spanish speaking meetings, but that wouldn't be a fit for Hickman. "Say, did I tell you I'm thankful for you coming with me?"

Hickman snaps out of his grogginess and smiles. "You let me know in various ways. Yes. I'm going to get something out of this, too."

"What do you mean?"

"Oh, from time to time I hear docs say how they are going to do a medical mission, or volunteer work. They have a hard time extricating themselves from work or their wives or husbands want to go on a vacation or blah, blah. They never do it."

"Are you one of those docs?"

"Yeah, so I'm grateful for you thinking of it. Being your sponsor sealed the deal to hook up with you and go."

"Actually, you initiated the idea. I just concretized how it was going to happen." There're amends that are a part of piecing together recovery, and some can't be directly made or fall flat. The first one is with Julie. I tried, but I didn't get any traction because her receptivity was like an impenetrable fortress. Closed up like an iron gate tightly locked, guarded against any entry. Because of all of my past lying, the amends seemed inauthentic to her, though she couldn't see I was a bleeding heart. And there was no back peddling from crossing the lines of propriety with Jackie.

I have respect and admiration for Hickman for telling me that perfection isn't the goal of our work together. It's just getting better. After all these years I've finally come to recognize the simplicity of what's obvious. The paragon of flawlessness is a false personal belief of grandeur that's nonexistent.

The amends list gets longer. My hand in what happened was I grew in size and decked my father. Based on my hurt and wanting to back him off, I can rationalize that he deserved it. But there was another way of getting through to him—compassion. I knew mom made him crazy with her infidelity when he was gone. And I knew he was spineless—supposed to be standing for military might—and didn't stand up to her and took it out on me. I was old enough to talk with him about his pain, but I was so angry that I punched him and laid him out flat on his back. I've come to realize that compassion is better than anger.

The second part of the amends is more telling. There were the family rules and codes of secrecy about my mother. I was in collusion with my mother's secret that constantly and alternatively stabbed my father in the back and then in the gut. My amends to him is my part in the conspiracy of secrecy, and for angrily decking him instead of compassion's evenness. The secrecy of the past is still the secrecy for today, though my father is dead. I don't have to live with it. Mom does. And I can't help that she wants to ferment in the cesspool of her life.

And there are the amends that would damage me or others. First up are all the patients I have treated where I either had drugs onboard or had been hung over. I screwed up follow-up with patients, but thank god there was never a procedural mishap. I can't exactly call every patient up and atone for operating on them when I was impaired. This could be damaging in some way to them—eroding doctor-patient confidence—and would certainly generate complaints to the medical board. My career would be deep-sixed.

Jackie's receptivity for making up for the past brought light during a dim and murky time. She understood what making amends was about. She bathed me in forgiveness.

Then there's the second part. Jackie said she had used me, as well. She was in pain about being smothered by a wet blanket marriage and used me for a release. Jackie and Tom were already separated when I made the amends to Jackie. I felt that I owed him one, too. I suspected by doing so would cause him more pain on top of the schism with Jackie. I spoke with her about it. Jackie confirmed it would be a disaster. This was one more case where a direct amends would serve no purpose other than being harmful.

Hickman says, "Hey Glen, where did you drift off to?"

"Just thinking about why we are doing the medical mission."

"Many people who get clean don't quite understand how the process of the journey back from addiction works. They're just so desperate there's partial understanding and they do the rest on faith. I think this is also the case for you. And faith fills in the blanks that would otherwise make you incomplete." Hickman nods. He purses and then wets his lips. "But I must say you have nailed down where it's fitting to do an amends and where it would be a disservice to someone else or you. And I love the idea of doing the medical mission as your way of making an amends where being direct isn't possible, or a bad idea."

"Well, thank you for guiding me down the twisty path." The corners of my mouth curl up. "You're quite a guy, Hick."

"Don't get all soft on me, Glen." Hickman laughs and slaps his thigh. I laugh along with him and I revert to not being so serious. Hickman has that effect on me.

• • •

The driver from the medical mission is in his early forties. He picks us up at the airport. Beto has a professional way about him, a starched white shirt that offsets his inky black curly hair and khaki colored pants. A clean-cut man. He drives us from Guatemala City down a mountain road into a valley where Antigua is located, and the town is forty-five minutes away. Antigua is situated in the central highlands of Guatemala. And when we roll into the town, Hickman and I are taken with the Spanish Baroque architecture and the colonial feeling of the settlement. And there is a combination of ruins and restored buildings. Beto says the ruins were caused by *terremotos,* meaning earthquakes. We pass the *Parque Central* with its gushing fountain and purple and red bougainvillea vines and jacaranda trees. The driver stops at the marketplace for us to see the flowers and vegetables and fruits and we buy a delicious mango on a stick. There's a fragrant floral smell and an infusion of fruit scents. Women wear multicolored hand woven full skirts and dresses, with their hair up in braids. And we hear Guatemalan music in the background, which is probably coming from the *Parque Central*—the sound of a marimba and guitars and smaller stringed instruments I don't know the names of, and *chinchines* that are rattles made from little gourds.

The town is surrounded by volcanoes. Their presence is striking and they tower and appear bluish through and translucent haze. The volcanoes stand shimmering by the sunlight cast through the atmospheric mist.

I ask a friendly looking man who is heavyset, *"¿Cuales son los nombres de los volcanes?"* I ask him the names of the volcanoes, interested since we occupy a valley surrounded by volcanoes that have a seismic influence on the town. He glances at me with a good natured stake at answering the question.

The Guatemalan limps toward me, as if his knee is bone on bone. He moves like his knee is a bother, but appears accepting as if that's just the way it is. The man points to the south and says, *"Volcán de Agua."* He turns west and says, *"Acatenango."* He moves his body to complete the triad of mountainous geological formations and says, *"Volcán de Fuego."* I understand the first and third names. The volcano of water and the volcano of fire, but the middle name is a mystery. Maybe it's some version, meaning to have respect, or maybe it's just a non-translatable name. He says, *¿Entendió?* He asks me if it's understandable.

I say, *claro,* meaning of course. The man bows. And we shake hands. He smiles again. He turns and limps away.

Hickman and I hear people making reverential sounds. Adjacent to *El Parque* there is a vaquero smartly dressed in ranchero clothing and leather boots, riding an Arabian stallion. The horse is fitted with a beautifully tooled saddle. The equine beauty prances. The vaquero pulls the reins, backing the horse up, and then he pulls the reins to the right and straightens his legs in the stirrups, working the magnificent powerful stallion like it is doing waltz movements. We happened upon a show we didn't expect. The vaquero tips his hat and smiles to the audience. He dismounts the Arabian and ties it to a lamppost, and speaks with a few people that crowd around him.

Hickman and I look at each other. Beto is waiting in the car. We decide to explore. There are shops with *artesanías* or regional handicrafts, and clothing stores that have exquisite hand woven clothes for women and men. And then there is a unique store that sells nothing but masks. We step inside

A middle aged man greets us in nicely polished English. He introduces himself as Alejandro. He has on streak of white hair at his right temple that elegantly sweeps back past his ear. His soft cotton embroidered shirt seems to fit the indigenous ambience of the shop. I know the material in Mexico to be *manta* that is a coarsely woven fabric. When he learns we have nothing in mind, he tells us to look around. I see a striking mask of a jaguar face. I ask the store owner about it. Alejandro mystically speaks using metaphors and symbols. He says the mask represents renewal. Its meaning corresponds to how one perceives the world. But it has more dimensions, since it stands for the fact that nothing is as it seems to be. The jaguar is a warrior. And it's central attribute is that it symbolizes transformation. I think, Jesus, how did I stumble onto this one?

I shift to a coyote mask. He says the coyote has intellect, but lives in secrecy. A knowledgeable creature that nonetheless disobeys rules...the trickster that defies rules. I wonder if this guy is reading me and then giving explanations for the masks, or if he is accurately explaining the mythology and symbolism of the masks. I walk out the store with both the masks.

Beto tells us the medical mission has lined up ten cases scheduled for us tomorrow, and another ten for the next day. Parents will be bringing their children for the procedure from near and far. After the first round in Antigua we will be moving onto Río Dulce. Beto says the digs in both locations will be nice, in spite of being on a medical mission to treat the poor. We arrive at a private residence that's set up for us. In the neighborhood there are poles with crisscrossed telephone and electrical wires in a mass confusion going every which way. Trees are sparse on the street, though other places in the town there's a tree studded lushness. Beto is good to his word. A Spanish-speaking housekeeper greets us. My Spanish from mostly growing up near the Mexican border is a tad rusty, but we get along fine.

I've already exchanged dollars for the Guatemalan quetzal, which is named after a striking green-headed bird with a red breast and white leading to its extravagantly long green tail. I tell Hickman that I want to hit the market and buy a case of bottled water. There is a man in the market that looks like an expatriate. I strike up a conversation with him, introducing myself as being here on a medical mission. He's interested. I invite him for a cup of coffee. We sit in a café. We're talkative.

He's an older slight-bodied man, looking like a survivor who has a weather beaten face. He's a person with stories about is life in Central America. He says that he lives next to a ruin that has been restored into an elegant hotel named Casa Santo Domingo. He describes his kitchen being part of a tunnel that runs underneath the borderline of the hotel grounds. We exchange names. Sam stories his early lucrative life being in the tobacco business. Maybe it's because I'm a doctor that Sam reveals how he was kidnapped in the 1980s by some leftist military group and handcuffed to a bed for three days. The equivalent of a SWAT team somehow got wind of the kidnapping and stormed the location where he was held and successfully rescued him. Physically, Sam was uninjured. He denies being traumatized, but he obviously was since he refuses to go out at night.

And then Sam tells me he had prostate cancer. He sought medical consultation in Guatemala City and was hospitalized to have his prostate removed. The man was put under anesthesia and recuperated for a couple of days. Afterward, Sam was still having medical problems when he visited the United States. A physician took his medical history and examined him. There was a scar from the incision, but his prostate had not been removed. At this point my eyes must be as wide as saucers, and my jaw drops. The doc in the U.S. operated and removed his prostate. I invite him to dinner with Hickman and me, and he reminds me that he does not go out at night. This fellow is full of stories, but I feel the pull to get back to our temporary residence. He adds a short story about forensic anthropologists who excavated a mass gravesite in the nearby countryside where the people had been murdered by extremist militants. I think I'm stretching out my time too long, away from our little casita. Sam and I shake hands goodbye. He's still not a go for dinner tonight.

I walk down the sidewalk, and again notice the far and few between dots of vegetation—just cobblestone and sidewalk. There is one solid wall lining the sidewalk which composes the front portion of each house. I recognize our door. I put the case of bottled water in the kitchen. Hickman is nervous when I get back to the house, "What took you so goddamn long?" Maybe he thought that since I was out of my element I might have stopped to get a drink or scored some drugs or wrangled a prescription at a pharmacy.

I tell Hickman about my further introduction to Guatemala and my interview with the expatriate. Hickman's watchdog anxiety dissipates and I apologize for being gone so long

I call Lisa and Jack on our house phone. It's a newsy conversation about being in Antigua and what's happened so far and the people and the lay of the land and architecture. Lisa says she drove by the old clinic site. The debris had been cleaned up and the forms had been put in for the foundation. I tell her about the jaguar and coyote masks. I'll gift them to Jack and tell him about the masks' mythological stories.

I hear Jack hysterically laughing his ass off in the background. I ask Lisa what's Jack cracking up about. Lisa says she doesn't have a hint about what the joke is. I beg her to hand the phone over to him.

"Hey big guy, I heard you going nuts laughing. Let me in on it."

Jack chortles. "Well, you should see mom while she's talking to you."

"Like what do you mean?"

"Honest to goodness, she's wiggling around so much, it's like a super excited black lab wagging its tail like crazy."

I hear Lisa scream, "Oh, Jack." At this point the three of us are laughing with Jack at his cleverness. And then our laughing spins into our own orbits. And we turn our laughing into circles that crisscross each other's paths. The laughing turns into laughing just to laugh, like we lose a grip on our minds as to what the joke is. I wipe a laughing tear off my cheek with the back of my hand. The silent attachment between the three of us seeps in.

That evening we go to a recovery meeting, followed by a late dinner at a restaurant called Meson Panza Verde. My long unused Spanish is good enough to learn that *panza verde* means green paunch or green belly and is a nickname given to the men of Antigua. The restaurant was so urbane with excellent food that I thought I was on vacation, rather than being on a medical mission. That will all change tomorrow.

● ● ●

Hickman and I arrive at the clinic at 0730 hours to assure all is set up for the first case at 0800 hours. There are more than forty people waiting, one child and two parents and sometimes a second child or more children in tow because they are part of the family. Apparently, they were told to arrive today and were not given specific times.

A staffer greets us. We are filled in with cultural stories that Hickman and I have forecasted, and we held on for the specifics. The children with the deformities have been shunned. They have been segregated in classrooms and rejected by other students. Many have simply stopped going to school. They are treated like pariahs, and the ones who make it to adulthood without the operation are unemployable. And then the staffer tells us stories about parents who have abandoned their children by roadside far away from their villages or towns. The staffer's face glows like it's illuminated by a private buried spiritual light. We have a clue why. She tells us she's glad we're here.

A lot of medical missions can last for extended periods of time. I'll perform surgery for forty children in four days and Hickman will assist me.

I go into the waiting area. All the adults immediately look at me. Their faces are permeated with hope and anxiety and doubt, and some seem blank. I walk through the waiting people and glance at each child. I knew there'd be a range of cleft palate deformities. Some marginal and some are quite severe. My practice in the States has been a dress rehearsal for today. The trauma surgery in Iraq is a closer training ground. Some will take more time, and some less.

For such a life changing procedure, the operation on average only takes forty-five minutes. And we'll give the scrub staff fifteen minutes between cases to prepare the surgical suite for the next patient. The staff will give post-operative instructions to the parents. Two ten-hour days back-to-back in Antigua and more work in Río Dulce isn't too much to make my amends. I'm touched helping these children, since in this part of Latin America resources for what we are doing are so slim.

After each case the parents are ushered into the recovery room to see their child. I take a minute to meet the parents while the scrub team is setting up for the next case. Hickman curiously hangs back and has me join the parents alone. In each case I'm moved with how stirred the parents are. A few of them say, *¡La cirugía de labio leporino es un milagro!*. Rusty

Spanish or not, it doesn't take much to translate they are saying the cleft palate surgery is a miracle.

At the end of the day Hickman and I have some exhaustion, but it's a good and satisfying fatigued feeling. We walk outside. I have an elegant twilight mood. The sun has faded down the backside of Acatenango framing the volcano in a dense orange crepuscular blush, bleeding into a pink outline above. And the darkening lapis lazuli blue heavens wait for the clear night's blackness to show the configurations of the universe's constellations. A brief flash of breeze brings the smell of smoldering rubbish and rotting fruit. And then I see a small statured woman who is one of today's parents leaning against a jacaranda tree. She straightens up, looking directly at me. She's waiting. The woman motions to get my attention. Hickman doesn't move. I step forward. I want to know how I can help her. *"¿En qué puedo servirla?"*

"Muchísimas gracias, doctor, por su ayuda." She's thanking me for my help, but I suspect there is more. Her eyes have a deep opaque cavernous look, yet superficially each pupil seems as if it had eclipsed the iris.

"El gusto es mío, señora. ¿Cómo se llama?"

"Lupe."

"¿Es un apodo de Guadalupe?" I tell her it was my pleasure to do the work and ask her what her name is.

"Sí." She goes by the nickname Lupe. *"¿Puede oírme?"*

"Por supuesto." She asks if I'll listen to her and I say of course.

"Mi marido dice que hera mi culpa porque nuestro hijo tenía la deformidad."

"Nadie puede pronosticar estos problemas con los labios." Her husband has told her that she is lacking in some way because their son had a cleft palate, and I tell her that nobody can predict these things.

"Despues del nacimiento de nuestro hijo él hera reservado y frío. Entonces, discubrí que había otra mujer." She says that after the birth of her son her husband became reserved and cold and then she discovered there was another woman.

I say, *"¡No me diga!"* You don't say which is the polite and a canned response.

"Sí, señor."

"Estas situaciones son muy complicadas, y algunas veces una persona tiene sentimientos y emociones que no son manejables. La persona entiende mal porque no tiene la capacidad de discutir sus emociones."

"Sí, esa es la realidad de la situación con mi marido." She looks hurt.

She puts her hands in a prayer position and bows. I feel like she has mistaken me for a priest. And then I realize if I helped her son that she is thinking the same person could help her. One problem bubbles into another, animating a dynamic energy, festering something unwanted and being trapped. *Mentiras producen obscuridad y la verdad hace illuminación y la luz. Quizás vaya a mejorar su suerte ahora."*

She says, *"Quizás, Ojalá. Voy a tener esperanza. Adios. Muchas gracias por todo."*

"Igualmente. Adios." Lupe turns and walks away. I see her silhouette fade into the shallow light of the shadows. I sink, not knowing her future. I recognize the fact that the only deformity her son will have is a razor thin scar on his upper lip. I look up at Acatenango and see the last sunlight slip away, followed by a rare atmospheric green flash.

I return to Hickman. He says, "What was all that about."

"The woman's name is Lupe. She said that her husband faulted her for their child's deformity. And then he blamed her. I told her cleft palates can't be predicted. But I left out that some kind of stress in the first trimester could possibly be associated with the deformity. And then she said that she had discovered that her husband began to see another woman after the birth of their son. She seemed to be asking for my opinion, but more so she wanted me to hear her. I understood what she was saying. She felt this though my compassion. I told her that sometimes a person will not quite be aware of themselves because of not having the capacity to discuss emotions. I inferred that her husband was confused and this caused him to seek another woman and blame Lupe. She felt this was the reality with her husband. I told her lies bring darkness and the truth makes for illumination and light. And possibly her luck will get better. She said that she would have hope and thanked me, I said the same and she left."

"You clearly have the experience, and now the sensitivity to be able to counsel Lupe."

"Yeah, maybe moving in that direction." I take in a breath. "It was mostly listening to her pain." I examine the towering volcano, and turn to Hickman. "Astonishing how members of mankind can cover up more than they lay bare."

I had the foresight to come by a SIM card for my cell phone to be able to call back to the States. "Hick, you recall by buddies in treatment, Dave and Mike, and our sordid conversations about how we were going to atone and make up for our pasts. They know my plan for coming to Guatemala for the medical mission. But right now, especially being affected by taking to Lupe, I feel an urgency to talk with them. Do you mind holding on while I give each one of them a call to say what's happened so far."

"Those two boys are plainly key players in you adding two and two to pull your life together. Knock yourself out. I'd like to overhear what you have to say."

I punch in the country code and area code and their individual numbers. And I have a charmed feel, since both of them pick up the calls. Hickman patiently listens, and nods at the touching parts of what we have gone through so far. After I hang up, I say to Hickman, "I'm reminded of an old Tibetan Buddhist saying. 'Struggling against pain often increases suffering.'"

Hickman sighs and laughs, "You're making headway. Hold on to that one. We all need to move through our stuff. And if you avoid doing that, you keep on hurting."

● ● ●

The next day is the same routine. But these operations aren't every day, or mechanical. Nor are the surgeries going through the motions of a routine plastics practice. Some of the cases were challenging. Contacting the parents afterward made me feel like I was contacting the real world in a way that filtered-out useless complexities. The children seemed to have a similar vulnerability as the traumatized soldiers in Iraq. The difference being the families are immediately there to have dialogues. Not having the families in Iraq caused so much isolation with the treatment—an empty and disconnected feel.

Hickman and I burned up the following day, traveling to Río Dulce, which means *sweet river* in Spanish. A spectacular river, high green and palmed banks and soaring hills rising out of the river. Boat traffic and exquisite bird wildlife, and lily pads don sections of the river. We pass by an old stone fortress. We stay in a beautiful setting containing various bungalows situated on the river. Our digs here are rustic, framed with timbers and thatched roofs. We're here to do our medical work, but we're thankful for being able to occupy a smidgen of Guatemalan heaven.

We arrive in time to attend our second recovery meeting in English. We are welcomed by expatriates who are attending the meeting. The expats seemed tired of hearing their own stories over and over again. They want Hickman and me to be fresh meat and tell our tales. We do and give them a wild ride.

The set-up for the next day at the clinic is similar to Antigua. We toil through the day, again leaving the kids with an advantage they've never had, and us satisfied. The next day I check the children waiting with their parents. One child has the worst cleft palate I have ever seen, in person or in a medical journal. Throughout the day I anticipate he will be the next case. I do the ninth case and realize the child with the severe lip deformity is last. The procedure goes beyond forty-five minutes, and then an hour passes. The complications have only to do with the severity of his misshapen lip. The child turned out to have the best outcome relative to the harsh condition of what we had to work with. A staff person told me the parents were anxious because we were taking much longer than the other cases.

The child is taken to the recovery room. The parents are shown in. After a few minutes I join them. The father has his arm around his wife, pulling her tightly into his side. The mother falls to her knees and says, *"Dios mío, es el major resultado,"* My god, by far the best result. The woman grasps my hand and kisses it. She doesn't need to know I'm an addict-doctor. I know. And I look at her child and I don't feel like an imposture. Her husband takes a small silver cross on a chain from around his neck and places it on me. Tears spill down his face. I clasp the man's bicep and say, *"Estamos benditos. Somos afortunados."* I take a stab at saying we are blessed and we were lucky. The father nods and curls his lower lip. His cheeks are wet.

This is the last case before heading back to the United States. And the parents don't have the faintest clue that they have given me more than I have given them by the opportunity to have operated on their child. Right now I'm not in an all-encompassing state of deliverance. But I'm a couple of steps closer to a sensation of freedom. As the mother said, *"Dios mío."* My god. The positive and negative forces of my life merge into one, and my past at this moment feels like my best asset.